A

DUCHESS

FOR

ST. UGUZO

A NOVEL

SUSAN GARZON

A Duchess for St. Uguzo
© by Susan Garzon

ISBN (Print): 979-83-5093-449-6

ISBN (eBook): 979-8-35093-450-2

For all those who, like Holly, are striving to find themselves and their place in the world.

January, 2022,
the Duchy of St. Uguzo

My dear Guzos (and possibly a few others),

Here at last is my account of the crisis that nearly destroyed the duchy in 1994. At the time, I was asked to keep this information to myself, which I did. But it all occurred nearly thirty years ago, and I believe that we can now share our memories, face up to past failings, and be grateful for the courage and steadfastness of our fellow Guzos. (Note: The council granted me its permission to speak now, with one abstention.)

As you can imagine, it hasn't been easy for me to look back at the forlorn young woman I was when I first arrived in St. Uguzo. With hindsight, it appears that a straight line has run unerringly through my life and brought me to the present moment. But I assure you, it didn't look that way when I was a failed graduate student barely scraping by in a Midwestern university town in the U.S.

So, we begin on a late September evening in 1994 at the Hungry Hawk Café and Deli, where, like a real-life Alice in Wonderland, I was about to tumble into my future.

With affection,

Holly

P.S. I'm afraid I can offer no advice on how to marry a duke, disappointing though that may be to a few readers.

P.P.S. You may want to keep a chunk of good cheese handy while you read. But I didn't need to tell you that, did I?

CHAPTER ONE

It was nine p.m., and my last customers of the day were hustling out the door of the café, when in stepped a beautiful woman in a midnight blue wool coat and burgundy beret tilted at a stylish angle. I recognized her at once. Gwen Renard. I had thought more than once that if I had an after-life, she was exactly how I would want to return—as a stunning blonde opera star with an exquisite soprano voice. Currently, however, she looked tired and a little frazzled.

"I know it's late," she said. "Please tell me you're still open." Her accent was intriguing, English with hints of French or some other European overlay.

At this hour, I usually sent customers on their way. But Gwen was different. "Come in," I said. "The kitchen is closed, but I could get you some coffee or tea. And there's a Danish roll left."

"Lovely," she said, crossing the room. She dropped onto a chair at the table nearest the counter and plunked her voluminous tapestry handbag on the chair beside her. "Tea would be perfect, if it's not too much bother."

I hurried over to the front door, turned the "Open" sign to "Closed," and went behind the counter to pour a mug of hot water, grab a bag of Earl Grey, and put the Danish on a plate.

I realized that this must be the last night of Gwen's four-day stay on campus. According to a friend in the Music Department, she had led several master classes, ending in a public concert that night. I had missed it, since I had to work Thursday evenings. Usually, I didn't mind working late, as my social life was currently pretty dismal. But I'd been sorry to miss this performance, which I knew would be glorious.

By the time I'd gathered the food, Gwen was speaking on a sleek mobile phone. A few of my friends had them, but I had not yet coughed up the money to buy one. (Yes, these were the days before everyone had a cell phone.)

"Oh no," Gwen moaned into her phone, "that's awful." She listened, her brows furrowed. "No, don't worry. I'll be perfectly fine. Yes. Yes. We'll do it another time. Take care of yourself." A moment later, Gwen dropped her phone into her bag and sank back in the chair. "Darn," she said dramatically.

I'd stayed behind the counter, not wanting to intrude, but now I set down the tea and pastry on Gwen's table and moved the cup of sugar packets closer. "Bad news?"

Gwen sighed. "My traveling companion just canceled. She fell and sprained an ankle, poor thing. We were leaving for the duchy tomorrow. I guess I'll have to go alone."

"The Duchy of St. Uguzo?" It was her homeland, I knew. Not only was Gwen a famous singer, but she came from a tiny country that hardly anyone had ever visited.

"That's right." Gwen peered at me with cerulean blue eyes. Her brows curved up at the far corners, like graceful wings, giving her face an open, cheerful demeanor. "You look familiar, but I can't think where we've met," she said.

"I'm Holly Hewitt. I interviewed you once," I said. "It was several years ago, for my high school newspaper. You'd given a concert, and you let me interview you afterward." I was a senior at the time, and I didn't think I had a chance in hell of gaining access to the famous Gwen Renard, but my journalism teacher had urged me to try, and Gwen had been very generous with her time.

Gwen's face lit up. "I remember you. Didn't we talk at some length about the duchy? You seemed genuinely interested." She lowered her voice. "A nice change, I might say, from the usual nosy questions about my love life." She poured sugar into her tea and took a sip.

I smiled. "St. Uguzo sounded magical to me." Later, I had looked up the duchy for my newspaper article, but there was little information online or at the library. (These were the pre-Google days, you understand.) I did come up with the following information, all of which I included in my newspaper article: St. Uguzo was a tiny, autonomous duchy situated in the Alps, on the French border, equidistant from Switzerland and Italy. It was governed by a council, which was headed by the duchess. The major exports were gourmet cheese and decorative postage stamps, and its residents spoke both English and French. I also discovered that St. Uguzo was the patron saint of cheesemakers.

I had only found one first-hand account of a visit to St. Uguzo. A trekker reported that the scenery was beautiful and the capital had a medieval charm, but the Guzos were unwelcoming. Not only was the place hard to find, but once you finally arrived, there was no lodging or camping for travelers. My hopes of one day visiting St. Uguzo had plummeted. Still, the place intrigued me, and I'd thought of it off and on over the years.

Gwen began to rummage in her handbag. "You know, in our last conversation, I failed to mention the absolute loveliest thing the duchy has to offer. Ah. Here it is." She took out a small wedge of something wrapped in wax paper. "I smuggled in some duchy cheese, and there's still a bit left. We may as well finish it off." She cocked her head. "It's been a long day, and we could both use a lift. Don't you think?"

I wondered if this was the gourmet cheese I'd read about. "Sure." I sat down across from Gwen, pulling a napkin out of the dispenser, and watched as she unwrapped the wax paper, revealing a small chunk of cheese with a dark orange rind. I fetched a knife from behind the counter, and Gwen sliced the cheese, placing half on my napkin.

I sniffed the cheese and hesitated. An unusual aroma emanated from it, earthy like most natural cheeses, but with another scent, a tang that I couldn't identify. Sort of spicy, but not identifiable. Gwen was watching me expectantly. I'd tried enough strange cheeses to know they could be good or mouth-wateringly revolting.

"Do try it," Gwen said. She popped a piece into her mouth and closed her eyes, her face relaxing into a look of serenity.

I broke off a corner and took a bite. The rind was hard, but it was creamy in the middle. At first, it tasted rather bland, but then the flavor erupted in my mouth, rich and sumptuous, like expensive chocolate, only better. I surrendered to pure pleasure, letting the cheese practically dissolve on my tongue before I chewed and swallowed. "Oh, my God. This is the duchy cheese?" I said, breaking off a larger piece. "It's superb. I mean, really."

Gwen grinned. "I'm glad you like it."

We finished the cheese, and I sat back. "That cheese doesn't contain hallucinogens, does it? Not that I would mind. It's utterly delicious."

Gwen laughed. "No, nothing like that. I'm told the flavor comes from the duchy water and the alpine grasses that the cows eat." She lowered her voice to a theatrical whisper. "But I've always wondered if there wasn't a secret ingredient."

"So, do people in the duchy eat it every day? How do they get any work done? They must be completely blissed-out."

Gwen chuckled. "No such luck, I'm afraid. We make very good goat cheese for everyday eating. This cheese is saved for special occasions. Like our big celebration coming up in two and a half weeks. It's only held every five years, so everyone is looking forward to it. it's a big event for everyone."

"Will you be able to attend?"

"As a matter of fact, I'm leaving for the duchy tomorrow. There's always lots to do in preparation."

"Sounds like fun," I said, still savoring the last tang of the cheese.

"Say," Gwen said, sitting forward, her blue eyes bright, "I have a splendid idea. You're interested in the duchy, and you are fond of our cheese. Why don't you come with me? You could help out with a play we're putting on. Nothing too strenuous."

A surge of excitement rushed through me. My God, a chance to visit St. Uguzo. But my enthusiasm was followed by the crash of reality. There were two home games coming up. "The Hawk" was a town landmark, and hordes of alumni and other football fans would crowd into the café. If I suddenly asked my boss for three weeks off, he would fire me on the spot. "I can't leave my job," I said. It was a crappy one, but it provided a paycheck, not something I could just give up to fly off on some spur-of-the-moment trip. Plus, I had forty-six dollars in my checking account, which wouldn't go very far in Europe, I was sure.

"I know it's dreadfully short notice, but you wouldn't have to worry about money. The round-trip airline ticket is paid for. You'd have free room and board and a hundred francs for spending money."

I dropped my gaze. Could I really go? But my stomach tightened, and a familiar gut-clenching anxiety filled me. What was I even thinking? The trip was impossible.

"Do come," Gwen coaxed. "I hate to travel alone, and you'll have a brilliant time. I promise."

"I can't. But thank you for the invitation. I know you'll have a fine celebration." Without me. Well, at least there was the renaissance fair coming up. As usual, I would play my penny whistle with my musician pals. If I couldn't have the real thing, I thought, I might as well embrace the American imitation.

Gwen pulled a card and pen out of her handbag and circled something. "I'm afraid I have a confession. I just broke up with a rather famous movie director, and once the word gets out, reporters will probably descend. If they take pictures, I'd like them to show me chatting happily with a friend, not looking alone and sad."

"Oh, I see." Poor Gwen. A bad break-up could leave you feeling vulnerable. I should know. I imagined the two of us whizzing around an international airport in dark, wrap-around sunglasses, and the idea made me smile.

Gwen must have thought I was coming around. "As you see, my little dilemma doesn't really change anything. You will have a perfectly marvelous time in St. Uguzo. But you will also be doing me a big favor."

"I would love to go," I said, "but I can't."

Gwen's face fell in what looked like genuine disappointment. She extended the card to me. "I circled my phone number. Do give me a call if you change your mind. The limo is picking me up at one o'clock tomorrow. You will think about it, won't you?"

"Sure," I said, just to be polite.

CHAPTER TWO

I walked the four blocks home along dark, leaf-strewn sidewalks, barely aware of the old Victorian homes and boxy one-story houses illuminated by street lamps. Had I made the right decision? The trip to St. Uguzo had sounded wonderful, but maybe it was a little too wonderful. It would have been just my luck if the promised money had never come through. And what if Gwen suddenly changed her mind about hosting me? I might have found myself abandoned in some godforsaken corner of Europe, where I didn't know anyone. My French was less than fluent, and I would be easy prey for anyone out to bilk a hapless traveler. No, it was best to be safe.

By the time I stepped onto the saggy porch of the small, stale-smelling house that I shared with three graduate students, I was convinced of the wisdom of my decision.

My housemate M.J. had a different take. "You've got to be kidding," she said, her small figure curled up in a threadbare armchair in the living room. "You turned down a free trip to St. Uguzo?" She shook her head, her dark brown eyes reproachful.

I'd expected a little commiseration, but I should have known better. M.J.'s computer studies might be dry, but she was always eager for an adventure. "I can't just run off for three weeks," I said testily. "I need the money." She couldn't argue with that.

The next morning, I woke up with the wisps of a pleasant dream floating in my mind. I'd been standing in an ancient building with stone walls, looking through thick-paned windows arched at the top. A tall woman in an elegantly draped medieval dress stood close beside me, her face partially hidden by a wimple. We felt comfortable together, almost sisterly, which didn't seem odd until I woke up. The image stayed with me as I dressed in jeans and my favorite renaissance fair t-shirt, but my mood soon turned to gloom. I wished that Gwen had never extended her invitation to the duchy. It had given me a dream that could only turn to disappointment when I awakened. What's more, she had looked genuinely disappointed when I refused her offer, and I felt bad about that, as if I had let her down.

When I entered the kitchen, the house was silent except for the hum of the old fridge. M. J. had already left for work at the university's technology support center, and my two other roommates were on an ecology field trip. I filled the tea kettle, turned on the flame under it, and dropped a bag of jasmine tea into a mug decorated with wildflowers. Breakfast was completed by a slightly smashed Danish pastry, one of the perks of working at The Hawk.

When I turned on the radio, it was dialed to the public radio station, as usual, and I listened to the news as I sat at the table waiting for the tea water to boil. I nibbled at my Danish through an update on the seemingly endless saga of the O.J. Simpson trial, followed by a report on the effects of the Brady Bill, which Clinton had signed into law a few months earlier.

In the international news, the final Russian soldiers had left Estonia and Latvia, and in Germany, the last American, French, and British troops were scheduled to leave West Berlin. Amazing, considering World War II had ended nearly fifty years ago. But then, I knew that the repercussions of war went on and on. My own family was proof of that.

I poured hot water into my mug as I heard about a dictator in a small South American country who had stolen a great deal of money and was now looking for a country that would take him in before he was imprisoned. I was sure there was a greedy dictator someplace who would welcome a kindred spirit. Probably for a price.

The phone rang in the living room. I couldn't imagine who would call at that early hour, but I walked over and picked up the receiver. It was M.J.

"I'm in the office of your evil advisor," she said. "Working on her computer."

"Dr. Ferris? Lucky you," I said.

"Yeah, but listen to this. I told Ferris about your invitation to the duchy. You know, just to rub her nose in it. And she got all excited."

"Seriously?" I was surprised Dr. Ferris had even heard of St. Uguzo. So few people had.

"In fact, she got so agitated she spilled a mug of coffee all over her blouse. She's in the john right now, rinsing it out." Over the phone, I heard a door unlatch.

"Um, gotta go," M.J. said. "Talk to you later."

Good old Dr. Ferris, I thought as I sipped my tea. I was pleased that she was going to spend the morning with an unsightly wet spot on her blouse. She was the professor who had supervised what was supposed to be my M.A. thesis. My task was to analyze a set of letters and recipes written by an English noblewoman in fifteenth century England. The materials had never been studied in any depth, and I was thrilled. I immersed myself in the life and language of the times, scouring sources for information on the lady's family, taking a close look at the words she used, what she said and didn't say. Little by little, I began to live in the 1400s, until I had to forcibly drag myself back into the twentieth century to perform the mundane chores of my life, like shopping for groceries or hauling my clothes to the laundromat. Only in the 1400s did I feel vital and alive.

All through the fall and winter, I had worked late into the night, day after day, until finally I had completed the drafts of four chapters of my thesis. But it was then that I made a horrifying discovery. A Ph.D. student at Yale had just published a three-hundred-page dissertation on the very same noblewoman and her collection of letters and recipes. Heartsick, I trudged over to my advisor's office and wailed that my project had been hijacked. I fully expected Dr. Ferris to express her sympathy and come up with some way to salvage my thesis.

Instead, she suggested that this might be a good time for me to take stock of my prospects as a scholar, particularly in light of my unwillingness to embrace critical theory. This included her own theoretical paradigm (paradigm being her favorite word), which she fully expected to revolutionize medieval studies.

To put a finishing touch on her bad news, Dr. Ferris had told me that I wouldn't be able to keep my research assistantship for the coming year. If I wanted to stay in the department (and she didn't seem enthusiastic about the idea), I would need to find my own funding. Thus, my job at the café.

I sat at the kitchen table, running my index finger around a stain in the Formica surface while the tea cooled and what was left of my pastry stared at me, sugary and stale.

The sad truth was, I suspected Dr. Ferris was right. I had been kidding myself, thinking that I had what it took to be a scholar. She was correct. I couldn't care less about most theory, especially the literary kind. My eyes glazed at the mere mention of it. I knew that theory was revered in academic circles, but for the life of me, I didn't see why. Theories came and went. From what I could see, they were all airy castles in the sky. And I preferred my castles planted solidly on the ground. Dr. Ferris was probably wise to push me out before I got in too deep, before I had illusions of fitting into the academic world. Waiting tables and performing at medieval fairs was probably the best I could hope for, at least for now. It wasn't a bad life, aside from being poorly paid. I might just as well get used to it.

Ten minutes later, Dr. Ferris called. "That computer tech, M.J., was just here," she said. "She told me you had an invitation from Gwen Renard. To visit St. Uguzo during their big celebration."

"That's right," I said, "but I turned it down."

"Well, you've got to call up Ms. Renard and tell her you've changed your mind. You can't just pass up an opportunity like this."

How likely was it that Dr. Ferris was looking out for me? Not very. "Too late," I said. "Gwen (I used her first name to show how chummy we were) is leaving this afternoon. Anyway, I have a job. I can't just up and leave."

"I have a proposition for you," Dr. Ferris said. "That celebration in St. Uguzo has been held every five years ever since the late 1500s, and I'm told it still has strong medieval elements."

"Really," I said nonchalantly.

"Look. I need one more chapter for my book, and a study of that festival would fit in well. Here's my suggestion. You go to the duchy, take lots of good notes on the event, and come back here. We'll write up the chapter together, and you'll still have material for an article of your own."

Of course, I thought. This proposition was all about her book, the one that was going to cinch her bid to chair an international scholarly society.

"Do this," Dr. Ferris said, "and I'll see that you get an assistantship for the rest of the year."

I gasped. Was it actually possible? "I thought that money was gone."

"Yes, well, it looks like there's a small chunk available."

I had heard rumors that the department was trying to lure a new grad student from some Ivy League school, using my assistantship as part of the bait. But the guy must have found a better offer at another school. Good for him. I hoped his new department was less back-stabbing.

Dr. Ferris broke into my thoughts, her voice softened. "This trip to the duchy is your big chance, Holly. Not everybody gets such a break, especially early in their career. You need to go." And for the first time I thought she might actually be thinking of me.

"Are you saying...I have a future in the department?"

She paused. "Let's just say it could be a step in the right direction."

I lowered the phone's receiver and considered. What if Dr. Ferris was right, that this was my big chance? Not only could I get back into the department on a more solid footing, but I would experience a historic celebration in a place that was closed off to most people. Gwen was providing me with an "in." If only I had time to think this over. But if I was going to St. Uguzo, I had to decide now.

I took a deep breath. "Yes, all right. We'll leave for the duchy this afternoon."

"Good decision," Dr. Ferris said. "And let me know when you arrive. Then I'll start the paperwork for your assistantship."

Gwen answered her phone right away. "Of course you're welcome to join me," she said, in her rich operatic voice. "You have a passport, right?"

"Yes." I'd gotten it for a trip to Mexico with my then-boyfriend the summer before last. "But wait. I don't have a visa."

"No problem. I'll take care of it."

My mind immediately filled with visions of being stranded in some foreign airport where everyone hated Americans, especially the ones who showed up without proper visas. Paris Orly, for instance. "Are you sure you can do it?"

"Believe me, Holly, I fly internationally all the time. I know how these things work."

I thought I'd better tell my mother I was going to Europe, just in case something awful happened and she had to contact the nearest American embassy to bail me out. My mother, who was in California, didn't answer her phone, and my message went directly to voice mail. It was just as well, since this way I avoided listening to all the reasons that I shouldn't go to the duchy. If I had trust issues, I knew just where they came from—my mother. I left a message, saying I'd be in the duchy for the next three weeks, and I'd call when I got back. I left the same message for my sister Valerie, who lived in D.C.

Next, I left a note to M.J. on the kitchen table telling her I was going to the duchy after all. She would be pleased, especially since she'd been instrumental in shoving me out the door.

Finally, I dialed up my boss. At the café, I was usually Miss Responsibility, and I apologized wholeheartedly for leaving on such short notice. As I'd predicted, my boss was unsympathetic. "Don't expect a job here when you get back," he said before hanging up.

At ten o'clock, I was at the bank, where I drew out all but five dollars from my checking account. Then on to the drugstore, where I bought notebooks, ballpoint pens, a sample-size shampoo, and a "family size" bag of M&Ms. I was going out on a limb, but I wasn't climbing out there without my comfort food.

Back at the house, I pulled out a suitcase from under my bed and viewed my wardrobe. For once, the laundry gods were with me; I had just washed two loads the morning before. And it was a good thing, because I only owned about a week's worth of clothing. On the plane, I would wear jeans, a long-sleeve shirt, my knee-length trench coat that could later double as a robe, and my sneakers. Into my bag I threw slacks, tights and matching tunic, a cardigan sweater, my least faded tees, a mostly wrinkle-free khaki skirt, and pajamas. Around these I stuffed underwear and a pair of black ballet flats. At 5'9", I didn't need to increase my height by wearing heels. Silently, I prayed that not everyone in the duchy was as stylish as Gwen. If so, I would look like the poor country cousin. As a last thought, I tucked my penny whistle in next to my pj's.

Fortunately, my shoulder bag was roomy and accommodated my wallet, passport, the chocolate, and assorted other items.

It was almost one o'clock. In the bathroom, I took a last glance in the mirror. My auburn hair was long and shiny, but it was in need of a trim. If only I'd had one more day to prepare. Well, too late now, I thought, as I pulled it back into a low ponytail. I dashed into the kitchen and threw together a peanut butter and jelly sandwich, which I ate outside while I waited for the airport limo to pull up. I was just brushing off the last crumbs when Gwen arrived, waving cheerily from the vehicle. I smiled, pushing down my premonitions of impending doom.

CHAPTER THREE

I peered out the window of our jet to New York City and was met by a whitish haze. Gwen sat next to me, her eyes closed, her face relaxed. I pulled my passport out of my bag and gazed at my brand-new visa for the Duchy of St. Uguzo. At the Cedar Valley airport, Gwen had pulled a stamp pad and ink out of her carry-on. And just like that, I had a three-month visa. She was a consular official for the duchy, she explained, with her apartment in New York City serving as an occasional consulate. She assured me that France and St Uguzo had an arrangement by which the French immigration agents would recognize the visa and allow me to pass through French territory. She further explained that we would catch a flight from Paris to the small city of Bois, in the French Alps, and from there, we would drive to the duchy. Gwen's confidence had helped to calm my fear that I was traveling with a shady and possibly illegal visa.

I tucked the passport into my bag and cleared my throat. "Um, Gwen," I said, "there's something I need to tell you," and I proceeded to explain my plan to gather data on the celebration for my advisor's book and my own scholarly article.

"Oh," Gwen replied.

"It's okay, isn't it?" I asked, my nerves suddenly in a state of high alert.

"I expect so," Gwen said after a longish pause. "But we'll have to take it up with the council."

I vaguely remembered that the duchy was governed by a council. Was I going to have to go through them? I only had three weeks. What if there was some kind of grueling bureaucratic procedure? "Will it take long?"

"Oh, no," Gwen said. "I know the council members. In fact, I'm related to most of them." She shot me an encouraging smile. "I'll talk to people when we arrive. We can work something out."

"But you aren't sure, are you? They might say no." A weight settled in the pit of my stomach. What was I going to do if they didn't give me permission? Dr. Ferris would yank away my assistantship in a minute.

Gwen paused, her brows creasing. "I'm almost certain. It's just that people in the duchy aren't used to outsiders. And I'm not sure how they will feel about being...studied."

I hadn't thought of it that way. In fact, I hadn't thought out this project at all. There hadn't been time. But I understood what Gwen was saying. Who wants to be observed, like some poor lab rat? I pressed my fingers one by one on my jeans, as if I were playing my penny whistle. It was too late to go back, and I really needed this data. "Maybe you could talk to the duchess," I said.

Gwen startled. "The duchess? Oh, my grandmother, you mean. No, she passed away last year. There's no duchess, or duke, for that matter. My parents died when I was a child, so there's no successor. But we have a council, with six members. They make the decisions."

"Oh, I'm so sorry about your grandmother," I said.

"Thank you. Actually, this will be my first time back in the duchy since Gran's funeral."

I mused over Gwen's comments. "If your grandmother was the duchess, wouldn't you succeed her? Become the next duchess?"

"Me? Heavens no. I sing opera. That means I travel around the world. In fact, I'm performing at the Met this fall. How could I ever find the time to be a duchess?" She shook her head at the seemingly preposterous idea.

I don't remember much of the flight from New York to Paris, mostly because that leg of the journey was overnight, but also because I was a little drowsy from the Dramamine tablets I'd swallowed before takeoff to ward off motion sickness. However, I did get a chance to read the play, Our Noble Beginnings, which we would be putting on in St. Uguzo. Gwen handed me a manila folder containing the script. This consisted of stapled pages that I realized were photocopies of mimeographed sheets. The pages included blocking for the duchess, which I assumed was Gwen's role.

"Have you played the duchess before?" I asked.

"It's my third time. Every five years, I come back to portray the first duchess and to sing the anthem at the Ceremony of Allegiance. It's an obligation, but it's one that I happily fulfill."

Returning to the script, I saw that the play wasn't long. However, it had six scenes, with flowery, Victorian-style dialogue and even some Shakespearean-sounding phrases, like "Mistress, what cheer?" and "How now, good Sir?" The writer was identified as Ernest Merrywether, a Guzo schoolteacher who wrote his small masterpiece in 1886.

"It's a charming story," I said, "but a little old-fashioned."

"Quite true, but the Guzos are fond of it. It's the history of the duchy's founding, after all. And the older people have seen it performed every five years since they were children. Did you notice the sword fight? That wakes the snoozers up. And people shout and clap and boo all the way through. At the end, when the duke and duchess pledge their loyalty to the duchy, everybody stands up and cheers. So there's plenty of audience participation."

The Guzos sounded like a rowdy Shakespearean crowd.

"Besides," Gwen said, "we can't ditch the play or even alter it very much, because there are still a number of Merrywethers in the duchy, and they are loyal to their ancestor, Ernest."

Soon after, dinner was served, and Gwen picked at her supper while I scarfed down the chicken and rice. I never understood why people complained about airline food. Clearly, they ate better at home than I did. After the trays had been cleared, I read through the script again, more slowly this time, realizing that this play might be one of the keys to a new thesis for me. Even scholars enjoy a little drama and romance, I thought, if it's presented in the context of research.

(Dear readers, I imagine most of you are familiar with the history of St. Uguzo, but for those of you who are not, here is an overview of Mr. Merrywether's fine play.)

The story begins at a Welsh convent in 1538. There, Anwen, a young noblewoman, is preparing to become a nun. Unfortunately, however, she begins to dream of her convent burning down. This scares the nuns and disturbs the abbess, who agrees to let Anwen travel with Philippe, a dashing French nobleman, to a convent in France, just to be rid of her. Along the way, the two young people fall in love. (Wouldn't you know?) Instead of going directly to the convent, they stop at the French royal palace, where Anwen dreams that three of the king's henchmen are plotting to kill the king. His wife, the queen, takes Anwen's dream seriously, and they set up a trap for the villains, who are caught, but not before they engage in some "spirited swordplay." In his gratitude, the king gives Philippe a gold medallion and grants him a duchy. Afterward, Philippe asks Anwen for her hand in marriage, and she accepts. In the last scene, the new duke and duchess have arrived in their far-off duchy, and they pledge their loyalty to their subjects, new and old. Everyone cheers.

I closed the folder. "I'm looking forward to helping out with the production," I said. "And delving into duchy history."

"We have a local historian," Gwen said. "Peter. He runs the museum. It's small but rather nice. If you tell him you're interested, I expect he'll give you some guidance."

"That would be great." I pictured myself at a tiny museum, listening to an old codger relate stories of the past. If I was lucky, he would be happy to find an eager listener. Young people so rarely were, from what I'd seen.

"You know," I said, "there's something that puzzles me. I realize that people in the duchy are bilingual in English and French. I read that online. But shouldn't the historical play be written in French and not English? I mean, St. Uguzo was a French duchy."

"Oh, I forgot to tell you. People in the duchy mostly speak English, a dialect of English, one could say."

"Yes, but why? Why not French?"

Gwen yawned, a hand covering her mouth. "It's a long story. Anwen spoke English, as well as Welsh and French. Many of the nuns that she lived with also spoke English. Several came to join her at the duchy later, as did a number of English Catholic families who wanted to escape persecution from the Protestants, starting with Henry VIII. So, we've always had ties with England. Then, after World War One, the Brits supported the duchy's campaign for continued independence, and that strengthened the bonds. You should ask Peter. He can explain it better than I."

"Oh, interesting." I stuck the folder into the pocket on the back of the seat in front of me and pulled a notebook and pen out of my bag, making notes on what Gwen had just told me.

"You know, I've been thinking," Gwen said. "The delay in getting approval for your project may work out well for you. You'll have a chance to get your bearings in the duchy. And you'll meet people at the play rehearsals. Then, when you're ready to gather information, they will already know you."

"I suppose that's true," I said.

She eyed my notebook. "But you might want to be careful at first. Don't take notes in front of people. You don't want to cause suspicion."

"Oh, right." I closed the book, as if the warning should take effect immediately. I realized that I'd imagined myself making friends among the duchyites. But maybe I was kidding myself. Right now, I felt like a spy going undercover.

Gwen nodded off not long after the cabin lights went out. In the darkness, I was afraid that all my worries would keep me awake, replaying themselves over and over in my mind, but the drone of the plane soon put me to sleep as well.

We touched down at the Paris airport in the early morning, local time. I was nervous about going through Immigration. Would they recognize my St. Uguzo visa? But the official just stamped my passport without comment. The customs agent rifled through my handbag, pausing when she saw the M&Ms. "You are not in Outer Mongolia," she muttered.

When I told Gwen later, she just laughed. "You needn't have brought the candy. France has lovely chocolate. And Swiss and Belgian chocolate are also available. We'll stop and get some in Bois."

A couple of hours later, we boarded a small two-engine plane that would take us to Bois, a town in the French Alps. All the time, I'd kept my eyes open for lurking paparazzi, greedy for photos of Gwen, but I hadn't seen anyone aiming a camera at us. Maybe they hadn't yet learned of her break-up with the famous movie director, whoever he was. I hadn't wanted to ask.

"Do you think we're free of the reporters?" I asked.

"The reporters?" Gwen looked puzzled, then her expression brightened. "Oh, yes. We were very lucky, weren't we?"

It was late afternoon when our plane circled the terrifyingly short runway outside Bois and landed without any fuss. Stiff-legged, I made my way down the metal stairway, and several minutes later, we were outside the car rental agency, storing our luggage in the trunk of a little red Renault Twingo.

We headed into Bois, which turned out to be a charming small city nestled among towering, snow-capped mountains. We passed a medieval-looking church with a tall spire, and I would have loved to get out and walk around, but Gwen was clearly in a hurry, and we stopped only to visit a candy shop, where I passed up the beautifully ornamented chocolates in the case and instead bought two plain chocolate bars. To pay, I dipped into the stash of French francs that Gwen had given me. (Euros were not yet on the scene.) Next door was a touristy-looking ski shop, and on the other side was a cyber-café, where Gwen assured me I would be able to get onto the internet later. The duchy had no access, but she assured me that the duchy had daily buses going to and from Bois, the first one leaving at eight-thirty on weekday mornings.

"We have no television either," she said. "But there's plenty of gossip. News travels amazingly fast that way."

Then we were driving out of the city and heading southeast, moving ever higher into the mountains. Gwen steered with a feverish joy, maneuvering through curves at gut-clenching speeds. But when I wasn't engulfed in fear, I was ecstatic. Here I was, in the Alps at last, and they were just as majestic as I'd imagined.

An hour or so later, we turned onto an unmarked road, and soon we came to a tiny wooden building with the sign "Fermé" hanging in a dirt-encrusted window. Closed.

"The French used to keep a border guard here," Gwen said. "The poor fellow. He must have been bored out of his mind. Then, France had a budget crunch, and they decided to close the office. St. Uguzo never had a guard."

A few yards away a large sign proclaimed in English, French, and Italian:

YOU ARE ENTERING THE DUCHY OF ST. UGUZO

"Huzzah! Home again!" Gwen crowed.

Farther down the sign, I read:

No Lodging

No Camping

No Fishing

All Visitors Must Leave By Sundown

My chest tightened. They might as well have put up a sign saying, "Stay out." I cleared my throat. "This sign isn't very welcoming."

"Oh, pay that no mind," Gwen said. "You'll be my guest. Everyone will be friendly." But I thought I noticed a hint of reticence in her voice.

We soon approached a rustic, one-lane wooden bridge. I looked out the window as we rumbled across. Below, water rushed across dark boulders. "This bridge is kind of narrow," I said.

"You should have seen the old one," Gwen replied cheerily.

On the other side, the road wound upward, past meadows and hillsides forested with mostly deciduous trees, their leaves turning shades of ochre in the chilly September air. I recognized oaks and elms as well as occasional stands of birch. High above them loomed the craggy mountain peaks.

"You'll have to come back in the spring," Gwen said. "The wildflowers are lovely—cowslips and gentian and primrose. I love the colors."

"Does this land all belong to the duchy?" I asked.

"Yes. We used to have more, but France and Italy have chipped away at it over the years."

The sun was descending, throwing long shadows across the flanks of the mountains, when Gwen pulled the car over to the side of the road.

"There it is," she announced. "My favorite view of the city of St. Uguzo."

CHAPTER FOUR

Day 1, Saturday Evening

Gwen and I climbed out of the car, and I followed her to an overlook a few feet away.

"Oh my gosh," I murmured, looking out on the vista. It was magnificent. In the distance, craggy mountain peaks, their recesses smudged with snow, reached upward to a sky so deeply blue it was practically cobalt. Below the peaks, evergreen trees carpeted the high slopes. Closer to us, a sparkling stream rushed down the mountainside, and parallel to it, a road. To the left of the stream was a patchwork of trees in an array of fall colors, like the ones we'd seen on the drive up.

Gwen pointed toward the mountain range. "Do you see the tallest peak? There, near the middle? She's the Guardian, La Gardienne, as we sometimes call her."

The peak was multi-faceted, as if its slopes had been carved out by some divine jeweler. "As guardians go, she looks kind of severe," I said.

"That's true, I suppose, but life can be difficult. And Guzos believe she watches over us, especially through the hard times." She paused. "And those times never seem to be far off."

I glanced at Gwen, surprised at the chink in her usually sunny demeanor, but she had already regained her good humor.

I continued tracing the course of the stream and the road next to it. To the right side of the road, the elevation of the slopes was more gradual. Houses studded the grassy hills, mostly visible by their pitched roofs, dark brown or gray in color. Goats, or maybe sheep, clustered in penned areas next to some of the houses. After about a mile of descent, the terrain leveled out, and a town appeared beside the road, a compact place with narrow, winding streets and a spacious town square.

"Oh. That must be your capital," I said.

"Yes. St. Uguzo City," Gwen said. "Do you see the plaza?"

I nodded. A few tiny human figures were walking across the square.

"The Ceremony of Allegiance is held there. At the far side there will be a big stage where the council members sit, all wearing their red sashes. Below them, the square will be crammed with Guzos—men and women, all there to pledge their loyalty to the duchy. It's quite stirring, really, a mass of people standing tall, their knives held high. They make the pledge, then huzzah for all they're worth."

"They raise knives?" I asked.

"Mostly hunting knives, a few daggers. In the old days, only men raised their weapons. Now women sometimes bring their kitchen knives. Everyone is ready to defend the duchy, symbolically at any rate. Although I like to think it's more than just symbolic. I do hope the day will be sunny. Then the sunlight will hit the blades and turn the plaza into a field of brilliance." She shivered. "It always gives me a thrill."

"The ceremony sounds exciting," I said. Dr. Ferris would be ecstatic to read about such a medieval-sounding rite—if, that is, I got permission to carry out the study. When I got permission, I corrected my treacherous inner voice.

Gwen slipped her hand through the crook of my arm. "You know, I travel around the world to sing opera. But this is where my heart lives." Her voice had softened and lost its cheeriness, and I realized I was hearing the true Gwen Renard, not the famous opera star. "My roots go deep here," she continued, "and that's true of every Guzo I know. The duchy is several hundred years old, but some of our ancestors have lived here for much longer, for thousands of years. This place is in our blood, in our bones. At the celebration, when we pledge our loyalty to the duchy, the words have weight. It is a sacred oath."

Gwen's words moved me, but I also felt a small stab of envy. I couldn't imagine ever making such a passionate declaration of love for the U.S. It wasn't that I wasn't fond of my homeland. Of course I was. But our pledge of allegiance had a far milder effect on me, maybe because I had said it by mindless rote so often as a school girl. Besides, the people in my country who claimed to be patriots were often hateful toward their fellow Americans, people of a different ethnic or religious group, in fact, anyone not just like them. They made patriotism feel sleazy. At least in this regard, I wished I could be more like the Guzos. "I suppose you have to be born here to feel such deep loyalty," I said.

Gwen hesitated. "Usually, but not always."

Just above the plaza, I spotted a hump-backed bridge that crossed the stream. It led to a narrow road that skimmed the forest edge and wound its way to a stone wall. Within the wall, a series of stone structures, including a tower at one corner, encircled a central courtyard. "What are those stone buildings?" I asked, "The ones beyond the bridge."

"That's the convent. Or what's left of it. A group of nuns arrived here from Wales a few years after the duchy was founded. The museum is inside the convent grounds. Beyond that is the cheesery. You can't see it from here because of the trees. That's where our marvelous cheese is made. You'll get a tour of the place, I'm sure."

"Do they give away free samples?"

Gwen laughed. "You can probably talk Fred into it. He's our chee-semonger. I'm sure you'll get to know him at play rehearsals. He's a marvel-ous actor."

I hated to leave the overlook, but I could see that Gwen was eager to be on her way. The truth is, I was getting nervous about arriving. The duchy was beautiful. But would the people be welcoming, and would I be able to carry out my study?

The sun was getting lower, sending ominous-looking shadows across the valley and further chilling the air. I buttoned my trench coat as we got back into the car, already wondering if I'd brought enough warm clothes. We drove on, no longer ascending, but circling down the mountainside. We finally crossed a stream and followed alongside it as it cut through a valley. It took me a minute to realize that we were now on the road that we'd seen from above.

From the car window, I had a better look at the houses dotting the hills. Many were wooden cottages with porches, while others were larger, resembling the pictures I'd seen of Swiss chalets. These seemed plainer, though, without decorative carving or colorful window frames. The ragged bleating of goats carried in the breeze.

Gwen slowed the car as we approached three houses standing in a line several yards up from the road. The first was a wooden cottage with a black Saab parked next to it. A black Saab, like the one my cousin drove, if I wasn't mistaken. The other two houses were two-story wooden chalets with stone foundations. The gray pitched roofs were covered with flat stones that looked like slate and projected well beyond the walls, sheltering everything below. Both houses had verandas in front and a balcony traversing the second floor. Lucky home owners, I thought. The view from the balconies must be stunning.

The cottage and middle house were dark, but a soft light emerged from the lower windows of the third house, and smoke billowed up from the chimney. Gwen pulled the car onto a narrow gravel drive beside the house in the middle. "This is where we'll be staying," she said. "It was Gran's house, and now it's mine, at least for the time being."

From the chalet next door, a coltish teenage girl appeared on the veranda. She had black hair in pigtails and was wearing slacks and a red sweater. Instantly, she disappeared inside. "Mum, Gran," the girl called, "Gwen is here."

A moment later, the door opened and the girl bounded out, followed by two women with lean frames and dark hair and eyes. I had expected everyone to be blond and blue-eyed like Gwen, but this family looked almost Asiatic, with their broad faces and almond-shaped eyes. The older woman, somewhere over sixty years, had an old-fashioned, country look, with a high-necked gray blouse and a calf-length skirt partly hidden by a white apron. The younger woman, in her mid-forties probably, looked more modern, in khaki slacks and a cardigan sweater with a bright blue border. Both wore sturdy walking shoes.

"What cheer!" the older woman called.

Gwen had jumped out of the car and was soon hugging one friend after the other. "How fare you all?" she asked.

"Well, as you can see," the older woman said.

"And excited to have you back," the younger woman said.

"My heavens, Kessie," Gwen said, placing her hands on the girl's shoulders, "it has only been a year, and you've grown into a young lady. How old are you now?"

"Thirteen," the girl said, rocking back and forth in her sneakers. "I'm to be in the play. A lady-in-waiting."

"How lovely," Gwen said. "We'll be performing together, then."

I'd gotten out of the car, but hung back, feeling shy about inserting myself into the happy reunion.

Gwen turned to me. "Holly, come and meet my friends," and she proceeded to introduce Rosamunde, her daughter Juliette, and Juliette's daughter, Kestrel.

"People call me Kessie," the girl said, peering at me with open curiosity.

"We're so glad you've come, Holly," Rosamunde said, her weathered face crinkling into a smile. "We were hoping you could join us."

"Oh, thank you," I said, "but I'm afraid I'm just a replacement. Gwen's friend had to drop out at the last minute."

Rosamunde patted my arm. "You are exactly who we were hoping for. You will be helping out with the play, n'est-ce pas?"

"Yes," I said, skipping a beat at the French phrase, but also starting to relax. "Gwen said some of the actors might need assistance with their lines. And I can help out with props or scenery or anything else, really." I'd worked on both high school plays and community theater, so I felt at home on a theater set.

"Brilliant," Juliette said. "Peter will be delighted to have you. He's the director this year."

"Peter?" Gwen said. "How did that happen?"

Juliette shook her head, her short bobbed hair shining. "Not by choice. No one else would step up, so he finally agreed. He's also playing the King of France."

"What a sport he is," Gwen said. "At least the monarch has few lines." I wondered if the reluctant director/king was the same Peter who was the duchy's historian.

"I haven't any lines in the play," Kessie grumbled.

"Oh, but all the actors are very important," I said. "And that includes those without speaking parts. Everyone's role is crucial to the success of the play." It's what I'd been told in my high school theater productions, when I ended up playing a crowd member. Tall girls didn't play leading ladies. The best roles I could hope for were character parts, but occasionally I had ended up as a bystander.

Kessie scrunched her face, apparently considering the idea. "The ladies-in-waiting are important," she said. "And Gran is playing the queen."

"Once again," Rosamunde said, chuckling. "The costume still fits, so I didn't have much say in the matter. "But come," she said, "let's get you both settled. Then we'll have a little supper and share all our news."

We hauled our bags up the stairs to the veranda and into the house. A hallway led to a stairway at the back. Gwen led us through a doorway on the right that opened onto a larger room. She flicked on an overhead light, revealing a large wood-paneled living room with a rustic feel, similar to a cabin my family had stayed at one summer in Minnesota. The air felt chilly and a little damp, although I noticed a stone fireplace with firewood stacked in it. The chairs and sofa looked comfortable enough, their wooden frames covered by blue checked cushions.

"I left a few things in your fridge—milk and cheese mostly," Rosamunde said. "And bread in the breadbox. I'll go next door now and finish up our meal. Come when you're ready." She bustled out.

"There are two bedrooms upstairs," Gwen said to me. "Mine is in the back, and you can have the front room. The balcony is right off it."

"Oh, thank you," I said. I couldn't believe my luck. A balcony with a view of the mountains, right outside my room.

We carried our bags upstairs, Kessie helping with Gwen's suitcases. My room was large, with four single beds accompanied by nightstands, and armoires against the walls. I wondered if more people would be arriving for the celebration. I headed for the one bed that was made up and set down my bag beside it. On top was a quilt with a pattern of interlocking circles in faded but still pretty colors. It was stuffed with goose down, judging from a feather peeking out of a side seam. My small bedside table was topped with a reading lamp.

At the end of the room was a door, presumably leading to the balcony. I crossed to it and stepped outside. The sun was setting, bleaching the valley of color, but the last golden light of day illuminated the towering alps in the distance. The Guardian and her sisters were watching over us.

When I walked inside, Kessie was perched on one of the unmade beds. "I could stay here sometime," she said, "if you wanted company."

"That's very sweet of you," Gwen said from the doorway. "We'll be sure and let you know."

After Kessie departed, somewhat reluctantly, Gwen and I took turns in the bathroom, a half-bath, really, with a toilet and sink, surprisingly modern. My energy had begun to flag, but a few splashes of cold water on my face helped revive me.

A few minutes later, drawn by the aroma of hot food, we scurried several yards to the house next door. After climbing the stairs to the veranda, I followed Gwen through the front door.

"Halloo," Gwen called out as we entered the pleasingly warm house. I followed Gwen from the hall to the living room, which had a similar layout to Gwen's place. A large gray cat was curled up beside the fireplace, which glowed with embers, and a carved grandfather clock ticktocked in one corner. We headed straight back to the large, farmhouse-style kitchen at the rear of the house. There, Rosamunde's family awaited us.

Supper was a cheerful, bustling affair. Rosamunde's husband, Rob, sat at the end of a long table with wide pine planks. He was a quiet man with graying hair and a weathered face, much like his wife's. But he also sported a full salt-and-pepper beard and mustache that gave him a mountain man look. When he got up to fetch more bread, I noticed that he was wearing baggy slacks, a collarless shirt, and a loose vest. His sturdy, grayish clothing was brightened by an emerald-green kerchief knotted at a jaunty angle around his neck.

Juliette's ten-year-old son nodded shyly when he was introduced to me as Ozzie, short for Osprey. He stood at one end of the table, looking as if he was ready to dash off at any moment. I wondered where Juliette's husband was. I would ask Gwen later.

The meal consisted of a hearty goat stew with carrots, parsnips, and potatoes. A loaf of fresh bread was sliced and passed around. The goat meat had an unfamiliar taste, but I decided I liked it well enough and ate with relish, mopping up the stew with a hunk of bread.

The other women hardly ate, sneaking in a bite here and there as they hashed over the local news. This included their neighbors' assorted injuries, illnesses, and deaths, a spectacular win by the local soccer team over the team from Bois, young people marrying or leaving the duchy for England or France, and old people going abroad to live with their grown children. It sounded like there was a fair amount of migration out of the duchy.

"Oh, and Clive Cotton has disappeared," Rosamunde said. "You remember him, the assistant cheesemaker."

"Clive? I've always liked him," Gwen said. "He has the best jokes. What do you mean, he disappeared?"

"Here one day, gone the next," Rob said.

Juliette frowned. "It turns out he has large gambling debts in Bois. Apparently, he was under some pressure to pay them. Who knows? Maybe a quiet escape was his best option. You remember his wife, Alice. She says she's heard nothing from him. Of course, she might say that to protect him. But I'm inclined to believe her."

"Poor Alice," Gwen said.

"Truly," Rosamunde said. "Clive's disappearance is taking a toll on her, as you can imagine. She's certain he wouldn't just take off without a word. She's afraid something terrible has happened to him. "

"Maybe he's dead," Kessie said ominously, her almond eyes wide.

"Oh, surely not," Gwen said.

Juliette shrugged. "It's been three weeks, and we keep waiting for some kind of news. But there's still have no clue. In the meantime, Alice has been promoted to assistant cheesemaker. She's experienced, and with two teenage children, she needed the job."

She turned to Ozzie, who had eaten most of his stew and was twirling his spoon on the table. "Did you finish your French homework?"

"Yeah," he said. Juliette gave him a piercing look. "Well, almost."

"Go and finish, then. I'll be up a little later to check it." The boy trudged off, his sneakered feet clumping up the stairs.

Rob finished Ozzie's stew, and we women cleared the table, stacking bowls in the sink and leaving the pots to soak. The pot of stew was almost empty, and I had to admit, I had done my fair share.

When we moved into the living room, a pleasant low flame was crackling in the fireplace, and Rob sat in a leather armchair by the fire, puffing on a long-stemmed pipe. Gwen and I sank onto a wooden sofa with green and red plaid cushions opposite the hearth, and Rosamunde and Kessie took matching chairs, forming a semi-circle around the hearth.

While we waited for Juliette, Gwen filled Rosamunde in on her recent U.S. singing engagements. I noticed that she mentioned nothing about her break-up with the famous movie director. Soon, Juliette pulled up a chair beside the sofa.

"We should tell you about the play," Rosamunde said to Gwen. "We've had a read-through and checked the blocking. I think everyone knows where to stand now. The first real rehearsal is tomorrow night."

"And who's playing the duke?" Gwen asked. "As I recall, Felix said he was getting too old for the part."

Rosamunde and Juliette exchanged a guarded look. "I don't think you've met him. Wilheard Fosse," Rosamunde said.

"Fosse? He must be related to Eglentyne. Where did he come from?"

"Some place in the U.S., apparently," Juliette said. "I tried to coax the information out of him, but he's close-mouthed about his previous life. A few months ago, he just showed up out of the blue."

Rob scowled. "He's a dodgy sort. Claims to work for some high-powered syndicate. He's told us often enough. Drives around like a lord in one of them BMWs."

"Anyway," Juliette said, "he's keen to stay and establish himself as a true Guzo. He practically demanded the role of the duke in the play. Not that there was any competition."

Kessie scrunched her nose. "He's too old and fat to be the duke."

Juliette shot her daughter a reproving look.

"Everybody says so," Kessie mumbled.

"I'm sure he'll be fine," Gwen said. Turning to me, she said, "we make do with the actors we have. One year the fellow playing the duke was a grandfather." She lowered her voice. "But quite a good-looking one."

"Old Donny's a brash one," Rob said. "Had his eye on Roz the whole time."

"What rubbish," Rosamunde muttered, but she exchanged a knowing look with her husband, whose eyes crinkled mischievously. "At any rate, Eglentyne seems fond of her cousin. It's not surprising, really. After her aunt and father died, she was the last remaining Fosse in the duchy. As to Wilheard's merits, we'll let you draw your own conclusions."

The grandfather clock standing against the wall chimed the half hour. Eight-thirty. Kessie glanced at the clock, then looked away quickly.

Juliette eyed her daughter. "Kessie, how are you doing with your maths assignment?"

"Oh, Mum, it's sooo boring."

"Yes, I know, but go on with you, and give it half an hour."

Kessie darted a look at the rest of us, as if someone might give her a reprieve, gave up, and trudged up the stairs.

Rosamunde faced Gwen. "You may as well know, the Bonnet Brothers are causing trouble again. Clamoring to open up the duchy to outside investors. And God knows what else."

"Now, Mum, it isn't just the Bonnet brothers," Juliette said. "But you're right. Some of the younger men have become quite insistent. And they've gained support for their demands. The mead hall is turning into a regular hotbed of dissension."

"A bunch of malcontents, they be," Rob grumbled.

"What sort of investments do they want?" Gwen asked.

"What don't they want?" Juliette said. "Some of the demands are fairly reasonable—money for a café, an inn, a brewery. But there are also calls for fast food chains, an upscale ski resort, and computers. At one point they were talking about an alpine theme park."

I gasped, shocked by the idea of a Heidi-Land, or Duchy-land, whatever it might be. Everyone turned to me, as if suddenly remembering I was there.

"They were probably joking about the theme park," Juliette said. "At least I hope so."

Gwen shook her head slowly. "It all sounds ghastly. I hope that no one has come to blows over these wild schemes."

"Not yet," Rob said.

A knock at the kitchen door was followed by a deep "Halloo." A moment later, a slender man in his mid-thirties with brown, unruly hair and hazel eyes appeared in the doorway. His brows were dark, but otherwise, they resembled Gwen's, with the same upturned wings at the outer edges. He was in jeans and a navy windbreaker, and he might have been attractive if it weren't for the gloom that hung over him like a storm cloud.

"Peter!" Gwen cried. She jumped up and raced over, flinging her arms around him. "It's so good to see you."

"And you," Peter said, his face brightening as he returned her hug.

Gwen took his hand. "I'm so sorry about Bren. I wanted to go to the memorial service, but I was in Strasburg and..."

"No, don't apologize. It was an informal gathering, put together quickly. Mostly neighbors, Bren's rugby mates, and a few ex-girlfriends. Lots of stories. Bren would have liked it, I think."

"Set yourself down, lad," Rob said, and Peter pulled up a chair in the space that Ozzie had vacated. Rosamunde offered him stew, but he declined, saying he'd just come from the dining hall.

"Holly, this is my cousin Peter," Gwen said. "He's the historian I was telling you about." She turned to Peter. "I persuaded Holly to leave the U.S. and join us for the celebration. And you'll be pleased to know, she has volunteered to help out with the play."

"Good. We can always use workers," he said, casting me a cursory glance. His speech sounded upper class British, at least to my American ears, different from Gwen's more continental pronunciation. So far, it seemed like every Guzo I'd met spoke a different dialect. It was interesting, but a little confusing.

"Holly is also interested in duchy history," Gwen said. "I thought she would enjoy seeing the museum."

"Why not," Peter said. "Come by some time. Let's see. Tomorrow is Sunday. I'll open around ten." His offhand manner tempered my high hopes. My visions of sitting around with a talkative old codger had vanished.

"Thank you," I said, summoning a bit of my now diminished enthusiasm. "I look forward to learning as much as I can."

"Yes, well, the museum isn't all that grand," Peter mumbled.

"Bah," Rosamunde exclaimed. "Whatever are you talking about? It's a very fine place." She turned to me. "Pay him no mind. I'll be at the museum about eleven. I can show you around, if Peter is occupied." She cast him a dark look.

Peter blanched, looking chastened. "Sorry," he said. "I seem to be a bit off my game tonight." He faced me. "I'll be happy to give you a tour when you come by. Holly, wasn't it?"

"Yes," I said, and Rosamund nodded at him approvingly, like a teacher satisfied with her pupil.

"And now," he said, pushing back his chair, "I'd best be on my way."

"Must you leave so soon?" Gwen asked. She looked so crestfallen I thought he would surely relent.

"Bonnie awaits," he said. "I just stopped by to welcome the travelers. I'll see you all tomorrow." He stood and let himself out the kitchen door.

"Who is Bonnie?" I asked, imagining a wife or young daughter.

"His dog," Juliette said. "An energetic young collie. If I'm not mistaken, he has begun using her as an excuse for weaseling out of social engagements."

"Now, daughter," Rosamunde said reprovingly. She turned to me. "Peter lost his younger brother about six months ago. A skiing accident. Between losing his grandmother and his brother, all within a year's time, he has been brought low."

"We've all been trying to cut him slack," Juliette said. "I was hoping the play would help revive him."

"Oh, I almost forgot," Rosamund said. "He's had more bad news. The council met this afternoon. They've refused to provide additional funding for the museum. Never mind that it had been promised a year ago. I did what I could to approve the funds, but we were deadlocked." She faced Gwen. "Now that your gran is no longer on the council, we are only six members. It's hard to get a majority vote."

I shifted on my chair. The duchy council was the group that would decide if my project would live or die. They didn't sound all that cooperative, despite what Gwen had told me on the plane. At least, Rosamunde was a member. I hoped I could count on her support.

"Poor Peter," Gwen said. "Back-stabbed by the council. No wonder he looked so glum. Why haven't they replaced Gran?"

"Several people have been proposed," Rosamunde said, "but they have all met with opposition from one side or another." She clucked her tongue.

"Oh, but shame on us. Burdening you with all this unpleasant business when you've just arrived."

"No, go ahead," Gwen said. "I'll have to face the situation sooner or later. It's best I'm prepared."

"Then you might as well know," Juliette said. "The progressives—that's what they call themselves—the progressives are talking about nominating a candidate for duke."

"What?" Gwen exclaimed. "How can that be?"

"It's not as strange as it sounds," Rosamunde said. "A law was passed about six years ago. Anyone born in St. Uguzo or their direct descendant may be declared duke or duchess, provided they live here, of course. They just need the council's approval. And the consent of the Guzo people, which was never defined very clearly."

"I don't remember that law," Gwen said.

"I believe you were performing in Japan at the time it was passed," Rosamunde said.

"Oh. Japan. I guess I had other things on my mind."

"Like a certain baritone?" Juliet said under her breath. She and Gwen shared a knowing smile.

Rosamunde continued. "Your grandmother introduced it. She knew that you didn't want to be duchess, and this was before Peter took the job at the museum, so he and Brendan were both living in England. She was afraid that none of her grandchildren would want the responsibility. So the law allows another Guzo to become duke or duchess."

"I see," Gwen said. "Well, I'm clearly in no position to object, since I'm one of the good-for-nothings who refuses the title. But it's not really a big deal, is it? I mean, the duke is a council member, just like the other six. And he has occasional ceremonial duties. That's about it. Maybe these progressives don't realize how little power the duke really wields."

"Maybe," Rosamunde said. "But he—or she-would carry a certain status. And he would represent us to the outside world. Become a symbol of the duchy."

"That's right," Rob said. "The last thing we need is some hotheaded plonker as duke."

Gwen frowned. "And who are the hotheads proposing?"

"Well, that's the good news," Juliette said. "They can't agree on anyone. You know how the families are. Each is afraid that another family will surpass them in power and prestige."

"It would be different if you wanted to be duchess," Rosamunde said, nodding to Gwen. "Or if Peter did. You are Duchess Anne-Marie's grandchildren, after all. Virtually all the Guzos would accept either of you as the rightful heir to the title. Even though Peter grew up in England. He did spend his summers here, of course. And he's lived here for the last four years."

"Well, I'm out of the running," Gwen said. "We've discussed this before. But I can have a little cousin-to-cousin talk with Peter. See if I can cheer him up a bit. And maybe talk him into accepting a nomination to become duke. He doesn't have Gran's prodigious moral authority, but he's no plonker."

"Good luck with convincing him," Juliette said. "Believe me, we've tried."

"You know," Rosamunde said, "if Peter is willing to be duke, now would be the ideal time to make it known. He could be put forward as a nominee at the Ceremony of Allegiance and be approved immediately by a raising of knives."

The conversation was fascinating, revealing one piece of news after another. But even so, my eyelids were feeling increasingly droopy, and I started to yawn, swiftly covering it with my hand. My two days of travel, plus jet lag, had finally caught up with me.

"We should be going," Gwen said. "It's been a long day for us both."

After expressing our thanks for dinner and the warm welcome, we said good night and hurried back to Gwen's house. I noticed lights on in the cottage next door. "Who lives there?" I asked.

"Peter. Maybe we can lure him over for breakfast in the morning."

"Are you going to lock up?" I asked as we stepped inside.

"Gran never did. The duchy is safe enough. Besides, the sheriff lives next door."

"Rob?" I asked.

"No. Juliette."

So, Juliette was the sheriff. This place was full of surprises. We climbed the stairs to the bedrooms, and Gwen halted at the top. "Oh, by the way," she said, "please keep to yourself everything you've learned tonight. It would do the duchy no good if our troubles were to leak out to the wider world."

"I understand," I said.

In my chilly bedroom, I shivered as I quickly changed into my jams and pulled on clean socks. The sheets were cold, but I trusted that my body heat combined with the quilt would produce enough warmth for me to fall asleep eventually. In the meantime, I lay curled up on my side, the bedding pulled up over my nose. My head swam with all the new sensations and ideas I'd been bombarded with since leaving home.

My first glimpses of St. Uguzo had been of a beautiful, idyllic mountain enclave, a place where ancient traditions still thrived. But it had taken only a couple of hours for me to be disabused of this peaceful fantasy and become immersed in the local drama. Dr. Ferris might be hoping for a report about a duchy captured in an earlier, even medieval time, like an insect in amber. But I could already see that she wasn't going to get it.

My last thought before I drifted into sleep was that it was surprising how willing everyone was to trust me with information about the duchy's problems. For a people known for their aversion to outsiders, Gwen's friends had readily gathered me into the fold. Or at least, ignored the fact that I was there.

CHAPTER FIVE

Day 2, Sunday

I woke when the morning was just turning gray, aware that my nose was cold but the rest of me was cozy. It took me a moment to remember that I was under a goose-down quilt, in an upstairs bedroom in Gwen's house. And this would be my first full day in the duchy. I popped out of bed, filled with the energy that surges forth when you've escaped your ordinary rut and awakened to a new and fascinating place.

I pulled my coat on over my jams and opened the balcony door to a blast of cold air. The view from the railing revealed the far-off mountains looming gray above the shadowy valley. But above them, wispy bands of clouds shone in luscious shades of pink and gold and tangerine. It would be a beautiful morning. A nearby cock crowed, then another and another, each one farther away. Goats baahed, eager to start the day.

Inside again, I stopped outside Gwen's room and listened. No sounds of stirring. After using the bathroom as quietly as possible, I pulled clothes out of my bag, donning jeans, a long-sleeve shirt, a sweater, and finishing with my coat. After two days on the road, my hair felt kind of grungy, and I pulled it into a pony tail, held in place by a black scrunchy.

Carrying my socks and sneakers, I started down the stairs, trying not to cause too much creaking. Memories of last night's conversation came back to me as I laced my shoes on the bottom step. The situation in the duchy seemed more explosive than Gwen had described it on the plane. I hoped the turmoil wouldn't cause problems for my study. In the kitchen, I drank a glass of water, then slipped out the front door.

From the veranda, I saw that the sun now illuminated the high peaks, brushing them with gold. A minute later, I was following the road uphill, away from the town. I didn't feel ready to face people on my own, and I wanted to see the landscape up close. It didn't take long before I was breathing heavily, and I reminded myself that the duchy must be at a fairly high elevation—one detail to fill in later for my study. I slowed down a little, enjoying the shushing, gurgling sound of the stream as it rushed over and around rocks.

On the other side of the stream, among the trees, I caught a movement in the underbrush. It was a small animal keeping an eye on me, no doubt. "Hello," I said softly. "I'm curious about you too." (Yes, I know. Most people don't engage animals in conversation, especially wild ones. But I've spoken to squirrels and birds and the occasional grasshopper since I was a child. I didn't expect a response, which was a good thing, since I never got more than an alert and puzzled stare. For me, it was enough to express my friendly intentions.)

About half a mile above the house, I discovered a natural bridge across the stream, consisting of several large, mostly flat rocks. I clambered down the bank, then gathered my courage and leaped from rock to slippery rock, narrowly avoiding a fall into what I was sure would be freezing water. With relief, my feet landed on the opposite side, and I scrambled up the bank.

A few yards away lay the entrance to a leaf-strewn footpath leading into the woods. For several minutes, I ambled along it, glancing up periodically to make sure the Guardian was still in view. As long as I could see her craggy outline, I shouldn't get lost in the forest. From a distance, the tree cover had seemed dense, but I now saw a few small grassy clearings through the trees, and assorted large rocks dotted the landscape.

As I approached a knee-high boulder, I spotted a squat, furry animal sitting on top, staring at me. A marmot. I had come across them when I was a girl, vacationing in the Rocky Mountains in Colorado, and I found them charming in a plump, waddly sort of way. This guy was attractive, with his sleek gray head transitioning into a bushy, golden brown coat.

"Hello there," I whispered. In response, he jumped down and disappeared into the trees, only to reappear on the path several yards ahead of me. He continued up the trail, looking back at one point. Then he headed into the trees once again. I trod onward, enjoying the early morning bird song and watching as the sunlight gradually traveled down the mountainsides and brightened the colors of the leaves.

A shrill marmot chirp halted my steps, and looking to the left, I realized there was a barely visible footpath that veered off the main trail. I hesitated, wondering if I should follow it. Then I caught sight of the marmot sitting on a large rock several yards down the path. He was peering at me with his dark brown eyes, and as I started after him, he did another disappearing act, this time into high brush.

I took the turn, and after several minutes, the trail curved uphill, the broad-leafed trees gradually giving way to fir trees, followed by a grove of stately birches. I have always loved birch trees, and these were beautiful, their white bark glowing in the soft morning light. They looked scarred, with their dark gray markings. But even so, there was something cheerful lighthearted about them, their yellow leaves fluttering in the cool breeze. And then, the trees gave way to a small clearing. I stopped at the edge. The area was nearly circular, with a diameter of about twelve feet. Oddly, the ground was bare, with no grass or other plants underfoot, the compacted earth touched only by dappled morning sunlight.

As I stepped inside the circle, an oddly exhilarating feeling enveloped me, as if the air surrounding me was electrically charged, almost alive.

What's more, I sensed that I wasn't alone. Oddly enough, I wasn't frightened. It was just an awareness I had, a knowing.

I stepped into the center of the glade, and the vibrancy surrounding me became even stronger. I had never felt so aware of the world around me. Turning in a very slow circle, I peered into the surrounding forest, alert to any unexpected movement or color or sound. But there was nothing, no one. I was alone in this glade. Alone and not alone. I closed my eyes, and almost at once, I was bathed in a feeling of complete and utter well-being. For the first time since I started this crazy adventure, I knew I was in the right place at the right time. Everything would work out. I didn't know how, but I knew in every cell of my being that I would be all right.

As I stood there, a wondrous, shimmery vibration flowed upward from the base of my spine to my belly, then my chest, my throat, up to my head, and finally through me, as if my body had opened to the cosmos. And then, in an instant, the other-worldly hum was gone. I opened my eyes, and I was still standing in the middle of the glade, with my sneaker-clad feet planted securely on the ground. Everything was back to normal. Normal, but changed. To my delight, my anxieties had vanished. I was entirely content.

I heard a rustling in the leaves and turned to see Rosamunde, in a long skirt and a rust-colored shawl. She was standing at the edge of the circle, the path behind her.

"You felt it, did you not?" she said. She wasn't smiling exactly, but her weathered face looked hopeful.

"Yes," I said. "That is, I felt something. What was it?"

Rosamunde cocked her head. "You can be sure you're not the first one to ask that. But I'm afraid I have no definite answer. Some say this glade is situated at a thin place. It's a spot where the boundary between earth and spirit is porous, where the two are able to touch."

"A thin place," I murmured, mulling it over. Had I been touched by something supernatural? If so, it was a first. If God had ever spoken to me,

I certainly wasn't paying attention. "I felt so peaceful," I said. "Then I had this strange, shimmery sensation. Like a hum moving through me."

"Yes. I've had that too."

What an extraordinary place the glade was, I thought. And it was close to Gwen's house. I could run over here every morning for a little mood lifter. In fact, I was surprised the place wasn't more popular. The path certainly didn't look well trodden. "Do Guzos come here often?"

"No. Actually, most people don't feel the sensation at all. They think the whole idea is rubbish."

I couldn't blame the nonbelievers. If I hadn't felt the sensation myself, I might have dismissed the idea as some kind of delusion.

"Even those who feel the hum are well advised not to dwell on it. They are better off tending to their daily lives—their work and families. There are stories about people who spent too much time here and became mentally unbalanced."

"I understand." So much for a daily trip to the glade. Rosamunde was right. I could imagine becoming addicted to this place, to the shimmer.

We started back along the path, walking single-file at first, then side by side when we got to the main trail.

"Has anyone ever studied the glade?" I asked. "I mean scientifically?"

"Two Englishmen came to the duchy in the 1930s. They were on a world tour, they told people, and they wanted a guide to show them around St. Uguzo. The Guzos considered them rather peculiar. Who would stop at the duchy on a world tour?"

"My father was a skilled hunter, and he knew the duchy well. So, he offered to show the Englishmen around. As it turned out, they weren't just on a tour. They were on a mission—a quest to find the remaining "*Thin Places*" in the world. I can't say if they were scientists, but they were very thorough in their methods."

I was intrigued. "Did they find other *Thin Places*? Besides the duchy?"

"Oh yes. They were especially taken with the Himalayas. They recorded lots of stories there, of gods appearing to people, of spirit visitations, that sort of thing."

"Did they themselves have such encounters?"

"No, and they were very disappointed. But one of them wrote up a fine report of their travels and sent a copy to my father. It's in the museum now. You should ask Peter to let you borrow it."

"I will," I said. It would make interesting reading, something to tide me over until I got permission to start my own research. I had to admit, my topic was not quite as intriguing as a search for *Thin Places* around the world.

By the time we came to the stream, my sense of well-being was beginning to ebb. Rosamunde traversed the rocks easily, but I hesitated. "The stones can be slick," she said, then crossed back half-way and extended her hand.

When we were back on the road, I realized that the day was warming up, and I took off my coat. Noises drifted up from the town below, the sound of people talking, shouting, laughing. Cart wheels rumbling over cobblestones. The bleat of goats.

"I should warn you," Rosamunde said, as we headed downhill, "sometimes people have vivid dreams after they've visited the glade."

"Nightmares, you mean?" It wasn't a happy prospect.

"Not necessarily. The dreams have a certain clarity. Sometimes they're more like visions. They can be pleasant. Or not."

"Do you have these vivid dreams?"

"Sometimes." She gazed straight ahead, her jaw set, suggesting that further information was not forthcoming.

We had stopped in front of Gwen's house when a question occurred to me. "How did you find me at the glade?" I asked.

She smiled with a hint of amusement. "Rob saw you walking up the road quite early. I had a hunch I would find you there. I hope you don't mind my keeping an eye on you. You know, we all want you to feel at home here." Her words were soothing, but I caught a touch of concern in her eyes. Maybe it was just the Guzos' customary wariness around strangers. Or maybe Rosamunde realized how wildly out of my depth I was.

CHAPTER SIX

Day 2, Sunday

When I got back to the house, I found Gwen sitting at a circular wooden table in the kitchen, looking comfy in soft gray sweats, her blond hair flowing down her back. Sunlight streamed in from a window above a deep enamel sink.

"You must have risen early," she said, smiling. She set a cup of steaming tea down on a china saucer. A slice of bread and jam sat before her, half eaten. "Help yourself to breakfast. The gooseberry jam is locally made, and the butter is fresh. Oh, and I set out a chunk of our everyday goat cheese, in case you want to try it."

"It looks great," I said, suddenly aware that I'd worked up an appetite on my adventure in the forest.

"There's hot water in the kettle. And tea bags here. She pointed to a dark blue metal container on the table. In case you're a tea drinker."

"I am," I said. Gwen had left an extra cup and saucer on the table. They were pretty, decorated with cheerful pansies, and I brought over the kettle and filled the cup. I sat and sliced a piece of bread, slathering butter and the juicy pink jam on it. I took a bite. Heavenly. "I've had gooseberry jam before, but it was green."

"Gran always made her jam with ripe gooseberries. That's why it's pink." All at once, her face crumpled, and she covered it with her hands. Her shoulders shook, and she sobbed quietly, then inhaled deeply and straightened, wiping tears off her cheeks. "Sorry. Every now and then some memory of Gran pops up, and off I go."

"I understand. I know how hard it is to lose a grandmother." I hadn't known my grandmother well. She and Mom hadn't been on the best of terms. Still, Grandma and I had loved each other, and she had always encouraged me to set worthwhile goals and work hard to attain them. For years, she had her own crop-dusting business, flying planes over the Midwest. In her younger years, she had been a pilot, and she knew that a woman had to stand firm to get what she wanted. When she died eight years earlier, my one-woman cheering section had vanished, and sometimes I wondered if my ability to persevere had vanished too.

Gwen sipped her tea. "So, tell me where you went at the crack of dawn."

I told her about visiting the glade, and she peered at me intently.

"My heavens," she said. "How ever did you find the place?"

"Oh, I just followed the trail." I was reluctant to admit to Gwen that a marmot had been my guide. I had come to the duchy as a serious scholar, after all. I finished my bread, savoring the Duchess Anne-Marie's jam. "Rosamunde said that not everyone feels anything at the glade."

Gwen nodded. "You were quite fortunate. I went there with Gran a few times over the years. Once or twice, I thought I felt something, but now I'm not so sure. I could have just imagined it—you know, to please Gran and feel satisfied with myself. It seems I'm sensitive to music but not so much to vibrations in the forest."

She got up and refilled our cups from the kettle while I cut another slice of bread and helped myself to a piece of the white cheese. One bite told me it was a little on the salty side, with a fairly strong tang of goat, but it was also pleasantly creamy. Nothing like the cheese we'd shared at The Hungry Hawk, but then Gwen had prepared me not to expect that.

"Good cheese," I said.

"I'm glad you approve," Gwen said. We continued our breakfast in comfortable silence. At one point, a truck must have rattled by, but otherwise everything was quiet.

"I should warn you," Gwen said, "it's best not to talk about the glade with others. Guzos are protective of the place, even those who don't believe in its power. They fear that outsiders will hear about it and come sniffing around. We had a small problem with that in the past."

I was immediately curious about the "small problem," but I didn't want to pry. Maybe I would ask her about it later, when we knew each other better. "Is there anyone I can talk to about the glade?" I asked.

Gwen took a sip of her tea. "For now, feel free to bring it up with Rosamunde and Juliette. And Peter. I don't know if he's a dreamer, but his mother is. I understand, the gift sometimes runs in families. Otherwise, it's best to stay mum." She looked at my empty plate and cup, popped a bread crumb into her mouth, and finished her tea. "Right. I suppose we should get on with our day."

After we'd cleared and washed the dishes, Gwen showed me the shower, which was in a bathroom at the rear of the house. "It's modern," I said, with relief. I'm not sure what I was expecting. A water spout and a bucket?

"Gran was quite the trendsetter," Gwen said. "When I was growing up, we bathed in a tub in the kitchen. Every Saturday night. Peter's mum and I finally talked Gran into installing a shower about five years ago. At first she felt terribly self-indulgent, but later she quite liked the convenience."

A few minutes later, I stood under a stream of hot water, letting it wash away the travel grime as well as the disquiet that clung to me from my astonishing experience in the glade. I emerged with clean hair (at last) and a sunny outlook. The morning wasn't even over, and already the duchy had opened up to me in a wondrous way. In the bedroom, I put on tan slacks, a short-sleeved shirt, my cardigan sweater, and sneakers. The rest of my things I stored in the armoire by my bed.

When I joined Gwen downstairs, she was transformed. Her blond hair was pulled back into a loose bun, and she looked demure in a gray, calf-length wool skirt and long-sleeved white blouse. A pale pink shawl covered her shoulders, crossing in front, and pinned into place, just as Rosamunde's had been. It was an unusual outfit, but it was attractive in a peculiar sort of way, the shawl's pink hue picking up the glow in Gwen's cheeks. Sturdy walking shoes and knit stockings, similar to the ones worn by Rosamunde and Juliette the night before, finished Gwen's ensemble. I guessed this must be the attire for traditional Guzo women. Gwen was asserting her Guzo-ness.

We struck out for the town, walking downhill at a brisk pace. Gwen informed me that she had errands to run, and I told her I was heading for the convent, where the museum was located. Houses, mostly trim chalets, soon lined the road.

An elderly woman appeared on a balcony behind a row of yellow and purple flowers in a planter. "Good morrow, Duchess," she called out.

Gwen winced but waved and said, "Good morrow to you, auntie." She scowled as we walked on. "People are going to have to get over this absurd notion that I'm to be the next duchess."

It occurred to me that I was soon going to be meeting a lot of people. "I'm not good with names," I said, "especially unfamiliar ones. I hope people will forgive me if I forget. I didn't catch Rosamunde's last name."

"Don't worry. We hardly use last names inside the duchy. You can call people by their first names. Actually, I'm probably related to everyone by blood or marriage. So I end up calling people 'cousin' or 'auntie' or 'uncle.' Even if we're not related, no one is likely to take offense."

"Where is Juliette's husband?" I asked. "I noticed he wasn't at the house last night."

"Oh, that's a sad story. He passed away about four years ago. A heart attack. He was the sheriff for years. He recruited Juliette as his deputy, and they eventually married. When he died, she became sheriff. She's very good at it, partly because she's a good listener. When people get into trouble, they know they can air their grievances, and Juliette will hear them. Also, she knows everybody in the duchy. I've listened to her dealing with young people. Sometimes all she has to do is tell them how bitterly disappointed their families will be if they learn about the kid's misbehavior. That's enough to put a stop to the mischief."

The duchy certainly didn't sound crime-ridden, even if there was a certain amount of political strife. And there was the unexplained disappearance of Clive, the assistant cheesemaker, now replaced by his wife. "What if Juliette can't bring conflicts to a resolution?" I asked.

"Then she goes to the council. The members meet, thrash out the problem with the parties involved, and make a judgment. It doesn't happen very often, which is lucky, because the whole duchy gets involved. I suppose that's one reason people don't let conflicts get out of hand. They don't want to become the object of endless scrutiny and gossip. A few people have left St. Uguzo rather than put up with it."

Near the plaza, the paved road turned to cobblestone, and the houses became taller and narrower, huddling next to each other as the hill leveled out. Our progress became halting, as we stopped to greet Guzos on our way. Everyone eyed me warily, at least until Gwen introduced me as her good friend from America.

Many of the people we encountered were middle-aged or older, and I observed them, mindful of the need to write out descriptions in my notebook when I got back to my room. The men mostly dressed like Rob, with baggy slacks, collarless shirts, and a loose vest or jacket, all made of sturdy fabrics. Some sported a floppy hat. A spot of color was provided by kerchiefs at their necks. The colors varied—mustard yellow, red, even a plum paisley print.

The women dressed soberly, either in a dress that skimmed the calf or a blouse and skirt. They all wore stockings and sensible shoes. In addition, every lady wore a scarf or shawl that covered her shoulders and either crossed in front or was tucked into her waistband. The colors were mostly soft and earthen, and I wondered if natural dyes were preferred.

"Ca va, Gwen?" said a pretty young woman with short blond hair, artfully spiked. She was wearing jeans and a faded t-shirt with Indochine printed on the front. Three silver rings pierced her right nostril. No shawl.

"Giselle," Gwen said delightedly. They spoke in French for a moment, saying something I didn't understand, which made them both laugh. I really needed to work on my high school French, which was not only limited but rusty from disuse. Gwen introduced me.

"Welcome to the duchy," Giselle said in English. "We are very happy you have come." She and Gwen exchanged a few more words, then we all said "au revoir" and were on our way.

I spotted a man and woman peering at us from the other side of the plaza, and a moment later they made a beeline for us. Both were blond and in their forties, but they seemed mismatched. The woman was thin, almost bony, and wore a maroon shawl tucked into her skirt. When she turned her head to address the man, I saw that her hair was tightly braided and circled into a bun in back. In contrast, the man looked more modern, dressed in neat slacks and a navy blazer. But his substantial paunch combined with plastered-down hair below a receding hairline gave him a slightly gone-to-seed air.

"I bet that's Wilheard," Gwen whispered, "the fellow that Rosamunde and Juliette were telling us about."

Kessie had been right. I had difficulty envisioning this guy as the romantic young nobleman who won Anwen's heart.

"What cheer, cousin," the shawled woman said primly as they drew near.

"Well met, Eglentyne," Gwen replied warmly.

"Gwen is granddaughter to our departed Duchess Anne-Marie," Eglentyne said to her companion. She slid her hand into the crook of his arm in a proprietary way and beamed at Gwen. "I would like you to meet my cousin, Wilheard Fosse. He has come all the way from America."

Wilheard looked Gwen over from bottom to top. I found his leering behavior offensive, but Gwen managed to keep a smile on her face.

"So you're the famous singer," he said. "Glad to meet ya." His voice was gravelly, and it reminded me of an actor from an old gangster movie, Marlon Brando, maybe.

Gwen introduced me as her American friend, who had come for the celebration. Wilheard and Eglentyne barely spared me a nod.

"Wilheard is settling down here," Eglentyne said to Gwen. "It's high time we Fosses regained our prominence in St. Uguzo. Don't you agree?"

"Absolutely," Gwen said. "I've always held the Fosse family in high regard."

Eglentyne quirked a smile, apparently satisfied with Gwen's response.

"And how fare you, Eglentyne?" Gwen asked. "Will you be in the play again? I always so enjoy your performances." Gwen was a talented diplomat, I thought, probably a skill she had learned from her grandmother.

Eglentyne adjusted her perfectly positioned shawl. "I am a lady-in-waiting to the French queen, as usual. And Wilheard is to be the duke. Quite an honor for our family." Wilheard puffed out his chest, a smirk on his face. "We'll see you both tonight," she said before they continued on their way.

"Where in the U.S. do you think he's from?" Gwen asked when they were out of earshot.

He hadn't said much, and even if he had, I was no expert on American dialects. "Hard to say. Probably not the south. To tell you the truth, he sounds like a tough, city guy." A thug, I thought, but didn't say it. "But I could be way off base."

"I was thinking mafia," Gwen whispered, and we both giggled.

CHAPTER SEVEN

Day 2, Sunday

Gwen and I parted company at the stone bridge. She headed down a narrow, cobbled street leading deeper into the town, and I crossed the hump-backed bridge over the stream. The water flowed smoothly here, pouring itself into a series of small pools downstream.

I followed a gravel road that bordered a graveyard extending across a broad field. Beyond it lay a wooded area. I kept walking until I came to a long stone wall, some ten feet high. It appeared old, the stone speckled stained with moss and pockmarked in places. Looking upward, I saw that the structure was irregular at the top, where blocks had apparently tumbled down. At the far end, rising above the wall, I spotted a church steeple housing a belfry, and topped by a spire. The belfry housed a bell, and I wondered if it still rang. I realized that the convent must be inside these walls. About half-way down the wall, I came to a double wooden gate, which was barred with a hefty iron lock securing the door.

The ancient ambience was marred broken by a dark blue van parked just up the road. On it were stenciled the words "Duchy Sheriff's Office." I looked around and saw no sign of Julicttc or of any disturbance that would require the sheriff's presence. Aside from birdsong and the hum of voices from across the bridge, everything was quiet. I continued walking until I arrived at the end of the wall and turned the corner. The steeple spire and bell tower rose above me, and I realized I must be standing just outside the chapel. Its tall, weathered door was closed but creaked open when I pulled on the brass door handle.

The temperature dropped as I entered the stone building, and I was glad for my sweater. It took a moment for my eyes to adjust to the low light. The church was small, more like a chapel, really, and it was clearly no longer in use, at least on a regular basis. The walls were bare, as was the altar standing at the end of the nave. I supposed a crucifix must have once hung above it, and I wondered where it was now. Half a dozen pews were arranged at the front, their dark wood lit by narrow leaded glass windows.

I walked forward and sat in the front pew. In spite of the austerity lent by the dim light and bare walls, I relaxed into the silence almost immediately, feeling a peacefulness akin to what I'd felt in the glade. I wondered if the nuns who worshiped here had found the thin place in the woods. And if they had, what did they make of it? Maybe they already lived close to the spirit.

"You're about sixty years too late for Mass," said a male voice behind me, and I turned to see Peter, the historian, standing in a doorway to my right. He'd entered from the south transept, if I had my terminology straight.

"I got here a little early," I said, taking in his casual jeans and faded long-sleeved shirt. "I hope you don't mind my nosing around."

"Not at all. I hear you're interested in carrying out research on the duchy. A study of our big celebration."

Gwen was right. News traveled fast. "Yes, if I can get permission from the council."

"They meet next Wednesday, a few days from now. In the meantime, I don't see why you can't gather a little background information." He sat down beside me, in the middle of the front pew, an arm's length away. "How much do you know?" he asked, his brown eyes peering intently into mine.

I swallowed hard. This was going to be embarrassing. I could hardly have been less prepared. "Not very much, I'm afraid. I have a little background from a paper I wrote some time ago." I didn't mention it was an article for my high school newspaper. "I only found out I was coming on Friday morning, and we boarded the plane that afternoon."

"Yes, I see," he said. "That doesn't leave much time for preparations. I take it you've read the play, Our Noble Beginnings."

"Twice, in fact. I read it on the plane."

"That's not a bad place to start."

I'd been prepared for Peter to dismiss the play as a fanciful, amateurish work, if he mentioned it at all. I must have stared at him in surprise.

"Something wrong?" he asked.

"No, not at all. Well, actually, I did wonder how accurate the play was. Historically."

"As a matter of fact, Merrywether didn't stray far from the historical record." Peter cleared his throat and launched into what sounded like a prepared lecture. "From what we know, Anwen left her convent in Wales in 1535. At the beginning of a disastrous time for the Catholic Church in England." Peter might be in jeans, but his voice carried a touch of academic pomposity.

I pulled my notebook and pen out of my shoulder bag, where I'd tucked them away, and began taking notes. "El leaves convent in 1535," I wrote. It was a period I'd studied in my English history classes. "That was shortly before Henry the Eighth started closing down the monasteries, wasn't it?"

"Indeed. Henry had declared himself head of the Church of England the year before. At first, he claimed he simply wanted to reform the monasteries. But it soon became clear that he wanted to do away with them altogether."

I thought back to the duchy play. The abbess was portrayed as quite a cruel figure. But I couldn't help feeling a glimmer of sympathy for her. "I imagine the abbess at Anwen's convent was afraid. It couldn't have been easy keeping up morale among the nuns. Not when the country was governed by a hostile king. And a ruthless one. Anwen's nightmares about the convent burning down would have made the abbess's job more difficult."

"Just so," Peter said, and I could see he was regarding me with greater interest now. "The abbess was in a tight spot. I expect she wanted to send Anwen packing, but the girl was from a prominent family with deep Welsh roots. And the convent would have been promised a sizeable dowry when Anwen took her vows. The abbess must have wanted to control the damage, so she told the nuns that Anwen was being assailed by demons, then isolated and nearly starved the girl. But still the visions came. Finally, a nun came from the mother house in France and saw what was going on. Her younger brother, Philippe, was visiting England on a diplomatic mission, and he agreed to escort Anwen to France. I imagine the abbess jumped at the chance to rid herself of the troublesome novice."

"So, Anwen's dreams—assuming they were real—were predictors of the destruction to come. Did the Welsh convent really burn down?"

"It appears so, but that came later, after the nuns were gone. There would have been lead in the roof and other places. It was valuable—for armaments mostly—and the easiest way to remove it was by burning down the structure. That happened a lot. Anwen's vision of fire could have been a realistic view of the future, but I suspect it was a metaphoric reflection of the imminent destruction of monastic life in England."

I scribbled more notes, then looked up. Peter was leaning back, looking reflective, an arm draped over the back of the pew. I lowered my pen. "Gwen said the nuns arrived here a few years after the duchy was founded."

"Yes," he said. "In 1540. A group of them had banded together to form a household in Wales. That was after they were kicked out of the convent. Somehow Anwen got word to them, inviting them to settle in St. Uguzo. So they came. Eight of them, plus two lay sisters. Fortunately for us, one of the lay sisters was a skilled cheesemaker."

He stood. "It's a bit chilly here, isn't it. What say we go for a stroll around the convent? I can give you more history while we walk."

We exited through the same door where Peter had entered. "Here is where the sisters lived," Peter said. Before me stretched a square, grassy area, with what looked like an herb garden in the center. The square was surrounded by a covered walkway leading to a series of rooms, the roof supported by simple stone columns. On the opposite wall, the double gate now stood open, probably opened by Peter before he joined me.

"As you can see," Peter said, "the convent was small, and the nuns weren't really cloistered. When the gate was open, anyone could enter the courtyard."

"That must have taken some getting used to," I said.

"Maybe not so much. By the time the sisters arrived, they had been living out in the world for a few years. I suspect many of their rules and expectations had loosened some. And the duke didn't have vast resources to spend on a convent. Everyone had to make do."

"I suppose they were grateful to have a home at last. And I imagine Anwen was happy to be among old friends." I looked down the shaded walkway paralleling the church, where several narrow, evenly-spaced rooms were lined up. Their doorways consisted of graceful arches, but the doors themselves were no longer in place, giving the spaces a barren, forlorn look.

"Those were the sisters' cells," Peter said. I tried to imagine a nun inside the nearest one, sitting on her bed, or possibly lying on a straw pallet, conditions being what they were. Either way, she was enjoying a moment of solitude, mindful of a crucifix on the wall, an anchor for her faith.

"We are less certain about some of the other rooms," Peter said. He led me down the second side of the square and motioned with his hand to a good-sized room. "This was probably the chapter house, where the sisters met for their daily readings. And next to it is the parlor. I'm guessing the third room was the infirmary."

We turned the corner to the third side of the square, where a large detached room took about half the space. "The kitchen," Peter said. I peered in and saw a huge fireplace on the far wall, with heavy-looking hooks inside. For holding pots, I supposed. The surrounding walls were stained dark from smoke.

Peter continued. "And next to it, the refectory, where the sisters ate. It would have had a long, wooden table. I am hoping to have such a table built when we refurbish the convent."

"You're going to renovate the place?"

"Eventually." He frowned. "If the council ever approves the plans and comes up with the money." I took more notes. "Oh, and there's a cellar that runs the length of the rooms on this side," Peter said. "It was used for storage—produce and wine, and the like. They also left cheese there to cure."

"Any chance I could visit it?" I didn't suppose the place had much connection with the celebration, but I had developed a sort of weird fascination with spooky underground places. A memento of the trip to Mexico, when I crawled through caves with my ex-boyfriend.

"We usually discourage people from going down there. You know, we don't want kids running around, getting into trouble."

"I won't take my roller blades," I said.

His lips formed a half-smile, but he said no more. It seemed odd that the cellar would be off limits when everything else was open. Were they storing something down there that shouldn't be seen?

We turned to the south side of the square. The colonnaded passageway was divided in two by the main gate, apparently open to visitors. The rooms on either side contained modern windows, and both had signs on their wooden doors. One read "MUSEUM," and the other read "SHERIFF." I remembered the van parked outside. "Isn't it odd to have the sheriff's office in a former convent?"

Peter shrugged. "It's the duchy."

The door to the sheriff's office was ajar. "Does Juliette come in on Sundays?" I asked.

"Once in a while. Actually, I rarely see her here, although sometimes she drops over for tea. Mostly, she walks around town, chatting with Guzos, keeping on top of things. I tease her that she gets paid for law enforcement, but she's really a social worker."

"Like an old-fashioned cop walking his beat," I said.

"Just so. She's even been known to deliver the mail. Now then, I promised Rosamunde I'd show you the museum. And here we are."

We crossed to the museum, which was padlocked. Peter took a key out of his pocket, and a moment later, we crossed the threshold. In one step, I went from bright warm sunshine to the dim coolness of thick stone walls. The room had a dusky, aged smell, but it was oddly pleasant.

When my eyes adjusted fully, I saw a large room with light flowing in from tall, narrow windows on two sides. Three round wooden tables, each surrounded by six chairs, were spaced around the middle of the room. I walked over to the new-looking shelves that lined the walls. They contained various items—silver candlesticks, a few ceramic pots, old-fashioned dolls, and other toys. Looking around, I saw that the museum lacked the kinds of implements often found in museums-things like old butter churns and spinning wheels. And I realized these tools might still be in daily use in the duchy.

In front of one thick-paned window stood a two-sided wooden lectern with a three-ring binder on top. I walked over, Peter behind me. He opened the book to a page marked with a ribbon.

I inhaled deeply. Before me was an illuminated manuscript, rich with graceful calligraphy and bordered by delicate, ornate figures in bright colors. This had to be a modern facsimile, I realized, the page further protected by a transparent plastic sleeve. The original book would be too valuable to leave sitting around.

"This room was originally the scriptorium," Peter said.

"Oh," I murmured in awe, my eyes sweeping the room. I had read about scriptoria in my English history classes. The great English monasteries all had them. This was where monks and nuns copied books and other documents, and where they created exquisite illuminated manuscripts. The Venerable Bede had worked in a scriptorium. The tale of Beowulf had likely been copied out in one.

"The sisters were part of an important scholarly tradition," Peter said. "Let's sit, and I'll tell you what I know about it."

I settled into one of the chairs, finding it surprisingly comfortable.

"From what I can tell," Peter said, "Anwen's Welsh convent had a sizable library. What's more, the sisters included several talented calligraphers and illuminators. As you may recall, when Henry VIII destroyed the monasteries, he also destroyed and sold off thousands of books. It was a tragedy for the English-speaking world, of course. But fortunately for us, three of the women from Anwen's convent managed to smuggle out books—four biographies of saints, one Bible, and one history of Wales. When the sisters arrived here, they set to work copying these books. It was an outmoded occupation in a way. By that time, printing presses had been in England for about eighty years. But these books were works of art, achievements of a different order."

"Do you still have the original books?" I asked.

"One of the biographies was lost, but I was able to locate the other four books or a copy. Sadly, they are in need of restoration, and we lack the means to do that properly. What's more, we urgently need a room that is climate controlled, where the books and the duchy artwork can be properly stored. Right now, they are being housed for us at the University of Leicester."

"Oh no."

"Yes," he said, clearly sharing my dismay. "But I will bring them back as soon as possible. In the meantime, they are well cared for. I lectured at Leicester before I came here to start the museum. That was four years ago."

He tapped his index finger on the lectern. "The council had promised to appropriate funds for the climate-controlled room this year, but they have recently reneged."

I wondered if this was the disappointing news that Rosamunde had mentioned the night before. No wonder Peter had been so disgruntled.

"But look," he said, "we have good-quality, modern copies of the books and artwork here, and you are welcome to take a look at them."

For the next hour, I pored over the photocopied pages of the biography of Saint Cadoc, a Welsh saint. It was written in Latin, of course. I had taken two levels of Latin, so I could understand or at least guess at most of what I was reading.

Peter disappeared into a small adjoining room that turned out to be his office. The door was open, and I peeked in. A desk made from a dark wood—walnut maybe—sat in the middle of the room with an office chair behind it and two straight-backed chairs with padded cushions in front. The desk was stacked with folders, loose papers, and a few thick books. Peter was flipping through books shelved on two tall bookcases dominating the facing wall. I withdrew before Peter could catch me in my nosiness, and a minute later, he stood over me at my work table. "Here's what I was looking for," he said and handed me a large volume, which turned out to be a Latin-English dictionary, well-thumbed. "This should help. How is it going?"

"Well enough. But the original book must have been moldy," I said, pointing to grayish marks that obscured the text. "And whole sections have faded badly."

"You should see Anwen's journal. The damage is even worse."

"What?" I said, sitting bolt upright. "The duchess kept a journal?"

"That's how I know that the information in the play is mostly correct."

"Oh my gosh," I said, marveling at the duchy's astonishingly good fortune.

Peter hesitated for a moment, then sat in the chair next to mine. "A lot of Anwen's commentary is pretty mundane—who is sick, changes in the weather, how the garden is doing. But later in her life, she wrote longer passages about the early days of the duchy."

"How fascinating," I said.

"Yes. I'm in the process of translating the journal into modern English, but it's slow going. And not just because of the poor condition of the manuscript. Anwen was well educated for her time, but even so, her writing skills were rudimentary. Sometimes she writes in Latin, but often she switches to English, an old regional dialect of English, spelled phonetically. And she scatters in words and phrases in Welsh. I have a colleague at the University of Wales who has been helping me decipher those."

Imagine, I thought. What an opportunity to delve into a distant time, to enter Anwen's mind and see the world from her perspective. It would be a pleasure even dealing with all the challenges, untying the stubborn linguistic knots. "It all sounds glorious," I said.

And this time Peter's face lit up in a broad smile, his winged eyebrows tipping up even higher. "It is. Bloody glorious."

CHAPTER EIGHT

Day 2, Sunday Evening

I resumed my study of St. Cadoc after Peter returned to his office. Deciphering the Latin words was tricky since the nun's handwriting was graceful but highly stylized. So, I was pleased when Juliette dropped by around noon to say that her mother and Kessie were coming with sandwiches for everyone. I shelved the photocopied biography and wiped off the table as Peter disappeared into a small room next to his office. Following him, I discovered a rudimentary kitchen. On a countertop, a blackened tea kettle sat on a hot plate. Next to them were a stained porcelain sink and a draining tray. Peter opened the doors of a cupboard over the sink. It housed a collection of cups, saucers, dessert plates, and a serving platter, all in off-white with a faded pattern featuring a sheaf of wheat.

"Those look like melamine," I said. "They remind me of my grandmother's set."

"Do they indeed? My gran donated them to the museum," Peter said. "I think she was glad to find a home for them."

Peter put on water for tea while I carried dishes to the museum and arranged them on the round table in the near corner. Our guests arrived soon after, and we wasted no time spreading out lunch and sitting around the table. The sandwiches turned out to be cheese and pickle (the everyday goat cheese, naturally) on hard-crusted bread, with gingerbread bars for dessert, everything wrapped in butcher paper.

Gwen appeared at the door, pulled up a chair, and proceeded to entertain us with the gossip she'd gleaned from running into old friends and kinfolk.

"By the way, Peter," Rosamunde said as we were cleaning up, "I was telling Holly that we had a report by that Englishman who came here in the 1930s. The one looking for *Thin Places*. Perhaps you could lend her the book while she's here."

"Of course," Peter said. He went into his office and returned with a thin volume. The title, *A Tour of the World's Thin Places*, was embossed on the front, over the author's name, Alastair Framton.

After lunch, Gwen and I headed back to the house. It was a slog going uphill. Fortunately, Gwen kept running into more friends and relatives, so I had a chance to catch my breath. I hoped that I'd adjust to the altitude soon. At one point, a bus came barreling down the road. The driver beeped, and Gwen waved. "Catholics on their way back from Mass in Bois," she said. "The church there is lovely, and I'm told it's a nice Sunday outing."

Back in the house, I sat on my bed, cross-legged, the door to the balcony open, giving me a glimpse of the mountains. I was eager to dig into *Thin Places*, but I knew I should revise my notes while everything was fresh in my mind. So I opened one of my notebooks and began by jotting down a short description of my arrival in the duchy. I debated whether I should record what I'd learned at the dinner table the night before about duchy politics, but Gwen had asked me to keep that information to myself, so I left it out. I did, however, expand on the notes I'd jotted down during my tour of the convent and museum. It warmed me to remember that Peter had shared with me some of the joys and hardships of his own work. I hoped he might recognize me as a colleague, if a very junior one.

After finishing my notes, I took *Thin Places* out of my shoulder bag and leafed through the book. It was soon clear that Framton and his companion had indeed circled the globe in search of *Thin Places*. There were several chapters on Europe. In addition to St. Uguzo, they included sites in Ireland, the Isle of Iona in Scotland, and a couple of places in Eastern Europe.

A section in the middle was devoted to photographs. The grainy picture of St Uguzo had been taken from the lookout where Gwen and I had stopped. The vista was very similar to my own first glimpse of the valley sixty years later, except the photograph showed a heavily rutted earthen road instead of the paved road we'd driven. The longest section in the book was devoted to the Himalayas, but the travelers had also visited Australia and the Americas, including a site in the Arizona desert and a place in Guatemala called the Valley of Los Ancianos. The next-to-last chapter was broken up into two sections: Supernatural Visitations and Vivid Dreams.

I started reading the introduction, which featured a description of Framton's growing interest in *Thin Places*. This interest, he assured his readers, in no way conflicted with his unwavering Anglican beliefs. That reminded me that I might need to choose which of my friends and family members I told about the thin place in the glade. Dr. Ferris? Maybe not. As I read on, my eyelids began to droop, and I lay back on the bed.

When I awoke, Gwen was standing beside me, giving my arm a small shake. "Rise and shine," she said. "Rehearsal is in half an hour." I sat up. Out the balcony door, deep shadows were graying the mountains, and the light behind the peaks was a yellow-orange shade. According to my Timex, which I had adjusted to duchy time on the flight from Paris, it was 6:30 p.m.

I headed for the bathroom, where I splashed cold water on my face, shocking me out of my nap-induced grogginess. A minute later, I picked up my sweater and bag and clomped down the stairs. In the kitchen, I took an apple from the fridge, and ate it while I waited for Gwen to join me.

When Gwen appeared, she had changed out of her duchy outfit and was wearing gray wool slacks and an off-white blazer over a turtleneck shirt. She was carrying her playbook. "Tonight the fun begins," she said with a wry smile. And we set off down the road.

The theater was in the gymnasium of the duchy's school, Gwen told me, as we hurried along. Opposite the plaza, we turned onto a cobbled street called the Dukesway. I had to trust Gwen on this, since I saw no signs for it, nor for any other street, for that matter.

As we passed a row of narrow, half-timbered houses, I heard the muffled sound of men's voices laughing and conversing loudly. It was soon apparent that they were coming from a long, white cement-block building across the cobbled street. Light shone from behind a row of curtained windows framed by dark blue shutters.

"That's the dining hall," Gwen said. "And the mead hall is attached to it. It's past dinner time, so it's probably the drinkers that we hear now."

"It sounds lively," I said.

"Both places are popular. The dining hall was mostly built for the old bachelor goat herders, so they would have a place to get together and eat. But we all use it sometimes. The duchy cheese—the gourmet cheese—pays for most of the food and upkeep. You're welcome to eat there any time, lunch or dinner. Free of charge.

"Thank you." Gwen had offered me room and board. This must be what she meant by board.

"Of course, people pay for their own beer and mead. Or find a friend to stand them a pint."

A few minutes later, Gwen and I arrived at the school, another one-story concrete block building, standing next to a playing field. The walkway to the entrance was bordered by holly bushes, neatly trimmed, with shiny green leaves. Gwen led me around the building and through a double door to a room that looked very much like my middle school gymnasium, the floor serving as a basketball court, with bleachers on one side, and a raised stage at the far end.

People were already milling about onstage. A tall, bald man stepped to the edge of the stage. He reminded me of Captain Jean-Luc Picard, but with a slightly roguish air. He waved to Gwen, his face alight. "That's Fred," she said, waving back.

"The cheesemaker?"

"And a talented actor."

As we neared the front, I looked for familiar faces among the assembled cast. Upstage, near the back, I spotted Peter and Wilheard, the thuggish American, engaged in some kind of argument. Peter was fingering the forest green kerchief at his neck as Wilheard shouted in his face. Meanwhile, Eglentyne stood to the side, hands clasped nervously. Peter tore his gaze from Wilheard and spotted us below. He shot Gwen a look of exasperation.

"I'd better go rescue our director," Gwen said, and she hurried up a set of stairs on the right side of the stage. I looked around me. Three rows of metal folding chairs were set up below the stage. A group of women were chatting in the second row, one of them knitting. All were decked out in comfortable duchy garb, their pastel shawls crossed in front. I took the next-to-last seat on the first row.

A swish of fabric and the subtle aroma of perfume made me turn to my left, where a forty-ish woman was seating herself next to me. Her black hair was styled in a sleek geometric cut, and she wore casual slacks and a vest. From her tiny waist, I could see that her figure was the kind described as svelte.

"Hello," she said in a smoky French accent. "I am Monique, a friend of Fred, from Bois. You are Gwen's American friend, n'est-ce pas?"

"That's right. I'm Holly," I said. Back home I hardly knew anyone who was truly chic, and I tried not to think about my own slobbishness. "Your friend makes excellent cheese."

"The best in Europe, probably the world. He is a man of many talents." Monique's gaze shifted to the stage. "Ah, there is Fred. And Gwen. And I see the Bonnet brothers are here." She raised a hand in greeting to one of three darkly handsome men, each wearing a kerchief of a different shade of red.

So, these were the guys stirring up trouble at the mead hall. "They are friends of yours?"

"Oh yes. We enjoy a beer together now and then. Also, they rent their bees to my brother every summer, to pollinate his crops. Of course, their mead is popular here. Have you tried it?"

"No. Gwen and I just arrived last night."

"You will, I am sure. It is not to my taste, but to each his own, non?" So, the Bonnet brothers kept bees and brewed mead, which was made from honey. They were beer buddies with Monique and volunteer actors. They didn't sound like such bad guys.

Peter raised his hands, hushing the group, and asked everyone to clear the stage. Soon, the actors and crew had filled most of the chairs around me and a few seats on the bleachers. From the stage, Peter launched into a speech. He reminded us of how important this play was to upholding the spirit of the celebration. "It is both our privilege and our duty to bring our very best work to this endeavor. I keep thinking of our duchess, Anne-Marie, who died a year ago. She would be proud of every one of you, gathered here to carry on this tradition. With your permission, I would like to dedicate this show to her memory." Sounds of approval rose up around me, and tears glistened in several eyes.

"Right, then," he said after a pause. "Tonight is our first onstage rehearsal. Our whole cast is finally assembled, as is our crew. We are going to begin with Act One and get as far as we can. With a little luck, we'll make it through to the end."

Peter then crossed the stage and descended the stairs. He nodded to me shortly before sitting down in the middle chair of the first row. "Places," he said. "Act One, Scene One."

Fred and Gwen climbed the stairs. Gwen remained behind the curtain to the right, but to my surprise, Fred crossed to center stage. Was he a narrator, I wondered? He had a true actor's presence, fully inhabiting the space. Then his demeanor shifted. He began pacing back and forth, his steps short and even graceful. And when he stopped, he raised his hand to his cheek in a motion that was, well, feminine. A few giggles erupted in the audience. I wondered who in the world Fred was playing.

Gwen walked onstage, and a rush of excitement swept through the audience. "You sent for me, Reverend Mother?" she asked, her head lowered.

I gasped. Fred was the abbess! As it turned out, Act One, Scene One had been converted into a comedy, with Fred portraying the abbess as vain and self-centered. As he postured dramatically, his voice comically shrill, the audience laughed and hooted. To her credit, Gwen let Fred dominate the first part of the scene. Her Anwen was a charming nun-to-be, sweet and humble. But as the scene progressed, its tone shifted to something more serious. The strength of Anwen's passion began to shine through. She was a young woman who trusted in God and knew that her tragic dreams of the convent in flames could not be denied. As the scene concluded, the abbess informed her she was being sent away to France, and good riddance.

"You leave tomorrow at dawn," Fred said, his voice still feminine, but not as loud or high-pitched. He seemed to be subtly transferring the weight of the scene to Gwen.

As Anwen, Gwen turned to the audience, her beautiful, noble face uplifted. "With the grace of God, I am ready for whatever may come." And we knew she was prepared for her future. Marriage to a young nobleman. A trek across the mountains. The founding of a duchy. Light applause rose from those of us in the audience.

"Good work," Peter called. "On to Scene Two." Fred started to stride off the stage, but paused. Reverting back to the comic abbess, he kicked up a heel and sent a flirty over-the-shoulder look to the crew members below. Laughter and hoots of approval rose up, and I found myself grinning along with them.

Monique leaned toward me. "He is magnifique, non?"

"Absolutely." Fred's humor was broad and even hackneyed, but he pulled it off with panache.

"Wait until you see him in performance. A comic genius." Monique sighed. "Mon cher Fred, he is wasted on the duchy. But that is life."

The second scene reverted to its intended formality. But there was a problem. It became evident early in the scene, when Wilheard, as Philippe, was introduced to Anwen by the abbess.

"Ah. Here is the Lady Anwen, Your Lordship," Fred said. "The companion on your voyage."

Wilheard kept his eyes fixed on his playbook. "My Lady," he said in his gravelly voice, "What is this?" He screwed up his face. "How pal-pallid you are. I must warn you. The j-jo..."

"Journey," Gwen whispered behind her hand.

Wilheard continued. "The journey is long and ar-ar-du..." I had a feeling Wilheard had given up on reading sometime around the third grade. Sounding out words had not worked for him. As obnoxious as he was, I was developing a little sympathy. I hoped he had street smarts, because he needed something.

"Arduous," Gwen said.

"Huh?"

"Difficult," Gwen said. "The journey is difficult."

"Yeah, all right."

Fred spoke next, in his high abbess voice. "Lady Anwen is young and healthy. I assure you, she will give you no trouble."

"My good lord," Gwen said, her voice silken, "have no fear on my account. I am a countrywoman who thrives on fresh air and sunlight. And I have ridden since I was but a small child."

"There. You see?" the Abbess trumpeted. "She will be no burden to you, my lord. None whatsoever."

Wilheard resumed reading. "In that case, it is my great p-pl... Oh hell!" He threw down his script and stomped to the edge of the stage, where he glared at Peter. "I told you this stuff is trash. Nobody talks like this." Behind him, Gwen was pressing her fingers to her temples, as if she had a massive headache.

Wilheard scowled. "This Philip, he sounds like some kind of queer. Nobody told me he was queer."

"He wasn't gay," Peter said. "That is, as far as we know. This is just the way people used to talk."

"Well, I don't buy it. I want new lines. Something short, like 'Get on your damn horse. We're going to the duchy.'"

I started to laugh but covered it with a cough. Snickers erupted around the room, and a murmur of righteous indignation rose from the seats behind me. The playwright's descendants maybe.

"That is quite stirring," Peter said. "And I take your point. The language is somewhat formal. It's an issue the council can take up before the next celebration. But for now, I suggest we leave the lines as they are. Just do our best."

He shifted his gaze to me. "As it happens, we have a dialogue coach with us. Holly, would you like to work with Wilheard on his lines?"

"Of course, I'd be happy to," I said. Calling me a dialogue coach was stretching it, but I was pretty sure I could help, given enough time. Besides, this would allow me to do my bit for the celebration.

"No dice," Wilheard said.

"Look," Peter said, "perhaps you and I should discuss this privately." He stood and faced the rest of us. "Everyone, take a ten-minute break."

The Guzos stood up from the bleachers and chairs, mumbling among themselves and looking uneasy, as Peter and Wilheard exited the gym. A moment later, Fred joined us. He kissed Monique, greeted me, and accepted our congratulations on his performance.

"Ready to go?" he asked Monique. "I don't see us rehearsing those scenes again, at least not tonight." She nodded, and we all stood.

"You're not going to stay to hear the outcome of the discussion?" I asked.

"I'll hear it all soon enough," Fred said. "Right now, we have more important business to attend to." He and Monique exchanged a smoldering smile, then headed for the gym door, Fred's hand on the small of Monique's back. A tiny wave of envy hit me.

I looked around, feeling at loose ends, a stranger among a close-knit group of people. To my relief, Rosamunde appeared at my side and introduced me to the three ladies who had been sitting behind me. They turned out to be the costume committee.

One of the ladies was Alice Cotton, whom I remembered as the unfortunate woman who was named assistant cheesemaker after her husband disappeared three weeks earlier. She was a small, compact woman in her mid-forties with tired, gray-blue eyes and sandy hair in a thick braid. Her pale yellow shawl, like Alice herself, appeared to have lost some of its vibrancy but was still pretty. When she reached up to adjust it, I noticed her hands looked sinewy and strong. Alice was no stranger to physical labor.

I sat down next to Alice, who pointed out her daughter, Jenny, a slim fourteen-year-old with waist-length caramel blond hair. She was deep in conversation with Kessie, whose dark hair was braided and pinned into a coil on the back of her head, making her look a little older than her thirteen years.

Alice also directed my attention to her gloomy, sixteen-year-old son, Tony, who was sitting on a bleacher, smoking a cigarette, his expression stormy. He had agreed to work on props, she said. The kid was handsome, with thick, blond hair and blue eyes widely spaced under surprisingly dark eyebrows. With his good looks, I could imagine him in a boy band, but with his troubled visage, he would be "the bad boy" of the group.

Alice clicked her tongue. "I don't know what's gotten into Tony. He used to be so well-behaved." She sighed. "Now he's surly and smokes those smelly cigarettes. I suppose it's just his age."

"Could be," I agreed, although I suspected that having his father mysteriously disappear could play a part in his altered behavior. My gaze shifted back to Kessie, and I realized she was staring at Tony with a lovelorn expression. I wondered if Juliette was aware that her daughter was infatuated with Clive Cotton's son.

Just then, Peter and Wilheard returned, their expressions upbeat if a little forced. Peter strode onto the stage and addressed us all. "There will be a change in the cast. I am pleased to say that Wilheard has agreed to play King Francis the First of France. I am certain he will be a very fine king."

"The king doesn't talk much," Alice whispered.

"Good," I said, although Wilheard's reassignment meant my coaching services might not be required. "But wasn't Peter playing the king?" Alice nodded.

"Unfortunately," Peter continued from the stage, "that leaves us without a duke. Would anyone here like to take the part?"

The cast and crew all looked from one to another, no one speaking up.

"Right," Peter said. "I'll read the duke's lines tonight, while we look around for someone else."

"Peter makes a very good duke," Alice said. "He took the part during our read-through."

"Oh? Where was Wilheard?"

She raised an eyebrow. "Off on business. Or so he said."

Ah. That's why no one knew that Wilheard couldn't recite the duke's lines. Why in the world had he insisted on playing the duke? He must have at least looked at the lines before he took the part. The rest of the play went relatively smoothly. As Gwen had predicted, the fight scene was lively. The would-be assassins, played by the Bonnet brothers, swaggered around, waving their cardboard daggers with zest. The king's courtiers, four guys of varying ages looking properly steadfast, fought them off, amid shouts and grunts. The audience members alternately cheered and booed both sides.

I wondered how Wilheard would do during the ceremony when he made Philippe a duke, but he rose to the occasion, only mashing up the words twice. While Philippe knelt before him, Wilheard lowered a gold medallion around his neck.

"The original medal was real gold," Alice whispered. "Embossed with the king's crest, a salamander below a crown."

A salamander? I wondered what that represented. "Do you still have the medallion?"

"It disappeared after the war.

"The war?" I asked. There had been so many.

"The Second World War. That was the last one that really affected us. There were German soldiers stationed here, you know. It was a terrible time."

We turned our attention back to the stage. The last scene was touching, with Peter and Gwen standing side by side, facing the audience.

"We have traveled long and far to come to this place," Peter said, as Duke Philippe.

"To this beloved place," Gwen said. "To our heart's home." Tears glistened in her eyes.

Peter's voice swelled, resonating against the gym walls. "You are our people now, and we are yours. We pledge our loyalty to you, and our protection, as long as God grants us life."

A hush filled the audience, and I sensed that the people around me on the chairs and bleachers had fallen in love with these two fine, handsome people, Anwen and Philippe, the ancestral duke and duchess. I gulped. Had they also fallen in love with Gwen and Peter, their descendants? Unfortunately, or fortunately, depending on your viewpoint, both had firmly rejected the title and the responsibility that went with it.

"All rise," Peter said. And they sang the short but rousing duchy anthem to a tune that sounded a little like "The Farmer in the Dell." Afterward, everyone cheered. Peter remained on the stage. "Thank you all," he said, as the crowd quieted. "We're off to a good start. Tomorrow we will work on individual scenes, beginning with Act Three. Everyone who's in the French court scenes, be here at seven."

Kessie had slipped onto the seat on my other side. "The duke and duchess were squatters. That's what my dad says."

I looked at her aghast, while Alice chuckled. "Some things never change," she said. "Not everyone wants somebody over him, telling him what he can and can't do. Especially when the orders come from an outsider."

A few minutes later, Gwen, Peter, Kessie, and I were climbing up the road together, since Peter's cottage was next door to Gwen's house. Now that I was walking uphill, I realized that the grade was steep, enough that I was soon breathing hard. The others seemed oblivious.

"Do you think anyone will volunteer to play the duke?" Gwen asked.

"What do you think?" Peter said, but it was clearly a rhetorical question, and the answer was no.

We'd almost reached our destination when Peter turned to me and stopped. "Do you have a proposal together for the council?"

A proposal. I took a few deep breaths. Of course, I had to come up with a description of my proposed research project. Dr. Ferris hadn't given me any directions, just told me to observe the celebration and take copious notes. But naturally, the council would expect a plan.

Peter must have read my panicky expression correctly, because he said, "Come by the museum tomorrow morning, and we can work on it."

"Thank you so much," I said, flooded with relief.

"Not at all." And he hurried up the road to his cottage and his collie, Bonnie.

CHAPTER NINE

Day 3, Monday

I was glad to be back in the house, ready to dig into *A Tour of the World's Thin Places*, the book that Peter had loaned me. Gwen and I said good night and went to our rooms. I changed into jammies, climbed into bed, and began reading the chapter on the Isle of Iona. After my long afternoon nap, I thought I might be awake into the night, but I only made it through three pages before I drowsily turned off the bedside lamp.

I can still clearly recall the dream that awakened me. I was in a room with Gwen, who was standing by a window streaked with rain, her golden hair flowing down her back. Oddly, I seemed to be a sort of silent bystander, off to the side. I watched with curiosity, rapidly turning to terror, as a shadowy, hooded figure moved stealthily across the room toward Gwen. Suddenly, he produced a long, heavy wire, which he threw around her neck. He pulled the wire tight as Gwen gagged and thrashed, her hands grasping the wire. Then she slumped, collapsing to the floor. All the while, I stood at a distance, powerless to move or speak. An observer to Gwen's murder.

I woke up, breathing heavily, the room dark and silent. The image of Gwen struggling against the assassin was etched into my mind, not fading the way dreams usually do. Then I remembered Rosamunde's warning. People who went to the glade sometimes had vivid dreams afterward. That was it, I realized. I'd just had a very scary, very vivid dream.

I pressed the little knob on my watch that made the dial light up. It was 5:50, not long before dawn. Further sleep was impossible, so I dressed in jeans with layers of clothing on top: a t-shirt covered by a long-sleeve shirt, my sweater, and coat. After making tea in the kitchen, I carried a cup up to my bedroom. There, I took my bag of M&Ms from the high shelf of the armoire, counting on the chocolate to take the edge off the icy horror I was feeling.

On the balcony, I dragged a chair to the end that overlooked Rosamunde's house. She and Rob had risen early the day before, and I was counting on them to get up early today so that I could run over and talk to Rosamunde as soon as possible. As morning slowly colored the sky and the valley below, I munched on the chocolate, one piece at a time. I'd gone through a third of the bag when a light came on in the second floor—a bedroom, no doubt. And a few minutes later, a room at the back of the house lit up, the kitchen where we'd eaten the night before. I waited another ten minutes, to be semi-civilized, before I ran across and knocked on the kitchen door.

"You're up early," Rosamunde said, opening the door.

"I had a dream. A vivid one."

She invited me in, and I sat down at the kitchen table across from Rob.

"Good morrow," Rob said, and I replied in kind, the strange greeting coming surprisingly easily to me. He drained his tea and scraped back his chair. "I'm off, then, wife."

"Don't forget your lunch," Rosamunde said, handing him a thermos and a canvas bag with a strap that he hung across his chest. "Give my regards to Herbert and Elsie." He clomped out the kitchen door.

"I hope I didn't run your husband off," I said.

"He likes to get an early start on the day," Rosamunde said. "Besides, he has business across the valley." She set down a cup of tea in front of me. "Now. Tell me about your dream."

I told her every detail, which wasn't hard because the dream was short, and it had fixed itself in my mind. Rosamunde said nothing, but nodded from time to time.

"I'm not sure where the dream came from," I said. "Maybe it was the Bonnet Brothers waving their daggers around."

"Perhaps." Rosamunde got up and served me a plate with a slice of bread and goat cheese. I ate while Rosamunde sat back on her chair, apparently pondering what I'd related.

"Holly, have you ever had a dream that came true? I mean a real dream, not a fantasy. Or a vision, perhaps. One that predicted something that occurred later."

I considered. My dreams were pretty mundane. Now that I thought of it, I seemed to specialize in anxiety dreams. In a recurring one, I showed up for a final exam in a class I'd never attended. And a few times I found myself standing in front of an audience, not knowing one lousy line of the play I was supposed to be acting in. But a lot of my dreams were just plain weird, jumbling together elements from my life. They never predicted anything.

"Not really," I said.

"That's fine," Rosamunde said and we drank our tea and munched on the bread and cheese in comfortable silence. Upstairs, I heard Ozzie yelling at Kessie to hurry up in the bathroom.

A memory popped into my mind. "Now that I think of it, there was one time," I said.

It was a dream I'd had when I was twelve. I hadn't thought of it in years, but it was so striking that it came back to me fully all these years later. In the dream, I was riding in my family's car up a highway with a steep incline. The road was carved out of a hillside, with stone walls on either side. I was admiring the way the multi-colored rock formed layers, one on top of another, when suddenly I saw a truck at the top of the hill. It was hurtling down the road, coming straight at us, and the second before it hit our car, I awoke, screaming. I sat up, my heart pounding. It took me a long time to go back to sleep, and I felt off balance the next day.

A few days later, my family headed west in our Chevy station wagon on our annual trip to Colorado. Dad drove and I sat behind Mom, next to my sixteen-year-old sister, Valerie. She was reading, and I was looking out the window, feeling bored, since reading in the car gave me headaches. Suddenly, I realized the stone walls on either side of the highway looked familiar. They were the same rock layers I'd seen in the dream. Fear gripped me as I remembered the truck.

I grabbed the back of my father's seat. "Nooo!" I cried.

"Pull over! Pull over!" Valerie shouted.

My father steered the car onto the narrow shoulder, and a second later a black pickup came over the hill, careening into our lane. It shot past us, missing our car by inches. If we hadn't pulled off, we would have had a head-on collision. We'd all be dead. Dad's hands clutched the steering wheel and Mom's hands covered her face. The fearful pounding in my ears began to fade.

Dad turned to face Valerie and me, his voice strained. "You two all right back there?"

Valerie and I both said we were. I dragged myself out of the car, my legs like water, and Valerie and Dad walked over beside me. "That was a close call," Dad said.

Mom staggered out of the car, her face ashen, her eyes round. "We could have been killed. Did you see that?" Her voice rose to a hysterical pitch. "We could have been killed!"

"But we weren't, were we?" Dad said. "We're all okay." He patted my shoulder. "Thanks to our daughters."

"I swear to God," Valerie said to me, "I'll never complain about you puking in the car again." I realized then that when Valerie shouted to Dad, it was because she thought I was carsick and was about to vomit all over the backseat, something I'd done before. The oncoming truck was just a coincidence to my family.

I didn't tell anyone about the dream. I'm not sure why exactly. I guess it was just too weird, too scary. Almost as frightening as the truck nearly plowing into us. Plus, somehow the dream didn't fit the story that we shaped into reality. The story was about my family surviving a near disaster. It was about my carsickness changing from a messy affliction to a saving grace. And it was about my dad's quick response to his daughters' alarm. It definitely wasn't about a weird, supernatural vision.

Two years later, Dad left us to start a new life with another woman, fulfilling my mother's longstanding fear of abandonment. After he moved out, Mom, Valerie, and I never brought up the near-collision again. And over time, it sank deep into my memory.

"There was one time," I said to Rosamunde, and I related the dream, along with its aftermath.

"I thought so," she said. "You're a vivid dreamer."

"Is that bad?"

"It isn't good or bad. It's just the way it is. Sometimes dreams—vivid dreams—can be helpful. Sometimes not. In the case of your car trip, the dream probably saved your lives."

"But I wasn't anywhere near a thin place," I said.

"People who are sensitive may not have to be close to a thin place. Besides, can you be sure there was no thin place nearby?"

I nibbled on a piece of cheese. Could I-80 be harboring a thin place? The idea seemed absurd, but then again, Native Americans had lived in the area for thousands of years. Who knew what dreams might have found them? "What about my dream last night? Do you think it was...prophetic?"

"Oh, you needn't worry. We'll keep an eye on Gwen. Nothing terrible will befall her."

I really, really hoped she was right. "Should I tell Gwen about the dream?" I was reluctant to disturb her with such a grisly story, especially if it had no bearing on reality.

"No, don't bother. I'll tell her later. We often chat about dreams and such."

When I crossed the lawn back to Gwen's house, the sun was fully up, and the evening's chill was receding. I crossed the veranda and stepped inside our house, where I was met by peaceful stillness. I climbed the stairs and slowly opened Gwen's bedroom door. She was lying on her side, her golden hair tousled, her chest rising and falling under her quilt. She was safe, and I was probably being idiotic to worry.

Back in my room, I picked up *A Tour of the World's Thin Places* from the bedside table where I'd left it, and went back on the balcony, where I sat across from The Guardian, her faceted slopes now bathed in sunlight. Below her, the trees in the valley glowed bright in their rich autumn colors. I peeled off my coat, leaving on a sweater and two shirts to stave off the chill. I hesitated before opening the book. I was eager to know what Framton had to say about vivid dreams, but also a little frightened. From what Rosamunde said, I was a vivid dreamer, although apparently not a very active one. Two dreams in my twenty-five years wasn't an impressive record. But they had each shaken me profoundly. First came the collision dream and then last night's dream, when I had watched in speechless horror as Gwen was garroted. I needed to know what they meant.

The book's table of contents guided me to the next-to-last chapter and the section entitled "Vivid Dreams." I began reading.

Among the most commonly reported phenomena associated with *Thin Places* are what I refer to in this book as "vivid dreams," a special class of dreams often experienced by people who have been in close proximity to *Thin Places*. These dreams are remarkably clear and life-like. In some cases, they are prophetic in nature.

My heart squeezed. Was the scene of Gwen's death destined to come true? But Framton had said some dreams, not all. And Rosamunde hadn't seemed overly disturbed by the dream. Surely she would know if there was real danger.

Not only are these dreams intense, but they remain engraved in the dreamer's mind. A number of individuals remembered their vivid dreams in detail many years after they occurred.

A theme common to many vivid dreams is an element of danger. Sometimes the threat is to an individual, as in the case of a death in the family, and other times to the community as a whole, as in an impending storm or earthquake. Understandably, a number of people expressed dismay and even guilt over their dreams.

The idea of guilt hit home. Now that I thought of it, after my family's near-collision, my twelve-year old brain had concocted the idea that I was somehow responsible for my family's scrape with disaster. In my mind, by dreaming about it, I had brought it into being. I wasn't sure I had ever quite shaken off that feeling.

In a few cases, the dreamers were actually able to fend off the calamity. One woman reported that when her mother was a girl, there was an active group of female dreamers in her village. By combining clues from their dreams, they were sometimes able to solve problems. In their most celebrated case, the women identified a culprit guilty of stealing half a dozen sheep. Piecing together scenes from the vivid dreams, the women guided the police to the thief, just as he was in the act of absconding with a prize ewe.

Here was some good news, at last. I wondered about the dreamers in St. Uguzo. Did they ever join forces? I would have to ask Rosamunde.

In some communities, vivid dreamers spoke openly about their visions. Generally, these were towns where they and their visions were accorded a certain respect. In other places, however, people were reluctant to discuss their dreams with us or anyone else, for fear they would be accused of witchcraft or sorcery. One man told us that when he was young, a neighbor woman—a kind, gentle soul, he said—was forced to leave her village after she predicted a landslide that seriously injured two people.

One of our most poignant conversations took place in a Croatian village, where we sat in a hut, drinking herbal tea with an elderly couple, both vivid dreamers, as well as our interpreter. (Note: As elsewhere in this book, I will use both "thin place" and "vivid dream" as translations for native folk terms.) According to the couple, vivid dreams used to be an important part of village life, a source of information and even wisdom. But in recent years, the nearby thin place had waned in strength, so that even the dreamers felt little energy there now. Many people in the area had begun dismissing both the thin place and the dreams it engendered as the products of superstition.

"The thin place is dying," the old woman said with genuine sorrow. "I expect a few people will still have vivid dreams now and then. But those dreams won't be seen as anything special. My own daughter gives no importance to hers. My fear is, once my husband and I have passed on, there will be no one to tell the young people about the thin place. About what it has meant to our people."

I closed the book on my lap, Framton's words whirling around in my head. In a way, it was comforting to know that people all over the world had vivid dreams. I was not alone in my peculiar ability. But as fascinating and insightful as the chapter was, it was also a letdown. Part of me had been hoping that Framton would write that the vivid dreams weren't really prophetic, that the belief was an old wives' tale without any true merit. That would mean Gwen was in no danger. But Framton had not.

Framton was no scientist, I reminded myself. He lacked a genuine commitment to objectivity. He had, however, gone to communities around the world and listened to people with an open heart and mind, accepting their experiences as valid. That was probably why all those dreamers were willing to confide in him. Oh, I supposed there were people who had spun a yarn or two, but the reports of vivid dreams crossed continents. I didn't think that all those people had contrived to weave the same lies. No. I was pretty sure that Framton had recognized the truth when he heard it.

If anything, Framton's book reinforced the idea that vivid dreams needed to be taken seriously. I shuddered at the memory of the savage attack on Gwen. What if it was an omen? Absently, I ran my index finger across the embossed title of the book. The prophecies could be reversed. I knew that from my own experience with the drunken trucker. And from what Framton wrote, in one village, the female dreamers had prevented the theft of a sheep. So there was hope. Maybe that was why Rosamunde had not seemed worried about my dream.

I looked up at the peaceful alpine scene spread out before me. What a strange place the duchy was, so old and beautiful, but also a land of mysterious danger and social upheaval. If I'd thought I was out of my depth earlier, I was now at the bottom of the pond.

A glance at my watch indicated it was almost nine o'clock. Oh my gosh. The museum should be opening soon. I'd totally forgotten about Peter's offer to help me with my proposal to the council. I inhaled deeply. It was time to set aside my worries about vivid dreams. After all, what could I do about them? Rosamund had lived here all her life. She knew the ways of the duchy, of the people and places. I would put my trust in her and those supporting her to protect Gwen. And I would turn my attention to my research on the celebration. That was why I was here.

I stood and stretched, then left the balcony and stored *Thin Places* in my wardrobe. As I descended the stairs, I heard two women's voices talking in the kitchen in low voices. Rosamunde and Gwen. Were they discussing my dream? I would leave them to it.

CHAPTER TEN

Day 3, Monday

I headed down the road toward the museum, exchanging a friendly "good morrow" with people I passed, many looking at me less suspiciously today than they had the day before.

Framton's information on vivid dreams was still heavy on my mind, but there was no point in dwelling on it, or on my own vivid dreams—if, in fact, that's what they were. No, I was here to study the celebration, not to delve into the supernatural aspects of duchy culture or to ponder my own weird abilities.

When I arrived at the convent, the gate was open, as was the door to the museum. I entered the former scriptorium to find that the main room was unoccupied except for Peter, who was sitting at one on the tables, a pile of manila folders stacked neatly beside him.

"Good morrow," I said.

He cracked a smile. "Good morrow to you. Ready to get started on your proposal?"

"Absolutely," I said, shaking off the last of my gloomy thoughts. I pulled up a chair next to him, and we got to work, Peter reeling off information while I scribbled notes. I learned that the Ceremony of Allegiance had its roots in the defeat of a predatory Italian duchy in 1690. For the next hundred-plus years, a celebration was held intermittently, often after some foreign incursion on duchy land. Finally, in 1824, the duchy began holding a celebration every five years, complete with the Ceremony of Allegiance, in which the men raised their daggers and hunting knives high and proclaimed their loyalty to the duke or duchess. Beginning in 1974, the women did so too, although it was often kitchen knives they raised.

Over the years, the celebration took on some of the features of a county fair. Guzos competed in various contests, among them sports—archery, wrestling, and foot-racing being favored; baking and jam-making; sewing; even yodeling. There was always live music played by musicians from the duchy and Bois. And starting in 1889, the play, Our Noble Beginnings, was staged.

"So," I said, "I need to concentrate my efforts on the years beginning in 1824." I wondered how in the world I was going to dig up information that far back.

"The archives going back to 1824 are pretty spotty. But as it happens, you're in luck for the later years. Between 1886 and 1974, the duchy had its own two-page weekly newspaper—except for 1944, when the duchy was occupied by German soldiers. But that's a story for another day. The best part for you is, every five years, a supplemental edition of the paper was printed, covering the celebration. Some of the supplements have been lost, but copies from eight years remain."

"Oh my gosh," I exclaimed, in awe at my good fortune. "That's fantastic."

"I thought you'd be happy. There's a list of all the contests, along with the winners, and photos are included. The pictures are pretty hazy in the beginning, but they improve over time. There are also sketches and a few wood engravings. And patriotic essays, many written by school children."

"Do I need permission to go through the supplements?"

"Yes, and I'm giving it to you. Actually, anyone can access the papers. I just need to keep records on who has used them."

"Is there any chance I could make photocopies?" My little stash of francs should stretch that far, and it would be great to have the original documents to work with when I was back home.

"I don't see why not. As soon as you receive the council's permission for the study, you can go to Bois and make copies. In the meantime, don't tell people that you've started work on your project."

"Understood." I sat back on my chair, grinning. I could begin my background research right away. By the time the council gave me their permission on Wednesday, two days from now, I would have a solid foundation for my chapter on the history of the celebration. For the first time, I felt genuinely optimistic about my chances of carrying out my study. After the council met, I would e-mail Dr. Ferriss and tell her the good news. Then I could look forward to an assistantship and a welcome back from the department.

Juliette arrived at the museum mid-morning, looking disheartened. She placed a cloth-covered basket on the table and sat down across from us. Whatever was in the basket smelled marvelous. "Alice stopped by," she said. "Again. I wish I had news for her about Clive, but there's still nothing. The police chief in Bois has put out feelers once again, but no one has information. And I checked back with clinics and hospitals in the region. None have had patients meeting Clive's description."

"Not too surprising," Peter said. "If he's in hiding from his debtors, he could be virtually anywhere."

"Not exactly. He left his passport and other identification at his house. If he's lying low somewhere, it's probably not too far away. But in that case, I'd think he would contact Alice, let her know he's okay."

"Very true," Peter said. "By the way, just how substantial are his gambling debts? Rumors vary."

"Alice thinks he owes around fifty thousand francs."

A quick calculation told me Clive owed almost ten thousand dollars.

Peter grimaced. "A burden like that could dampen one's spirits."

"Yes, but that's the odd thing. Alice says that Clive was in a good mood before he disappeared. For a month or so, he'd had ample spending money, enough to pay the butcher's bill and even buy a bottle of wine. And he said more money was on the way, enough to satisfy all his creditors and even buy a good, late-model car. He didn't sound like a man weighed down by his debts."

"Strange indeed," Peter said. "Whatever his plan was, something must have gone awry."

Juliette shook her head. "If only I knew what that rascal is up to. I feel like a total failure."

"I don't see what more you can do," Peter said. "You've questioned everyone who had any contact with Clive. Half the duchy, I'd say. Besides, you're a sheriff, not a detective."

"Tell that to Alice," Juliette said. "And all the other Guzos who keep expecting me to solve the case."

"Clive will turn up sooner or later," Peter said. "Then you can put this all behind you."

I was beginning to see that Juliette used Peter as a sounding board. He was in the unusual position of being a Guzo who was brought up outside the duchy, so he had a certain perspective on Guzo affairs. The two had an easy, comfortable relationship, and I wondered if Peter confided in Juliette too.

"Now then," Peter said, "what's that in the basket? Something tasty, if I'm not mistaken."

Over tea and orange scones, baked by Rosamunde, I told Juliette that Peter and I had put together an outline for my project and explained that a major component consisted of interviewing people who had carried out various roles in the celebration over the years.

"I'll also devote a chapter to the play," I said. Since I would be present during nearly all the rehearsals, I could describe both the preparations and the performance. I turned to Peter. "I'll need the approval of the actors and stage crew. Do you think that will be a problem?"

"I wouldn't think so," he said. "You already have the director's approval."

I smiled. "Thank you."

"Of course, there is one unknown," he said. "Wilheard. But I imagine he'll cooperate if everyone else does."

We finished our tea, and Peter cleaned up while Juliette thought of Guzos who were talkative and civic-minded and might be good to interview. My list of names kept growing.

The museum door creaked open, and Rosamunde walked in. I thought for a moment that she was there to join us for a neighborly cup of tea, but the grave expression on her face suggested otherwise.

"Well come," Peter said. "Is anything wrong?"

Rosamunde sat down next to me. "I have bad news. Gwen has left the duchy. She says she'll be back in time for the Ceremony of Allegiance."

"What?" I squeaked. I stared at Rosamunde in dismay. Gwen was my hostess, my guide, my go-between with the council. What was I going to do without her?

"What happened?" Juliette asked.

"It's her throat. You know how careful she is about it. She started coming down with a sore throat last night, and by this morning she sounded bull-froggy. She's afraid if she talks at all, she'll damage her vocal cords. So she has gone into seclusion. She drove off twenty minutes ago."

How could it be? Gwen hadn't said anything about her throat the night before. "She sang the anthem," I said. Although, come to think of it, I hadn't really heard her voice. At the time, I thought she was reluctant to drown anyone else out with her operatic volume.

"She didn't want to worry us," Rosamunde said, "in case the soreness was temporary. But she realized this morning that it wasn't."

"Poor Gwen," Juliette said. "She just got here."

"What about the play?" Peter asked. "Will she be back in time to perform?"

"I'm sorry. You will need to find a new duchess."

Peter dropped his head into his hands and moaned.

"I know," Rosamunde said. "It's dreadful news."

Peter slammed his fist against the table. "Blast it. What am I going to do now? I have no duke and no duchess."

"Hold tryouts?" I asked meekly.

He shot me a sour look. "Why not? Maybe two talented actors will crawl out of the forest." He stretched out the "r" in "crawl," so that I pictured creatures with long talons clawing their way out of a swamp. I recoiled, regretting my suggestion.

Peter sagged back in his chair. "Sorry," he said. "I didn't mean to jump on you like that." He ran his fingers through his hair, defiant brown strands poking up. "All right. We'll hold tryouts. Let's make it tomorrow night at 6:30. Before rehearsal. That will give people a chance to prepare."

"That's the spirit," Rosamunde said. She rose. "I'm going to make a few calls on people, let them know about Gwen. Perhaps you and Holly could go to the dining hall for lunch, make an announcement there. Surely someone will want to play the duchess."

Would they? Gwen was going to be a hard act to follow, almost an impossible one. Who would want to replace her? Then again, maybe one of the ladies-in-waiting would like a promotion, a chance to play a duchess. Alice Cotton's daughter, for instance. She was young and pretty, and her family could use a little happiness. Maybe her father would even sneak back for the performance.

"Oh, I almost forgot," Rosamunde said, pulling an envelope out of her skirt pocket and extending it to me. "Gwen left you a letter."

"Nothing for me?" Peter asked sardonically.

"She felt terrible about leaving. I think she was hoping you'd understand."

"Not bloody likely."

I opened the letter, which was written in graceful but somewhat untidy cursive.

My dearest Holly,

I apologize for taking off with such haste. The unpleasant fact is, opera singers must sometimes put their voices first, even before their duty to friends and family. I do hope you will stay and pursue your study. Rosamunde and Juliette are good people, and they will help you in any way they can. You have only to ask. I am certain that Peter will also assist you, although he is probably in a monumentally foul mood just now.

I promise I will return to the duchy in time to sing the anthem at the Ceremony of Allegiance on the final day of the celebration. After that, you and I can catch up.

I must go. Take care of yourself, my friend. I will see you soon.

Gwen

She had called me her friend. Did she really mean that? Or was it her phony celebrity side talking? I looked up to find all eyes on me. "She thinks I should stay."

"Of course you should," Rosamunde said.

I wasn't so sure. This felt like the kind of abandonment that my mother had taught me to expect in life. "You can't depend on anyone," Mom had told me repeatedly. "Not even the people who supposedly care about you." I knew she was mostly referring to my dad, but the principle could extend to anyone. When things go south, she had instructed me, cut your ties and move on.

"I can't say I'm hungry," Peter said to me, "but we should probably head for the dining hall. I can beg for actors while we're there."

"Sure," I said, gathering up my notes. I could always consider a getaway later, if the council refused my request and I found myself truly alone. I still had my return airline ticket and enough money to get me home.

Rosamunde must have been reading my mind, because she slipped her hand in the crook of my arm and took me aside. Standing next to her, I was aware of how short she was and how much gray was invading her thick black hair, pulled into a braid. "Now then," she said, "I don't want you making any big plans without talking to me first." Her dark eyes locked onto mine. "Promise me."

No one had looked at me with such earnest caring since my grandma died. "I promise." A thought had been pressing on me since the announcement of Gwen's departure. "Rosamunde, please tell me. Did my vivid dream have anything to do with Gwen's decision?" What if I had scared her away from the duchy? Just when we needed her."

"Gwen has done this before, taken herself away to protect her voice. She is a fanatic about her vocal cords. You shouldn't concern yourself."

A few minutes later, Peter and I were crossing the bridge on the way to the dining hall.

"Do you ever have vivid dreams?" I asked him.

His expression clouded. "Ah, like the ones described by Framton. I don't concern myself with such things. As far as I can see, dreams—whether vivid or otherwise—are of no use. I keep my attention on what is real and verifiable." He didn't say, "and you should too," but it seemed implied.

"I see," I said. Clearly, I shouldn't tell Peter about my dream of murder. But I couldn't help wondering why he seemed so accepting of Anwen's dreams, which sounded pretty vivid to me, while he wanted nothing to do with such dreams in the here and now. I should probably also omit any mention of the marmot who had led me to the glen.

We walked on, skirting the plaza and entering Dukesway Road. Despite Rosamunde's reassurance, I couldn't shake the idea that Gwen's hasty departure had nothing to do with her voice and everything to do with my dream. Was it fear of murder that had sent her packing? If so, I was no longer a disinterested observer of a quaint celebration. My life was becoming entangled with the life of the duchy. And maybe with its fate.

CHAPTER ELEVEN

Day 3, Monday

As Peter and I walked into the dining hall, I was assailed by the aroma of fresh bread and hot food. I paused inside the doorway to get my bearings. Although it was a little early for lunch, the dining hall was nearly full, with a cheerful buzz coming from a dozen tables seating groups of two or more. Near the middle of the room, a long table was half occupied by a group of elderly men. To my left, multi-paned windows illumined six potted red geraniums perched on the sills.

Best of all, one wall was mostly covered by a charming mural. The scene was a colorful landscape with houses climbing up a steep hillside that overlooked a cerulean sea. Diaphanous clouds in a pale blue sky adorned the top of the painting. The landscape looked like Italy or Greece, and it transformed the rather plain dining hall into an open, airy space.

"Our chef, Violet, painted that," Peter said.

"It's marvelous."

"And behind the double door on your right is our mead hall. It opens around four. You should stop in sometime."

We walked to the far end of the room and approached a serving line with two women standing behind a large pot of what looked like stew and a basket filled with crusty rolls. Peter and I each took a tray, then Peter introduced me to Violet, the artist and manager of the dining hall, a sixty-ish woman with a good-natured, gap-toothed grin. Blond-gray hair peeked out from a headscarf decorated with tropical flowers, and a matching apron covered her skirt and blouse.

"Your mural is heavenly," I said, as Violet filled my bowl with stew.

"Thank you kindly," she said, beaming.

The young woman who served us bread flushed and cast her eyes down when Peter addressed her. He seemed oblivious to her discomfort, which was clearly evidence of an unrequited attraction. For the first time, it occurred to me that Peter might have a number of admirers in the duchy, even a lover.

Peter surveyed the hall. "There's room with the goat herders," he said, walking in the direction of the long table. The men were dressed like the guys I'd seen earlier on the road, in collarless shirts and loose vests. Each had a kerchief at his neck, no two colors alike. "May we join you, gentlemen?" Peter asked. Seven wrinkled faces peered up at me.

"I don't know about you, historian," boomed an elfish-looking guy with a surprisingly deep voice, "but your lady friend is welcome to keep us company." Beside him, an even smaller fellow with a weathered, deeply wrinkled face mumbled what sounded like nonsense syllables. "Aye, Oswin," that's right," the elfish fellow said. "It's the lady Yank what's come to see us."

Peter smiled wryly, and we sat. He introduced me, explaining that I was from the U.S., information that seemed to surprise no one. The elfish gentleman was named Roderick.

"I was once in New York," said a wiry man with a crooked nose sitting near me. He was missing some teeth, and he had to repeat himself before I understood he had been with the British Merchant Marines.

Across the table, a rosy-cheeked fellow with unkempt gray hair and a matching beard confided that he had a brother in Wyoming, but he'd never visited him. "Too many rattlesnakes. Wyatt, he's killed four of ‹em. Cut their heads clean off. Vicieux, they was. They got rattlers where you live?"

"No," I said. "They're mostly farther west."

I wasn't that hungry after the scone earlier, but the stew tasted good, full of sausage, potatoes, cabbage, and peas. The men dunked their rolls in the stew, and I followed suit, feeling like a kid, slurping up gravy with my bread.

The men turned to their own conversation, about half of which I understood, even with a concerted effort. Their speech consisted of some strange dialect of English, interspersed with French words and phrases. As the old fellows talked, they wheezed and laughed and snorted in a congenial way. Actually, the goat herders reminded me of the farmers who gathered at coffee shops across the Midwest, except these guys didn't wear caps with seed company logos.

Juliette appeared at the end of the table, holding a tray with a bowl of stew. She greeted everyone and sat down next to Peter. "How goes it?" she asked.

"Well enough," Peter said. "Oh, and that reminds me." He stood and disappeared into the kitchen. A moment later, Violet appeared with a large metal pot and spoon. A mighty clang sounded and everyone looked up.

"Listen, friends," Peter said in a voice that carried to the back of the room. "I have some news. In case you haven't heard, our friend Gwen has been called away suddenly." The diners responded with low murmurs. Peter held up his hand to regain everyone's attention. "As a consequence, we are in need of a duchess for our play. Ladies, I urge you to consider taking the role. And please tell others who might be interested. We will have tryouts tomorrow night at 6:30. We are also in need of a duke. Men, if you have even the smallest interest, please come. No experience necessary. And I assure you, the duke will not wear anything unmanly. So give it some thought. The duchy needs you." He sat and everyone resumed their meal.

"I wish you luck," Juliette said. "I might be able to talk Kessie into trying out. Do you want a thirteen-year-old as duchess?"

"Maybe. Let me see who shows up at the tryouts."

I raised my eyes to see Wilheard barging toward us, Eglentyne trailing behind, eyeing us nervously.

"You looking for a duchess?" Wilheard demanded of Peter.

Peter affected a civil smile. "Yes, as I said."

Wilheard grabbed Eglentyne's arm and pulled her forward. "My cousin wants to play the duchess."

"Ah, Eglentyne. You're welcome to try out," Peter said. "Six-thirty tomorrow evening, at the gym. I'm sure Wilheard will lend you his playbook." Peter turned back to his meal. I couldn't really blame him for wanting to rid himself of the Fosses. But Englentyne still stood there, hands tightly clasped. She looked like she was about to say something, but then her shoulders slumped, and she began to turn away.

My heart went out to her. "You know," I said, "I always find auditions frightening. I have to summon all my courage just to show up."

Eglentyne looked at me as if she'd just noticed me for the first time. She nodded in agreement.

"Is there anything troubling you?" I asked. "Any questions about the tryouts?"

"It's just...well, the duchess is a young woman. Whereas I am... more mature."

Peter looked up from his stew. "You can't be much older than Gwen."

"I know," Eglentyne said, "but Gwen is the duchess's granddaughter." Her voice dropped to a whisper. "I wouldn't like people laughing at me, thinking I'm deceiving myself about my age."

So that was it. Eglentyne looked like she was in her early forties, rather old to play the young duchess. But she clearly wanted the part. "I don't see why you couldn't play the role," I said, hoping that Peter wouldn't mind my forwardness. "You have a slim figure, and you'd be amazed at what a little stage makeup can accomplish. It's really just a matter of acting youthful."

"Do you think so?" Eglentyne asked.

An idea occurred to me. After all, wasn't I the designated dialogue coach? "Look," I said. "Why don't you and I get together. We can read through the duchess's lines, and you can see how they feel. If you are comfortable with the part, you can try out. If you decide the role isn't for you, you can skip the audition."

"Good idea," Peter said.

"If you're sure you don't mind," Eglentyne said to me. "I'm busy today, but I'm free tomorrow morning. Perhaps we could meet then. Say nine thirty?" I could see she was getting back the assertiveness she'd displayed when we'd met on the road and she had proclaimed the importance of the Fosses.

"The museum is usually quiet at that hour," Peter said. "If you want to meet there."

"Perfect," Eglentyne said, smiling broadly. She strode off with Wilheard, both in noticeably good spirits.

The door to the dining hall opened, filling the air with exuberant young voices. A moment later, Kessie was standing behind the chair next to her mother.

"Shouldn't you be at school?" Juliette asked.

"Miss Fishburne is sick. She had to go home."

"Not again. What about the substitute?"

"She's visiting her son in Lyon. His wife just had a baby. And Mr. Clark says he's very sorry, but he refuses to let his small students be overrun by a horde of barbarians. That would be my class."

"What a bother," Juliette muttered.

"Mum, I know you don't like me hanging around, bothering you. What if I go to Bois? Some of the kids are talking about taking the bus."

"You were there a few days ago. What would you do?"

"Oh, you know, just walk around, look at things. Maybe see a film."

"What film?"

Kessie's gaze shifted to her hands, which were gripping the chair back. "Oh, whatever is playing. I'd need thirty-five francs. For the cinema and a treat."

"I have a better idea," Juliette said. "Holly has hardly seen anything of the duchy. Why don't you take her to visit the Falls." She turned to me. "It's a lovely spot. A waterfall with a pool below. We often picnic there in the summer."

"Okay," Kessie said, without enthusiasm. She turned to three girls standing near the door and shook her head. Their faces fell.

"And we can have popcorn tonight after your rehearsal," Juliette said.

"With a soda?"

"Sure. Why not? Peter and Holly can join us. We can celebrate Holly's arrival. And your first part in the duchy play. We haven't done anything to celebrate that."

Kessie brightened. "Okay. I'll be back in a minute." She headed over to her friends, who would no doubt commiserate over her mother's veto of the excursion.

"Thanks for helping me out," Juliette said to me. "I keep an eye on the cinema. There is nothing in Bois right now that is suitable for a thirteen-year-old. And I don't want my daughter loitering around the streets."

"I would love to see the Falls," I said. I would probably have started working on interview questions that afternoon. But Juliette was right. The duchy was a beautiful place, and I'd seen little of it so far. It was a cool, crisp autumn day, and there was no reason my study couldn't wait until tomorrow.

CHAPTER TWELVE

Day 3, Monday

Kessie and I met in front of my house, where Kessie handed me her brother's canteen, filled with water. According to Juliette, the hike to the waterfall was about forty minutes each way, maybe a little longer since I was still getting used to the elevation. The walk started with a steady, easy incline, as Juliette had said, but it got steeper about ten minutes from the Falls.

We headed up the road and crossed the creek over the stepping stones that I'd taken the day before on my way to the glade. I felt more confident this time as I leaped across. We followed the same path into the woods, but this time I noticed that it ran parallel to a small stream a few yards away. Its waters must empty into the creek.

Kessie kept up a steady flow of chatter as we strode along side by side. It was a good thing, because after several minutes, the path rose and became rocky, and I didn't have much breath for conversation. By the time we arrived at a line of birch trees, I had learned that Kessie was indeed smitten with Alice Cotton's son Tony, and that he was oblivious to her existence. She also told me that her good friend Jenny, Tony's sister, thought that Tony was acting weird—sulky and easy to anger. What's more, he had stopped confiding in Jenny, which pained her more than anything. His schoolwork had also started to slip, not surprising, since he rarely showed up for classes.

"I imagine Tony is upset about his father's disappearance," I said. "That could explain a lot."

"Yes, but he started changing before that, like, a few weeks earlier. I remember. When Clive disappeared, Jenny wanted to talk to Tony about it, but she couldn't. He had already pushed her away, like he didn't care about her. Like they weren't mates."

"That's too bad," I said. Maybe Alice was right, and Tony's behavior was just a teen thing. "It sounds like Tony is going through a rough time, but he'll probably pull out of it later. Then Jenny can get her brother back."

The path hit a relatively level stretch, and I worked up the nerve to pose a question I'd been wondering about for some time. "Peter seems like a good guy. Does he have a girlfriend?"

"Not in the duchy," Kessie said. "But I've heard he has a lady friend in Bois. He goes there a lot. And he lived with a girl in England. She came to visit once a long time ago. I only saw her from a distance, but she was a stunner."

I shouldn't be surprised that Peter had a gorgeous woman in his past and a love life now, his partner kept at a distance from the worst of duchy gossip. I resolved to keep him securely parked in the mental compartment I reserved for male colleagues. It was just as well. I would be here such a short time, it would be unwise to let my emotions run amok.

Kessie raised her brows. "Do you like him?"

"Yes, of course, but not that way. He's more of a mentor." I hoped I sounded convincing.

The afternoon sun was warm, and I'd worn a sweater, which I now took off and draped around my neck. I realized that we must have passed the turnoff to the glade without even seeing it, not surprising since we had no marmot lookout to signal us. The trail was leading us upward in the direction of a wall of granite peaks. After about half an hour of walking, the trees bordering the trail turned from oaks to pines, and I could hear a rush of water.

"Listen to that," Kessie said. "It's the Falls. We're getting close."

The path became steep, and we scrambled over rocks, winding our way upward, my chest heaving. Finally, the path leveled, and after skirting a stand of lofty pines, I stopped in awe-struck wonder. Beside me was the top of a majestic waterfall. Curtains of water dropped down a sheer rock face, crashing into a pool below. A misty spray rose into the air.

"There are steps down to the pool," Kessie said, and as soon as my breath had returned to normal, she led me down a series of flat stones jutting out from the steep hillside. As we got closer, I could see that the pool was roughly circular and about twenty feet in diameter. It was deep, with rocks clearly visible several feet down. A path circled the pool and led down the hill.

"We can go back that way," Kessie said, indicating the trail. "It's easier. But I thought you'd like to see the falls from above first."

"Yes, thanks," I said. Boulders rimmed the pool, and we sat on two of them and drank from our canteens. Kessie pulled a couple of partially smashed cookies wrapped in butcher paper out of her pocket and offered me one. I peered at the ridge above, where the wall of water began. "This place is so beautiful," I said and took a bite of my cookie. Ginger.

"It's more exciting in the spring," Kessie said. "The water is super loud, like thunder, and it comes crashing down into the pool." She threw out her arms. "Keblooie!"

"Awesome," I said.

"Hardly anybody comes to visit now." She went silent, staring across the pond, to a spot behind a fallen pine tree. "That's odd. I see something." She jumped down from her rock and walked to the edge of the water, then continued a few yards around the pool.

I eased off my boulder, my legs stiff from the climb. "What is it?"

Kessie turned to me. "Something orange. A kerchief, I think, the kind the men wear."

Joining her, I peered to the other side, near the falls, where rocks and the fallen tree partially obscured the pond. The cloth had gotten caught in a low branch. Below it, the branches dipped into the water, where they had ensnared more detritus, including what looked like the remains of a large animal. A doe maybe.

"Clive wears a kerchief that color," Kessie said. "Jenny's dad."

A bad feeling swept over me. "The guy who disappeared?"

Kessie nodded, her eyes wide.

I continued walking around the pool, slowly now, Kessie right behind me, until I had a clear view of the detritus. It was no animal I was looking at. It was the bloated, decomposing body of a man lying face down in the water.

"Oh no," Kessie moaned. Ginger-flavored bile rose in my throat, and I looked away fast, barely holding down the remains of the cookie.

"We'd better get your mom," I croaked.

"I'll go," Kessie said. She pivoted and raced down the path. It was immediately clear that I had no hope of keeping up with her. I reasoned that I might be of some help when Juliette arrived, so I sat down in a weedy spot beside the pool, hugging my knees tightly, out of sight of the fallen pine and what lay under it.

In less than an hour, Juliette showed up with the three Bonnet brothers and a lanky fellow I hadn't met. They were dressed in matching bright blue jackets, and it turned out they were the local alpine rescue team, accustomed to removing people from dicey situations. I pointed out the branch that had captured the orange kerchief, then walked back to my out-of-the-way spot and sat cross-legged on the ground.

Taking care not to look directly at the body, I watched as Juliette bagged some soggy-looking objects and took numerous photos. Then she walked slowly up the stone steps, gazing around her as she climbed to the higher level, where she looked around the area overlooking the Falls, then disappeared from view. Several minutes later, she climbed down the steps, exchanged a few words with the men, and walked toward me, looking weary, her expression strained.

I stood. "Is it Clive Cotton?" I asked, as she lowered herself to the ground beside me.

"I think so, but we'll have to wait for positive identification."

"I'm sorry."

"Me too."

"Did you find anything helpful?" I asked.

"Not really. It looks like the body probably dropped from above, but how it happened is anyone's guess. For now, anyway. The body has been in the water for a while, maybe since Clive disappeared three weeks ago. We've had afternoon rain showers a few times since then, so there are no footprints or other tracks visible. Nothing left behind on the path or in the area above." She shook her head. "No physical evidence that I could see, beyond the body itself."

I supposed there were four possible causes for the fall. Some sort of natural cause, like a heart attack, could have been involved. Or Clive could have tripped and fallen, maybe under the influence of alcohol or some other substance. Suicide was also possible, and lastly, murder. Hopefully, it wasn't either of the last two, for everyone's sake.

Together, Juliette and I observed the men as they hoisted the corpse into a body bag and onto a stretcher.

"What a nightmare for Alice," I said. "And for the kids."

Juliette picked up a pebble and threw it into the pool, setting off ever-widening ripples across the still, deep water. "Alice was convinced that Clive would never have taken off without sending her word. I guess she was right."

Juliette asked me to describe how Kessie and I had found the body, which I did. She took notes, then flipped her notebook shut and dropped it into a jacket pocket. "If you wait, I'll walk down with you," she said. "The police van is parked beside the road, and Baptiste will drive the body into Bois. The medical examiner there will perform an autopsy. As sheriff, I get the hard job, telling Alice the bad news."

Juliette made her way back along the path to Baptiste, the oldest Bonnet brother. They stood close to each other, silently observing the other team members' final preparations. Then he put his hand on her shoulder and bent his head down to say something to her. She gazed up at him, and something clicked in my mind. They were lovers, or something very close.

The three Bonnet brothers and the lanky guy carried the stretcher with Clive's bundled-up body down the path, and Juliette and I followed. We were mostly silent on the trek, and I suspected that Juliette was choosing the words she would use to tell Alice that we had found a body that was probably her husband's. I was pretty sure that friends and family would gather around Alice, for comfort and support. That was the benefit of close-knit communities.

It would have been a pretty, scenic hike down the mountain and along the stream if we hadn't been constantly aware of the tragic circumstances. By the time Juliette and I parted company, late afternoon shadows were falling across the road outside Gwen's house. "I'm sorry you had to go through this," Juliette said. "Next time I'll let Kessie go to the cinema."

Once inside the quiet house, I dragged myself up the stairs and collapsed onto my bed. What a day. I had been awakened before dawn by a horrifying vision of Gwen's murder, and in the afternoon, I'd climbed to a waterfall and discovered Clive's corpse. Between those grisly events, I'd outlined my project with Peter, learned of Gwen's departure, and agreed to coach Eglentyne. It was too much to absorb. After lying on the bed for several minutes, I hauled my stiff body up and opened my wardrobe. From the top shelf, I took out my bag of M&Ms and my penny whistle. It was time for some comfort.

With the sun going down, the air had turned chilly, and I pulled on my coat and stuffed the candy into a pocket. As I descended the stairs, penny whistle in hand, I heard tapping at the front door. "Halloo," Rosamunde called as she entered the hallway. "Ah, Holly, how fare you? I know you've had a terrible shock."

"I'm okay," I said. "I think."

"Tonight's rehearsal is canceled. I knew you'd want to know."

"Thanks. That's a relief." I had no energy for another rehearsal. "How is Kessie doing?" I hadn't seen her since I glimpsed her disappearing down the trail.

"She's still shaken, but she'll be all right. Shall we sit?" We went into the living room, where we sank onto the sofa.

"You don't have more bad news?" I asked, alert for the worst, whatever it might be.

"No, nothing like that. I was thinking you might like some company at the house tonight, now that Gwen is gone. Peter offered to sleep here while you're alone in the house.

"Do you think I'm in danger?" A murderer could be nearby, I realized with a start.

"Oh, no, it's just that the house is large for one person, and you had two scares today, first the dream, then finding poor Clive. If it were me, I wouldn't want to sleep alone." She was right. Now that I thought of it, I could hardly bear the idea of a night alone in the house. But at the same time, I hated to be a bother. "That's very generous of Peter. But I don't want to inconvenience him."

"He'll be happy to come. He's just next door, and this was his gran's house, so he has spent lots of time here. He'll be right at home. I thought he could take the bedroom downstairs. The bed is already made up." "In that case, I won't say no."

A moment later, we both headed for the door. "You're a musician, I see," Rosamunde said, pointing to my long brass penny whistle.

"Of the very humblest sort." I accompanied her outside, said good-bye, then followed the veranda as it curved around the house. By the kitchen, steps led to a grassy slope with occasional stones jutting out. I made my way up the hill, until I found a relatively level, rock-free spot with an unobstructed view of the mountains, and I sat cross-legged on the ground. I ate a handful of chocolate as I pondered the tunes that I knew well. It was the traditional Celtic melodies that came to mind, haunting and melancholy, matching my mood, but bringing beauty to it, allowing the pain to flow freely into the air.

I picked up my simple flute, placed my fingers over the holes, and brought it to my lips. I blew, lifting my fingers, as I played the tune of "Loch Lomond," the words echoing in my mind. "By yon bonnie banks and by yon bonnie braes, Where the sun shines bright on Loch Lomond." The music poured out of my penny whistle, soft and mellow, and I relaxed into the sound. At the end, I stopped, the notes still ringing in my ears. I heard a chirp and looked toward a large rock several feet away. A marmot sat on top, its bushy tail golden in the slanting sun. "I'm glad to see you," I said. "Did you cross the road to visit?" He peered at me with his dark, oval eyes, then twitched his tail and disappeared behind the rock.

As I started in on "Barbara Allen," I became aware of a rhythmic drum beat and looked across to the slope above Rosamunde's house, where Kessie was standing, a shallow drum tucked under her arm and a short drumstick in her hand.

"Come on," I called, and she loped up the hill and parked herself on the ground at my side. "You doing okay?"

"I keep seeing him," she said.

"I know. I do too." We were both marked by what we'd seen. I placed a hand on her shoulder and gave a small squeeze. Then my gaze shifted to the drum. "That's a bodhran, isn't it? It's a beauty."

Her expression brightened. "It was my dad's. He lived in Ireland for a few years when he was young, and he brought this back. Now it's mine." Her brow furrowed.

"I'm still just a beginner."

"I'm learning too," I said. "Do you know 'Barbara Allen'?"

"I've heard it." She kept up a steady rat-a-tat as I played the bittersweet notes. "'Twas in the merry month of May, When green buds all were swelling, Sweet William on his death bed lay, For love of Barbara Allen."

We were on the third repetition when I heard the warm tone of a violin and looked down the hill, to see Peter poised on the veranda behind his cottage, the fiddle cradled against his chin and the bow sweeping across the strings. Kessie and I both stood. "Come join us," I called, and we waved him over.

It was when the three of us began playing "Amazing Grace" that Juliette appeared, walking slowly up the hill and singing the lyrics in a rich alto. Amazingly, Juliette knew the lyrics to all the verses. When we finished the last one, Juliette suggested that we sing the first verse together. So we laid down our instruments and formed a circle. Then we lifted our voices, the sound flowing up and out into the darkening world.

Amazing grace, how sweet the sound That saved a wretch like me. Who once was lost, but now am found, Was blind, but now I see.

By the time the final notes died out, tears slipped down Peter's face, and Juliette had placed a comforting hand on his shoulder. He took a long, shaky breath, and I remembered that his younger brother had died recently. It wasn't only Clive we were mourning. I turned toward Juliette's house and saw two figures on the back veranda, barely visible in the pale light. It was Rosamunde and Rob, leaning into each other, his arm around her.

"Soup's on," Rosamunde called. "Come, dear ones, let us eat."

CHAPTER THIRTEEN

Day 4, Tuesday

I woke up to sunlight streaming through the closed balcony doors. It was seven-thirty, and I had slept for ten solid hours. But my sense of well-being vanished as a picture of Clive's bloated corpse flashed across my mind. I groaned, realizing that the scene was probably etched forever in my brain. I sat up in bed, steeling myself against the morning chill, when another thought hit me.

The worst is over.

Now that Clive's body had been discovered, his family could get on with the process of grieving. My own recovery from the horror had begun last night with the music and the gathering of friends—Kessie, Peter, and Juliette. Rosamunde's hearty potato soup had nourished us, and the M&Ms hadn't hurt.

Last night, I had crashed in bed before Peter moved in, and now I listened for sounds of him downstairs, but heard nothing. After gathering my shower gear, I padded down the steps, passing Peter's room, which was next to the bathroom. His door was open, but he wasn't there. The room, however, looked lived-in, with clothing piled on a chair and the quilt askew on the bed.

Back in my room, I dressed in my khaki skirt and a lavender t-shirt that I'd picked up at a Celtic music festival. When I walked into the kitchen, there were two bowls on the floor in a corner, one filled with water and the other containing a few pellets of dry dog food, so I knew that Bonnie had spent the night as well.

Peter had left me a note on the table:

Bonnie and I are going for a run.

Eggs and bacon in the fridge.

Help yourself.

I had just dragged a skillet out of the cupboard when I heard footsteps outside the kitchen door. I looked up to see Peter in the doorway, flushed from exercise and the brisk morning air, Bonnie beside him. She dashed to her water bowl. Peter hadn't eaten yet, he told me, so while he showered, I took out three strips of bacon and three eggs and fried them up, savoring the smoky aroma. I never ate bacon at home, and it felt like a delicious, self-indulgent treat.

Rosamunde had pressed me to take a round, hard-crusted loaf of bread the night before, and I was cutting thick slices of it when Peter emerged, looking smart in slacks and a pale blue button-down shirt, his brown hair still wet. A few strands flopped over his dark, winged eyebrows. The purplish circles under his eyes that I'd noticed when we first met had now mostly faded. Had he sung away some of his sorrow last night?

We sat at the table, and as I poured tea, Peter described the route that he had followed that morning, along a path up into the hills behind our houses. I confessed that I was more of a walker than a runner. After that, our conversation paused as we applied ourselves to slathering jam on our bread and enjoying our hearty breakfast. I had drunk the last of my tea when Bonnie came over to sniff me. She allowed herself to be scratched behind the ears before she lay down on the rag rug by the door.

"Are you ready for Eglentyne this morning?" Peter asked, and I remembered my nine-thirty appointment at the museum.

"Do you think she'll show up after everything that happened yesterday?"

"I don't know her well, but she seems like the determined sort. Actually, I was surprised she was so reticent yesterday at the dining hall."

"Do you suppose her fears are realistic? Could people criticize her for playing the duchess?"

"I doubt it. Not unless she's genuinely terrible. And even then, Guzos are pretty forgiving. But the Fosses have a long-standing sense of inferiority, and it can make them touchy."

"Why do they feel inferior?" I asked.

"It goes way back. The family has always played a lesser role in the duchy. They are descended from Philippe's cousin, an ambitious young man. Judging from Anwen's journal, he was one of the rare people she never warmed up to. Unfortunately for him, he never achieved his goals of wealth and status, and he was bitter about it. The family has never let go of the notion that they should have risen higher."

"After three hundred years? It's a long time to hang on to a grievance."

Peter shrugged. "This is the duchy."

We washed and dried the dishes. Then I collected my play book, and Peter and I walked to the museum together. On the way, people greeted him with "good morrow," but they said nothing to me. Even people I'd met on the previous two days looked at me askance, refusing to make eye contact. "They don't imagine I murdered Clive, do they?" I asked Peter. "No. They're just edgy. When people die here, it's usually from some ailment of the elderly. Actually, I suppose you might be under a little suspicion. You know, a stranger who finds a corpse at their favorite picnic spot. But they'll get over it."

I hoped fervently that they'd get over it by the next day, when the council would consider my request to study the celebration. I was eager for good news that I could pass on to Dr. Ferris.

A small dog that looked like a terrier mix ambled over to us, and we stopped while she gave Peter a good sniff. "A friend of Bonnie's," he said before we resumed our walk.

Eglentyne arrived at nine-thirty sharp for our session. We sat at the table farthest from Peter's office, and it was immediately clear that she had prepared. She read Anwen's lines with some fluency, although her delivery was stilted. We talked about Anwen, how she probably felt, what was going through her mind as she spoke. Little by little, Eglentyne's performance improved, the lines sounding more natural, a hint of youthful sweetness entering her delivery. I read lines with her, taking the parts of the abbess and Philippe. By ten-thirty, I felt like she was ready to try out for the duchess, and apparently Eglentyne did too from the pleasure she radiated.

"You know," she said, "I've always wanted to play the duchess, ever since I was a girl. But someone else was always chosen. Someone better suited, I suppose."

Gwen, she probably meant. Gwen's sudden departure still stung, but if her absence meant that Eglentyne would finally get to play the duchess, maybe it wasn't all bad.

Eglentyne had brought a basket with her, the contents covered by a tea towel, and when Peter emerged from the kitchen with a tea pot and mugs, she pulled out a beautifully braided sweet bread, studded with candied fruit. I wiped off the table, and we sat down to eat.

"What do you think?" Eglentyne asked Peter. "Have I a chance to play the duchess?" He had clearly had the opportunity to eavesdrop.

"I'd say a good chance," he replied. His eyes crinkled impishly. "And Holly should try out for the duke."

"Very funny," I said. "Although, it's true that you can do a lot with makeup. And a good fake beard."

"Wilheard's boss is arriving this afternoon from New York City," Eglentyne said. "I'm sure he'll want to watch the rehearsal. It's good that we're performing Act Three, since the King of France appears in it. I know that Wilheard will be splendid." A few minutes later, she gathered her things, leaving the remains of the bread, and took off for home.

Juliette appeared just as Eglentyne was leaving, sinking into the chair beside mine. I poured her a cup of tea, then set the bread and a plate in front of her. Her dark, almond eyes appeared troubled.

"What's wrong?" Peter asked.

"The medical examiner in Bois called." She explained that his findings were inconclusive. Clive had died from impact, no doubt the result of falling from the top of the waterfall and landing face-down in the pool. But he had an injury to the back of his head, perhaps caused by crashing against a rock when he fell. Or by a blow to the head with a blunt object.

"So he could have fallen by accident, hitting his head," Peter said. "Or he could have been struck on the head and shoved over the cliff."

"And we can't completely rule out suicide," Juliette said. "At this point, we can't eliminate anything."

It was aggravating and sad. If only the autopsy could have been more conclusive—and benign. Death by a heart attack or something like that. Anything that crossed off murder from the list of possibilities.

Juliette took a swallow of tea. "In any case, he had been in the water for about three weeks. Since around the time he disappeared."

Peter frowned. "I can't see Clive killing himself. Or stumbling over the cliff, for that matter. He wasn't a heavy drinker."

"I know," Juliette said.

Peter rubbed his fingers over his temples. "Assuming for the moment that Clive was murdered, the next question is, why the hell would anyone want to kill him?"

Juliette sighed. "After he disappeared, I asked everyone: 'Who might want to harm Clive?' But I came up with absolutely no one. Clive was a mischief maker. He adored practical jokes, but he was a good sport, even when he himself was the victim of a prank. Everyone liked him. And of course, everyone loves Alice."

"What about the gamblers in Bois?" Peter asked.

"According to the police chief, they are wealthy, generally law-abiding citizens. Not the sort to kill off people who lose at cards. The worst they would do is bar Clive from future games. Really, I can't imagine how Clive got into the high-stakes table in the first place. He certainly had brass."

Juliette laid a slice of bread on her plate. "You know what really troubles me? Clive's notion that he was coming into a large sum of money. I wish to heaven he had told Alice how he was going to get it."

I thought of my conversation with Kessie on our way to the waterfall. "Actually, Clive's son Tony might know something. Jenny told Kessie that her brother had started acting troubled some time before their father's disappearance. Clive may have been in a good mood, but apparently, Tony wasn't."

"I spoke with Tony," Juliette said, "but his answers were all monosyllables, and I had to pry those out of him. If he knows anything, he's not talking. At least not to his mum or me. It sounds like I should speak with Jenny again." She shook her head. "I hate to upset the girl further."

"So, what now?" Peter asked.

"I'll go to the council and see if they have any suggestions for how to handle this. If I treat it like a full-scale homicide investigation, I'll have to interview people all over again, looking for means and motive. I'm not sure how that will go over, especially right now, two weeks before the celebration."

At noon, Peter went home to check on Bonnie, and Juliette was out, so I walked to the dining hall by myself. Sandwiches were on the menu, and

I didn't feel like facing any of the other diners' slitty-eyed looks without moral support. So I approached Violet, the chef, whose apron today had a pale lilac print, which was pretty, but still in tune with the somber mood. I asked if I could take out my sandwich.

"Of course," she said kindly. She packed up two egg salad and watercress sandwiches in brown paper for me, then handed me an apple. "Take care of yourself, dear."

Back at the museum, I sat down to eat my lunch and work on interview questions for my study. When I had done as much as I could, Peter read through them, suggesting ways I could simplify a few questions. He also advised me to add questions about how the subjects' parents and grandparents participated in the celebration. Not only would it show me patterns of behavior within families, he explained, but it would extend the time range.

Peter gave me several sheets of lined paper, and I carefully copied out my project outline and interview questions, all in longhand.

A little before five, Rosamunde dropped in, and Peter and I joined her at the table near his office. "The council met this afternoon," she said. "We didn't see much point in having Juliette repeat all the investigations she carried out after Clive disappeared. She will continue to look for leads, of course, and follow up on any that arise, but she will try not to stir up people more than necessary."

"Do you think people will accept such a low-key investigation?" Peter asked.

"The council members will all talk to friends and family, explain our reasoning. With the celebration fast approaching, I expect most Guzos will see the wisdom of it."

"I don't suppose Alice or her children will be at rehearsal tonight," Peter said, "but I'll have a word with anyone who brings up Clive's death. Let them know that the council has met and Juliette is at work."

"Yes, would you?" Rosamunde said.

All through the conversation, my anxiety level had crept up. "And my study?" I asked Rosamunde. "I'm ready with my presentation. Will they consider my request tomorrow at their usual meeting?"

"I'm sorry, Holly. We won't be meeting tomorrow. And this isn't a good time to make your request. The council members are anxious, and they would probably just refuse. It's better to wait another week and let things settle down. You'll have a much better chance of receiving approval then."

"Oh, no," I moaned. That would leave me only a week to work on my research before the celebration. And the last few days, everyone would undoubtedly be busy preparing for the festivities. I would have to seriously pare down my list of potential interviewees. And that was assuming I received permission to go ahead with my study, which was far from a sure thing.

"Everything will work out," Rosamunde said. "I'm certain of it."

Peter and I ate dinner at the dining hall. As we walked in, I noticed that everyone was either silent or speaking in low voices, as if the whole duchy was in mourning. Actually, once we sat down with our bowls of stew, I was only vaguely aware of the other diners, as I was enveloped in misery over the council's unwillingness to consider my proposal. Rosamunde was right, I knew. It would be a mistake to be pushy. What's more, my troubles were minor next to those of the Cotton family, who had just lost their husband and father. Still, I was disappointed.

I had agreed to e-mail Dr. Ferris when I arrived in the duchy, but I'd decided it would be better to wait until I had permission for the study—which I had thought would come tomorrow. But that wasn't going to happen, and I couldn't wait any longer to contact her. I would have to hit the cyber-café in Bois tomorrow and tell Dr. Ferris I was still waiting for the council's okay. I had been told that the first bus to Bois left the duchy every morning at eight.

At one point, Giselle, the pretty blond woman with the pierced nose, stopped by our table. "I hope you are well," she said to me, her English words spoken with a slight French accent. "I know it was terrible for you, finding Clive that way." She seemed genuinely concerned, and I assured her I was doing okay.

"Soon Gwen will return," she said, "and we will all feel better." I fervently hoped so. Maybe Gwen would come back early. Her very presence would impart a sense of stability. And she could help to convince the council of the worthiness of my project.

By the time Peter and I arrived at the school gym, half an hour later, Eglentyne was already there, waiting for her audition. She easily won the role of the duchess, partly because she read well, but also because no one else tried out. Unfortunately, nobody wanted to play Philippe.

"Damn," Peter muttered.

"Want me to buy a beard?" I asked.

He flashed me a half-smile. "Not quite yet. I'll try throwing myself at the mercy of Felix and Donny. They have both played the duke at past celebrations."

"Isn't one of them a grandfather?" I asked.

"They both are. And Donny is in a wheelchair. But he gets around, and he's still a popular fellow. And as you say, make-up can do a lot."

A few minutes later, the cast and crew started dribbling in, and not long afterward, Peter called the actors to their places for Act Three. Since he would be onstage most of the time, playing the duke, he had asked me to take notes on anything I noticed, so I sat in the middle of the front row with a pen and notepad. So far, there wasn't much to report. One of the ladies-in-waiting needed to speak more loudly during a scene with Anwen and the

French queen. And the youngest Bonnet brother kept turning away from the audience in the scene where the traitors were plotting to kill the king.

The fight scene began, and my pleasure was heightened now that I was aware that three of the villains, the Bonnet brothers, were also the core of the alpine rescue team. I tried to cheer equally for the loyal courtiers and the scoundrelly Bonnets, but my heart was with the brothers. The blades on two of the cardboard daggers bent over during the course of the battle, and I made a note of it.

Peter called for a break, and when I looked up from my notepad, a tall, good-looking man in his mid-thirties stood in front of me. He wore khakis and a white t-shirt, a wool sweater tied around slender hips. Wavy strands of chestnut brown hair fell forward, nearly to his gray eyes. I wished I were so skillful with styling gel.

"Hello," he said. "You must be the visiting American. I'm Sebastian, Wilheard's employer. And friend."

"I'm Holly," I said, "Gwen's friend. His hand shake was firm.

"May I?" He sat down next to me without waiting for a reply. He sounded American, but with a trace of Brit, and maybe something else. Up close, I could see that he had a faint scar that extended down from the base of his left nostril and bisected his upper lip. A tiny imperfection in an otherwise flawless look.

"Are you here on business?" I asked.

"Not at all. Wilheard has been urging me to visit the duchy for a long time, and I finally managed some vacation time. I have to say, the duchy is every bit as charming as he told me."

"It is, isn't it?" Except for the corpse in the pool.

He crossed his legs. I'd seen suede leather boots similar to his in a J. Crew ad. "How is the play coming along?" he asked. "I understand you're short a couple of actors."

"Would you like to audition?" I blurted, not entirely in jest. "We need a duke."

He laughed. "I'm strictly here to relax and enjoy the scenery. And of course, I'm looking forward to the big celebration." He leaned toward me, lowering his voice, as if we were co-conspirators. "Especially the ceremony with all the Guzos raising their knives. Very rousing and medieval, don't you think?"

"Yes, I understand it's the highlight of the celebration. Although the play should be very good too."

The rehearsal resumed, moving on to the moment when Wilheard, as the French king, entered to thank his loyal courtiers and send the traitors to the dungeon. He handled "Off to the dungeon" well.

"That was exciting, eh?" Sebastian said, with a grin. As the actors moved around, getting ready for the next scene, I jotted down a couple of observations about costumes. When I looked up, Sebastian was eyeing me.

"I'm looking for ways to entertain myself while I'm here," he said. "If you don't mind my asking, what do you do when you're not taking notes on the play?"

"I'm afraid I won't be much help. I'm interested in history, so I've been spending a lot of time at the museum."

"Very commendable," Sebastian said. "I admire people who delve into the past."

I had the sense his admiration didn't go very deep, but then, not everyone was fascinated by history.

"Perhaps we could meet for coffee tomorrow," he said. "Compare notes on St. Uguzo."

"I'd like to, but I'm planning to go to Bois, check out the cyber-café."

"Really. I need to send a few e-mails. Could I give you a lift?"

Absurdly, my mother's warning about accepting rides from strangers popped into my head. "Oh, actually, I was planning to take the bus."

"But a car is so much more convenient. We could make it a quick trip or do a little sightseeing while we're there. Say nine-thirty? I could pick you up at your house. It's on the road out of town, isn't it?"

A small alarm went off in my head. "Well, yes. How did you know?"

"I see I've spooked you," he said. "Rest assured, I'm not a stalker. Wilheard gave me the grand tour. And I have a good memory for places and people. It comes in handy in my line of business."

Peter called for the next scene to begin.

"I'll leave you to your task," Sebastian said, rising. "Are we on for tomorrow?"

"Sure."

"Good. Nine-thirty. I'll be driving a red Ferrari convertible." And he moved away.

A Ferrari. I'd never ridden in one, but what the hey? I could be a member of the elite for a day.

CHAPTER FOURTEEN

Day 5, Wednesday

The next morning, I had the sunny kitchen in Gwen's house to myself. The room was starting to feel homey to me. I liked the bright yellow-and-white curtains that framed the window above the sinks, as well as the round, oaken table that seemed to invite tea and conversation.

I was eating bread and jam when the kitchen door opened, and Peter came in, red-cheeked, in his navy sweat pants and long-sleeved shirt. In the light from the window, copper highlights shone in his chestnut brown hair. His dog Bonnie headed straight to her water bowl, while Peter poured himself a cup of tea from the pot I'd left on the table, then flopped down on the chair next to me.

"Have a good run?" I asked.

"Bonnie did. I jogged along and tried not to fall too far behind." He took a big swallow of tea. "By the way, I met Wilheard's boss last night after rehearsal. Sebastian, his name is."

"So did I. In fact, I'm driving into Bois with him this morning."

"Ah. In his little red Ferrari. I saw it yesterday." He said it with a touch of disdain, but I suspected there was envy not far below. What man wouldn't want to own such a car? And a lot of women would too, for that matter. "I hope you enjoy your outing," he said dryly.

"Actually, I'm not looking forward to the trip, but I have to find an internet café to e-mail my adviser, tell her that I'm still waiting for permission to start the study."

"Yes. I can see how that could be touchy. But then, field work always has its obstacles. I expect she'll understand."

I thought of Dr. Ferris and her earlier willingness to dump me from the department. "I'm not so sure."

After breakfast, I had rummaged around the mud room behind the kitchen and found a laundry basket with a bag of wooden clothespins like the ones my grandma used to use. I washed a pile of clothes in the double kitchen sink, including the jeans, shirt, and sweater I'd worn to the Falls. I scrubbed and rinsed them thoroughly in an effort to rid them not only of dirt but of the web of sorrow that seemed to cling to them.

After hanging the clothes to dry on a clothesline behind the house, I took Framton's book to the veranda and read more about *Thin Places* in Ireland, specifically looking for further information on vivid dreams. Sure enough, Irish nuns and monks and other people with a spiritual bent sometimes had prophetic dreams, often envisioning tragic events. I couldn't help wondering if any of the dreamers in St. Uguzo had witnessed some element of Clive's death. I would ask Rosamunde.

Shortly before nine-thirty, I was sitting on the front veranda, waiting for Sebastian, dressed in one of my few remaining outfits that wasn't sopping wet—black tights and a sage tunic that brought out the green in my eyes, as well as my ballet flats.

The low-slung red Ferrari zoomed up the road and stopped in front of the house. Sebastian jumped out and opened the passenger door as I walked down the path from the house, clutching my shoulder bag.

"Good morrow," I said, showing off my tiny knowledge of Guzo expressions. I lowered myself onto the cushy seat.

"Good morrow to you. We seem to be going native, eh?"

I laughed. "Not really. I don't even own a shawl."

He strode around the car and settled in. "Maybe we can find one for you in Bois. I suppose I should look for a kerchief. Want to look my best for the celebration."

"Good idea," I said, pulling my sunglasses out of my bag. I should really have the pricey wrap-around kind for racing around in a Ferrari, but I would have to make do with my drugstore variety. Sebastian put the car into gear and we shot forward, the engine purring happily. I was glad I had pulled my hair back in a low pony tail, or it would have been sailing around my face.

"I understand your friend Gwen left in a hurry," Sebastian said, as we drove up the road.

"For health reasons," I said. "A problem with her throat."

"Too bad. Is it true that she might be the next duchess?"

He had wasted no time in becoming acquainted with duchy gossip. "I doubt it. She's an opera singer, you know. It would be hard to juggle both jobs."

"Still, the prospect could be enticing, don't you think? To be a genuine duchess?"

I shrugged. "I'm not sure that's important to her."

We reached the top of the ridge and passed the overlook. Sebastian shifted gears as the car raced downhill. "Is Gwen in Bois?" he asked. "If you'd like to drop in on her, I'll be happy to take you."

"Actually, I don't know where she is."

"Really? That's a bit odd, isn't it? She brings you here, then disappears without a trace?"

I also found it more than a little peculiar, but I didn't want to admit it in front of this stranger. "She's very protective of her voice. Opera singers have to be."

"I get it. She needs to guard her privacy. Still, if you want me to drop you off somewhere, I won't say a word about it."

I was getting irritated. "Thanks, but I just need to go to the cyber-café." And afterward, I thought, I'd stop at the chocolate shop down the street. I wasn't out of chocolate, but I liked to have a little cushion, just in case life took a turn for the worse.

We flew around curves, often crossing the center line, as we followed the road down through the mountains. At one point, my ears popped. After several minutes, we rumbled across the narrow wooden bridge. On the other side, a sign announced that we were entering France. Back to the modern world, I thought, even though it was a foreign one to me.

Sebastian turned onto the two-lane highway, and the car quickly accelerated, pressing me back into my seat like a weight against my chest. The engine roared as the scenery raced by. We had to be going close to eighty miles an hour. Sebastian glanced at me, a glint in his eye. "You should see how fast she can really go."

"Eglentyne said you flew in from New York," I said, hoping to dampen his testosterone surge. "Is that your home?"

"One of them. I keep apartments in New York, London, and Milan." The car slowed a little.

"How convenient," I said, trying not to show how dazzled I was by his lifestyle. "So you travel a lot. Is it difficult living that way?"

"Not really. My parents are diplomats, so I'm used to moving from one country to another."

I was impressed. To me, being a diplomat had always been the pinnacle of success—to lead a life that took you to exotic places, where you carried out exciting and important work. "I used to think I'd like to work for the Foreign Service when I grew up."

"Why not?" he said. "You're smart and adaptable. You've fit right in to the duchy, from what I've heard."

Really? Who could have told him that? I was clearly floundering, and I had apparently inspired suspicion in a number of Guzos. But maybe I didn't look as lost as I felt. Or maybe Sebastian was a shameless flatterer. "You said you need a good memory for your job. Do you mind if I ask what you do?"

"Not at all. I have the best job in the world. I work for an international corporation. It's the type that's well known to people in the highest financial circles but unknown to the general public. My job is to travel around to beautiful, charming towns to scout out places where my outrageously wealthy clients can retire. They prefer to live together with others of similar means—in an enclave, so to speak. So I find locations that can easily accommodate several individuals with large homes."

"Isn't that hard to do? It seems like the townspeople might not want a bunch of rich strangers moving in."

"You're right. The locations that I identify are often out-of-the-way places, remote from cities. At first, the locals are skeptical about the idea of wealthy neighbors. But then I explain about the improved infrastructure we'll provide: well-maintained roads, a reliable energy grid, a small airport, internet access, not to mention shops and a couple of nice restaurants. My company basically provides whatever is lacking. Plus, of course, there are jobs for the locals. We employ gardeners, chefs, that sort of thing. Pretty soon the townspeople are begging us to come."

"That must be gratifying for you."

"Actually, the only hard part of the job is when I have to tell the town leaders that their spot is not quite right for our clients."

"Why would that be?"

"Oh, any number of reasons. Some towns are just too set in their ways. Even when most people are keen for us to come, a few families may be resistant. Or there's no single leader we can deal with, like a mayor. That makes everything more difficult. And then a few places have simply been too remote."

"And is St. Uguzo a possible site?" I asked. The duchy was certainly a beautiful place and not that far from major French cities.

"This isn't a work trip, Holly. I'm here on vacation. I hadn't taken one in two years, and my boss told me it was either use my days or lose them. Wilheard had always spoken highly of the duchy, and now that he's living here, he thought it would be a perfect opportunity for me to visit. I must say, I haven't been disappointed."

"So, you aren't even considering the duchy for your rich clients?"

He grinned. "Actually, I did consider it. How could I not? But realistically, the place is too closed, too traditional. We require almost one hundred percent buy-in from the populace, and I can't see that happening here." He glanced at me. "Can you?"

"Maybe not." Although he would probably have some support, especially among those who wanted to open up the duchy to the outside world. And who wouldn't like internet access? Or a nice restaurant where you could get a glass of wine and order something other than goat stew?

"As it happens," Sebastian said, "we're set to sign a contract with a beautiful seaside town in Italy."

"Really? Where?" Not that I'd recognize the town, but I could look it up later.

"The name is confidential until the contract is signed, which will be very soon. In fact, the closing date is the day after the duchy's celebration. I'll have to leave very early that morning to arrive in time."

A pick-up truck loaded with what looked like cabbages turned onto the road. Sebastian beeped, and we zoomed around it.

"Enough about me," Sebastian said. "Tell me about your life. What do you do for entertainment?"

Entertainment. I hated to admit that for me that was probably reading a good book, walking around a park, or playing my penny whistle. "Well, I do belong to a musical group that specializes in traditional folk music.

We perform at renaissance fairs and local festivals around the Midwest. Sometimes at schools, that sort of thing."

"Excellent," he said. "I imagine you've been to some interesting places."

I thought of all the small towns surrounded by cornfields that I'd visited. "Nowhere sensational, but I like to stop in small towns and neighborhoods, chat with the townspeople, try out the cafés. My friends and I search for the ones that sell fresh-baked pies. You can't beat a good strawberry rhubarb pie. Or coconut cream."

He cocked his head. "You know, we've been looking for an agent in the American Midwest, someone who knows the region, feels comfortable in small towns. It's a great job. Excellent pay with full benefits. Not to mention the perks. You may have noticed my transportation." He patted the dashboard and gave me a knowing look."

Oh my gosh. The company would give me a sporty car to drive around in?

"Plus, there are lots of opportunity for advancement," he said. "I could put in a good word for you if you're interested."

My mind was sailing around in the clouds, but I brought it back to earth with a thump. "That's very kind of you. But I'm in graduate school." Or at least, I hoped I would be, if Dr. Ferris came through with the assistantship.

"The job wouldn't have to be full time, especially to start. Would you be free over the summers and school breaks?"

"I suppose so." Seriously, did I have anything better to do?

"Let me be candid. You're a bright, straightforward, friendly person. And you're flexible. Those aren't qualities that one comes across every day. You know how it is. Most people put up a front, try to pass themselves off as more than they are. But I can see that you're genuine." He beamed a smile at me.

"Oh, well, thank you," I said, my face warming. I had to admit, I was tired of being a student and a waitress—an undervalued peon. Was it possible that

Sebastian saw the real me? The woman with career potential just waiting to be realized? At the same time, I couldn't quite picture myself working for some international corporation. Did they want someone who blushed uncontrollably? "I'm not sure I'm the person you're looking for."

"You can think about it. I'm certain we'll have an opportunity to talk more before I leave. One word from you and I can call up the head of human resources. She's a good friend, and she trusts my instincts about people."

As we drew nearer to Bois, I tried to imagine myself driving around lakeside towns in Minnesota and Wisconsin in a sporty little car, talking to mayors and City Council members and folks from the Chamber of Commerce. Small town leaders who wanted the best for their communities. Lots of Midwestern towns were slowly dying, and this could be a chance to revive a particularly nice one, give it the boost it needed to thrive again. I had to admit, the job was starting to feel do-able.

Sebastian found a parking spot just up the street from the internet café. I'd never been inside one.

I was pleased to find that this place was bright and attractive, with framed geometric prints on the walls. The aroma of fresh coffee wafted out from the front of the building, which was devoted to a coffee bar and small lounge area. Sebastian and I signed up for computers and were directed to the back, where computer stations lined the walls. In addition, six round tables each held four work stations. I shared my table with three other people. A young woman with stylishly crimped blond hair looked up, and we exchanged a bonjour.

It only took a minute to get onto my server and find e-mail waiting for me from Dr. Ferris, my housemate M.J., my mother, and my sister Valerie. I opened Dr. Ferris's first.

Holly, I trust you are doing well in St. Uguzo. Just to let you know, increasing competition has developed for the assistantship that we discussed. Please let me know the status of your research ASAP so I can nail down your funding.

Marilyn Ferris (followed by all her academic information)

My stomach clenched. The department was battling over what I thought was my promised assistantship. That meant my funding could disappear at any moment. I wondered just how hard Dr. Ferris was fighting for me.

I took a deep breath and composed my reply. I explained that I was settling in well. With help from the duchy historian, I had written up a project proposal, including a detailed outline. The governing council would meet soon, and I was optimistic that they would approve my plan. I considered adding, "Please hang onto my funding!" but I decided that sounded too desperate, so I typed "Holly" and hit "Send."

M.J.'s note had better news.

I am SO jealous, just thinking of you in the ALPS! Are you learning to yodel? We could add it to the Rovers' repertoire. BTW, the Rovers have an Oktoberfest gig the third weekend of October in a suburb of Chicago. MJ

I was happy to learn that our group of musicians, The New World Rovers, had a job coming up. But Oktoberfest in Chicago seemed far away and kind of unreal. Here in the duchy, I was going to participate in an authentic, historic celebration. Then a few days later, I would go home to perform at an Americanized re-creation of a German festival. Beer and brats. Maybe pizza. Possibly a polka band. I replied to MJ that there might be yodeling at the celebration. I would check.

My mother had sent her e-mail from her new husband's account. Her message urged me to go to the nearest American consulate if I ran into trouble. There was one in Strasbourg and one in Lyon. She listed the addresses and phone numbers. "Remember," she said, "you are an American citizen and entitled to assistance." I replied to Mom that I was doing fine.

Finally, I opened the message from my sister Valerie.

Looking forward to hearing about St. Uguzo. Stay safe!
Valerie

Stay safe? That was weird. She certainly hadn't told me that when I left to go spelunking in Mexico, an activity that I considered fairly dangerous. She had just told me to have a great time.

I typed in "Thanks. I'll have lots to report," when I felt someone behind me and turned to see Sebastian at my shoulder.

"Hey," he said. "Are you about ready to leave?"

I signed the e-mail with "Holly," clicked "Send," and faced him. "I am now."

He asked me if I wanted to walk around before we went back, and the beautiful cathedral beckoned me, but I realized I would rather tour it with Peter—not that I thought that was likely to happen. Between the museum, directing the play, and running with his collie, he didn't have a lot of free time.

"Maybe another day," I said.

A few minutes later, after a quick stop at the nearby chocolate shop, we got into the car and zoomed away. Once we were past the center of Bois and heading toward the highway, Sebastian asked me if I had found e-mail waiting for me. I replied that I had heard from my advisor, housemate, and family members.

"Where does your family live?" he asked.

"My dad's in Minnesota, my mom's in California, and my sister is in D.C."

"All over the country. What does your sister do?"

"She works for the government. I'm not sure exactly what she does. She says she's a bureaucrat, does low-level stuff for one of the federal agencies."

"Ha," Sebastian said. "You know what that means, don't you? If she can't tell you who she works for or what she's doing?"

I've never liked being quizzed. "I suppose it means she doesn't feel like explaining it to her little sister."

"It means she's working for an intelligence agency. Probably the NSA or CIA."

I shook my head. "She would have told me."

"I assure you, that's the last thing she would have done."

I mulled it over for about three seconds and decided he didn't know what he was talking about. After all, Sebastian knew nothing about my sister. To suggest that Valerie was part of the spy world was laughable.

We entered a hilly, no-passing zone, where we found ourselves behind a boxy-looking sedan driving at what seemed like a reasonable speed. Sebastian pulled the Ferrari right behind the car, so we were tailgating it in a way that I considered both dangerous and rude. After half a mile, the sedan pulled off onto the shoulder, and we sped forward. Sebastian grinned. "Ferraris rule," he said and sped up.

I was glad half an hour later when Sebastian pulled up in front of Gwen's house.

"I hope I didn't put you off with my driving," he said. "I've been told my foot is a little heavy on the accelerator."

"No problem," I said, and thanked him for the ride. He started to open his car door, but I told him not to bother and climbed out of the car.

"By the way," he said, "have you tasted the duchy cheese? The good stuff?"

"I have. It's awesome."

"Wilheard is arranging for a tour of the duchy cheesery. Would you care to join us?"

"I'd love to," I said. The truth was, a day hadn't gone by that I hadn't thought of the tantalizing cheese. Now that I had met Fred, our very own abbess, I felt confident we could talk him into giving us samples during the tour.

"I'll let you know when we have a time," Sebastian said, and drove off.

CHAPTER FIFTEEN

Day 5, Wednesday

I walked up to the house, aware that my academic career could be heading for a final crash, but buoyed by the idea that a career in international business might be in my future.

A note was taped to the front door:

Lunch at the museum. Join us if you can.

Rosamund

It was almost noon, so I used the bathroom, then washed up and headed down the road. When I got to the museum, food was spread out on one of the tables— bread, cheese, cabbage slaw and apple cobbler. Rosamunde, Juliette, and Peter were eating their desserts as I filled a plate and dug in. They asked about my trip to Bois, and between bites of food, I reported on the e-mails I'd exchanged, including Dr. Ferris's suggestion that I would lose the assistantship if I didn't act fast to get permission for my study.

"That is worrisome," Rosamunde said. "But I'm sure the approval is coming. Your Dr. Ferris needs to have more faith in you." Not likely to happen. I knew from experience that Dr. Ferris was stronger on ambition than faith.

I also told them about my conversation with Sebastian, starting with the description of his job. They all listened attentively.

Juliette sat back in her chair. "So that's what he and Wilheard do for a living."

"Or that's what they claim they do for a living," Peter said. "You say Sebastian didn't give you the name of the corporation?"

I shook my head. "He said I wouldn't recognize it."

"Wilheard told me the name after some coaxing," Juliette said. "It's International Strategic Solutions, Inc." I've made inquiries among my law enforcement contacts. No one has heard of them."

"Do you suspect the company of something criminal?" I wondered if I had just driven to Bois with a con man.

"Not necessarily. I often do a background check on visitors, any stranger who is here for a while. And now that we have a possible murder to investigate, diligence is more important than ever."

I thought back to my conversation in the car. "Sebastian seemed pretty secretive. He wouldn't tell me the name of the town they're currently working with."

"Typical," Peter said.

"By the way," I said, "Sebastian offered to recommend me for a job with his company." I described the job, in which I would travel around the Midwest, looking for towns with potential as a retirement site for rich people. "Of course, I know it's nothing I can depend on."

Rosamunde, Peter, and Juliette shared a skeptical look. "The position sounds very fine indeed," Rosamunde said. "And I'm sure you'd be excellent at it..."

I heard the "but" in her voice. "You think there's something wrong with the offer, don't you?"

"Look at it this way," Peter said. "The chap hardly knows you, and he dangles a fantastic job in front of you. Does that strike you as a bit odd?" He raised an eyebrow. "Did he offer you a posh new car?"

I winced. "Okay, I admit it, I'd been considering a Mustang GT."

Peter groaned.

"I mean, he did mention perks," I said. I sank back in my chair. Rats. For some unknown reason—desperation probably—I had convinced myself that maybe, just maybe, Sebastian had peered into me and divined my stellar qualities. But Peter was right. I had to be pretty gullible to believe that a smooth character like Sebastian was being straight with me. "Okay. But why did Sebastian bother with his promise of a recommendation for a juicy job? What was in it for him?"

"It could be a genuine offer, of course," Juliette tapped her finger on the table. "Let's suppose for a minute that Sebastian has some ulterior motive. What would he gain by enlisting you? Making you an ally?"

In my mind, I replayed Sebastian's comments and questions. "I wonder if this has something to do with Gwen. He was convinced that I knew where Gwen was. I told him I didn't, but he didn't seem to believe me. He even offered to drop me off at her place but keep it a secret."

"Interesting," Peter said. "It appears that Sebastian wants to locate Gwen through you. The question is why. He must see Gwen as someone who can help him...or harm him. But I don't see how. She's not even here. It's not as if she were planning to become duchess. She's going to return in several days, sing the anthem, and leave."

Rosamunde and I locked eyes, and a chill went through me. I had dreamed of Gwen's death. Was she truly enough of a threat to someone to make her a target for murder? And how was Sebastian tied in with all of this? I was becoming increasingly glad that Gwen had left town.

"Maybe I'll have another word with Sebastian," Juliette said. She excused herself to return to work, and Peter went into his office and closed the door. That left me with Rosamunde, who sat patiently while I finished my cobbler. In spite of my worries, it still tasted marvelous.

"Any news about Clive's death?" I asked.

"Nothing yet."

"I've been wondering," I said. "Are there many Guzos who are vivid dreamers?"

"Five or six. Perhaps a few more who don't wish to admit it. And others, who have yet to recognize their abilities."

"And did any of them dream about Clive's death? You know, before it happened?"

"If they did, they never confided in me. But then, someone might have dreamt of the waterfall or the pool and had no idea of its meaning, that it would be the scene of Clive's death. Dreamers rarely see the whole picture. At best, we see a fragment and maybe an emotion to go with it. Fear or anger, occasionally even joy, if it's something the dreamer was wishing for. Your dream of Gwen was unusual. You saw a great deal of the action."

"But not the murderer," I said.

"Sadly, no. I hope the villain has become discouraged and given up."

"You know," I said, "in the Framton book, there was a group of women who pieced together information from their dreams. They caught a sheep rustler that way."

Rosamunde smiled. "I remember that. It was very clever of them."

"Have you tried it here? Getting all the dreamers together?"

She shook her dead. "It isn't the Guzo way. Besides, it's too late to save Clive. The deed is done." She sighed. "But there are other currents, an atmosphere of danger that I've sensed, like something toxic in the air. And a few other dreamers have felt it too. Unfortunately, no one has a clear vision of what it is or how to respond."

I didn't know what to say. I routinely lived with a feeling of impending doom. It was hard not to, world news being what it was—with massacres in Rwanda and the prospect of war in the Persian Gulf. And lately, apart from a few encouraging incidents, my own life seemed increasingly destined for failure.

When I got back to the house, I took my clothes off the line and hauled them to my room. They smelled great but felt a little stiff, just as they did at my grandma's house.

Peter had loaned me copies of the newspaper supplements covering the duchy celebrations, and I sat on my bed, reading through them and taking notes. I hoped the effort was not a wasted one. Then I took my penny whistle up the slope behind the house and played Beatles tunes. The music-appreciating marmot sunned on a rock not far away, but chose not to accompany me with his sharp whistle.

I arrived for an early supper at the dining hall, where the elfish goat herder—Roderick, his name was—invited me to join his pals at the long table. They all greeted me politely, then went back to their own conversation, which suited me fine. I finished my stew and applesauce, then headed for the school gym.

I got to rehearsal fifteen minutes early, but even so, I heard people moving around backstage. When I went back, I found both Peter and Tony, Alice Cotton's son, rummaging among the props. The boy looked old for his sixteen years, or maybe it was just a weariness about him.

"Ah, Holly, you've arrived," Peter said. "I was just telling Tony here that we need to survey the props and see what we need to replace. There's a little money set aside in the budget for that purpose." He held up a cardboard dagger, which flopped over when he waved it. "I believe we need new weapons."

"There's a toy store in Bois," Tony said. "I bought a sword there for my nephew last Christmas. It looked wicked, but the blade was rubber."

"Excellent idea," Peter said. "Look. Why don't the two of you make a list of what we need? Then you can organize a small shopping expedition."

Tony and I set to work. Some objects needed to be replaced, while others just needed a little mending. The queen's crown was bent, and Tony offered to cut out a new one if we got some cardboard. I suggested we look for some shiny paper or spray paint to cover it. We could transfer the fake jewels from the old crown to the new one. When I picked up the king's crown, I realized it also needed to be replaced.

"Wilheard will need a new crown too," I said. It should look impressive, or at least not tacky.

"Let the wanker buy his own crown," Tony muttered. What could that be about? Wilheard rubbed me the wrong way, but Sebastian had told me he was popular among the men.

I picked up the gold cardboard medallion that the French king would bestow on Philippe. There was the salamander under a crown, just as Alice had described. The image was drawn on, and it was a little crude, but from a distance, no one was likely to notice.

When I looked through the make-up, I discovered it was mostly dried out, so we'd have to buy fresh supplies. Eglentyne was going to need heavy-duty cosmetics, as was Fred, since he was playing the abbess. And if Peter convinced one of the grandfathers to play Philippe, he would need them too.

"Could we go to Bois together?" I asked Tony. "I should probably select the make-up. But I don't know my way around town, and my French isn't the best."

"Sure," he said. "You want to go tomorrow?"

"Don't you have school?" He looked down, and I remembered that he'd been skipping classes. "What time do you get out?" I asked.

"Three o'clock. But I can leave early. All I have to do is say that I'm working on the celebration, and the teacher will let me go." He paused. "There's a bus that leaves the plaza at eight-thirty."

Why not? I bet the kids weren't getting a whole lot done in school with the celebration approaching. And at sixteen, Tony was old enough to make his own decisions. "Great. I'll be there."

"Sweet," he said, which I took as a step forward in our relationship. It was only six years since I was a teenager, but the adult-teen boundary was already firmly established.

The cast was assembling onstage when Tony and I exited the stage. I took my seat in the front row, taking my notebook and pencil out of my bag. Tony had left the gym. It occurred to me now that his father must have a funeral soon. It had to be strange for Tony, making plans and carrying out normal activities at this unsettled, transitional time.

Breathing in the scent of perfume, I looked over to see that Fred's girl-friend from Bois, Monique, was taking the chair next to mine. We exchanged a greeting.

"I was sorry to hear about Clive," she said. "He always made me laugh with his jokes. And his poor wife. It is too sad. Is it true that you found the body?"

"Unfortunately, yes." I hoped that wasn't my new identity—the Yank who discovered the body.

"Frederic is upset, of course. He and Clive were old friends. And co-workers."

"The whole duchy is in mourning," I said.

"Yes, of course." She looked uneasy and clasped together her manicured hands. Was she worried about the murder? Or was there trouble with Fred? They had seemed so happy together last time I saw them.

"I have news," she said. "I fear it is bad news, and I am not sure who to tell. Of course, I would like to tell Frederic, but he is very troubled about his friend."

Oh no. I felt like I'd had enough bad news for the day. On the other hand, it was usually best to get problems out in the open, so they could be dealt with, one way or another. "Tell me, if you like," I said.

"Let us go outside."

Intrigued and apprehensive, I followed Monique across the gym floor and out the door. A few yards from us lay the soccer field, now deserted, while above us, the moon floated over a distant mountain, its face alternately shaded and revealed, as wispy clouds passed over it.

Monique took a packet of cigarettes out of her clutch bag, offering me one. I waved "no," and she lit one, inhaled, and blew out a breath of smoke.

"I was at a party in Bois last weekend," she said. "It was in the home of a friend. He is a patron of my little theatre troupe, a very generous patron, and I do not wish to reveal his name. But you should know, he served duchy cheese at the party. The gourmet cheese." She looked at me, gauging my reaction, I suppose. But at that point, I had no idea how upsetting her news would be. Monique continued. "Of course, the guests were all delighted. Except me. Frederic has told me that no one in this region is allowed to buy or serve duchy cheese. No one."

"I see," I said, although really, I didn't. I couldn't see that it was a problem if somebody in Bois had gotten hold of a little duchy cheese.

"Please inform Juliette," Monique said. "She will know what to do. You may tell her that I am the source of this news. But she must not reveal it to others. I will tell Frederic later, when the time is right. But not now."

"All right," I said. "I'll tell her tonight. She lives next door. Thank you for letting me know."

Peter was rehearsing Acts One and Two, and they had already begun when I slipped back into my seat. Monique had remained at the rear of the gym, where Fred would join her later. I forgot about her revelation as I watched the rest of the rehearsal, taking occasional notes for the actors and crew. Peter was still playing Philippe, but he seemed more comfortable in the role tonight. When the rehearsal ended, I delivered my notes to him, and he read them over, then passed on the information to the actors and crew concerned.

I waited around to tell Peter that Tony and I were going on a shopping trip the next day and would need some money. He pulled a few twenty-franc bills out of his pocket and handed them to me. "I'll need receipts," he said.

"Of course."

"You haven't been to the mead hall yet, have you?" he asked. "Juliette is there. What do you say we meet her there for a beer?"

Peter and I entered the mead hall at the entrance farthest from the dining hall and were immediately assailed by men's voices rising through a cloud of hazy tobacco smoke. The room was large, with a bar against the far wall and two long trestle tables down the middle, with benches on either side. A companionable seating arrangement, like something out of a medieval Great Hall. The benches were nearly full, taken by men of varying ages and a few women. I inhaled the smell of sweat and musk, probably a familiar aroma in a Great Hall as well.

Sebastian and Wilheard sat near the far end of the closest table, engaged in what looked like a spirited conversation with a couple of the younger men. On every surface sat mugs of what I assumed was beer or mead.

Against the wall to our left was a series of booths that ended at the connecting door to the dining hall. Because of their placement, the booths were half hidden from the rest of the room, giving their occupants a measure of privacy.

Peter led me down the row until we found one with Juliette sitting in the far corner, a mostly full mug of beer in front of her. She looked like a spy, sitting alone in the shadows. I slid into the booth across from her.

"Much action tonight?" Peter asked, still standing.

"It's been pretty peaceful. At least no liquor-fueled demands to overturn the council."

"Glad to hear it." He turned to me. "What can I get you? You have three choices: beer, mead, and hard cider. They're all brewed in the duchy."

I'd been hoping for a glass of wine. "I'm not really a beer drinker. And isn't mead quite sweet?"

"How about cider? It's dry, not sweet."

"Cider it is," I said, and Peter strode over to the bar. A minute later he was back at our booth with two mugs of a golden drink. He slid in beside me. I took a sip. The cider had a tart apple flavor, but it was very dry, nothing like the cider I grew up with. With the second sip, I decided I liked it.

"The cider is good, no?" Juliette said.

"Yes, it's very nice."

She sat back and pushed a strand of her short bob behind her ear. "You might be interested to know that Sebastian addressed the drinkers for quite a while. He described some town where his company brought in a group of new residents who had money to spare. Apparently, these rich newcomers provided the funding to enlarge a local brewery and begin international distribution of their beer. The citizens are all overjoyed." She turned to me. "Sound familiar?"

"It must be one of the towns where Sebastian's company settled its clients. Did he give the name of the place?"

"Not that I heard," Juliette said. "I'll ask him later."

Peter smirked. "It sounds like Sebastian is making himself popular among the mead hall crowd. That story of his must have gone over well with the Bonnet brothers, Bruno and Bernard anyway. And I suppose some of Sebastian's aura of success is rubbing off on Wilheard. I wish I knew what they were up to."

"And what it has to do with Gwen, if anything," I said. I couldn't shake my uneasiness over Sebastian's prying interest in her.

"How was rehearsal?" Juliette asked.

"Fine," Peter said. "But no one has stepped up to be duke."

I'd forgotten about Peter's search for a replacement, including the two former men who had played the duke, who were now elderly. "What about the grandfathers?"

"They said they'd think about it, but I know it was just a way of getting rid of me."

"Sorry," Juliette said.

"It's all right. I'll play Philippe and hope that people don't start thinking of me as a real duke."

"By the way," I said, "a piece of information was passed to me in confidence at the rehearsal."

"How mysterious," Juliette said. "You're in the thick of things already."

"Not by choice," I said. "Monique spoke with me, and I'm telling you this on the condition that you not reveal her as the source of the information."

"All right," Juliette said. "What's the news?"

I told them about the party in Bois where Monique had been served duchy cheese.

"What!" Juliette cried. Peter groaned and covered his face in his hands.

I couldn't believe they were getting so upset about a little cheese.

"Who was hosting the party?" Juliette asked, her voice stony.

"Monique didn't want to say. Apparently the guy is a patron of her theatre group."

"Merde," Juliette mumbled. "I'd better go tell Fred. If the cheese was stolen, he needs to know. And maybe he'll have some clue about the host." She slid across the bench and stood up from the booth. "Let's keep this quiet for now."

"You won't let Fred know that Monique told me, right?" I asked.

"No, but he may guess. Anyway, that's the least of our worries."

She strode past the line of booths and out the door. I turned to Peter, who was slumped against the bench, looking miserable.

"I'm sorry," I said. "I didn't realize the news was that terrible." No wonder Monique chose to tell me, an outsider. She wouldn't have to deal with a Guzo's emotional outburst.

"Not your fault," Peter said. "You won't be shot for bearing bad tidings." He sounded like he might have considered it.

"Seriously," I said, "what can it hurt if a little duchy cheese is served at a party in Bois?"

Peter cast me a dark look. "Time for another history lesson. You ready?"

"Sure." His lessons were always interesting, but this time I wished I didn't feel like I was being chastened for my ignorance.

He took a long swallow of his cider and began. "Right. Let's go back to 1926. That's when an Englishman was given permission to build a hunting lodge in the duchy. At the time it was constructed, it was quite a grand place, and it brought in extra income for the Guzos who worked there.

"One October, there was a group of hunters at the lodge when a freak blizzard cut the place off for a week. My great-grandfather, Duke Archie, and Rosamund's father skied in with enough liquor and duchy cheese to keep everyone happy. The Guzos became chummy with two of the guests, a savvy British entrepreneur, and a banker with ties to the English royal family. In the course of several conversations around the lodge hearth, the men devised a scheme to boost St. Uguzo's income, which was distressingly low. Duchy cheese was at the center of the plan."

I wondered if this plan would explain why I never got duchy cheese with my meals.

"Duke Archie sent out word to certain wealthy individuals that duchy cheese, in small quantities, would be made available to a very exclusive group of cheese lovers around the world, people who were willing to pay a frankly outrageous price for the privilege of buying it. The duke also leaked out the information that a prominent member of the British royal family, who had asked to remain unnamed, was the first to obtain permission to buy duchy cheese.

"Who was it?" I asked.

"That, I can't divulge. Sorry."

He took another swig of his cider. "You can imagine what happened next. Wealthy cheese connoisseurs from around the world started getting in touch with the duchy. By that time, we had a council, and the members decided that between one and three individuals per country would be allowed to buy a license to acquire our cheese. Such restricted access meant that the cheese would be very valuable, conferring high status on the people who bought and served it. The permission would be immediately revoked if the purchaser sold the cheese to third parties. This system has worked very well. Until now."

"Are there Americans on the approved list?" I asked.

"In fact, there are. One is a philanthropist in Pennsylvania and the other a married couple in California. They are well known in the cinema industry. But they have to be discreet. Our cheese isn't pasteurized or sufficiently aged to be legal in the U.S. It has to be smuggled in, which, of course, only makes it more coveted." He must have read my expression because he said, "Oh, don't worry. Duchy cheese is perfectly safe."

I sipped my cider, enjoying its tart apple taste, and let the information soak in. "Okay. I'm beginning to understand. If a bunch of unauthorized people in Bois, or anyplace else, start obtaining and serving duchy cheese, the cheese will be devalued. And wealthy buyers around the world could stop purchasing it. Or refuse to pay the high price."

Peter nodded. "Exactly. And if that happens, the duchy will quickly be brought low. No money for the dining hall and little for the school or the clinic. Definitely no money for the museum. As you can see, the duchy cheese has been responsible for a small economic miracle. It has allowed the Guzos a level of prosperity and a degree of security we never had before. And that could disappear in a flash."

"I get it," I said. I had no idea that the slice of cheese that I shared with Gwen was so valuable. Thinking back, I'd practically swooned with pleasure at my first bite. But Gwen hadn't mentioned that the cheese was responsible for the duchy's welfare.

"Come on," Peter said. "Let's go home."

We left the mead hall and walked down Dukesway, turned at the plaza, and started climbing up the steep road. After a long day, I would have been happy for a lift, but Guzos seemed to walk everywhere in the duchy without complaint.

"It's too bad that only wealthy people can afford duchy cheese," I said.

"Not quite. At Christmas, every Guzo family is given a wedge of the cheese. The size depends on the number of people in the household. Families often serve it at birthdays and other family celebrations. But I know what you mean. I would like to see a world where everyone had access to the good things in life, not just the rich."

A few minutes later, we entered the house and started walking down the hallway. Peter paused at the living room. "One of these days we'll light a fire in the hearth. On an evening when there's no rehearsal and no crisis to deal with. Should such a time ever arise."

"I would like that." We continued to the bottom of the stairs, with Peter's room to the left. There we halted under the dim overhead light. Peter was only a little taller than me, and I found myself looking straight into his blue-gray eyes. They were soft now, not intense, the way they were when he lectured. I liked them this way.

"I'm sorry about your job offer," he said. "It was thoughtless of me to jump on it the way I did."

"It's okay. I had to come to my senses eventually."

He frowned. "I couldn't bear to think of that weasel taking advantage of you."

"A weasel with a Ferrari."

His lips curved up in a half-smile. "All right. I confess, I have difficulty trusting a man who drives around in a flashy sports car. Unless I know him quite well, that is."

"And I'm sorry about the cheese showing up in Bois," I said.

"Don't worry. Juliette and Fred will get it sorted. Fred will figure out who could have sold the cheese, and Juliette will coax a confession out of the guilty party."

"Juliette seemed to think the cheese was stolen. But isn't it just as likely that some Guzo sold his own cheese?"

"It's possible, of course, but such things are very rare. The only case I know of was in the 1950s. A married fellow with two children wanted some extra cash, and he sold his family's wedge to an acquaintance in one of the nearby towns. When the misdeed was discovered, the man was hauled in front of the council. It was a great scandal, so of course, the room was packed with onlookers. You can imagine the shame for the fellow and his family. Anyway, the council ruled that the man's household would receive no duchy cheese for five years."

"So the punishment fit the crime."

"Indeed. But there's more. The fellow's wife was so disgusted with her husband that she threw him out of the house. He lived with his goats for six months."

I laughed. "You're joking."

"I'm not. At least, that's the story I was told."

Peter was standing close to me, and I was aware of his faint scent of rosemary and juniper. An oddly appealing combination. I'd noticed the aromas before, without figuring out what they were. I stood there, feeling a little awkward but not wanting to let go of the moment. My emotional walls were starting to crumble, and I didn't care as much as I should.

Peter rubbed his chin, with its faint brown shadow. "Monique was heroic for telling us about the cheese, ratting on her friend. The duchy should reward her in some way."

"Hmm. Maybe you could make her an honorary Guzo and give her a wedge of cheese at Christmas."

"I like that," he said, his eyes smiling, tiny wrinkles fanning out at the edges.

I lowered my gaze, aware of the quiet enveloping us. "I never thanked you properly for coming to stay in the house with me."

"It's my pleasure." He smiled. "And not just because of Gran's hot shower." He leaned toward me, his hand rising. For a moment I thought he was going to touch my cheek. Or kiss me. Then he seemed to think better of it and stepped back. "I'd better go fetch Bonnie." The pup spent most of her day in Peter's cottage, so she wouldn't run around destroying Gwen's house.

"Yes. She'll want a run before bed, I expect."

"Good night then," he said.

"Good night." I turned and climbed the stairs to my room, wishing that Peter had kissed me. Then I flashed on Kessie telling me that Peter had a lady friend in Bois. And who was I? A visitor here for a couple of weeks. What a fool I was.

CHAPTER SIXTEEN

Day 6, Thursday

I woke up to a light drizzle on Thursday morning, the mountains in the distance veiled in haze. My bedroom had the kind of damp cold that seeps inside you, so I put on my coat and hustled downstairs to shower. Back upstairs, I dressed quickly while I was still warm, pulling on jeans, my meerkat t-shirt, sweater, and sneakers. After towel-drying my hair, I pulled it into a low ponytail.

Downstairs, the kitchen was empty of Peter or Bonnie, and I mixed a heaping teaspoon of gooseberry jam into a cup of my new yogurt. I ate it slowly, savoring the sweet creaminess. As I'd hoped, the jam mostly hid the earthy tang of the goat milk yogurt.

It was eight-fifteen when I grabbed my shoulder bag and hurried down the hill to meet Tony at the plaza. The drizzle had let up, and patches of cerulean sky appeared out of the haze. Tony was already at the bus stop, as were about a dozen other people. He was the youngest and trendiest of the group, in denim jeans, a well-worn leather jacket, and sneakers. His blond hair was clean but disheveled, and his teenage cuteness was marred only by his troubled expression. I hoped the shopping trip would lighten his mood.

When the bus pulled up, we sat near the front. I was happy to note that the seats had a little padding, and the windows were large and clean, but as I breathed in, I realized that some Guzos did not believe in frequent bathing. I gazed at the Guardian, watching over the hills and valley below it. I started to say something to Tony about the beauty of the day, but when I turned to him, he was scowling.

"Anything wrong?" I asked.

"I hate this place," he mumbled.

"St. Uguzo?" I asked, startled.

"Yeah. Especially the mountains. They're everywhere. All around us. It's like they're trapping me."

I didn't know what to say. I loved the towering peaks that surrounded us. Even with their cragginess, they made me feel protected. But I suspected that it was more than the scenery that disturbed Tony. The death of his father had to be weighing him down, especially since the killer still hadn't been found. But his dissatisfaction might also stem from being sixteen years old and living in a close-knit community, where he was always sure to be under scrutiny.

"You'd like to get away?" I asked.

"Yeah. Someplace wide open. Where you can see the whole sky, from one horizon to the other. You ever been in a place like that?"

"Yup. My hometown for one. There are hills, but nothing high. Once you get away from the buildings and trees, you can see a long way."

"That's where I want to go, a place like that. Someplace far away."

"You know, I used to feel the same way. I wanted more than anything to get away from my hometown."

"Oh yeah?"

"To me, it was the most boring spot in the world. All around me, all I could see were cornfields. Cornfields and bean fields. They were everywhere, for miles and miles. All those cornfields were oppressive to me. Maybe like the mountains are to you."

"Weird," he said.

"I wanted to get out of my hometown, go where I hadn't seen the same people and places a million times. But mostly I wanted to live in a city, one where people didn't know every stupid mistake I'd ever made. From the time I was a kid."

"I hear you."

The bus let us off just before the bridge in Bois. We crossed the stream, which whooshed over jutting rocks that gleamed in the morning light. From there, the toy store was three blocks away. It was easily identified, with "Jouets de Jacques," Jacque's toys, written in bright red letters above the door, and a display window with a variety of toys, from dolls to building sets to board games.

Inside, the shop had tables stacked with new, flashy items and three long aisles behind them. I saw only one other customer, a young woman browsing in the first aisle. Tony led me down the third aisle to the toy weapons, where we chose knives for the courtiers, daggers with gold pommels and hard rubber blades. The price seemed reasonable and wouldn't break our budget.

"Maybe I can borrow one of these for the celebration," I said. "Not that I can vote or anything."

Tony's blue eyes brightened. "Let's find a better one." He strode back up the aisle to a table with a display of Star Wars stuff, including Jedi light sabers. He pulled out a stubby sword, and with a flick of his wrist, the blade extended.

"Whoa," I said.

"Here." He handed it to me with a grin.

The saber was clearly not up to Luke Skywalker's standards, but it was appealing in a somewhat flimsy, far-future sort of way. "Hey. The box says the blade glows red, green, and blue. I just have to get batteries."

"You know what?" Tony said. "We could get these for all the courtiers."

"No kidding." So much for historical accuracy. "Can't you just see the Bonnet brothers flashing these around? We could load the swords with batteries, and they'd glow."

"I have an idea," Tony said. "We could turn out the lights and the men could battle in the dark. The audience would love it. And more people might show up if we let everybody know there would be a battle with special effects."

"Yes!" I could imagine the colorful swords blazing in the dark. Besides, it was a pleasure to see Tony so enthusiastic. I tried not to think what Peter's reaction would be. Or the toll on our budget.

I stepped back into the aisle and put down my shoulder bag. With a swooshing noise, I waved the sword around. I'd taken a semester of fencing in college, so I knew a few cool moves.

Tony pulled a saber out of a box and raised it, then lowered it so it extended toward me. "En garde," he said with a menacing grin.

"Allez," I cried. Assuming my fiercest expression, I lunged toward him, arm and sword fully extended. He responded immediately, gently blocking my thrust with his saber. From there, we dueled, jabbing and lunging and crossing swords, moving up and down the aisle, swooshing as we went. As I charged and retreated with my Jedi saber, all the stresses of the last several days drained out of me.

All of a sudden, I took a misstep as I was moving backward and executed a perfect pratfall, landing on my bum in the middle of the aisle, sword still in hand. I let out a hearty "oomph." Then the sheer absurdity of the situation overwhelmed me. Me, the avid scholar, landing on my butt in a French toy store, sword at the ready. I burst into great, gasping, snorting gales of laughter. It must have been contagious because Tony doubled over, laughing uproariously too. Tears rolled down my cheeks and my nose started to run as I tried, unsuccessfully, to gain control. Finally, Tony came over and extended a hand to help me up.

It was then that I heard clapping and saw a portly man with a dark, neatly-trimmed beard standing at the end of the aisle. "Bravo," he cried. I stood just in time to see Tony's grin drop away and the blood drain from his face.

Sobering fast, I pulled a tissue out of my jeans pocket to wipe my nose. The man approached us, seemingly oblivious to Tony's distress. "Ah, Tony, it is you, no?" He beamed at us. "Such energy, such passion. You must both join our local theatre troupe."

"Thank you," I said, rather pleased, "but I'm just visiting. I came for the duchy celebration."

"Oh, yes, the celebration. It is coming soon, no? Monique mentioned it." He turned to Tony, who had backed up against a shelf full of board games. The man lowered his voice. "My party was a great success, thanks to you. When can I expect another delivery?"

Tony glanced at me, his expression weighed down with guilt and a little fear. I had a flash of understanding. The delivery was duchy cheese.

Tony glanced at me, then the two men held a short conversation in French. I couldn't understand most of it, but the older man's face fell, and I made out the names Clive and Alice. The bearded man, now solemn, laid a hand on Tony's shoulder. "Je suis désolé, vraiment désolé," he said. He was truly sorry. Then he bade us adieu.

I faced Tony, who looked away. The heady sci-fi moment had passed for us both. We trudged back to the Jedi display, where a stern, gray-haired man was waiting for us—the owner, I was guessing. Three wide-eyed children hovered nearby. I looked at the price tag and winced. "We can't really afford these," I mumbled. Tony said something in French to the man, and he looked the swords over carefully, then returned them to their places. I retrieved my purse while Tony picked up the daggers we'd set down earlier. Following the owner to the front, we passed the kids, who were gathered around the light saber display, talking in animated voices. I paid for the knives and we left the store.

Outside, we stood for a moment in the bright sun. "Look," I said, "let's finish the shopping. Then we can talk." He agreed with a nod and led me around the corner and up a block to a department store. There, he took charge, finding an older clerk with brassy red hair, who was familiar with stage makeup. She was pleased to help us when Tony told her about the duchy play. She pulled out an assortment of cosmetics, including thick pancake makeup and even phony blood. (I'd seen no ketchup in St. Uguzo.) I would have had a good time picking out the supplies if I hadn't been dreading the coming talk with Tony. As the red-haired clerk arranged the supplies in a bag, she said something about how she was sure the Guzo play would be très charmante, and I detected more than a touch of condescension in her voice.

We completed our shopping at a store selling paper products, glue, and such, before heading back toward the bus stop. I still had a few coins left from Peter's money, but not many. Near the bridge, a squat, middle-aged vendor was selling soft drinks and snacks, and we bought lemon-lime sodas and small bags of potato chips, then crossed the bridge, the stream babbling beneath us. I checked my watch. We were a little early for the eleven o'clock bus back to the duchy. Setting down our bags, we settled onto a bench overlooking the stream and gulped our drinks. I hadn't realized how thirsty I was. Fencing and laughing hysterically will do that to you.

"I know about the duchy cheese showing up in Bois," I said. "So do Juliette and Fred. What we didn't know was how it got there."

Tony gazed downward.

"You were delivering the cheese, weren't you?" I asked softly.

"Yes. But I didn't steal it. I would never steal the duchy cheese. Never." His handsome face crumpled and his lean, long-legged body slumped back on the bench. Clearly, he was involved in the theft.

"Who stole the cheese?" I asked. I was pretty sure it was Clive, but I needed to hear it from Tony.

"Dad." Tony raked his fingers through his thick, blond hair. "Look. Don't get the wrong idea. Dad was a good man and a good father. But he gambled too much, and he had debts he couldn't pay. So he decided to steal a little cheese. Just a little, he said, nothing anybody would miss."

It must have been easy enough for him, I thought, working as the assistant cheesemaker. "He stole it at work?"

"No, he didn't dare. Fred saw everything, he said. Dad went back to the cheesery in the evening, when it was almost dark. He had a key, so it was easy. He took me with him as a lookout. I didn't want to go, but he told me I had to. Our family was depending on me, he said. So I went. Twice. But I never stole the cheese. I just waited outside."

"I understand," I said.

"Are you going to tell Juliette?"

"It's better if she hears it from you. Or your mother. Don't you think?"

Tears brimmed in his eyes. "What difference does it make now?" he demanded. "Dad is dead, and there will be no more sales. Can't we just leave it at that?"

If only we could. This was about more than just stealing a little cheese. Tony's father was dead, and I didn't know if the two events were connected.

"Tony, Juliette is looking for the person who stole the cheese. Who do you think she will look at first? The people with the easiest access to it. And that includes your mother. Do you want Alice to be a suspect?"

"Merde," he mumbled. We sat quietly for a moment. "Okay. I'll tell Mum."

"Juliette also needs to know," I said.

He nodded. "I know."

Guzos gradually arrived at the bus stop, carrying shopping bags, large and small. They greeted us as they walked by, then left us alone. It was clear that Tony was grieving, so it was natural to allow him some space, and I was carrying my own measure of sorrow. I felt rotten that I had to confront

Tony, a teenager who had been forced to assist his father, his beloved father, who was a thief and a traitor to the duchy.

On the bus, I sat down, and Tony took the seat beside mine. It surprised me a little, since I had thought he might retreat to the back. We munched on our potato chips and said nothing. I thought of the brassy-haired cosmetics clerk and her superior attitude. It occurred to me that the people in Bois probably looked down on Guzos, whom they hardly knew. I imagined they saw the duchy as insular, backward, and just plain peculiar. Certainly, I had found it that way when I'd arrived, and if I was being honest, I still did to some extent. But I was beginning to see that St. Uguzo was a great deal more than that.

The duchy was the site of a mystic "thin place" hidden in the forest, and it was home to prophetic dreamers and companionable marmots. What's more, from what I had seen, St. Uguzo provided for its old people and dispensed justice in a basically humane way, thanks to Juliette and the council. But most important for me, it had some genuinely fine people, including a knowledgeable, generous historian who also happened to be decidedly hot.

As the bus passed the lookout, and the valley spread out before me, I thought about Tony and wondered if he and I would be able to preserve the friendship that had just started to develop. Or if I'd gone too far as an authority figure. The bus pulled up beside the plaza, and Tony and I got out. He nodded to me and turned to go.

"Tony," I said, "you are a terrific Jedi."

He quirked a smile. "You too, Holly."

The rehearsal went reasonably well that night. Eglentyne had memorized many of her lines and only glanced at her playbook occasionally. That was more than I could say for her cousin Wilheard, who only had a few lines but hadn't bothered to learn them. Naturally, I was dying to take Peter or Rosamunde aside and tell them what I'd learned about Tony's involvement in the sale of the cheese, but I had decided not to say anything until Tony had had a chance to make his own confession. I hoped that would be soon.

Kessie came up to me at the end of the rehearsal, since we had planned to walk up the road together. "I would have gone to the toy store with you," she said in a pout.

"Weren't you in school? Anyway, it wasn't much fun, just a trip to buy props for the play."

"That's not what I heard. I heard you and Tony had a battle. With Jedi swords."

Good grief. How did that get out? And so fast? "It was a spur-of-the-moment thing."

"It's true then." Kessie's brown eyes widened. "Are we getting light sabers? If so, I want one."

"Sorry," I said. "I would love to arm the ladies-in-waiting. But the swords were a little pricey, even for the men. We bought them daggers with rubber blades instead."

Eglentyne appeared at my side. "What say you? Are we arming the ladies?"

Oh no, I thought. More gossip in the making. "We were just kidding. The women will not carry weapons."

"Unfortunate," she said. "Sometimes a lady must protect herself."

"Very true," I said. "By the way, you were very good tonight. An excellent Anwen."

"I'm glad you think so. Actually, I came over to invite you to my house for tea tomorrow. You were so generous to coach me, I wanted a chance to say thank you. My Aunt Bessie took pictures of all the celebrations for years. She passed away last year, but she left me her photo album. I thought you might like to see it."

I felt genuinely touched and also eager to see the album. "That's so kind of you. I would love to see your aunt's photos."

"The house is a bit distant," Eglentyne said.

Kessie piped up. "I know where it is. I can take her there."

"In that case, you're both invited," Eglentyne said. "Say tomorow at four? It will be a traditional tea, just like my aunt used to host."

I thanked her. Then we said good-bye, and Kessie and I started down the Dukesway.

"Eglentyne is a terrific baker," Kessie said. "I can hardly wait."

"Me either," I said. I hoped that Eglentyne's offer was a good omen for my project.

CHAPTER SEVENTEEN

Day 7, Friday

I awoke early, as the night was just beginning to give way to dawn. In spite of the dim, grayish light, I felt optimistic, my spirits buoyed by the prospect of Eglentyne's afternoon tea party, where I would see Aunt Bessie's photos of past celebrations. I quickly showered and towel-dried my shoulder-length hair, then dressed, bundling up in layers against the cold morning air. Stepping onto the balcony outside my room, I was just in time to see the sun rise above the mountains, illuminating the fiery autumn colors of the trees below.

From the grassy hillside above the house, a man and dog stepped onto the road. I felt a rush of pleasure as I recognized Peter in his gray sweats. Beside him traipsed Bonnie, whose puppy energy was flagging after her morning run. Peter was nearly at the house when he looked up and saw me. His face burst into a grin, one that warmed me through the morning's chill. We both waved a greeting, and a minute later he and Bonnie passed out of my field of vision, onto the veranda below me. The kitchen door banged shut.

I was thinking about going in and starting breakfast when I spotted a chubby reddish-brown animal moving through the underbrush across the stream. My marmot pal. The name Monty came to mind, and I decided to call him that, now that we were surely on a first-name basis. I watched him for a while and resolved to make time to walk in the forest later. Maybe I'd take my penny whistle, since Monty seemed to like music.

Out of the corner of my eye, I spotted Rosamunde leaving her house and striding toward mine, carrying a small basket covered with a cloth. Pastries? I hastened through the door to my bedroom, where I shed my coat and combed my hair. Descending the stairs, I breathed in a mouth-watering whiff of lemony baked goods.

In the kitchen, Peter was breaking eggs into a frying pan while Rosamunde poured water into the tea kettle. She lit the burner with a long kitchen match that she took from a box on a ledge over the stove.

"Ah, there you are," Rosamunde said cheerily. "Good morrow."

"Good morrow," I replied, getting out the plates and cutlery and setting the table. A basket of neat, triangular scones sat in the middle. "Any news this morning?" I hoped that Tony had visited Juliette the evening before and told her about his father selling cheese in Bois. I was pretty sure that Juliette would have passed on the information to her mother.

"There is," Rosamunde said, and we both sat. "The council has agreed to consider your proposal officially at the meeting next Wednesday. Peter has graciously offered to present it for you. We think that will work best."

"Oh, thank you," I said. "Thank you both."

"No problem," Peter said without turning from the stove.

I only wished Wednesday weren't so far away. "I'm afraid that I won't have much time for interviews." I fixed Rosamunde with an imploring gaze. "Is there any chance you could tell me about your own family's participation in the celebration?"

"Of course," she said. "The minute you receive the council's permission." I was hoping she would bend the rules and let me talk to her earlier, but no chance.

The kettle whistled, and I popped up and poured water over the tea bags sitting in the teapot. Peter spooned scrambled eggs onto everyone's plates, finally scraping the remains into Bonnie's bowl. Bonnie instantly gobbled down her treat.

Peter sat, and we all reached for the still-warm scones, split them open, and passed around the butter. I took a bite, my senses surrendering to the lemony flavor. "Delicious," I said.

"Mmm," Peter murmured in agreement as he finished off his first scone. "You know, Holly," he said, reaching for his second one, "you might consider staying for a week or two after the celebration. You could talk to more people that way."

I hadn't thought of postponing my trip home, but another week or two would give me the time I needed for the interviews, and I was pleased the suggestion had come from Peter. An additional week's worth of data should satisfy Dr. Ferris, and I would have enough material for a solid article. Besides, I could already tell that it was going to be hard to drag myself away from the duchy. "Would that be okay?" I asked. "I mean, do you think Gwen would let me stay at her house? And could I continue to eat at the dining hall? I could help out."

"I don't see why not," Rosamunde said. "Of course, in that case, you might like to carry out a small assignment for the museum. As a way of showing your appreciation."

"Sure," I said, figuring I would end up scrubbing the convent floors, or worse. "What did you have in mind?"

"It's a small project," Rosamunde said, "one you could work on while you're waiting for Wednesday to come around. In fact, we believe you're just the person to take it on. It will be a service to the duchy." She turned to Peter. "Wouldn't you say so?"

"Absolutely," Peter said. He turned to me and assumed his historian's voice. "You probably don't realize that St. Uguzo served as an underground station during World War II. Refugees and downed airmen, mostly Americans, passed through here. Guzos usually guided the refugees through the mountains to Switzerland. The airmen preferred a route that led them to a group of French partisans who could help them escape to England."

I took a bite of my eggs and nodded my understanding, wondering where this was going.

"Unfortunately, St. Uguzo was occupied by German soldiers during much of the war. In those days, we had a small hotel near the plaza, and the Germans commandeered it. As you can imagine, their surveillance made it risky to provide temporary refuge to travelers and an escort through the mountains."

"The Guzos must have been very brave," I said.

"Indeed," Peter said. "And they were helped by a young American who remained here in the duchy. He was an experienced mountain climber, and he joined the team of Guzos who led people to safety. Or at least to their best chance for safety."

"I see," I said. I had never cared much for the history of World War II, and I was starting to feel uneasy about the project. "But what does this have to do with me?"

"The American kept a journal," Peter said. "We only discovered it recently, and we need someone to transcribe the entries. Another American would be ideal, someone familiar with your idioms."

Rosamund beamed at me. "Naturally, we thought of you."

I smiled weakly.

"The fellow wrote in pencil in a small notebook," Peter said. "I'm afraid the text is in poor condition. But his reflections provide a small window into a harrowing time in Guzo history. There is hardly any other personal writing from the time. Guzos have never been keen on diaries, and people wrote few letters, since there was little or no mail service. Rosamunde and I thought perhaps you would take on the transcription. It would be your contribution to the museum."

They both gazed at me expectantly.

"How long is the journal?" I asked.

"About twelve pages," Peter said, "but they're small."

"Sure," I said. "I'd be happy to work on the book." How could I say no? Especially given all the free meals I was eating. Besides, it would be satisfying to know that I'd left something of value behind.

As I gathered my bag and writing materials from my bedroom, my thoughts returned to Tony. I hoped that he hadn't put off telling his mother about Clive selling cheese in Bois.

By the time I started down the road to the museum, my attention had turned to the new project, and doubts began preying on me. I'd always hated hearing stories of World War II. For me, it was personal. My own grandfather was an Army soldier who had deserted someplace in Europe. Grandma didn't talk about him. Mom forbade it. Grandma just told me they had loved each other, and he had died in the war. I could forgive my grandfather. Sort of. We knew a lot more about PTSD in the 1990s than they had in the 1940s. Still, he had deserted Grandma and my mother, an infant at the time.

So, now I was going to read and transcribe the words of a courageous pilot. The exact opposite of my grandfather. And probably me as well. If there was a gene for cowardice, I had no doubt inherited it. When danger loomed—a tornado in the distance or a menacing bully, for instance—I was among the first to run and hide.

I was in a gloomy mood by the time I crossed the hump-backed bridge leading to the convent. But I had agreed to transcribe the journal, and I could not back out now. My grandfather was long dead, I reminded myself. His misdeeds had no power over me.

When I got to the museum, I found that Peter had already placed the pilot's small notebook at the table nearest his office. As soon as I sat, he appeared at my elbow. "I'm afraid the fellow didn't write down his name." He set down a large, round magnifying glass with a handle. "Good luck," he said and disappeared into his office.

I gazed at the notebook, with its cardboard cover, stained and mildewed. Peter had entrusted me with the original copy because, as he said, that would be hard enough to decipher. Photocopied pages would have been even worse.

Opening the book, I noticed that the first pages had been ripped out, and the last several pages were blank. The remaining twelve pages were covered in faint, badly smudged, penciled writing. Paper must have been scarce, because the young man had written in tiny block letters, with the writing filling not just the printed lines, but the lines between them. Apparently, the pilot hadn't realized that he wouldn't finish the journal.

I picked up the magnifying glass. A scan of the pages told me that the writer had used initials to identify the names of people or places, understandable given the possibility that his notes would someday be found by the Germans. Most of the entries consisted of what looked like a date, followed by a brief description of the weather, such as "heavy fog," or "windy," or of his condition, such as "cough continues," or "tired and hungry."

I figured out that "M" probably stood for "mission," since it was followed by a sketchy description of the people he had helped to escort, either airmen or refugees. Later in the journal, he had written longer passages, apparently recording his thoughts. I looked forward to deciphering those when I got to them.

I decided to call the pilot Al, just to make him more of a person. Al's first entry read:

9/12 Said good-bye to Y and Z. No turning back now.

How had he ended up with this assignment behind enemy lines? Had he volunteered, or was he ordered to go?

I picked up my pen and wrote out the words on the legal pad that Peter had given me. For the next hour or so, I kept going, trying to decipher Al's blurred printing. Sometimes I wrote "BG," in parentheses for "best guess." A few times, I left four dots to indicate that a word or phrase was unintelligible. Slowly, I read about days getting colder and Al's shoulder healing—from what ailment or injury, I couldn't tell.

On 9/18, Al wrote:

B brought potato soup. Stayed to talk.

I wondered who B was—some kind Guzo, I supposed.

On 9/19, Al wrote:

Lonely.

With that one word, I felt his aching heart at being so far from home and the people he loved.

At the morning break, Peter, Juliette, and I were sitting around the table drinking tea and eating biscuits (cookies to me), when Alice Cotton walked into the museum, looking anxious. She was wearing baggy slacks and a jacket, and I wondered if she'd come directly from her job at the cheesery. I hoped she was there to report Clive's theft.

"How can we help you?" Peter asked.

"It's Juliette I need to see," Alice said.

Juliette pushed back her chair. "Shall we go to my office?"

Alice looked from me to Peter. "It isn't necessary. I don't imagine this will come as a great surprise to any of you."

She sat, refusing a cup of tea, then began. "When I was looking for something in the cupboard this morning, I found a small wedge of duchy cheese hidden in the back." She pulled a handkerchief out of her jacket pocket and carefully opened it to reveal a slice of cheese. "I asked Tony if he knew anything about it. He told me that Clive had stolen duchy cheese from the cheesery and sold it in Bois."

"Oh no," Juliette murmured.

"Oh yes. Tony was certain that his father was providing cheese to some prominent citizen. I don't know who. I suppose this wedge was the last of it." Alice sat back. "This explains why Clive claimed that our money problems were over. He was paying off his gambling debts by selling cheese. And he was keeping some of the cheese for himself." She pushed the handkerchief across the table to Juliette, her eyes downcast. "I know that what Clive did was unforgivable. But he will be buried tomorrow. I hope this story can be buried with him. For my children's sake. And mine."

"I don't see why it would have to be public knowledge," Juliette said.

Alice looked relieved. "Does anyone else know about the missing cheese?"

"Your boss, Fred. At least, he knows that duchy cheese has shown up in Bois. I'll ask him not to say anything." Juliette paused. "But as you know, it can be difficult to guard a secret. All of us here will keep the information to ourselves. But even so, the story could leak out in other ways."

"Thank you. That will have to do."

After Alice had left, I told Juliette and Peter what Tony had confessed to me about delivering cheese. "I imagine Alice was trying to protect her son, by not revealing his involvement. I can't say I blame her."

"I agree," Juliette said. "Tony is young, and he was following his father's orders. Still, if Alice is holding back that information, I wonder if there's anything else she's hiding from us."

Peter rubbed his chin. "I hate to cast doubt on Alice's story, but Clive had major gambling debts. I don't see how he could have made enough money to pay off his debts and buy a car. I can't imagine anyone in Bois paying thousands of francs for cheese."

"That bothers me too," Juliette said. "Then there's Clive's death. Could it be connected to the theft?"

"If only we knew. You think someone could have found out about Clive's activities and decided to kill him?"

"That's a pretty extreme response," Juliette said. "It would make more sense for a Guzo to denounce Clive and let the council pass judgment."

I pondered the possibilities. "What about blackmail? Someone could have found out that Clive was selling cheese and demanded a share of the money." (I had read a lot of murder mysteries.)

Juliette frowned. "That's a thought. I suppose the blackmailer could have killed Clive when he didn't turn over the money. Out of anger maybe." She shook her head. "Alice's revelation certainly opens up new possibilities. Unpleasant ones, I'm afraid."

We cleared the dishes and took them to the sink in the little kitchen next to Peter's office. "I'll wash up," I said.

"Thanks," Juliette said. "I have an idea who the bearded theatre patron is—the one that Holly and Tony ran into at the toy store. But it would help to hear it from Tony. I'll see if I can find him."

While I washed the few plates, cups, and saucers, Peter dried. "Clive is being interred tomorrow?" I asked.

"The family is Catholic. As I understand it, there will be a small service at the cathedral in Bois in the morning. Then in the early afternoon, Clive's body will be buried in the cemetery behind the convent. Lots of Guzos will go to pay their respects. You don't need to attend if you'd rather not."

Back at the house, I put thoughts of theft and murder out of my mind as I freshened up for Eglentyne's tea, and dressed in my skirt and my best blouse, one with a little embroidery at the collar. I'd eaten light at lunch to leave room for the pastries I knew would be served.

As Kessie and I walked to Eglentyne's house, I was glad that she had offered to accompany me. The path to the chalet was barely visible in places as it wound among the hills above the town and passed through a forested area. I could easily have taken a wrong turn.

From a distance, Eglentyne's house was pretty—a two-story chalet with a balcony, similar to Gwen's. But as we got closer, I saw that the house had a sad, rundown look. The red paint on the shutters was peeling, the steps up to the veranda sagged in the middle, and an attic window was boarded over. If Wilheard was staying with Eglentyne, it seemed like he could help her with repairs.

I spotted a teenage boy chopping wood next to a large pile of logs beside the house. "Who is that?"

"Sam," Kessie said. "He's a schoolmate of mine. A little slow, but he tries hard. He does chores for Eglentyne." She called to him. "Halloo."

Sam broke into a grin and lowered his axe.

"I'll just say hello," Kessie said, and hurried off to meet her friend. She joined me at the door a minute later. "Sam says that Wilheard and Sebastian are both staying here, but they're out now."

Good. I had little desire to have tea with those two. I knocked at the door, and Eglentyne appeared, looking pleased. "Do come in. I hope you're hungry," she said as she ushered us in. We assured her we were.

Off the hall, I glimpsed a formal-looking parlor with heavy, dark, Victorian furniture. Against one wall stood a tall bookcase with knick-knacks and a few shelves of books.

"I see you're a reader," I said.

"The Fosses have always been educated," Eglentyne said. "If you don't mind, I thought we could have tea in the kitchen. "There's more light, and we can spread out the album on the table."

Kessie and I agreed that the kitchen would be perfect, and we continued down the hallway to the sunny, spacious room. A sturdy table held two plates filled with small cakes, half of them round and the other half square, all iced in white and topped with pastel-colored frosting in the shape of flowers, rabbits with floppy ears, pine trees, and a couple of ibex, the symbol of the duchy.

"Oh, how delightful," I said.

Eglentyne beamed. "People do say I have a talent for decoration."

Kessie and I sat while Eglentyne poured tea from a pot with a delicate rosebud design. The matching cups and saucers had a few tiny cracks and chips, but they were still lovely. "I admire your tea set," I said.

"It belonged to my great-grandmother. She was a lady of quality. My mother always said she had an eye for beauty."

We drank our tea and oohed and aahed as we sampled the cakes. Then Eglentyne cleared the tea things and stepped into the adjoining parlor to get the album. "Oh dear," she said. Kessie and I hurried to the parlor.

"Is something wrong?" I asked. I was afraid the book might have disappeared or been ruined somehow.

"No, but the album is on the top shelf. I hadn't thought it would be so hard to get down."

"I'll get a chair," Kessie said. She darted back to the kitchen, and a moment later returned with a sturdy wooden chair. She positioned it in front of the bookcase and climbed up. "Which one is it?" she asked.

"The large book lying on its side," Eglentyne said. Kessie reached up and lowered it, then handed it to Eglentyne before climbing off the chair.

"Thank you, dear," Eglentyne said. "You can leave the chair there. I should have fetched the album earlier, but I became so involved with the cakes that I quite forgot."

We trooped back into the kitchen, where I sat on one side of Eglentyne and Kessie on the other. Eglentyne placed the photo album, a three-ring binder, on the table in front of her and ran her hand lovingly over the dark green faux leather cover.

"My Aunt Bessie was very protective of her album," she said. "She wouldn't let just anyone see it."

"It's very kind of you to share it with us," I said.

"I'm sure my aunt would have been pleased that someone cared about the way we celebrated in earlier days. My own family played quite a prominent role back then." She opened the book to the first page. Six black-and-white photographs were affixed to the page with triangular black corners. "Those are my grandparents," Eglentyne said, pointing to the top-most photo on the left. "It was their wedding portrait, taken in 1912."

"It's lovely," I said, peering at the solemn young man in a dark suit and his bride in a frilly white blouse and a cameo brooch.

"Oh, but I'm sure you're not interested in a lot of family photos," Eglentyne said.

"I love old photos," I said, "especially when they're connected to people I know." Kessie leaned back and glared at me behind Eglentyne. "I know that Kessie enjoys them too." I shot her a wicked grin.

"Well, in that case..." Eglentyne said, and she proceeded to point out pictures of various relatives as small children, her parents' wedding portrait from 1950, and family picnics by the Falls. I shuddered inwardly at the sight of the pool.

She turned the page. "Ah, here are photos of a duchy celebration." At the top of the page, "1959" was penned. The first photo featured a line of smiling, costumed people standing in line across a stage. I was pretty sure we were still using a few of the same outfits.

"Look," I said. "It's the duchy play."

Eglentyne pointed to a middle-aged blond woman wearing a crown. "There's Duchess Anne-Marie, Gwen's mother. She must have played the French queen that year." She moved her finger to a pretty, blond teenager, standing in the middle. "And who could this be playing Anwen? Oh, I know. It's Lillian, Anne-Marie's daughter. Peter's mother." She clucked her tongue. "What a shame that she went off and married that foreigner. But she visits often. I expect she'll be here for the celebration."

Eglentyne's finger trailed to another photo below it, in which three rosy-cheeked women were standing behind a table loaded with fancy braided breads. "Fosse ladies," she said. "As you can see, the women in my family have always been skilled bakers."

Another photo was underexposed, but I could make out a crowd of Guzos dancing. There were people of all ages, paired off in various combinations—men dancing with women, women together, and children dancing with parents or playmates.

"There's always a dance in the town square in the evening," Eglentyne said. "People bring their musical instruments, and everyone has a lovely time."

"Maybe I can take my penny whistle," I said.

"Indeed you may," Eglentyne said.

In the final photo, six men lounged by a woodpile, holding mugs.

"What is it they're drinking?" I asked.

"Mead, probably. They drink a lot of it during the festival. The night of the ceremony especially."

"It's mostly women and children who attend the play," Kessie said. "By that time, most of the men are sloshed."

The last photo of the group was taken from a vantage point above the square. Below, a sea of knives was raised into the air.

"In the early days, it was only men who swore allegiance to the duchy," Eglentyne said. "But then Duchess Anne-Marie said, 'Enough with that. Women are Guzos too. They can raise their own knives.' Some people found it scandalous, but no one had the nerve to oppose her. Since then, the women have shown up with their kitchen knives and held them high, with pride. We're very modern now, you see."

Kessie rolled her eyes, apparently not impressed with the duchy's progressiveness. Eglentyne saw her and raised an imperious eyebrow. "These days, women can do anything that men can. Just look at your mother, Kessie. Sheriff of the duchy and a very fine one at that."

Kessie lowered her eyes, looking properly abashed.

The next few pages consisted of color photographs of the aunt's travels in France and England, followed by postcards of the Statue of Liberty and the New York City skyline.

The next page featured people posing outside a boxy, two-story house, the younger women in short-skirted, brightly colored summer dresses and the men in suits with wide ties. A notation at the top read "Bingham, Indiana, 1962."

"That must have been my cousin's wedding," Eglentyne said. "And look. I think that's Wilheard." She pointed to a scruffy kid of about ten with a hangdog expression. "He was a handsome child, don't you think?"

She didn't wait for an answer, but moved on to the next picture, this one of a bride cradling a bouquet of mixed flowers and her young groom in a dark suit with a boutonniere.

Suddenly Kessie gasped and pointed to the photo of the bridegroom. Around his neck was a gold medallion. A gold medallion with a carving of a salamander under a crown. "Isn't that—"

I started to peer closer, but Eglentyne drew in her breath and slammed the book shut. "I'm sorry. That's all for today," she said, clutching the book. "I'm feeling a bit peaky." In fact, her face was ashen, and her hands trembled.

"Can I get you something?" I asked. "More tea, or an aspirin maybe?"

"No, no, I just need a little lie-down. That's all. Please excuse me."

A moment later, Kessie and I were out the door and on the path back to town.

Kessie halted abruptly and faced me, her eyes bright. "Did you see it? That was the duke's gold medallion. Wilheard's family must have swiped it. Those dirty, low-down Fosses. Stealing from the duchy."

I looked around to see if anyone was nearby, listening to us accuse a Guzo family of a traitorous crime. But we were alone. I'd only gotten a glimpse of the medallion, but it was enough to see that it looked like the medallion in our props box, the one that the king had bestowed on Philippe. Only this one had looked a good deal finer. "It could have been a reproduction," I said. "Do other people have medallions like it?"

"No," Kessie said, her face scrunched in disgust. "It's stolen, all right." She gazed at me, her eyes narrowed, as if taking my measure. "We've got to get the album back and show it to Mum. She needs to see what Wilheard's family has been up to."

"I don't think Eglentyne is going to hand the photo album over to us. Did you see the way she hung onto it?"

"I have an idea," Kessie said, rocking back and forth in her sneakers. "We'll wait until tonight when everyone is at rehearsal. I'll sneak back and get the album."

I groaned. "Kessie, that doesn't sound either legal or safe. What if Wilheard came back and caught you in the act? I vote no."

Kessie scowled, which was almost comical on her soft, young face. "Oh, all right," she said. She kicked a pebble out of the path and sent it flying.

Kessie led us back to the road, and we divided up our tasks. She would find her mother and tell her about Eglentyne's tea party while I told Peter. I wondered if Kessie would ask Juliette to authorize a raid on Eglentyne's house. I would have loved to see Juliette's response.

There were no visitors at the museum, as was usually the case, and Peter willingly set aside his work on Anwen's journal to join me at a table in the main room. I described the photo that Kessie and I had seen of the medallion that looked very much like the duke's medal, and I also recounted Eglentyne's abrupt reaction after we'd seen it.

"You know," Peter said, when I'd finished, "a group of Fosses sailed to the U.S. shortly after the War. And it was not long afterward that people realized that the medallion and other duchy treasures were missing. Maybe it's more than a coincidence. I would love to take a look at that photo."

"I wish I'd seen it better. But Kessie was convinced that the medallion was the real thing."

Peter rubbed his chin. "It may be. And I'm sure that Juliette will look into it. Eventually. But my immediate concern is the play. Eglentyne is obsessed with the Fosses' reputation. And Wilheard has a bad temper. If they're already on edge, either of them could throw a fit and disrupt the rehearsal. I suggest that we act as if nothing unusual occurred at the tea party."

The rehearsal was late getting started as we waited for Wilheard and Eglentyne. That gave me a chance to hand out props. I climbed the stairs to the stage with my bag of rubber daggers and passed them out to the male courtiers, who appeared pleased with their improved weapons.

"No light sabers?" the youngest Bonnet brother whispered.

"Not this year. Sorry," I said. And I was a little sorry. I could picture Bernard brandishing a Jedi sword. With that unruly black hair and dark flashing eyes, he would have looked smashing. As would his brothers.

I returned to my front row seat. Finally, Wilheard walked through the gym door alone and headed for Peter, who was standing below the stage.

Peter put on a smile. "Good to see—"

"My cousin is leaving the play," Wilheard said. "She's too busy preparing for the celebration."

Peter's smile vanished. "What? She can't quit now. The celebration is a week away."

Wilheard smirked. "That's your problem, isn't it?" He shot me a dirty look. "People shouldn't go poking their noses where they don't belong." He shoved Eglentyne/Gwen's playbook at Peter. "Here. My cousin's got no use for this now." He strode off to join some of the men in the crew.

I was sitting in my usual spot in the front row, and Peter sank into the chair beside me. "What am I going to do now?" he moaned. "Where in God's name am I going to find another duchess at this late date?"

"I'm so sorry," I said. The unfortunate fact was, Anwen had a lot of lines, and some of them were convoluted in an old-fashioned way. Who would want to learn them on such short notice? Besides that, the part had originally been Gwen's, and we already knew that women were reluctant to take her place.

"You know what this means, don't you?" Peter said. "You'll have to read Anwen's part tonight."

"Me?"

He handed me the script. "It's only temporary, until we find another Anwen. Look. I'd rehearse an act where Anwen doesn't appear, but there isn't one."

"It's okay," I said. "I'll muddle through."

When the cast and crew had all assembled, Peter made a little speech, explaining our predicament. He suggested that one of the ladies should consider switching parts and taking the role of Anwen. For a moment, his gaze focused on Kessie, who immediately looked down. When no one volunteered to take on the role, Peter announced that I would play Anwen that night.

The rehearsal went reasonably well. I was familiar with many of the lines, since I had coached Eglentyne on them. At the end of the practice, Peter announced that there would be no rehearsal the following night, out of respect for Clive's family. Alice, Jenny, and Tony were all valued members of the production. We would resume our work on Sunday evening.

As people streamed out of the gym, I stored the new makeup and the rest of the props backstage. By the time I finished, Kessie had left with Rosamunde, and Peter suggested that we walk home together.

"You are quite a fine Anwen, you know," he said, as we walked past the narrow half-timbered houses on the Dukesway.

"I recall saying something similar to Eglentyne just last night."

"You think it's bad luck to tell the leading lady that she's good? In that case, I won't tell you that you greatly outshine Eglentyne. Which happens to be the truth."

His words warmed me, but I had to be realistic. "Thanks, but I'm well aware that Anwen needs to be played by a Guzo. And anyway, by the time of the performance, I'll be busy collecting data on the celebration."

"Right. Maybe I should talk to Monique. She isn't Guzo, but she's an actress, and she knows a number of people here. I wonder how Fred would feel about playing the abbess opposite his girlfriend."

"I suppose you could ask Monique," I said. Peter could do worse, although I couldn't say I was comfortable with the idea. Monique was another outsider, besides being a little old and worldly to play Anwen. We walked past the plaza and started up the road.

"I don't believe Eglentyne really wanted to leave the play," I said. "She was dying to play the duchess. Remember?"

"You think somebody talked her out of it?"

"I'm betting she told Wilheard that Kessie and I saw the medallion in the album. He got worried and told Eglentyne that she had to stay away from us. That she couldn't be in the play."

"You might have something there," Peter said. "I wouldn't put it past Wilheard to boss Eglentyne around."

"Maybe we should pay her a visit, see if we can talk her into coming back. She can't possibly want to see me or Monique playing Anwen."

"That's not a bad idea," Peter said. "But we'll have to wait until Sunday. Tomorrow will be devoted to Clive Cotton."

As we trudged up the hill toward Gwen's house, we talked about our own limited acting experience. Oddly enough, our first roles in secondary school were in Blithe Spirit. I played the eccentric medium, Madame Arcati, and Peter played Charles Condomine, a novelist. Among our other humble accomplishments, we had both had small parts in A Midsummer Night's Dream. We reminisced about dress rehearsals gone hilariously, horribly wrong, and relived the thrill of applause at the curtain call.

By the time we reached home, I had somehow come to feel hopeful about the duchy play and its chances of success, even though the major players kept pulling out, leaving Peter scrambling to assemble a workable cast. But after all, wasn't Peter's predicament pretty typical of life itself? We had to take the weird, imperfect resources that fate sent our way and somehow assemble them into something good, or at least moderately viable.

The thought brought Grandma to mind. She'd brought up a daughter single-handed, managed a small farm, and run an aviation service with her trusty biplane. In hindsight, I could see that she had cobbled together a good life through grit, determination, the support of friends, and a belief in the ultimate goodness of life.

CHAPTER EIGHTEEN

Day 8, Saturday

I awoke the next morning to a clear, crisp day, but it was shadowed by the knowledge that Clive would be laid to rest that afternoon in the cemetery behind the convent. After breakfast, I waited for Peter on the veranda while he dropped off Bonnie at his cottage next door. When he re-appeared, he was wearing a black kerchief around his neck.

"How goes the journal?" Peter asked as we headed down the road.

"Slowly. But pretty well, I think. So far, the entries are brief. But even so, as I write down Al's words, I feel like I'm entering his thoughts."

"Al?" Peter asked.

"That's what I call him."

"Airman Al." He shot me a lop-sided grin. "Why not." We nodded a greeting to a mother and her school-age daughter, both wearing black scarves on their heads.

"And I know what you mean," Peter said. "There's something about copying the words, especially in longhand. The thoughts sort of creep inside you. As if your mind was merging with the writer's. I've found that with Anwen's journal." That would be amazing, I mused, to have such an intimate connection with a woman from the 1500s.

Back at the museum, I settled at my usual table. As I continued transcribing Al's journal, I occasionally cast back to Peter's observations. On some level, was I merging with the young pilot who had sojourned here during that dark time?

At one point, I came to a slightly longer mission entry:

M.2. Family of refugees. Hungry, exhausted. Man stumbled, wrenched knee. Nearly turned back. No Germans, TG.

I had wondered about TG, which appeared now and then, and I finally decided it probably stood for "Thank God."

10/3 Frost this morning. B brought vegetable soup, chunk of bread. Stayed to talk. Told her about C.

So B was a woman, and a good listener, it seemed. And who was C? A girlfriend back home or a close friend, maybe. An enemy, even.

M.3. Airmen. Well-fed, but not used to mountains. G was strict. I brought up rear, said nothing. In my Guzo clothing, they didn't know I was American. Better that way.

That must have been hard for Al, I thought, being with a group of fellow countrymen and not able to share his thoughts with them. But on reflection, I recognized that the less the airmen knew, the safer it was for everyone. If the men were captured, they couldn't reveal that an American lived among the Guzos.

Around nine-thirty, I needed a break, so I crossed the courtyard outside the museum and stepped through the convent gate. Across the road lay the duchy's cemetery, a broad grassy field studded with clusters of headstones. The land rose gradually on the far side and was bordered by forest that crept upward toward the mountains. I noted that none of the headstones were large or elaborate. Guzos appeared to be an egalitarian lot, at least in death.

I gazed to my left, where the end of the bridge was visible at the spot where it bordered the cemetery, right above the road running in front of the convent. Four sturdy Guzo men strode off the bridge and entered the cemetery carrying shovels and spades, and I realized they were there to dig a grave. Like Peter, they all wore black kerchiefs. They stopped near the far edge of the field close to a stand of green fir trees, and began their work.

An hour later, I was making tea when Rosamunde stopped by to chat and to drop off a black scarf for me in case I wanted to join the mourners.

Juliette arrived just as her mother was about to leave. "Well, I tracked down the fellow who bought the cheese in Bois. Claude Toussaint, his name is."

"Well done," Rosamunde said. "Tony told you his name?"

"He didn't know it, but his description led me to Toussaint. The fellow's a theatre patron and also a high-stakes gambler. Clive owed him several thousand francs. Toussaint said that Clive had paid off part of his debt in duchy cheese."

"That comes as no surprise," Peter said.

"There's a little more. Clive assured Toussaint that he would soon have the rest of the money. Unfortunately, he didn't mention how he was going to get it." Rosamunde had poured her daughter a cup of tea, and Juliette took a sip. "I suppose Clive could have found a wealthy buyer for duchy cheese."

"One with a penchant for murder?" Peter said.

"I know," Juliette said. "It doesn't sound very likely."

Peter rubbed his chin. "Or maybe Clive found another source of money, something entirely unrelated to cheese."

"Are you suggesting some kind of criminal activity?" I asked.

Juliette shrugged. "Who knows?"

Rosamunde frowned. "I hope Clive didn't get mixed up with underworld characters. You know, daughter, I don't like you taking unnecessary risks."

"Don't worry," Juliette said. "The police chief in Bois didn't say anything about organized crime in Bois. And I can't imagine such a group taking a serious interest in St. Uguzo. If they did, we would certainly have heard about it." Juliette sipped her tea. "Besides, I'm sure I can count on Baptiste for back-up, if things heat up."

"So, what's your next step?" Peter asked.

"I'll talk to Clive's family again. I'm not sure they've told me everything they know. But I'll have to wait a few days, let them mourn Clive's death at least a little before I start prying again. In the meantime, I thought I might go to the mead hall and see if anyone has heard of any get-rich-quick schemes, something that Clive might have bought into."

"I'll ask around too," Rosamunde said. "My friends might have heard of something."

"And I'll let you know if I uncover anything," Peter said. "Of course, my networks aren't as extensive as either of yours."

"I wish I could help," I said, feeling useless.

"You've been immensely helpful already," Peter said. "You passed on the information about cheese showing up in Bois, and you uncovered Tony's involvement in the sale."

"Exactly," Juliette said. "But now I think you should take a break from the investigation. Unless you chance on something useful, that is." She stood and thanked us for our support. "I'd better put on my scarf and get ready for the afternoon's service."

Lunch at the dining hall was a somber affair with vegetable soup and chunks of crusty bread. Even Violet, the artistic chef, had traded her bright, floral aprons for a solid brown one. When I arrived back at the convent, Guzo families were already starting to gather for Clive's interment. I stood outside the convent gate, with its view of the cemetery, and watched as the early arrivals crossed the bridge and headed toward the grave site. As the numbers swelled, they spread out across the cemetery grounds, a sea of Guzos, women with black scarves on their heads and men with black kerchiefs around their necks.

A hum of voices drifted across to me, a mixture of quiet conversation and occasional low laughter. Maybe Clive's friends were recalling the practical jokes he was famous for. A baby cried, then hushed.

Peter moved next to me, and we watched as the priest appeared in his long black cassock, striding solemnly across the cemetery, his curate a step behind him. A few minutes later, the crowd parted as six brawny Guzo men carried what looked like a simple pine coffin across the field to the grave site. Behind them came Clive's family, walking at a dignified pace. Alice wore a black calf-length skirt and a black shawl over her blouse. A veil extended down from her brimmed hat. She was flanked by Tony and Jenny, then two older people behind them—Clive's parents I guessed.

"Shall we join the mourners?" Peter asked. I placed Rosamund's black kerchief on my head, tying it under my chin. We made our way to a slight rise at the rear of the crowd, where we exchanged nods with the folks around us. I made a quick estimate of the people before me—some three hundred, I guessed. All assembled to remember Clive and to care for his family.

We barely heard the priest's voice as he prayed over the grave, but the hush of the crowd enveloped us like a cloud. A man had died, far too young, I thought, ripping his family apart and leaving them to grieve. A violin played in the distance, the bittersweet strains of "Morning Has Broken."

Memories of Grandma's funeral flooded me. The same song had been played, but on a harp. I choked back a sob and felt Peter's arm encircling my shoulders. If only Grandma hadn't left us. I pictured her at her kitchen table as we shelled peas, telling me what a fine future I had in store for me. What would she think of this unexpected turn in my life? Would she think my research project, collecting data to help out Dr. Ferris, was a worthy goal? For the first time, a tiny doubt surfaced. Was there something more important I should be doing with my life?

I looked at Peter, whose eyes were brimming with tears. This sad event must be bringing back memories for him as well. And his memories were fresh—of the burial of his grandmother and brother. I heard a sniff from a woman near me, and looking around, I realized that many people—men and women—had tears streaming down their faces. Clive's death had touched them all.

After the interment, Peter and I joined the streams of people leaving the cemetery. He and I returned to the museum, but I found I couldn't concentrate on the pilot's journal, so I headed back to the house, where I climbed the stairs to my bedroom and removed one of my French chocolate bars from the small cache in the armoire. I sat on the edge of my bed and slowly ate it, the rich flavor smoothing me out, although I had to fight the urge to eat one more bar.

I spent the late afternoon sitting on my bed, propped up with a pillow against the headboard, reading more of *Thin Places*. I'd finally made it to the section on the Americas, starting with the Southwestern U.S. It seemed that *Thin Places* often showed up in remote desert locales.

In the midst of the duchy's problems, it was comforting to read about sacred places that had survived over the centuries. I'd been thinking off and on of the thin place in the glade. It was so near; I couldn't help feeling drawn there. I certainly didn't want another violent dream. Still, I wondered what information the glade might hold for me. But every time I considered another trip to the clearing, I remembered Rosamunde's warning about people who had visited it too often and gone bonkers. I wondered how many visits it would take. Would two be safe, or was I asking for trouble?

Just as I was getting hungry, Peter appeared at the door to my room. Ozzie, Kessie's ten-year-old brother, had come to invite us to dinner next door. I was relieved, since I had little desire to walk back into town to the dining hall. Plus, I'd finished my yogurt and didn't want to sponge off Peter, who made a weekly grocery run.

Rosamunde's kitchen was warm, and it felt good to sit around the plank table, crunched in between Peter and Juliette, and across from the kids. Rob and Rosamunde sat at the head and foot of the table. Rob said a short grace, giving thanks for our blessings and asking for comfort for Clive's family. After amens, we tucked into shepherd's pie, one of my favorite comfort foods. It was topped with swirls of beautifully browned mashed potatoes, and the heavenly aroma brought back memories of dinners at Gran's house.

"Gwen called," Rosamunde said. "She was sad to have missed Clive's interment. But she says she's doing well and is eager to return to us."

I realized with a start that I had practically forgotten about Gwen. In a way, it was a good sign. Work at the museum had filled my hours, and I felt myself among friends. Mostly.

"Did she say when she's arriving?" Peter asked.

"Saturday morning, probably. She wasn't sure." Rosamunde turned to me. "She said she hoped you were getting along well. I told her I was confident the council would approve your project soon."

"Thanks," I said. "My fingers are crossed."

"You know," Rosamunde said, "there will be dancing on Saturday night after the Ceremony of Allegiance. I'm sure we'll all want to join in. After the play, that is."

"I won't," Ozzie mumbled.

"That's okay," Juliette said. "It will be past your bedtime anyway."

A horrified look crossed Ozzie's face, before he saw the tiny smile on his mother's face and realized she was joking. I imagined that all the duchy kids would be up late on the night of the celebration.

Rosamund continued. "There will be a few traditional Guzo dances, and Holly might not know them. Suppose we have a little dance lesson tonight. I'm sure we could all use the practice."

"What will we do for music?" Peter asked. "Should I get my violin?"

"No need," Juliette said. "One of the musicians recorded music from the last celebration, five years ago. It's on a cassette. The sound isn't great, but it should be good enough."

I put down my fork, having finished my last bite of shepherd's pie. "You don't think your neighbors will hear us and object, do you?" I asked. "Dancing on the evening of Clive's funeral?" There were no houses close, but you never knew when someone might pass by.

"Not a worry," Rob said. "If Clive were alive, he'd be the first to join the party."

"In that case," I said, "I would love to learn the dances." If I mastered the steps, I could teach them to my friends in The New World Rovers. We occasionally danced in addition to playing historical music. M.J., my apartment mate, was particularly light on her feet.

"I'm not much of a dancer," Peter said. "At the last two celebrations, I sat in with the band."

"Well, as you like," Rosamunde said, but I could tell from her expression that she was disappointed.

Peter gave me a sideward glance and cleared his throat. "But come to think of it, it wouldn't hurt me to soak up a little more duchy culture. I've been to the last three celebrations, but I'm sure there's a lot I missed."

I remembered that Peter had only lived in the duchy full-time for four years, although he'd been a frequent visitor when he was growing up.

After cleaning up the dinner dishes, we women trooped into the living room. The men had pushed the furniture against the walls, and Rob was at the fireplace, where he had placed a log at the back, and was now coaxing a carpet of glowing coals into flames. It was a cozy fire, one that took the chill off the evening.

A smallish black apparatus that I recognized as an audio cassette player sat on a straight-backed chair, together with a few cassettes in their plastic cases, one of which Peter was examining.

"We have some very fine country dances," Rosamunde said. "Square dances, I think you Yanks call them. But they aren't well suited for the evening entertainment." She must have noted my disappointment because she said, "Oh, but you can watch them earlier in the day. We have an excellent folk-dance group. They will perform in the plaza."

Juliette looked up from a cassette that she'd been examining. "You have to understand, it's late when the dancing gets underway. By that time, people are tired, and a lot of alcohol has been consumed. So, the footwork isn't very fancy."

"What say you, wife?" Rob said. "Shall we start with a couple of circle dances?"

"Yes. Why not?"

We formed a circle, Kessie and Peter on either side of me. Rob explained that we would skip to the left, stomp our feet three times, and skip back to the right.

"I'm not sure I remember how to skip," Peter mumbled.

"It will come back," I assured him.

Rosamunde stepped out of the circle to press the push button on the tape player, and a spirited tune much like an Irish reel filled the room. I made out an assortment of fiddles, pipes, guitars, and a drum or two.

"The squeaky fiddle is mine," Peter whispered to me.

I smiled back, not believing him for a second. I'd heard him play.

After several bars of music, Rob called out instructions. We skipped to the music's lively rhythm. Then we stopped and stomped enthusiastically before skipping back. After a few repetitions, I was warmed up and feeling at one with the music.

"Well done, revelers," Rob said. We all grinned foolishly. In fact, I was pleased with our performance, although I knew the steps hadn't required any great skill.

Next, we practiced a few step-hops, then joined hands and launched into another circle dance, this time taking eight step-hops to the left, another eight to the right, and moving to the center of the circle and back. Then we combined some of the hopping with energetic hand clapping, laughing good-naturedly at our efforts. Ozzie excelled at occasional zesty whoops.

Juliette paused the music, and she and Kessie brought out a jug of apple cider and glasses. By that time, we were all rosy-cheeked and thirsty, so the sweet liquid went down well.

"Dad, maybe you and Mum should show us a pairs dance," Juliette said. "The courting reel?"

I perked up, curious about how duchy couples danced together.

"Right you are," Rob said. He extended his hand to Rosamunde, who laid her hand demurely in his. The music began, and they held each other in waltz position, his hand supporting Rosamunde's back and hers resting on Rob's shoulder. They looked sweet together, this sixtyish couple so comfortable with each other. They both took a slide step, moving toward the center of the room, and closing with the other foot. This was followed by another slide, then a hop. Then they repeated the steps, moving to the side of the room. Finally, they step-hopped in a small, graceful circle. They repeated the sequence, moving around the room.

"The dance is a schottische," I said to Peter, who was standing beside me. "You know it?"

"I've danced similar ones."

"Wish I could say the same," he said.

I turned to Juliette on my other side. "Your parents are terrific dancers."

"They performed with the folkloric group when they were younger. That's how they got to know each other. Dad grew up in a village on the other side of the valley."

After that, we paired off to learn the dance—Rob with me, Rosamunde with Peter, and Juliette with Kessie. Ozzie manned the tape player. Rob was indeed a fine dancer, holding and directing me with a light but sure touch. When we took a break, Rosamunde was reassuring a frazzled-looking Peter that he almost had it down. Just a little more practice, she told him, and he'd be ready for the ladies at the celebration. "But that's enough for tonight," she said. Peter looked relieved.

"I wish I could stay longer," Juliette said, "but I need to head down to the mead hall. See if I can gather some information on get-rich-quick schemes."

"Not a problem," Rosamunde said. "I'll see the children off to bed."

"Would you? Thanks." Juliette put on a jacket and knitted hat. "Mum, as I recall, there's other music on that cassette. Something more modern. We don't want Holly to think we're stuck in the past."

We wished Juliette luck on her mission, and a moment later the door at the end of the hallway creaked open and closed.

Rosamunde followed the kids upstairs as Rob prodded the coals in the fireplace, then walked over to the cassette player. "I'll leave you young people to it," he said. He hit the "play" button and left the room. To my surprise, the music that had been copied onto the tape was American. It only took a few soaring bars to recognize "Endless Love."

"Oh, my gosh," I said. "That's Diana Ross. And Lionel Ritchie." I was in middle school when I first heard the song, and it had stirred up my powerful adolescent fantasies of romance.

Peter extended his left hand and I placed my right hand in it, my other hand on his shoulder. His right hand fit against my back, warm and solid. We fell easily into a gentle two-step, moving in flow with the music. Peter might not have mastered the schottische, but he could dance.

Now that I listened to the song again, it was mostly the lush harmonies that moved me, but I had to wonder if I had really left behind my romantic illusions. "There must be a confirmed romantic in the duchy," I said.

"Possibly more than one," Peter replied. His blue-gray eyes were soft, and I wondered if maybe, down deep, he was one of them.

The song ended before I was ready. "That was nice," I murmured.

"Yes," Peter agreed, his eyes gazing into mine, causing me to feel both desirable and desirous.

The next song came on, an equally dreamy American duet—"Tonight I Celebrate My Love." For you, I thought, completing the title line. "Roberta Flack," I said. "I love her voice. And Peabo Bryson is good too."

"Mmm." Peter slipped his arms around my waist, and I raised my hands behind his neck, my fingers nestling among soft locks of brown hair. After several bars, the two-step turned into a slow rock. I closed my eyes and leaned into Peter, feeling his warmth and breathing his scent of juniper and rosemary. When the song ended and the cassette player clicked off, I opened my eyes reluctantly. Peter and I were still enclosed in each other's arms, and I was feeling decidedly amorous. But we were in Rosamunde and Rob's house, the family upstairs, aware of our movements.

"It's getting late," I said, hating to break the mood. Peter nodded, and we retrieved our coats from the chair where Ozzie had dumped them. Peter turned out the parlor light as we walked to the front door.

Outside, the air was cold, and the only light came from the upstairs windows. Peter took my hand, and we paused on the veranda to kiss, warm lips holding back the chill. Then we walked to Gwen's house. Inside, Peter flicked on the hall light. There, in the hallway, he pressed one hand against my lower back, as if we were still dancing, then cradled the nape of my neck with his other hand, tilting my head back just a bit. We kissed again, long and sweetly, a deep yearning coursing through me.

Footsteps sounded on the terrace outside. "Merde," Peter mumbled, and we drew apart. At a knock on the door, he opened it to find Juliette.

"I saw your light on," she said. "I hope I'm not interrupting anything."

"Not at all," Peter said graciously. "Come on in. "What's the news from the mead hall?"

"It's a mixed bag," Juliette said.

"Would you like some tea?" I asked, trying not to show my disappointment in the interruption.

"If it's not too much bother." We filed back to the kitchen, where I put on water to boil. Peter detoured to his room and returned, placing a bottle of rum on the table.

"Unfortunately," Juliette said, once we were seated, "no one at the hall has heard of any get-rich-quick schemes. Nothing that would have attracted Clive's attention. But you might be interested to know that Sebastian and Wilheard were there, and they were stirring up unrest. Again. Only this time, Wilheard was haranguing his listeners about moral decay in the duchy.

"Moral decay?" Peter said, looking like he'd smelled something bad. "Wilheard has only been here a few months. When did he become such an expert on duchy morality?"

"He pointed to Clive's theft of the cheese as a prime example. But here's the surprising part. Tony was there. When Wilheard criticized Clive, the boy jumped up. He was furious and said that Wilheard was in no position to criticize anyone, when his own hands were dirty."

"Interesting," Peter said. "Did you talk to Tony about it?"

"I intended to, but everybody wanted a word with me, and by the time I'd worked my way across the room, he and Sebastian were standing in a corner, deep in conversation. Not long after that, they walked out together. By that time, Wilheard had stopped shouting about moral decay, and everyone had settled down."

Glowering, I pictured Sebastian acting all kindly and avuncular on his stroll with Tony. "You think Sebastian promised Tony my sports car?"

Peter and Juliette stared at me, then burst into laughter. Peter shook his head. "I can't get a fix on Sebastian and Wilheard. What do they have to gain by riling people up?"

"That's the big question, isn't it?" Juliette said.

I poured tea, and we all topped it off with rum. "Isn't Tony a little young for the mead hall?"

"He's sixteen," Juliette said. "Old enough to drink, but only duchy beer, which is weak. The adults keep an eye on him."

She and Peter shifted to a discussion of preparations for the celebration. Dozens of former Guzos would start streaming in as early as Thursday night, and while everyone would be happy to see old friends and family members, there would be unavoidable crowding and confusion. Juliette had already enlisted several trustworthy Guzos to help her keep order.

Next, Peter talked about his plans, which included tours of the convent, similar to the one he'd given me, on Friday and Saturday morning. I was surprised that he'd said nothing to me about this, but then, I'd been immersed in the pilot's journal for the past few days. As I listened, I couldn't help noticing how a lock of his hair kept flopping onto his forehead and how laugh lines appeared at his mouth when he smiled. He had a beautiful smile.

By the time we saw Juliette out, it was after midnight, and we'd drunk half a pot of tea with rum and munched on a plate of goat cheese and a couple of sliced apples. After mutual wishes for a good night's sleep, Peter closed the door behind Juliette.

I was pretty tired, and my romantic mood had dissipated with the news from the mead hall combined with the realization that my cozy duchy world was soon going to change dramatically.

"I guess we should call it a night," I said, with more than a little regret. I was aware of how deliciously close Peter was.

"I'm not so sure," Peter said and drew me into his arms.

CHAPTER NINETEEN

Day 9, Sunday

I lay in bed the next morning, feeling pleasantly warm and drowsy, my hand reaching for the pillow next to me, searching for Peter. He wasn't there, but I heard sounds from downstairs as he and Bonnie prepared for their run. It was Sunday, and I was in no hurry to rouse myself. Lying there, sun streaming in through the patio door, my senses wandered. I remembered the delicious warmth of Peter's body, his beautiful hazel eyes as they gazed into mine, his spicy scent. Today, everything felt new, as if we'd turned a page or even opened an entirely new book. I hoped that Peter had similar thoughts.

Finally, I got up and prepared for the day. I put on jeans and a green t-shirt and pulled my hair into a low pony tail with a matching green scrunchy. Downstairs, I set to work making French toast with some old bread, eggs, milk, and butter. I heard the front door open and recognized the sound of Peter and Bonnie arriving. I was standing over the frying pan a few minutes later when Peter walked up behind me. "Morning," he said. He swept my pony tail aside and planted a kiss on the nape of my neck. My body tingled.

"Good morning to you, too," I said, smiling. I could definitely get used to starting my day this way. A minute later, the French toast had a buttery crust, and Peter put a jar of gooseberry jam on the table, in the spot where the bottle of rum had sat the night before. Bonnie had finished her kibble and now stretched out on a rag rug, while Peter and I spread jam on our French toast.

Unfortunately, my warm glow was replaced by worry as I thought of our excursion to Eglentyne's house that afternoon. I shouldn't be so nervous, I told myself. After all, the visit had been my idea. My last trip, with Kessie, had ended badly, with our being practically shoved out the door. But this time Peter would be with me.

"Do you think Eglentyne will return to the play?" I asked Peter.

"I'd say we stand a good chance. We'll appeal to her pride as a leading member of the Fosse family."

"Good idea. And I'll beg, if necessary." I felt strongly that I wasn't the right person to play Anwen in front of an audience of patriotic Guzos.

He laughed. "Let's hope it doesn't come to that. If it does, I may be down on my knees too." He finished his tea. "I think I'll go into the museum around ten."

"I'll join you," I said. "I'd like to transcribe more of Al's journal." If I kept at it, I could probably finish on Monday.

*Half an hour later, Peter and I were ambling down the road. "There's something I've been wondering," I said. "Where did Al stay while he was here?"

"There was a hut up hidden in the mountains. A rendezvous point for escorts bringing people as far as the duchy. It was torn down a couple of years ago. That's when a workman found the book, hidden inside a wall."

"What luck."

"Indeed. And I'm told that airmen sometimes stayed in the convent cellar. Refugees too. They would spend a few days there when a delay occurred in moving them along. Sickness or bad weather, or too many Germans in the area." He paused. "I'm thinking about including a visit to the cellar in my tours this weekend. Most people have never been down there. I'm hoping it will stir up a little interest."

"I'll be there." I'd wanted to take a look at the cellar, and now that I knew about people hiding there during the war, I had more reason to see it.

"Would you like a private tour? I need to look it over before I take groups down there." I happily agreed. There were perks to being friends with the local historian.

When we arrived at the museum, Peter stepped into his office and returned with two flashlights, passing one to me. "There's no electricity in the cellar," he explained. We walked down the corridor and entered the big convent kitchen. The last time I was there, I had noticed a large, very faded rug in the far corner of the room, and now I saw why it was there. Peter pulled back the carpet to reveal a large trapdoor with an inset metal handle. He yanked the handle, grunting with the effort, and the door swung upwards, revealing a long wooden staircase next to a stone wall. I shone my flashlight down, and saw that the cellar floor was packed earth.

Peter descended the wooden stairs, which creaked at each step.

"They're sound enough," he said, and I followed him down.

At the bottom, I found myself in a large room with stone walls that exuded a cold dampness. High on the far wall, at ground level, two narrow, dusty windows let in a pale light. The walls were lined with wooden racks housing deep shelves, all standing empty.

"The nuns probably stored produce and other foodstuffs here," Peter said. "The cellar would have stayed cool in the summer but wouldn't have frozen in the winter." In my mind, I pictured baskets of potatoes and cabbages and apples.

Peter led me through a doorway to an adjoining room, where several more racks, each about five feet tall by four feet wide, stood against walls. In some there was ample space between shelves, while in others, the shelves were more closely stacked.

"The nuns made rosehip wine," Peter said, walking over to a large rack. "The barrels would have fit easily into these larger spaces. When they decanted the wine and poured it into bottles, the bottles could have been stored on the smaller shelves. And we think the nuns stored their cheese down here for aging. The rounds would have also fit on the shallower shelves. Our cheesemaker, Fred, tells me that storing rosehip wine next to the duchy cheese undoubtedly contributed to the flavor of the cheese."

At last. I had my first clue to the mysterious flavor of duchy cheese. "Do you still make rosehip wine?"

"Indeed. There are a few families across the valley who make it. It's just for local consumption. We drink it at holidays mostly. The wine is nothing grand, mind you, but people here like it."

I gazed at the empty shelves and wondered if cheese and wine were still stored here during World War II. Probably not. They would surely have been hidden away before the German soldiers arrived. "You said that people were sometimes hidden down here during the war. But wouldn't the German soldiers have raided the place and found them?"

"The story goes that the Guzo leaders actually invited the Germans to examine the cellar. But the Guzos explained that they themselves didn't come down here because lepers had lived here for years."

I shuddered.

"No. Don't worry," Peter said. "It was just a tale to scare the soldiers. Apparently, the Germans made a cursory inspection and never returned. So the visitors were safe, including your airman, when he was here."

"How were people smuggled in?" I asked.

"Very carefully and usually at night. Also, according to the old-timers, the Guzos built a tunnel from the convent cellar to a small, hidden cave in the hills."

"There are caves up there?"

"A number of them. Small grottos, really, nothing very scenic. Over the centuries, there were landslides in the foothills, and some of them resulted in caverns forming between the larger rocks. I've visited a few of the caves in the hillside beyond the forest, and I understand there are a couple more above the cemetery.

I tried to picture a tunnel extending from the convent to the nearest foothills. A few hundred yards at least. "Building the tunnel must have required some skill," I said.

"Indeed. But I came across a likely explanation in the archives. A couple of young Guzo women traveled to Wales around 1918. They were quite taken with the place, and they ended up marrying a couple of miners. When the mines in the area closed down a few years later, the women brought their husbands back to the duchy and settled down here."

"So," I said, "the men would have known how to dig a tunnel."

"Just so. And I'm told there was a chap who had studied engineering in England before the War. People say he was some kind of mathematical genius. Guzos still speak of him with awe. I wouldn't be surprised if he contributed to the planning. So, there was enough combined expertise to build a tunnel. Even so, it was somewhat rudimentary, I'm told. Still, it provided a relatively safe passageway. And if the Germans ever returned to the cellar, the plan was that the refugees would sneak into the tunnel."

"Where is the entrance?" I asked, looking around the room.

Peter shook his head. "Darned if I know. I've looked a few times and never seen it. Wherever it was, I imagine it's been sealed off. And I'm not sure where the cave is either. The entrances to the grottos are hard to find. They are usually little more than narrow gaps between large stones, and they are often hidden behind bushes and other vegetation. I've always thought I'd like to hike around up there one day, see what I could find. But I've never gotten around to it. Anyway, it's just as well that the entrance and exit have disappeared. After all these years, I'm sure the tunnel would be unsafe. I won't mention it on my tours. We don't need people nosing around, looking for it."

I stood in the middle of the cold, damp room and imagined Al spending days and nights down here alone, with little more than bedding and maybe a table. Maybe he'd stayed here when he was sick. "B" could have easily visited him and brought food.

What a sad time that was, I thought. It had to be tough for the refugees, bringing their families to such a bleak place. But then it occurred to me, maybe they hadn't minded the cellar. For a few days, they could rest from their travels, in a place that was reasonably safe. And it must have felt like a great blessing to be treated with kindness, by people who were willing to share their food and other resources, as limited as they were.

My thoughts turned to the present-day people from Central America, refugees fleeing the violence and privation in their homelands, hoping for safety in the U.S. In my country. I wondered how much kindness they met along the way. From what I'd read, it wasn't very much.

One more room lay on the other side of this one. As we walked in, I realized we must be right below the scriptorium. Once again, the walls were lined with shelving. Most of the shelves were close together, probably repositories for cheese. Like the other two rooms, this one had two high, narrow windows up at ground level. "That's the cellar," Peter said. "I hope the visitors aren't too disappointed in it."

"I bet we could bring some things down here, like baskets of produce, so people could see how the nuns used the cellar for storage."

"Right," Peter said. "And maybe I can come up with some makeshift bedding to show how the refugees would have slept. Straw pallets would work." He rubbed his chin. "I guess I should look for a couple more stories to tell on the tour. A few of the old goat herders were young men during the war. And the older women might also have memories of people hiding down here."

We climbed the stairs, and Peter closed the trapdoor in the kitchen floor. As we walked back to the museum, it occurred to me that some of the older Guzos might remember where the tunnel's entrance and exit were located. It would be worth asking.

Peter and I set off for Eglentyne's house a little before two that afternoon. Actually, we weren't alone. When Kessie found out about our excursion, she wanted to go too. At first I was against taking a teenager on such a delicate mission, but I finally relented for practical reasons. I hadn't paid close attention to how we got to the house the first time, and Peter had never been there. Eglentyne didn't have a phone, so our arrival would be a surprise. A happy one, I hoped. Kessie showed up at our house in a voluminous jacket, her grandfather's, she said. Before we started out, she promised to say nothing to Eglentyne about the photo album or the medallion.

Several minutes later, we arrived at the end of the path leading to the Fosse chalet. There was no car parked nearby, so I took that as a sign that Wilheard and Sebastian had gone elsewhere.

"Halloo," Peter called, and soon, Eglentyne appeared at the door, wearing a long white apron over her skirt and blouse.

"I wasn't expecting guests," she said warily.

"It's just a friendly Sunday visit," I said.

She hesitated. "Oh. Well then, come in. I'm in the midst of baking."

"We won't stay long," Peter said.

"Maybe we could talk in the kitchen," I said. "Then you can keep an eye on things." I wanted to avoid the dreary parlor.

We headed to the kitchen at the back of the house. The room was toasty, with heat radiating from the oven. The pleasant aroma of baked goods filled the air, and I noticed two loaves of bread on the counter beside a couple of mixing bowls. Cookie sheets rested in the sink. Eglentyne wiped off the table, which had trails of flour and dough, and we all sat.

"You have been busy," I said.

"Just so," Eglentyne said stiffly.

"I was telling Peter about the charming tea party we had on Friday," I said.

"I'm glad you enjoyed it," she said. "I was sorry to end it so abruptly."

"No problem," I said. "Are you feeling better?"

"Oh yes. Much better, thank you."

Kessie sat up straight. "Have you any iced cakes left? I liked the ones with the rabbits."

I lowered my voice. "Kessie, hush. We didn't come to beg for food."

"Oh, but you must have something to eat," Eglentyne said, rising. "I do indeed have a few cakes left. I daren't give them to Wilheard and Sebastian. They would only make fun of me." She walked over to her pie safe, a wooden cabinet with narrow slots in the door for cooling. (My grandmother had owned a similar one.) "No bunnies," I'm afraid," she said, pulling out a plate of cakes. "But I still have some flowers. And ginger biscuits. Let me just heat water for tea." She looked more comfortable now, as she got into her element as a baker. Kessie shot me a triumphant look.

Peter and Kessie sat at the table while Eglentyne bustled about, gathering cups, saucers, plates, and forks, which I set out before us. Eglentyne removed loaves of bread from the oven, and I poured hot water into her tea pot, before we finally gathered at the table to munch on cakes and cookies, praising our hostess highly. We talked about everything except the play, including Peter's plans for tours of the museum during the celebration.

"You ladies might want to join us," Peter said, facing Eglentyne. "I plan to include a visit to the cellar below the convent. Most people haven't visited it."

"How intriguing," Eglentyne said. "You know, in all these years, I've never seen the cellar. I'd forgotten it was there."

Peter ate the last crumb of his cake and set down his fork. He shot me a meaningful glance before turning to Eglentyne. "You know, cousin, you were sorely missed at the last rehearsal."

Eglentyne flushed. "I did feel sorry to drop out," she said, eyes cast down on her lap. "Oh, but I'm sure you'll find someone else to play Anwen."

"No one can replace you," Peter said. "I asked Holly to take the part on Friday, but she isn't comfortable in the role, as you can imagine."

Eglentyne smiled at me sympathetically, but with a tinge of satisfaction, I thought.

"It would be superb to have a Fosse in the role," Peter said. "A first for us. You have no idea how pleased I was when you volunteered. Of course, Wilheard is a very fine King of France. But the part of the duchess, well, that is very special."

"Indeed," Eglentyne said, and the way she worked her jaw suggested she was chewing over the idea.

Peter leaned toward her. "I can see how busy you are. But you've already memorized your lines. That's the most time-consuming part. And we only have five more rehearsals, with a night off before the performance on Saturday."

Eglentyne clasped her hands on her lap. "I would like to return..."

Kessie slipped off her chair. "I'll just visit the loo," she whispered and headed for the parlor.

Peter gazed at Eglentyne. "I need hardly point out that your performance would bring honor to the Fosse family. I feel certain that it would raise the Fosses to their historic position in the duchy. A position of unquestioned prominence."

Eglentyne's eyes glistened with tears. "I would like to remain in the play. Truly I would. That's what I told Wilheard. But he got it into his head that I should withdraw. He was quite insistent, and I don't like to cross him."

Her brows furrowed. "I wouldn't be surprised if that friend of his-Sebastian—talked him into it."

"Perhaps I could have a word with your cousin," Peter said. "He's new to the duchy. Maybe he doesn't understand how important it is for you to play the duchess. Important to us all."

"You might be right," Eglentyne said. "Wilheard wants to be a good Guzo. Perhaps he'll listen to you."

A scraping sound came from the parlor. I tensed, wondering where Kessie was, but the noise stopped.

Peter seemed oblivious to the interruption. "In that case," he said, "I'll have a word with your cousin. I only hope I'm successful. You may as well know, if you don't return, I will be forced to invite Monique, the actress from Bois."

Eglentyne gasped. "Monique? To play Anwen? She is totally unsuitable. Surely you—"

A harsh male voice boomed from the parlor. "You little brat! What are you doing?"

"Nothing," Kessie cried, followed by a crash. Peter shot up and dashed into the parlor, Eglentyne and I on his heels.

A chair had tipped over in front of the bookcase, and Sebastian, his face contorted with anger, was clutching Kessie by the arm. I groaned. Kessie had promised not to talk about the album, but she hadn't promised not to steal it.

"Let go," Kessie pleaded. "You're hurting me."

"I know what you're up to, you little thief," he said. As I looked on in disbelief, he slapped Kessie hard on the cheek and shoved her to the floor. With one long stride, Peter reached him and smashed his fist into Sebastian's jaw.

Sebastian recovered fast and flew at Peter with a powerful jab. Peter evaded it, but after that, both men threw themselves into the fight. Even the sound was awful, the crunch and slap of fist against jaw or stomach, and the puffing and grunting of the men.

Eglentyne and I had retreated to the hall doorway, but Kessie was sitting huddled against the far wall. As soon as the battle moved to the other side of the parlor, I rushed over. "You okay?" I asked, as I helped her to her feet.

She nodded, her eyes bright with tears, and I pulled her to the doorway. From there, Kessie, Eglentyne and I kept our eyes glued to the parlor, where the two men were still duking it out. Both were experienced fighters, it seemed, matching blow for blow. I recoiled every time Peter was hit, my gut tightening, but he always rallied. Eglentyne breathed in sharply whenever they got close to a piece of furniture.

A table overturned, and Eglentyne lunged forward, barely catching a ceramic shepherdess that was hurtling to the floor. She straightened, cradling the figurine against her chest. "Stop it!" she shouted at the men, but they didn't spare her a look. Sebastian hit Peter in the face, and blood spurted from Peter's mouth.

"Eew," cried Kessie.

I stepped beside Eglentyne. "We've got to separate the men. You take Sebastian. Grab him from behind. I'll take Peter." I didn't know if it would work, but we had to do something.

But just then, Sebastian landed a blow to Peter's gut that sent him reeling backward onto an end table. Peter and the table both crashed to the floor.

"See what you've done?" Eglentyne shrieked, her face and neck a blotchy red. "You've broken my aunt's table."

Peter struggled to a sitting position, grimacing as he tried to brace himself with his left hand. "I'll have the table repaired," he said. I helped him up, careful not to jar his left arm.

Eglentyne turned on Sebastian. "And you. I don't care if you're Wilheard's boss. I wish you'd never come. You're a brute and nothing but trouble." Pivoting, she fixed Kessie with a cold stare. "What have you to say for yourself, young lady? You were after my aunt's album, weren't you? Admit it."

Kessie bowed her head. "I'm sorry," she squeaked.

Finally, Eglentyne turned her wrath on Peter and me. "A friendly visit, indeed. You wanted that photograph. And don't pretend you don't know which one."

Peter shook his head vehemently. "It's not like that. Please believe me, we—"

"Get out, the lot of you," Eglentyne said. A sob wracked her, and she hurried out of the parlor and up the hall. Her footsteps clattered on the stairs.

Peter, Kessie, and I filed out the door, ignoring Sebastian's malevolent gaze. We trudged down the path, stopping to take stock once we were out of view of the house. Peter had a bloody lip and his left eye was already beginning to swell.

"How is your arm?" I asked. He lifted it, and I saw that his wrist was limp. Broken, possibly.

"I'm sorry," Kessie said. "It's all my fault. And I didn't even get the photo album. They must have moved it." She looked at us both imploringly. "Are you going to tell Mum?"

Peter fixed her with a stern look. "I suggest you tell her, the whole story. Before she hears it from every busybody in the duchy."

"She's going to kill me," Kessie muttered.

"It was nice knowing you," Peter said and turned to continue down the path. Kessie's shoulders slumped.

"I'll talk to your mom later, if you like," I said. "I know your intentions were good."

"Okay," she said miserably.

I fell into step with Peter. "We'd better get you to a hospital. I'm sure they'll want to x-ray your arm."

"I suppose," he said. "The closest one is in Bois. We can take my car, if you don't mind driving. It's a Saab with automatic transmission."

"Sure. No problem." We continued down the path. "I thought Swedish cars were mostly manuals."

"My girlfriend wanted me to buy an automatic," Peter said. "So I did."

"You have a girlfriend?" I blurted. Kessie had mentioned a gorgeous young woman who had once come to visit.

"Had a girlfriend. When I lived in Leicester."

"Oh. What happened to her?"

"I came here. She stayed there."

So it couldn't have been much of a love match, I thought, and I was more than a little relieved.

Several minutes later we arrived at our houses, where Kessie agreed to let Bonnie out for a short run while Peter cleaned up. There was no telling when we'd get back from Bois. I headed for the kitchen to look for ice to use on Peter's eye, but the freezer didn't contain any. I found Peter in the bathroom, dabbing at his mouth with a washcloth. "How is it?" I asked.

"Not bad. I still have all my teeth." I told him I couldn't find ice, and he said that it was probably too late to do any good. His eye was nearly swollen shut, so he might have been right.

I went up to my room and fetched my coat. It occurred to me that I might be sitting around a waiting room for a while, so I put *Thin Places* into my shoulder bag. Downstairs, Peter emerged from his room, a jacket thrown over his shoulders. He handed me his car keys, and a minute later, I was getting into the driver's seat of the Saab parked next to Peter's cottage. He maneuvered, one-handed, into the passenger seat, then sat back, eyes closed.

"You okay?" I asked. "I guess you'll be riding shotgun."

He startled, then his lips quirked up in the shadow of a grin. "Sure. I'll ride shotgun."

I started the car, drove down the hill, and turned onto the road. As I accelerated, it occurred to me that it wasn't so long ago that I had traveled along here in the passenger's seat of Sebastian's sporty Ferrari. At the time, he had seemed so charming and altogether awesome—a successful businessman, at ease in the world. I was pleased that he had deigned to give me a ride.

But now I was getting a fuller picture of Sebastian. I'd already become aware of his talent for manipulation, which he'd used on me, dangling a job with perks before my eyes. And from what Juliet had said the night before, he had probably turned his powers of persuasion on Tony. I wouldn't be surprised if we heard no more from Tony about Wilheard's misdeeds. And now I was seeing an even uglier side to Sebastian. He had manhandled Kessie, a fourteen-year-old girl, apparently without a second thought.

I guided Peter's car past the valley overlook and started the descent on the other side of the ridge.

I snuck a glance at Peter, wondering if this was a good time to talk about Sebastian. But the poor guy was slumping in his seat, his good hand cupping his bad eye. This was maybe not the best moment for deep analysis.

"How's your eye?" I asked.

"It's still there." I hoped he could get some relief at the hospital. Now that I thought of it, the biggest surprise of the day was not Sebastian, but Peter. Who would have guessed that he was so handy with his fists? So much for my stereotype of shy, retiring historians.

"You know," I said, "you're quite a good fighter.

He snorted. "I grew up in a town where boys learn to defend themselves. And I had a scrappy younger brother who was always getting into fights."

"So you went to his aid."

"Sometimes."

"Well, I was impressed."

"Not much to be impressed about," he said. "I have a wrist that's probably broken, a swollen eye, and a split lip. And God only knows what kind of internal damage. Plus, I have to replace Eglentyne's beloved table."

"True," I said, steering the car around a large rock that had fallen onto the road.

"But what's worse, I've lost the respect of Eglentyne, a prominent member of the community. I admit, she isn't my favorite Guzo, but I've always respected her. Now she thinks we went to steal her photo album. Had I not launched myself at Sebastian, I might have had a chance to explain."

"I'm sorry things turned out so badly," I said. "But you did come to Kessie's defense. And that's no small thing." Peter grunted his acknowledgment. "Besides," I said, "I get the feeling Sebastian usually gets what he wants. Now he knows that he can't just push Guzos around and expect to get away with it."

"You might be right about Sebastian," Peter said. "And I appreciate the vote of confidence. I'd give you a kiss, but my mouth is in no condition."

Rats. No kisses. "Now I really hate Sebastian," I mumbled.

Peter started to smile, then winced.

"By the way," Peter said, "my mother is arriving on Thursday. I expect she'll stay in Gran's house with you. I hope you don't mind another housemate."

"Of course not. I'm glad I'll have a chance to meet her."

We rode in silence until we had crossed the bridge and entered France. Peter stared straight ahead, a brooding look on his face.

"Will you be glad to see your mother?" I asked.

"What? Oh, sure. Mum and I get along well. Although, I hate to have her see me like this."

With good reason. By Thursday, his bruises would no doubt be a deep purple. "We have the pancake makeup I bought for the play. Maybe we can use it on you. You'll just have to avoid bright lights, so your mom doesn't catch on."

A laugh turned into a moan. He raised his hand to his mouth in a protective gesture.

"Sorry," I said. "Seriously, I'm sure your mom will be pleased to see you, even in your present condition."

"There's something else," he said. "I haven't seen Mum since my brother died. It's been six months. Everything is different now, without Gran and Bren."

I could see how that would feel strange. To pick up their relationship again, now that their family was so diminished. "Any chance your father might come?" I asked.

"Dad isn't big on the duchy. He and Bren have always been happier at home, busy with sports and hanging out with their mates. But Mum is looking forward to the celebration. Anyway, that's what she said on the phone. She'll bring her flute. She likes to play with the band."

A flutist. I hoped that Peter's mother wouldn't look down on my humble penny whistle. Or dislike me for other reasons, like the fact that I was an American visitor clearly fond of her son.

Fifteen minutes later, we were in Bois, where Peter directed me across the city to the hospital, a modern, three-story concrete building, with a large glass window running along the first floor.

Peter signed in at the counter across from the entrance, then joined me in the waiting area, where we sat quietly on comfortable chairs that were a combination of molded plastic and shiny metal. Soon, a pretty, athletic-looking nurse in her twenties led Peter down the hall.

After getting a long drink at a water fountain, I returned to my chair and pulled out my copy of *Thin Places*, turning to the chapter on Guatemala. As I read, I realized that Framton's discovery of a thin place there was serendipitous. He was traveling through Central America when he was invited to a party at the British Ambassador's residence in Guatemala City. There, he met an American businessman who became intrigued when Framton explained his search for *Thin Places*.

"I have an Indian worker you should meet," the American said. "A Maya." He explained that the fellow's ancestors had migrated from some place far south after their leader had visions of a place with sacred powers. His followers finally settled in a valley in the Guatemalan highlands. Framton arranged to talk with the worker the following day, with the American acting as translator.

Framton recorded the Indian's words:

My people traveled and traveled, always in search of a holy place. One day, they came to a valley. "Let us camp here," the leaders said. That first night, my people had dreams. Amazing dreams. Oh, they were so clear, like spring water. Some visions were beautiful. Some were sad. But they all had the taste of truth. A sacred truth, sent by the spirits. So my ancestors knew they had arrived at their new home. Oh, how they rejoiced!"

The taste of truth. Had my vision of Gwen's murder had the taste of truth? Maybe. Usually, when I woke from a nightmare, I was immediately relieved that it was only a dream. Even when the mood lingered, I knew it was only a hazy remnant. But that hadn't happened when I envisioned the murder. It felt real as I dreamed it, and it still felt real when I awakened.

I returned to the book, where Framton speculated that the group had been in search of a thin place all along, and they had finally found one. Naturally, he was eager to visit the valley, but the Indians had been displaced when the Spaniards arrived. The Valley of Los Ancianos was incorporated into a plantation, its current owner ignorant of the site's special properties.

Framton had visited Guatemala in the 1930s, I reminded myself. Would the valley still be owned by an oblivious plantation owner some sixty years later? Or had the Indians finally gotten their valley back?

I set down Framton's book. The account set me to thinking. Were there people who were drawn to *Thin Places*? And if so, how did they find the locations? Maybe these spots, like the forest glade in the duchy, sent out some kind of signal, a vibration maybe, that certain sensitive people were attuned to. Poor Framton had never experienced a vivid dream or vision associated with a thin place. But even he might have been unconsciously pulled to such places. And what about the duchy? Was it the thin place in the glade that had brought Anwen all the way to the very edge of French territory? Maybe other people had been attracted to the duchy over the years for the same reason.

It was nearly five o'clock when Peter finally emerged from the clinic's inner sanctum, his lower arm enveloped in a cast and cradled in a sling. "The wrist is broken," he said, "but there was no displacement."

"Thank goodness for that, at least." The nurse had also cleaned him up and covered his swollen eye with a gauze bandage. But he still looked like he'd been in a brawl. "Do we need to stop at a pharmacy?" I asked.

"No. I've got enough pain meds to get me through the night. I can stop off at the duchy clinic tomorrow if I need more."

Back in the parking lot, we got into the car and headed out of the city. Peter sank back in his seat, letting out a deep sigh.

"I read more of *Thin Places*," I said, and told him about the valley in Guatemala, hoping I could take his mind off the disastrous afternoon. He remembered the chapter vaguely.

"Do you think there are people who are drawn to *Thin Places*?" I asked. "Like Anwen maybe?"

"Hmm. It's not impossible, I suppose. She was certainly keen to settle here. Unlike Philippe, who had little desire to live in such a remote area."

"Why did he agree, do you think?"

Peter stroked his chin with his good hand. "Hard to say. Anwen must have been persuasive. Plus, the politics of the French court could be toxic. Maybe he wanted to escape that. Who knows? Anwen never explained it in her journal."

"I figured Anwen wanted land that wasn't already claimed by another family."

"Oh, it was claimed all right." Peter was looking more alert now that he was delving into his favorite topic—Duchy history. "By the Wiskara, as they were called. They'd been here for centuries, millennia probably. Naturally, they had their own culture and language. I'm sure they were in no hurry to surrender their autonomy to a bunch of French intruders." He adjusted his injured arm and winced.

"Oh. Kessie told me that Anwen and Philippe were squatters. I guess that's what she meant."

Peter tipped back his head and laughed. His pain killers must have kicked in. "She would say that."

"What happened to the Wiskara?" I asked.

"They're still here. In fact, Rosamunde and Rob's families are descended from the original inhabitants. Some historians think the Wiskara were related to the Etruscans, or the Basques possibly. Who knows? There has been so much intermarriage over the years, it's impossible to know what the original Wiskara looked like. We think they probably had dark hair and almond-shaped eyes. Attractive people, possibly with Asian roots. Well, I'm sure Guzos all have some Wiskara blood, but some families are more invested in it than others."

I thought of the play, where Anwen and Philippe pledged their loyalty to the Guzos. Instead of applauding their new rulers, the assembled crowd could have been smoldering with resentment. "Did the Wiskara ever revolt?"

"There's nothing in the historical record. Judging from Anwen's journal, her family and the Wiskara were willing to accommodate each other. And things loosened up more after Philippe left."

What? I searched Peter's face, to see if he was joking. "Philippe left the duchy?"

"Went back to his father's chateau, where he died of smallpox."

"Oh no," I groaned.

"Yes. Several of his courtiers went with him."

"It must have been devastating for Anwen, having her husband die hundreds of miles away."

"One would think so. But she was quite stoic in her journal comments. She wrote that he left with his men and later that word reached her that he had died. A Mass was conducted in his honor. That was about it. No words of longing or grief. It made me wonder if Anwen and Philippe had had a falling out. I'm not even sure he had ever intended to return."

"So, Anwen and Philippe didn't live happily ever after." Too bad, but such a rosy ending didn't always stand up under the wear and tear of daily life. My own family could attest to that.

I kept mulling over *Thin Places* and vivid dreams as the land gained in elevation, the road heading deeper into the mountains. I wondered if Rosamunde's Wiskara ancestors were the first to discover the glade. Probably.

Several minutes later, we came to the turnoff to St. Uguzo. Beyond it was the bridge, which had seemed decrepit the first time I'd crossed it in Gwen's rental car. Now, as I steered the Saab across the bridge, it struck me as perfectly sound.

I glanced at Peter. "Have you ever had a vivid dream? You know, a prophetic one?"

Peter's expression turned stony. "I pay no attention to dreams. As far as I can see, they're useless." His response seemed odd after all the time he'd spent poring over Anwen's journal. She was so clearly a vivid dreamer, as were others in the duchy. Come to think of it, hadn't Rosamunde mentioned that Peter's mother was a dreamer? I glanced at Peter, but by the set of his jaw, I recognized that he had nothing further to say on the subject.

The road followed a curve, heading upward and passing a grassy meadow. At the edge, a hawk eyed us from atop a young cedar tree. They were handsome, noble birds, I thought, although I knew that mice and other small animals would view them quite differently.

"So, you think that Anwen and the Wiskara got along well?" I asked, guiding our conversation back to duchy history.

"Yes, as did her children and grandchildren. In fact, the two groups joined forces a century later. The duchy had been steadily losing land to neighboring principalities. Settlers moved in and occupied land on the borders, eroding duchy territory. The French rulers, far off in Paris and consumed by their own problems, offered little assistance. Finally, the duke and a couple of the Wiskara leaders formed a delegation and went to visit the Pope, asking for his help. In the end, he declared the duchy a sovereign state, placing it under the joint protection of a high-ranking Catholic bishop and the French monarchy. That was in 1653."

I had wondered how the duchy became autonomous. Now I knew, and it was a story of cooperation between two groups who had reason to be opponents. That must surely bode well for the duchy today. Clearly, there were rifts between progressives, who wanted to open up the duchy, and traditionalists, who wanted to limit outside influence. But Guzos could draw on a long history of cooperating for the common good.

We said nothing further until we arrived at the overlook leading down to the valley. "Do you suppose we should cancel rehearsal tonight?" I asked. Peter looked beaten up, and he had to be sore.

He fixed me with his one good eye. "Why would we do that?"

Peter and I arrived early at the gym and turned a couple of chairs in the front row so that we had a view of the door. I fervently hoped there would be no last-minute withdrawals from the cast. Peter's scowl didn't bode well for anyone bringing bad news. He tensed, and I spotted Sebastian at the doorway, where he paused before striding across the gym toward us.

"What the bloody—" Peter muttered.

"I come in peace," Sebastian said from half-way across the gym. He raised his arms high, as if in surrender. He was full of his usual bravado, but his cheek looked swollen, and he was walking with a decided hitch, favoring his right leg.

"Look. He's limping," I whispered with satisfaction. Peter grunted in reply.

Sebastian came to a halt in front of Peter. "I'm here to apologize," he said, looking suitably contrite. "I was way out of line this afternoon. I've already talked with Kessie and her mother, and you'll be happy to hear that I received a proper dressing-down from the sheriff."

I couldn't help feeling gleeful at the image of Juliette lambasting Sebastian.

"That must have been unpleasant," Peter said, betraying no emotion.

"Believe me," Sebastian said, "I don't usually go around disciplining teenagers. God knows I got into plenty of mischief at that age." If Sebastian was trying to win us over, it wasn't working on me. Slapping Kessie and knocking her to the floor wasn't my idea of an enlightened approach to discipline.

Sebastian shook his head, as if he himself was bewildered by his actions. "I don't know what came over me. It was seeing the girl trying to steal from my friends, I guess. It set off an internal alarm, and I reacted without thinking. What can I say? It will never happen again."

"Glad to hear it," Peter said.

"Oh, and I've told Eglentyne that I will have her table repaired. Either that or replace it with a better one."

Peter nodded. "Decent of you."

"Look, Dr. Ericsson, I don't want any ill will between us." Dr. Ericsson? I hadn't heard anyone use Peter's title, although I knew he had a Ph.D. I'd seen the diploma hanging in his office. "Not at such an important time, with the celebration only days away. I know how important your play is to everyone."

"Indeed."

Sebastian cocked his head and broke into an ingratiating smile. "What do you say? Can we put this behind us? For the sake of the duchy? After all, we both got in a few good swings. Nothing to be ashamed of there. And we're both still standing."

Peter's shoulders relaxed, and I could see some of the tension drain out of him. "Yes, all right. The fact is, it wasn't my finest hour either."

Sebastian extended his hand, and after a tiny hesitation, Peter shook it. In a way, I hated to see Peter cave. I was pretty sure that Sebastian was manipulating him, winning him over, just as he'd manipulated me with the job offer. But Peter couldn't very well reject Sebastian's peace offering, not without appearing churlish. Besides, I had to admit, Kessie had been misbehaving.

Sebastian turned to me. "By the way, Holly, Fred has offered us a private tour of the cheesery. Tuesday afternoon at one-thirty. Can you join us?"

"Sure," I said. "Thanks for arranging it." I would have preferred other companions on the tour, but it was generous of Sebastian to include me. Clearly, I was not immune to his peace offerings. He left the gym as the first actors walked in the door.

I turned to Peter. "Do you suppose he promised Kessie something to appease her?"

"Who knows? What do teenage girls want? A shopping trip? A horse?"

I thought back to the way that Kessie had gazed at Tony Cotton. "Or maybe a date with a cute teenage boy."

CHAPTER TWENTY

Day 10, Monday

I was making scrambled eggs the next morning when Peter trudged into the kitchen, clad in navy sweats. I'd heard him outside, calling Bonnie earlier, so I knew he'd been up for a while, and the pup had enjoyed at least a short run.

Peter lowered himself slowly onto a chair at the table. A purple bruise had spread across his jaw, and he had removed the bandage from his left eye, so I could see that his eye was swollen almost shut. It hurt just to look at him. On the positive side, the fingers protruding from his cast didn't look swollen. He had dispensed with the sling and somehow had managed to tie the laces on his sneakers.

"How are you feeling?" I asked.

"Like I was run over by a lorry." He poured milk into his cup, followed by tea from the pot I'd left on the table.

I turned back to the gas stove, where the bright yellow eggs were shiny and solid. After turning off the flame, I sliced half of a loaf of quick bread that Rosamunde had dropped off the night before when she came over to check on us. To my delight, the bread contained dried cherries and (gasp!) little chunks of chocolate. I put the bread slices on the table, divided up the eggs on two plates, and sat down next to Peter.

"Smells good," Peter mumbled, and took a bite of egg, chewing slowly, as if his jaw hurt. "I might stop by the clinic this morning. I'll get to work a little late."

"No problem. I want to work on Al's journal, so I can open up the museum, if you like." If I kept working, I might be able to finish the transcription by the end of the day. It would feel good to complete the task. Besides, I wanted to know what happened to Al.

"Thanks again for driving me to the hospital yesterday," Peter said. "And for everything else."

"Glad to be of service." In this case, "everything else" had included helping him out of his clothes the night before. By the time we got home from rehearsal, Peter had been so tired that he hadn't objected to my removing his shirt, shoes, and socks. The rest, he'd assured me, he could deal with on his own.

I took a bite of the quick bread, savoring its moistness and flavor. This had to be the perfect breakfast food, even if it was a little on the sweet side. I could already feel myself mellowing out.

Peter lowered his fork. "I'm sorry you've been dragged into the duchy quagmire. I swear, it didn't use to be like this. No violent deaths, and I certainly never got into a fistfight."

"Maybe things will improve once the celebration is over," I said. "I wish our talk with Eglentyne had gone better. For a minute there, I thought she was going to agree to play Anwen."

"As did I," Peter said.

"You were very persuasive."

He cast me a sardonic look. "Shameless, you mean."

It was true that Peter had poured it on thick, appealing to Eglentyne's boundless pride in the Fosse clan. But he didn't need to be so hard on himself. "Actually, I found your pitch quite stirring. I only wished I were a Fosse."

"Oh yes?" His eyes crinkled into a smile, and I leaned over and kissed him on the cheek, on a spot that didn't look bruised. I had intended it to be a friendly peck, but I'm afraid I lingered a little longer.

"I'm feeling better all the time," Peter said. He placed his good, if slightly scraped, hand over mine. "You know, I'm really not all that incapacitated." His unswollen eye had a gleam that I recognized from two nights earlier.

Some time later, after a brisk walk down the road, I unlocked the museum door. The sheriff's office was open, and I went over to tell Juliette I would be alone in the museum.

"I apologize for Kessie's behavior yesterday," she said. "We've had a talk."

"Is she feeling okay? She did take a nasty tumble."

"She's a little sore, but she'll recover. How's Peter? I hear he broke his wrist."

I gave her the details. "He's moving slowly, but he'll be in later."

"Maybe we can all have tea," Juliette said. "Talk over what happened yesterday. I have some serious concerns about Sebastian."

"Sure," I said. I wasn't eager to rehash the visit to Eglentyne's house, but it would give me an opportunity to put Kessie's mischief in the best light, focusing on her admirable intentions, bravery, and ingenuity.

Back at the museum, I retrieved Al's journal and my writing pad, then sharpened pencils over a wastebasket with a little hand-held sharpener. Finally, I set to work, seated at my usual spot at the round table nearest the window.

The transcription was going faster now, since I was accustomed to Al's minuscule handwriting and most of his abbreviations. I was even able to go back and fill in a few words that had confounded me earlier.

Some of the entries were moving.

M5. Light snow. Parents, 3 school age kids. Sighted Germans passing below us. Hid among rocks. Child snuggled against me till they passed.

M7. 2 men, escaped from Nazi camp. Walking skeletons, but survived trip. I don't know how.

10/14 2 warm days in a row. Washed socks, what's left of them. Dreamed of C. How I miss her.

11/2 Sick for a week. B looked after me. Still weak. Must build up strength. Lives depend on me.

11/20 Very cold. D arrived last night, one of 3 Americans. Recognized me at once. We talked about men in our squadron. Several now dead. D talked about his girlfriend, I talked about C. Later, I wrote a letter to my parents and a longer one to C. D will mail them if he survives the journey to England. My parents won't understand my decision to stay here, but C will. At least, I hope so. She was afraid my reservations about bombing civilians would get me shot or thrown in prison. She may have been right. I don't see myself surviving this war. And if I do, what then? I can't go home.

I paused, lowering my pencil. I'd assumed that Al was assigned to St. Uguzo. Even if he'd volunteered for the duty, I imagined it was with the consent of his superiors. But maybe not. Was it possible that he had chosen to remain without authorization? He was performing an invaluable service, guiding airmen and refugees through the mountains. But what if he'd refused to return to his unit? The American military might not care about his reasons.

Al continued:

Here is my plan: C and I go to a warm, friendly country. Mexico maybe. I do carpentry or learn some other skill. We have kids. They're smart and brave and kind, just like their mom. I wake up every morning and give thanks for the blessings of my life.

It was a sweet vision of the future. Finally, I came to the last entry.

12/6 Dawn in the cabin. Woke from a nightmare, a vivid dream, as B calls them. In the dream, J and I are guiding a refugee family, the same ones who arrived yesterday. We file into Ibex Pass, J at the front, me at the rear.

I look up. Germans on the hillside, with machine guns. I shout a warning, but it's too late. An ear-splitting sound: rat-a-tat, rat-a-tat, rat-a-tat, rat-a-tat. Bullets rip into J. His body jerks and he collapses, covered with blood. The father and mother are killed too. The children clutch each other. I try to pull them back, but the bullets mow us down, our bodies spewing blood and guts. Rat-a-tat, rat-a-tat, rat-a-tat, rat-a-tat. Finally, silence. And then, without warning, I am floating high above the scene, looking down at our ravaged bodies, large and small, and at the rocks and dirt around us, splattered and stained with blood. On the hill below me, the Germans stand. One shakes his head. You can't kill children without feeling the weight of it on you. Not if you're human. Of course, some would say humanity is a an indulgence in war. Something to be discarded. But can they ever get it back? The Germans collect their gear and start down the mountainside. Their job is over. I wake up, shaking. I have seen my death. But enough of dreams. J is at the door, and the family is starting to rouse. I have to go.

The last entry left me shaken, especially since nothing followed. Just blank pages. I glanced over at Peter's office and saw that his door was open. He must have come in while I was absorbed in my work. I walked over and stood in the doorway, and he looked up from a stack of papers on his desk.

"What happened to Al?" I asked. "The journal entries just stop." I had guessed his story didn't end well. Still, I had held out hope that he had survived the war. Now I was filled with dread.

"He had a sad ending, I'm afraid. Killed by German soldiers. Fortunately, the family he was escorting made it, and so did two Guzo guides, but Al didn't."

"Oh." I sagged against the door.

"I know," Peter said. "Al seemed like a fine fellow. He deserved to live. Like so many others who didn't survive the war. Look. You should ask Rosamunde about that last mission. I think her father led it. She'll know more of the details."

"Her father was J?"

"I believe so." He turned back to his work.

I left the museum, crossed the bridge, and trudged up the hill, my mind immersed in a winter half a century ago, when the duchy was a stop for downed airmen and hungry, exhausted refugees. German soldiers were here also, a menacing presence. I reminded myself that they too were far from home and were surrounded by people who despised them.

When I arrived at Rosamunde's house, I found her in the kitchen, cooking a pot of applesauce. As soon as I told her I'd like to know more about Al's final mission, she turned off the flame under the pot and removed her long apron. "I'll tell you," she said, "but first, there is something you need to see."

"Where are we going?" I asked, as she put on her shawl.

"The cemetery."

"Is Al buried there?"

"Yes." It was only fitting, I realized, that I should see where he was interred. Once I'd completed the transcription of the journal, I could write a postscript, including information on Al's last mission and his burial. That should fulfill my obligation to the museum.

A minute later, I was hurrying to keep up with Rosamunde as we headed down the road.

"I suppose you've been wondering about the people mentioned in the journal," she said. "J was my father. His middle name was Joseph, you see. He led nearly all the missions. I was a girl at the time, and I remember my mother was deathly afraid the whole time Papa was gone."

"And B? The woman who looked after Al when he was sick?"

"Anne-Marie. Later, she would become Duchess Anne-Marie. She was in her twenties and very pretty. I suspect she felt some affection for Al. Affection mixed with sympathy, no doubt. As for the others, D was a pilot in Al's squadron. You probably figured that out. Y and Z, the two fellows mentioned in the first entry, crash landed with Al. They left and he stayed behind."

"And C was his sweetheart back in the States. Or his wife?"

"A young woman he met in training. They fell in love and were planning to marry after the war. He adored her, from what I can tell."

I thought of Al's doomed plan to go to Mexico and raise a family with C. "Did you ever learn her name?"

"I'll tell you when we get to the grave site." We crossed the bridge and entered the cemetery, where we followed the central path through the graveyard, then crossed the field at a diagonal to the road, past clusters of gravestones, some upright and some leaning. We finally halted at the edge of the cemetery, at a spot bordered by rugged oak trees, their remaining brown leaves rustling in the breeze. A simple gravestone stood alone, and I bent down to read the rustic inscription:

Albert Becker Fleming, 1924-1944.

"Albert," I said. "My gosh. I was right about his first name. What are the chances of that happening?" I looked back at the dates. He was twenty years old when he died. So young. I had pictured the man who kept the journal as older, but then he had been forced to grow up fast.

I peered again at the engraving, and a shiver ran down my spine. Albert Becker Fleming. I'd seen the name before, but I couldn't think where. "His name is familiar," I said.

"I'm not surprised," Rosamunde said. "He is your grandfather."

Her words hit me like a blow, and I stepped back. "What? No, that's not possible. My grandfather was a soldier in the army. Not the Air Force. And I'm sure he was an enlisted man, not a pilot. Don't pilots have to be officers?"

"Albert was an airman, but he wasn't a pilot. He was a crew member on a bomber. And you're right. He was in the U.S. Army, the Army Air Corps."

I stared at the gravestone, my mind reeling. "Okay. Albert wasn't a pilot. But what makes you think he was my grandfather?"

"You remember D, the Yank who was in Albert's squadron. Daniel McCleary, his name was. Danny."

I nodded, and Rosamunde brushed a bit of dirt off the headstone. "Among the downed airmen, Danny was one of the lucky ones. He made it back to England, and when he did, he mailed Albert's letters to the States. Then, after the war, he visited your grandmother. You see, he always credited Albert with saving his life. Apparently, on their trek through the mountains, he'd slipped and fallen half way down a cliff. Albert had climbed down, at great risk, and dragged him back. After that, Danny felt it was only right that he keep an eye on your grandmother and your mother."

"So C was my grandmother, Clara Beecher." I thought back to Grandma's male friends, and I remembered there was an old aviator, a friendly guy named Danny, who used to visit now and then. He had helped Grandma out with loans for her crop-dusting business. "So, all this time, Danny was keeping track of my family?"

"Yes. And he also stayed in touch with people in St. Uguzo, especially Anne-Marie and my father. You understand, most people wanted to forget the war years. But Danny wasn't like that. He understood the meaning of loyalty and of gratitude. He was our link to your family, passing on news to us. You can imagine how overjoyed we were to learn that Albert had a daughter. We had known that he had a fiancée back home—your grandmother. But Albert had no idea she was with child. He died, never realizing he had a little girl. Your mother."

I continued gazing at the gravestone, trying to make sense of everything. The old family story of desertion was starting to crack. Everything I'd learned about my grandfather—well, it wasn't false, exactly. But there was a whole other side.

Overhead, a bird cawed, and I looked up to see three crows perched on the barren branch of an oak tree. Witnesses to my confusion. And my growing understanding.

"Why did he stay here in the duchy?" I asked. "Why didn't Albert go back to his unit?"

"I only know what my father told me, and that wasn't very much. Albert felt terrible about dropping bombs on civilians, many of them women and children. He couldn't see them from the air, of course, but he knew they were there. Ordinary people just trying to survive. It was a heavy weight on him, knowing he was bringing death to all those innocent people. Finally, when he saw a chance to end his part in the killing, he took it."

"By staying here in the duchy."

Rosamunde nodded. "At first, the Guzos weren't sure they wanted him. He was another mouth to feed, and it was dangerous to hide him. But he had grown up in the mountains—the Rocky Mountains, I believe. Papa said he was like a mountain goat, sure-footed and steady. When there was a mission, your grandfather always took part. And he helped out in other ways too, chopping wood, hauling water. He fixed things too. He was very handy that way. Over time, people became fond of him."

"Tell me about Albert's final mission. Your father must have led it." (I couldn't quite bring myself to say 'my grandfather' out loud. It was hard to wrap my head around the idea that this young man, whose journal I'd read—a man who was younger than I was now—was my grandfather.)

"I'll tell you as much as I know." Rosamunde paused a moment, apparently gathering her thoughts. "The team was taking a refugee family to their next stop. As usual, my father took the lead, and Albert brought up the rear, so he could help anyone who started to lag behind. A young Guzo went with them, a boy on his first mission. You've met him, I believe. Roderick."

"Roderick? The old goat herder who looks like an elf?"

Her face softened into a smile. "Yes, I suppose he does resemble an elf, just a little." The smile faded. "The route they were going to take was the usual one, going through Ibex Pass. But the Yank—that's what Papa called Albert—the Yank said he had a bad feeling about it. So, at the last minute, they changed their plan, taking a longer, rockier path, one that would avoid the pass. My father had led the small group through the most treacherous section when he looked behind him. The Yank had stopped several yards back. He waved my father on insistently, but he himself stayed put. Papa stepped up the pace, guiding his little band into a wooded area.

"Just then, my father heard movement below him and spotted a German patrol coming in their direction. He signaled to his group to hunker down behind the trees, and they waited. But Albert didn't move. He stood in plain sight until a cry came from one of the soldiers below. Papa realized that the Germans must have spotted Albert.

The Yank struck off on a boulder-strewn path, one that would lead the Germans away from Papa's group. His plan worked. Papa hurried his little band around to the other side of the mountain, never once seeing the soldiers. But after half an hour or so, Papa heard machine gun fire in the distance. He wanted to go back to investigate, but he knew he needed to keep going. Too many lives were at stake. A few hours later, he delivered the refugees to their next rendezvous."

Rosamunde paused, taking a deep breath before she continued. "When Papa and Roderick finally retraced their path, their worst fears were realized. They found your grandfather's body lying on the ground, riddled with bullet holes." She lowered her eyes, and when she raised them, they held tears.

"Oh," I murmured. All my life, I had imagined that my grandfather was alive somewhere, even though Grandma assured me he'd died in the war. He'd died honorably, she'd said, but Mom told me she just said that to make us feel better. Deserters didn't die honorably.

"I was a child at the time," Rosamunde said, "but I remember how deeply my father grieved Albert's death. Now I understand. Papa and the Yank were more than friends. They were like brothers, entrusting their lives to each other, again and again."

"Yes, I see." I was happy to know that my grandfather, in his last days, was among people who truly cared for him. Even if that couldn't be Grandma.

Rosamunde placed her hand on my arm. "Holly, dear, I'm sorry that your mother grew up without a father. I can imagine how hard it was for her. Danny tried to explain what your grandfather had done, all the lives he'd saved. But your mother refused to listen."

Poor Mom. I could see now that she had always been too busy building barriers against a hostile world to really listen to people who wanted to help her. "I think Mom was just too wounded," I said. "She grew up ashamed of being born to a single mother. It was a big deal in those days. She might have been okay if her dad had died a war hero. But he was a deserter. And somehow everybody in our little town knew it, even the kids at school."

Rosamunde clicked her tongue. "It wasn't fair for a child to bear such a burden. We hoped that you and your sister wouldn't carry it too. Danny is living with his son in the U.S., but he's old now and in failing health. He didn't think he would ever see you again. So, we decided this was the time to bring you here. We wanted you to know the truth about your grandfather. Danny thought you might be more open to it than your mother was."

"What? Wait a second." I thought back to that evening at the Hungry Hawk, of the crazy coincidence that had resulted in Gwen inviting me to the duchy. "My meeting Gwen at the café. That wasn't by chance, was it? I wasn't a last-minute replacement for Gwen's friend."

"Not at all," Rosamunde said.

I gazed, unseeing, into the distance, trying to process this latest information, which was both creepy and sort of comforting. All through my life, people that I didn't even know had been keeping an eye on me. And now they had brought me here, to the duchy.

The crows on the branch above us cawed raucously and flew off over the forest, toward the mountain peaks. "Perhaps we should start back," Rosamunde said.

We turned, heading toward the path that led out of the cemetery. Thoughts tumbled through my brain, as if tossed by a blustery breeze. "Albert dreamed about his own death, didn't he? Do you think he recognized it as a premonition?"

"It's possible. He was clearly a vivid dreamer. Even so, he didn't accept his fate, not entirely. As you'll remember, he convinced my father to change their route through the mountains. Between that decision and Albert's choice to divert the soldiers, he saved six lives—six people who would have been gunned down in the pass." Her voice lowered to a whisper. "Including my father."

"Oh, Rosamunde, I'm so thankful for that." I was glad that Rosamunde's father had lived and that Grandpa hadn't given up, in spite of the dream. Still, he had deliberately put himself in harm's way. His actions were brave but suicidal. "Do you think Albert was convinced he was going to die? In a way, he'd already experienced his death, even if it was a dream."

"It's something I've wondered about," Rosamunde said. "In fact, I discussed it with my father once, shortly before he died. He pointed out something to me. Even if the Yank believed that he was fated to die, in the end, he did it on his own terms. He didn't die as a victim, gunned down in a narrow pass. No. He chose to dupe the Germans, to lead them away. He sacrificed his life for the good of his friends and the people under his care."

"So, his death had meaning."

"Very much so. Afterward, some people thought that Albert should be made an honorary Guzo. But I'm sorry to say, nothing ever came of it."

I thought back to my own vivid dream of Gwen's murder. Albert had changed the course of events. Could we do the same? "Do you think we can keep Gwen alive?"

"We've taken precautions already. And we will take more once she comes back to us. So, yes, I am confident we can keep her safe." She sighed. "Of course, it would help if we knew who wanted to kill her. And why."

As we walked across the graveyard, the convent's spire and bell tower and walls came into view above the stone walls on the other side of the road. I now understood that it was my own grandfather who had spent time hidden away in the convent's cellar.

Just then, a disquieting idea struck me. "What about Peter? Does he know that Albert is my grandfather? Oh, my God, does everyone in the duchy know?"

"No, no, only Gwen and I do. The dreamers may have their suspicions, of course. And Peter too. He's always been intuitive."

I parted from Rosamunde at the entrance to the cemetery and walked back to the convent, then into the museum, eager to talk to Peter. He was in his office.

"Did you find out about Al's last mission?" he asked.

"That and more." I explained that Al was my grandfather, and Rosamunde and Gwen had contrived to bring me here to allow me to learn about him. Peter looked sympathetic but unsurprised.

"Whew. That's a lot to find out in one morning." He got up and gathered me into his arms, a little awkwardly at first, since one arm was in a cast. I nestled against him. Then suddenly, unexpectedly, I broke down, sobbing against his shoulder, while he patted my back. I'm not sure where the tears came from. It felt like some kind of psychic dam had cracked and burst open, releasing a torrent of emotional pain, generations worth. By the time I stopped crying, I felt drained, but in the way that a good long cry can wash away the worst of your grief or disappointment.

"Peter, tell me the truth. Did you know all along that Albert was my grandfather?"

"No, I didn't. Although I have to admit, the possibility did cross my mind. Rosamunde was surprisingly keen on having you read the journal."

A few minutes later, we were sitting at my work table. There, we talked more about Albert and about World War II in the duchy. Finally, I offered to write an introduction for the transcribed book. "I suppose we should get a photo of the grave," I said.

"I can do that," Peter said.

"You don't suppose anyone has a picture of Albert?" It occurred to me that I'd never seen a photo of my grandfather. Or had I? Maybe it was time to go through Grandma's old photographs.

"There are hardly any photos from World War II," Peter said. "But I can take a look. You know, I imagine some of the old goat herders will remember your grandfather. They should be at the dining hall for lunch."

I looked at my watch. Half past twelve. We hurried out of the convent, across the plaza, and up the street to the dining hall. When we walked inside, we were surrounded by savory aromas and friendly chatter. Six old goat herders, including the elfish Roderick and his small sidekick, Oswin, were assembled at their long table. We walked over and stopped at the far end.

"Welcome," Roderick said in his rich baritone. He looked at me and cocked his head. "Anything wrong?" I realized my eyes must be puffy and bloodshot after my crying jag.

"Actually, we have good news," Peter said.

"In that case, set yourselves down," said the gray-bearded guy next to Peter. I remembered he was the one who had a brother in Wyoming and a fear of rattlesnakes.

Peter and I pulled chairs over and sat.

"What's the good news?" asked Roderick.

Peter cleared his throat politely. "Remember the Yank who lived here for a time during the war?"

"The airman, you mean?" Roderick asked.

"That's the fellow," Peter said.

"And a fine bloke, he was," said the guy with the crooked nose and missing teeth, the one who had been in the Merchant Marines. "For a Yank." The others nodded and murmured their agreement.

Peter leaned forward, enunciating clearly, presumably for the goat herders who were hard of hearing. "I'm happy to report that Holly here is the Yank's granddaughter." I blushed madly as everyone's eyes turned to me. "She found out today when she visited the Yank's grave."

"So that's it," Roderick said, slapping his leg. "I reckoned there was something familiar about you, my girl. I knew your granddad, I did. I was little more than a boy at the time. But I looked up to him. He knew his way around the mountains, as if he'd been born among us. But he never showed a speck of pride in it. And he always had a kind word for everyone."

Oswin, his wrinkled pal, began to chant happily. "Yank-o-lass, yank-o-lass, yank-o-lass."

"That's right," Roderick said, grinning. "The lass is the Yank's granddaughter."

From there, the men took turns coming up with stories and anecdotes involving the Yank, many featuring Rosamunde's father and occasionally Anne-Marie, the future duchess and Albert's friend.

The stories warmed me and allowed me to form a fuller picture of my grandfather and his place among the Guzos. At last, I thanked them for sharing their memories. "I read my grandfather's journal," I said, "the one he had hidden in the cabin. I think he cared deeply for the people of St. Uguzo. And now I understand why."

Violet, the chef, appeared at Peter's elbow, wearing her apron and head-scarf with the bright tropical colors. "If you want lunch, it's now or never," she said. Peter and I thanked her and headed for the serving table, where we picked up trays. Violet filled bowls with stew and laid small loaves of bread beside them. "Wait here," she said, and returned with bowls of stewed apricots with a dollop of whipped cream on top. "This is to celebrate your fine news," she said, grinning. "I was eavesdropping, which I imagine will come as no surprise." I could see that Violet was probably an active link in the duchy gossip chain.

We thanked Violet and returned to the goat herders' table, where we ate our lunch as the men proceeded to discuss goats, weather, and a recent soccer game, leaving Peter and me to eat, undisturbed. Actually, their conversation hardly registered with me, since a jumble of thoughts kept swirling through my head.

When we were finished eating, a young woman bussed the table, and the men pulled out their pipes. They turned to me, plying me with friendly questions. How was my visit going? Did I like the duchy? I told them I liked the duchy very much and described my activities transcribing the journal and helping out with the play. I also said I was looking forward to Gwen's return in time for the Ceremony of Allegiance on Saturday.

"Gwen is a fine lass," said Gray-Beard. "Odd to find out she's a spook. And you too. I would never have pegged you for a spy. Imagine that, work-ing for the CIA."

I had taken a swallow of water, and I spewed it out across the table. "A spy?" I croaked between coughs. "What are you talking about? I'm not a spy."

Gray-Beard laughed. "They said you'd deny it right quick."

"And who are they?" Peter demanded, red-faced. "Who's telling these lies?

The men shifted on their chairs and glanced among themselves. "It was just talk," said Gray-Beard. "Foolish jabber."

"Yes, but who started it?" Peter said. "This is important. Think back."

The men conferred for a few moments and decided it was Wilheard who had come up with the story. Or maybe Sebastian. Or both.

"Sebastian," Peter hissed between gritted teeth. "I might have known."

"Well, none of it is true," I said. "I've never worked for the U.S. government and certainly not for the CIA. And from what I've seen, Gwen is one hundred percent Guzo. I can't imagine her stooping so low as to spy for another country. Even a friendly one."

The men nodded their agreement. "I thank you for setting us straight," said Roderick.

Gray-Beard harrumphed. "I never believed all that rot. There's folks have nothing better to do than spread lies about their betters."

After a warm farewell, Peter and I left the dining hall and strolled down to the plaza, where we stopped to watch men erecting the stage where the dignitaries would sit at the Ceremony of Allegiance. I'd heard the sound of hammers and saws from a distance but hadn't watched the workers up close. Their job looked nearly complete, the stage rising well above the plaza and nearly stretching across one side of the open space.

"I guess I'll go back to the house," I said. The fact was, I was feeling shaky. I wanted to be alone, eat chocolate, play my penny whistle, and process everything I'd learned.

"Right," Peter said. "You know, you can skip rehearsal tonight, if you like. I can find someone else to read Anwen's lines. By the way, I called Monique and left a message on her phone machine, asked if she would be willing to play Anwen. I hope I'll hear back soon."

"So do I," I said. I still wasn't thrilled with the idea of Monique as Anwen, but better she than me. And once she signed on, I could return to working on props. I hadn't seen anything of Tony since his father's burial, which was worrisome, since he and I seemed to be the Props Committee.

Peter leaned over and kissed me on the cheek. "Take care of yourself. I'll see you later."

I climbed the grassy hill behind the house, sat on a fairly level spot, and played my penny whistle, starting with a couple of my favorite seafaring songs: "The Hills of Isle Au Haut" and "Shenandoah." Their haunting melodies put me in mind of people far from home who missed the people they loved, ideas that resonated strongly with me. I would love to sit and talk with my roommate, M.J., or my sister Valerie, to describe everything that had happened to me here, to make sense of it.

After a while, I noticed that my pal, Montie the Marmot (or a close relative,) was sunning himself on a large rock nearby. He stayed through a medley of spirituals, beginning with "Balm in Gilead" and "Go Tell it on the Mountain," a song that seemed appropriate for my surroundings. I finished with the Beatles' "Let It Be." Happily for me, Montie's taste in music was eclectic. By the time the afternoon shadows had lengthened, I was feeling calmer.

At six-thirty, I met Peter at the dining hall. Over a bowl of Violet's tasty squash and apple soup, he told me he'd learned that Monique was out of town until Friday, so she wouldn't be playing Anwen in our production. He didn't bother saying the obvious, that it was looking increasingly likely that I would take the role of the first duchess.

The warm soup and fresh bread performed their revitalizing magic. "I should be able to attend rehearsal," I said.

"Thanks," Peter said. "Since we're doing a run-through, I'm not sure how I would have managed without you."

"I also intend to confront Wilheard, find out why he accused me and Gwen of being spies." I wasn't looking forward to it. I'd never been good at standing up for myself, especially with overbearing men, but I wasn't the only one who had been maligned. I had Gwen's reputation to think of too. So, I couldn't just let it go. It was true that Gwen had let me down by leaving the duchy, but she had also gone out of her way to get me here. And now I understood why. I thought back to the interview she had given me when I was in high school, working on the school paper. She must have known who I was, even then.

"Would you like backup for your confrontation?" Peter asked. "I'll be on my best behavior. I promise."

I patted his good arm. "That's okay. I think I can handle it."

Several minutes later, I was standing outside the gym, waiting for Wilheard to show up. As the actors and crew arrived, they all remarked on the news that I was descended from the Yank. Apparently, they had all heard of him in one way or another. One of the king's courtiers said I must be glad to have such a heroic grandfather. If only Mom could hear this, I thought.

Wilheard was late as usual. It was dark out, and I was standing outside the glare of the overhead light, so he didn't see me as he barreled to the door.

I gathered my courage and stepped forward. "I'd like a word with you. In private."

"Can't now," he gruffed. "I'm late."

I stepped between him and the gym door. "They can wait."

He mumbled a curse. "Oh, all right. I guess I don't need Peter's girl-friend on my case."

Peter's girlfriend? We had become an item, it seemed. Wilheard and I walked a few yards away, to a shadowy bench with a view of the soccer field. We sat at opposite ends.

"What's this all about?" Wilheard asked. "The photo album? I thought Sebastian took care of that."

"This is different. There's a story going around that Gwen and I are spies for the CIA, and I understand you started it."

He barked a laugh. "Oh, is that all? I heard it too, at the mead hall. Nothing to do with me."

I suddenly remembered my conversation with Sebastian at the internet café, when I had told him that my sister Valerie worked for the government. He had immediately decided she was an intelligence operative. "It was Sebastian, wasn't it? He started the rumor."

"I told him it was a bad idea. But he wouldn't listen." So, the accusation wasn't some spur-of-the-moment thing. Sebastian had planned it ahead of time. Wilheard was facing away from me, gazing into the distance. He had lost his bluster, and in the shadowy light, he looked tired and forlorn. I remembered the photo of him as a scruffy kid in Indiana. A moody child, maybe destined to have a hard life. For the first time, I saw him not as Sebastian's friend and partner in crime but as his boss's unhappy minion.

"Wilheard," I said, "what's going on? Why does Sebastian want to turn people against me? And against Gwen?"

He frowned, and I waited, growing impatient, until finally he mumbled something like, "Oh, what the f***. If you really want to know, Sebastian thinks that Gwen will come back and proclaim herself duchess. And you're hanging around the duchy, waiting to tell her when the time is right."

"What?" I thought back to my trip to Bois with Sebastian, when he had repeatedly offered to drop me off at Gwen's hideaway. "First off, I have no idea where Gwen is. As I told Sebastian more than once. And second, Gwen has no intention of being duchess." I paused. "And third, as I understand it, nobody can just proclaim himself duke. Or duchess. The council has to agree. Anyway, why would Sebastian care if Gwen became duchess? He's not a Guzo."

"It's complicated."

"Complicated how?"

"Just...complicated." He picked up a pebble and hurled it off into the darkness. "The fact is, I'm getting tired of the guy. He doesn't fit in here, and I don't like how he treats Eglentyne. But I'm stuck with him."

"I know he's your boss," I said, "but he's a troublemaker. Can't you get rid of him somehow?"

"It's too late for that."

I stood, frustrated by Wilheard's unwillingness to take on his boss. Maybe it was just too much to ask.

"Hey," Wilheard said, "you're still going on the cheese tour tomorrow, aren't you?"

"Count me out." The prospect of spending even an hour with Sebastian was stomach-turning. I could put up with quite a lot for a piece of duchy cheese, but this was too much.

"Look. You have to be there. Fred only set up the tour because he thought you wanted one. If you don't show up, it will look bad."

I didn't mind embarrassing Sebastian, but Wilheard sounded desperate. Maybe it would reflect badly on him if I didn't show up. Besides, Fred had been kind to set up the tour, especially to please me. And then, there was the cheese. "All right. I'll meet you at the cheesery. But Sebastian had better show up with a heart-felt apology. For me and for Gwen. He can't just go around destroying people's reputations."

"I'll pass on your message," Wilheard said, and his smirky smile suggested he didn't mind telling his boss.

Peter had been right to suggest that I skip rehearsal. My head was still in World War II with my grandfather, when I wasn't obsessing over

Sebastian's nerve at calling me a spy. Needless to say, this didn't help my performance. Even reading from the play book, I missed cues and stood in the wrong places. When the rehearsal finally ended, I stuck around to check props, but Peter stopped me. "Go home," he ordered. "We'll have a technical rehearsal tomorrow night, and we can deal with props then."

Back at the house, I trudged up the stairs, brushed my teeth, and went to bed. But sleep didn't come. Instead, I lay under the quilt, my exhausted brain reeling through a series of disjointed images: my grandfather's tombstone, a secluded hut in the woods, Clive's corpse in the pool below the Falls, his wife and children walking across the cemetery, Tony at the mead hall shouting about Wilheard's dirty hands, and a mysterious, lethal figure—like the one in my vivid dream—skulking among us.

Slowly, my befuddled mind quieted, and my thoughts turned back to the young airman who had come here fifty years before me. I whispered his name, my grandfather's name. "Albert Becker Fleming."

And then I remembered where I'd seen his name written. It was in a book of poetry by Robert Frost. I'd found it when I was a kid nosing around Grandma's house. On the first page were words written in careful cursive: "With warmest regards, Albert Becker Fleming." At the time, I was surprised to find the book, because Grandma wasn't a big poetry reader. And of course I was curious about the man who had signed it. I showed her the first page. "Who is this guy?" I'd asked, greedy for information, the juicier the better.

She flushed and took the book from me. "A boy who courted me once. A long time ago."

And now I knew who had courted her. "Grandpa," I whispered, "I have found you at last."

And in spite of all I'd been told, I now realized that Albert Fleming was no coward. Not by a long shot. He was a man of principle and courage. And perhaps that meant that I too had bravery in my genes.

CHAPTER TWENTY-ONE

Day 11, Tuesday

Tuesday morning was sunny, with a chilly breeze, alerting us that winter wasn't far off. I ate yogurt and jam for breakfast. Since coming to the duchy, I'd eaten lots of hearty meals, and I was sure that it was only the multiple daily slogs up and down the road that had kept me from putting on weight. Across the table from me, Peter shoveled down eggs, cheese, and bread with his good right hand. If only I had his metabolism. I was happy to see that both his beautiful hazel eyes were now open, although the bruises around his eye and on his jaw had turned a deep purple.

Peter had gotten in late the night before, and we hadn't had a chance to talk. So I filled him in on the conversation I'd had with Wilheard before rehearsal. Peter wasn't surprised that Sebastian had started the rumor about Gwen and me working for the CIA. "I think Wilheard and Sebastian have had a falling out," I said. "Or are about to have one. Wilheard doesn't like the way his boss treats Eglentyne."

Peter raised an eyebrow. "Interesting. I suppose that reflects well on Wilheard."

"I'll see them this afternoon at one-thirty. For the cheesery tour. I was going to pull out, but I guess Fred is expecting me."

I sipped my tea, remembering that the council would come to a decision about my project tomorrow, and with any luck, I would start collecting data on the celebration right away. "Do you still think the council will approve my project?" I asked, eager for reassurance.

"I don't see why not," Peter said, slathering jam on his bread. "Rosamunde and I will back you. Besides, now everyone knows that you're the Yank's granddaughter. That will be in your favor too."

He had a point. I still felt a little glow from the warm greetings I'd received the night before at rehearsal.

"In that case," I said, "I think I'll take the bus to Bois this morning. Any idea where I can find a cheap camera and a tape recorder?"

"No need to go to Bois, unless you really want to," Peter said. "I have an extra camera and a few rolls of film. You're welcome to use them. In return, you can share your photos of the celebration with me. And the museum has a tape recorder. Borrow it if you like. There are several empty cassettes. Just replace them before you leave."

I thanked him heartily and planted a kiss on his cheek in a spot that wasn't bruised. I hadn't been sure if my small stash of francs would stretch far enough to pay for the equipment. Surely, no student had ever started a field work project as ill prepared as I was. But now, with my equipment needs taken care of, I could dedicate my morning to doing laundry and bringing my personal notebook up to date.

After climbing the stairs, I sat cross-legged on my bed, with my notebook on my lap, trying to remember what the goat herders had told me about my grandfather the day before. I should have jotted everything down immediately, but it didn't occur to me until I got up that morning that I could probably use some of the old guys' memories in my foreword to my grandfather's journal.

When I'd finished with my notes, I gathered up my dirty clothes and took them downstairs. As I scrubbed my clothes in the deep kitchen sink, my thoughts turned to my mother. Mom was a tall, attractive brunette with a short, feathery perm. She had survived not only the trials of bringing up two daughters, but a nasty divorce from my father, and periodic setbacks in her career as a small-town realtor. In fact, for all her fears of abandonment and disaster, she had mostly thrived.

A couple of years after Dad left us, I had a long talk with him at his new house. He had loved Mom, he said, in spite of all her fears and gloomy predictions. What finally turned him against her was her inability to forgive. He proceeded to remind me of a time when Valerie and I were small.

"I was working in a carpentry shop," he said. "The owner was a good salesman, but he was a lousy carpenter. He always wanted me to take short-cuts, to save on time and materials. One day, I'd had enough, and I up and quit. That night, when I told your mom, she was furious. Okay. This happened right before Christmas, and maybe I should have talked to her first. But we weren't that bad off. I mean, we had to cut back on gifts and decorations. Still, we weren't sleeping in the street. And I found another job a few weeks later. But she never let me forget that Christmas. She held onto every grudge for months, even years. I don't want you and Val to be like that."

I knew what he meant about Mom. Not only had she never let go of her bitterness over her absent father, she had allowed it to spill over into all our lives. Valerie refused to take on Mom's grievances, but I had an unfortunate tendency to hoard my own. Valerie could shrug it off and advised me to do the same, but I wasn't as successful.

Okay, Mom, I thought. It's time you learned the truth about your father. And maybe you can even forgive him. At least a little. In a week or two, I would go back to the States, where Mom and I would have a long moth-er-daughter chat.

But in the meantime, I needed to concentrate on the duchy celebration. As soon as I got the okay, I would let Dr. Ferris know, either by phone or e-mail. Then I would be very busy for the next few days, as I observed the preparations and the festivities, interviewed people, and helped out with the play, all the time soaking up duchy culture. After that, I'd have a week or so to finish up my data collection and spend time with Peter. Maybe take a leisurely walking tour of Bois.

That afternoon, I walked directly from the dining hall to the cheesery, only stopping at the museum to tell Peter I'd be back soon. The cheesery lay beyond the convent but on the same road, across from the cemetery. it was a modern, one-story concrete building. The entrance had glass windows, but the rest of the building had none. I'd walked around the building one day but had never stepped inside. The convent and museum had attracted me like a magnet, and I hadn't felt much need to stray.

Outside the building sat a navy-blue van with the words "Duchy Cheesery" stenciled in white on the door. And across the road, I spotted Sebastian's little red Ferrari, with Sebastian and Wilheard inside. It was unusual to see a private car, since everyone in the duchy walked.

Sebastian got out. "Greetings," he said, walking toward me with a slight limp. A lock of dark brown hair fell across an eyebrow, and his gray eyes were alert. "Wilheard tells me I owe you an apology."

"And do you?" I asked, frostily. He would have to work hard for my good will.

"I assure you, Holly, this spy thing is all a misunderstanding."

"So, you're saying that you never called me or Gwen a spy for the CIA?"

He cocked his head in a way that might have been endearing if I didn't distrust the guy. "Let me provide a little context here," he said. "A few nights ago, Wilheard and I were at the mead hall, kidding around with the men. I admit, I'd had too much of the local mead. Have you tried it?"

"Not yet."

"Well, let me tell you, it packs a punch. You think you've been drinking moderately, and suddenly you realize you're completely blotto."

I stared at him, an eyebrow raised, not giving an inch.

"Anyway, I must have blurted out something about you and Gwen being spies. It seemed hilarious at the moment. Wilheard and I both laughed. Who would have thought anyone would take it seriously?"

"The goat herders did."

"Those old geezers. Could they have been pulling your leg? Pretending they believed the story?"

"I don't think so." They had seemed serious to me, and Peter appeared to think so too. Was it possible that we'd both been taken in by a duchy prank? I could see how a little drunken humor could get out of hand.

"In any case, you have my profoundest apology. I meant no harm." He shook his head. "God. I hope that's my last apology for a very long time. I've eaten a lot of humble pie this week." He turned to the car and beckoned Wilheard, who unfolded his hefty figure from the sporty car and joined us.

As I said hello to Wilheard, I noticed that he was looking jittery. "Are you okay?" I asked.

"Yeah," he mumbled.

"He's just nervous about the cheese," Sebastian said. He lowered his voice, as if we were pals sharing a secret. "He's not very good with new foods. And duchy cheese has quite a reputation."

Oh dear. Poor Wilheard. I knew people with food phobias, including my freshman year roommate, who would never try anything new. No Indian food or Thai. Just burgers, pizza, and anything white.

"Don't worry about the cheese," I said. "It's delicious." Wilheard smiled weakly.

We all walked through the doors into a sunny room with a long counter, chairs on two sides. A large poster on one wall looked like an enlargement of a photo and showed cows grazing in a pasture against the backdrop of snow-peaked mountains.

A moment later, Alice came through a swinging door from the back. She was dressed in a long white apron over slacks and a blouse. Her sandy hair was pulled into a braid that wound around the back of her head. "Good day. We've been expecting you," she said, smiling. Her gray-blue eyes looked clearer than they had the last time I'd seen her. Maybe she was starting to recover a little from the trauma of her husband's death. "If you'll have a seat, Fred will be right with you."

She ushered us into a room off the entrance, where a dozen chairs were set up in three rows, facing an easel supporting a large whiteboard divided into several squares, apparently outlining the cheese-making process. The three of us sat in the front row, Wilheard next to me.

Fred swept in, making a dramatic entrance, his tall, fit figure covered by a white apron over gray slacks and a long-sleeve shirt. His bald head gleamed under the overhead light. "Welcome to the duchy cheesery," he said. "I'm glad you could all make it." He explained that Clive usually conducted the tours. "He was an excellent cheesemaker and a great deal more amusing than I am," Fred said. I glanced at Alice, whose eyes were downcast.

Fred proceeded to guide us through the squares on the whiteboard, each one with a photograph or drawing. "Here is a group of our fine duchy cows," he said, pointing with a long stick to a smaller version of the photo on the wall, with plump cows spread out across a pasture. "They spend the summer in the upper pastures, but now they are back in their winter digs." He then pointed to the second picture, which showed four milk cans sitting on a cart. "Here at the cheesery, we receive milk twice a day from the cow herders. The raw milk is kept cool overnight before the cheese-making process begins the following day."

Sitting next to me, Wilheard fidgeted, one thumb nervously rubbing the palm of his other hand. I was surprised that Eglentyne hadn't shared her cheese with him. Then he wouldn't be so scared of it.

Fred pointed to the third picture, which featured a large vat and a man in an apron, holding what looked like a thermometer. "The milk is first heated gently and held for about two hours. This allows the organisms that contribute to the final, unique flavor to develop. These, by the way, are all naturally occurring bacteria of several sorts that are native to our locale."

Wilheard's foot tapped audibly.

"Next," Fred continued, "we mix in rennet to begin forming the curd."

Sebastian eyed Wilheard, then stepped forward to stand beside Fred. "I say, mate, this is very informative. But might I make a suggestion? Could we sample the cheese now?"

"The tasting comes at the end," Fred said, shooting Sebastian a look of disdain that would have been in character for the abbess he would be playing that evening.

"Yes, I'm aware of that," Sebastian said. Then he moved in closer and whispered something in Fred's ear. Fred glanced at me, hesitated, then nodded to Sebastian. I was pretty sure that Sebastian had fingered me as the one who couldn't sit through a lecture on cheese making. What a jerk.

"All right," Fred said. "Just this once." He turned to Alice, who was standing at the back of the room. "Let's serve the cheese."

Alice left the room, returning a minute later, holding a tray with a large wedge of cheese, about a fourth of a wheel, which she placed on a table beside the easel.

Fred picked up a shiny silver cheese slicer and cut three narrow wedges of cheese, which he placed on squares of butcher paper. "This cheese has aged for nine months. I think you'll find it has an excellent flavor and texture." Alice stepped up and passed out the cheese.

After Sebastian's insistence on tasting the cheese immediately, I expected him to dig right in, but instead he said, "Ladies first."

It was an outmoded sentiment, but my senses were already prepared for the sublime treat, so I broke off a piece and took a bite. A horrible, noxious taste erupted in my mouth. "Eew!" I cried and spit the cheese out on the paper, my eyes tearing.

Fred stared at me in horror, broke off a piece from my wedge, and popped it into his mouth. Instantly, his face crumpled in revulsion, and he too spit out the cheese. "It's adulterated!" he croaked.

Alice gasped as she stared, wide-eyed. "It can't be. Can it?"

I hoped that adulterated didn't mean poisoned. I hadn't swallowed the cheese, but even so...

Fred groaned and raised his broad hands to cover his face. Poor Fred. Poor Guzos! I could only imagine what disasters would ensue once word got out that the duchy cheese was bad. Or even poisoned. Had all the cheese been ruined or just that one wheel?

While Fred bent over the large wedge of cheese, examining every inch, Wilheard and Sebastian returned their samples to the table. Wilheard looked relieved. He hadn't had to taste the cheese after all, and his wariness was vindicated.

"Bad luck," Sebastian said. "Does this sort of thing happen often?"

"Never!" Fred boomed, causing Alice to stumble backward, nearly upsetting the easel. Fred returned to his examination of the offending cheese.

"I'll get Juliette," I said, and dashed out of the cheesery.

The door to the sheriff's office had been open when I walked into the convent courtyard, and I hoped that Juliette would still be there. But when I hurried down the road, I saw her striding ahead of me, heading for the bridge.

"Stop!" I shouted. "Juliette, stop!" She turned and saw me. My voice must have conveyed serious alarm, because she started jogging back in my direction.

Peter must have heard me too, because he appeared at the convent gate. "What's going on?"

As the three of us headed for the cheesery, I explained about the inedible cheese.

In the cheesery, Fred was pacing, but he stopped abruptly when he saw Juliette. "Someone has adulterated the cheese," he declared, his broad face stormy. "It's a wanton, criminal act."

Juliette maintained her calm. "This is very disturbing. But could it be the result of an accident? Some ordinary contaminant that somehow got into our cheese?"

Fred cast her a hard look. "I am a master cheesemaker. I'm familiar with the usual culprits. Fungus, of course, and various pathogens—listeria, e. coli, salmonella, and others. I assure you, I would know if any of them was responsible. Besides," he said, "I examined the cheese wheel closely and discovered a tiny hole the size of a needle. The site of an injection, if I'm not mistaken. And I'd wager it wasn't done recently. The contaminant—whatever it is—has spread through the cheese. That would take weeks or even months."

It suddenly occurred to me that I could have tasted something toxic. I hadn't swallowed anything, but still...

"Right," Juliette said. "You've made an excellent start. Why don't you and I inspect the premises and make sure no one has been hiding out here. Then we can all sit down and establish the facts, as we know them."

"I'll look outside," Peter said. "See if there are any signs of disturbance."

Meanwhile, I made a dash for the ladies' room, where I repeatedly rinsed out my mouth. Wouldn't it be just my luck if I came to the charming Duchy of St. Uguzo and died of poisoned cheese. I stood in front of the mirror, staring at the green-eyed girl looking back. Aside from a little flushing and slightly bloodshot eyes, I seemed to be okay. My throat hadn't closed up, and my extremities hadn't turned numb. I'd probably be okay, although I'd really like to know what was in that cheese. I suspected that the memory of that one disgusting bite would linger for a long time.

When I came out, Wilheard and Sebastian were sitting on molded plastic chairs under the big cow poster, and I sat down next to Alice in a chair along the adjoining wall, facing the windows. Alice's hands were clenched together on her lap. "I had thought the worst was over," she said quietly. "And now, this."

I pressed my hand against her arm. "I know."

"I only hope no one thinks my family was involved," she whispered.

I shared that hope. But both she and Clive had worked at the cheesery. And we already knew that Clive had sold cheese in Bois, against duchy rules. Even Tony had been drawn into the illegal sales, although Juliette hadn't divulged that information. It was only natural to wonder if Clive's misdeeds and death were connected in some way to the adulteration of the cheese.

I snuck a look at Wilheard, who was looking calmer, if a little pale. Could he be tangled up with the crime in some way? He'd been pretty nervous earlier. But he was such a gung-ho Guzo, it was hard to believe he would do something to endanger the duchy.

I gazed out the window, where the cemetery, with its groupings of headstones, filled my view. The poor duchy. It was sad that these calamitous events were occurring shortly before the celebration. Or was that part of someone's devious plan? I couldn't even begin to make sense of it all.

Fred, Juliette, and Peter returned soon, having found no signs of anyone lurking around the cheesery. They sat, and Juliette explained that she would like to ask everyone a few questions. Peter took notes, using a pad and pen that Alice had passed to him before settling next to me again.

Juliette asked Wilheard and Sebastian to describe their experience at the cheesery that day. Sebastian went first, explaining that he had asked Fred to let us sample the cheese early. "In deference to the lady," he said, nodding to me.

"Actually," I said, "I was enjoying the lecture on cheese making."

"In any case," Sebastian said, "I certainly didn't notice anything unusual." Wilheard basically repeated Sebastian's account. Juliette thanked them for their cooperation and told them they could go.

"I'm glad to hear that we're not suspects," Sebastian said.

"Until this is solved, everyone is a suspect," Juliette said. "But I have no reason to detain you."

"Good enough, Sheriff," Sebastian said, standing. He gave her a small, brisk salute.

"But I have one request," Juliette said. "Please keep all this to yourselves, at least until the council has had a chance to meet. I expect they will address the duchyites later today. In the meantime, the last thing we need is a bunch of wild rumors circulating." She eyed them both sharply. "Do I have your word that you'll say nothing until the council has met and made their announcement?"

"Absolutely," Sebastian said.

Wilheard nodded solemnly. "You have my word."

"Do you trust those two?" I asked Juliette after Sebastian and Wilheard had left the cheesery.

"Wilheard, maybe. Sebastian, I'm not so sure. Information is power. And those CIA rumors suggest that Sebastian knows how to manipulate information. The council needs to get on top of this, make a public statement before news of the contaminated cheese leaks out and people start to panic." But seriously, I can't just lock up the two of them until the council meets.

Juliette had already questioned Fred while they were looking around the cheesery, and Alice had little to add now. The day had been an ordinary one, aside from their preparations for the tour.

I described the tour pretty much as Sebastian and Wilheard had. "Oh, but there was one other thing. Wilheard was nervous about trying the cheese. I think that was the real reason that Sebastian wanted to get the tasting over with. Wilheard was a wreck."

Juliette and Peter exchanged a look.

"Apparently he has a fear of unfamiliar foods," I said.

"He told you that?" Juliette asked.

"Yes. Well, no, Sebastian did. You don't think that Wilheard is involved in ruining the cheese? I had to admit, he was pretty nervous about trying the cheese. Maybe a little too nervous, even for someone with a food phobia.

"We'll keep it in mind," Juliette said. She turned to Fred. "You said the cheesery is padlocked at night."

"Here's my key," he said, removing a keychain from his apron pocket. "When Clive worked here, he also had one."

"I have it now," Alice said, holding up her key. "My husband kept it behind the pickle jar, and so do I."

Unfortunately, Fred admitted sheepishly, security was lax during working hours. When he stepped out to run an errand or worked in other parts of the cheesery, he sometimes left the door unlocked. The padlock was rusty and hard to turn, he said, and he didn't like to bother with it.

"In other words," Juliette said, "it would have been fairly easy for someone to sneak in, inject the cheese, and sneak out."

"So it would seem," Fred said, glumly. "But who would do such a thing? Outsiders hardly ever find their way to the cheesery. And no Guzo in his right mind would sabotage the duchy."

"It's a puzzle," Juliette agreed. "So, let's continue collecting the information we need to solve it."

Fred nodded. "We'd better get the cheese analyzed, find out what's in it." Fortunately, he had a friend who was a chemist at a reputable lab in Lyon. "With your permission, I'll give LaBecque a call."

"Yes, please do," Juliette said. "We'll cover the cost of the testing, whatever it is." With that, Fred strode into his office, closing the door behind him.

"I suppose we should notify the council members," Peter said. "That won't be a pleasant task."

"No, but the sooner the better. I'm afraid Claude lives across the valley. And he doesn't have a phone, so he can only be reached by foot. Or contacted by a good yodeler."

"I'm afraid my yodeling skills are rusty," Peter said, grinning. "But I know where he lives. I'll find him." After a little discussion, he and Juliette decided to schedule a council meeting in the group's usual spot, a side room at the dining hall. Juliette suggested they tentatively schedule the public announcement for five o'clock at the plaza.

A laugh carried from Fred's office, and a minute later, Fred emerged, looking a little more upbeat. "LaBecque says they're swamped right now, but he'll give our cheese top priority once I get it to the lab."

"You must be very good friends," Juliette said.

"He'll get a wedge of duchy cheese in return for the favor," Fred said. "I trust you don't mind."

"This is a crisis," Juliette said. "Rules can be bent."

He and Alice quickly packed up the tainted wedge of cheese, as well as a few wheels of cheese from different locations in the cheesery, and loaded them into the cheesery van. Fred climbed into the driver's seat, and we wished him bon voyage, knowing he would be on the road for several hours.

A few minutes later, we all left the cheesery. I headed back to the house and up to my bedroom, where I wrote in my personal notebook about the disastrous morning. Even if I could never use these notes for anything formal, it helped to get the words out. The notebook had become like a close friend, one who would listen to my seemingly endless worries without complaint. I am embarrassed to say that I wasn't thinking only of the calamity set to befall the duchy. It was my own prospects that stressed me out most. How upset would the council members be? Enough to turn down my project? I would have liked to talk to Rosamunde, but she was on the council and had no doubt been rounded up for the emergency meeting.

I was at the stove, making tea when I heard Peter come in the front door. A moment later he stood at the kitchen doorway. He looked tired and disheveled; a lock of brown hair stuck to his damp forehead.

"Did you find Claude?" I asked.

"Finally. I hiked across the valley only to discover he was visiting his daughter over here."

"Oof," I said with a grimace. "But at least the councilors have all been notified, right?"

"Yes, and they've gathered at the dining hall. I understand they're coming up with an announcement, even as we speak." He walked over beside me and leaned back against the counter. I put my arms around him, and he enclosed me in a long, warm hug, made only slightly clunky by the cast on his arm.

"I'm making tea," I said. "Want a cup?"

He nuzzled my ear. "I have a better idea."

Half an hour later, we were at the kitchen table, slurping tea and nibbling cashews from Peter's private stash.

"Are things really as bad as they seem?" I asked.

Peter sank back in his chair. "Once word gets out that our cheese is adulterated, I doubt if any of our clients will order more. Even if the damage is limited, and we're able to destroy all the bad cheese, people will still be reluctant to buy it. All it will take is a rumor of contamination to put people off for a very long time."

I grimaced. "But you'll be all right for a while?"

"For a few months, maybe. But once sales start to dry up, the museum will be the first thing to close down. I may as well get my resumé up to date, because I'll soon be looking for a job."

"Oh no," I moaned. The museum meant everything to Peter. He loved the place and his work there.

"Afraid so. And I don't know how much longer the old goat herders will receive free meals. Then there's the clinic and the school. I suppose enough money can be scraped up to keep them going, but it will be hard."

"That's so sad." The duchy had seemed so idyllic, a tiny, mostly comfortable nation, where everyone's basic needs were met. Like Sweden or Denmark, only much smaller and quirkier.

"Actually, if truth be told," Peter said, "something like this was bound to happen sooner or later. We've depended on the cheese for too long. Everyone knew we needed to diversify, to open up new channels of revenue. But the council lacked the cooperation and willpower they needed to make the necessary changes. Now they will have to. I just hope it can be done wisely and not in a crazy panic."

A bell tolled in the distance. Bong. Bong. Bong. Bong. "It's the bell in the convent tower," Peter said.

"So it really does ring." It must have sounded familiar and even reassuring as it called the sisters to prayer hundreds of years ago. But it could also have warned Guzos of an attack or some other danger. Just as it did now.

Peter scraped back his chair. "Time for the council's announcement," he said.

"Do you think they'll manage to put a positive spin on it?"

"This is the duchy. I expect they'll tell the unvarnished truth. Fortified with an appeal to Guzo patriotism."

The day had cooled, and I shrugged into my coat before walking down the road beside Peter. When we neared the plaza, I saw that a crowd of a hundred or more had already formed, their voices raised in clamorous excitement. We nudged our way forward, the Guzos in front of us making space, then closing ranks around us.

At the plaza, the stage had already been set up for the Ceremony of Allegiance, and all six members of the Duchy Council, plus Juliette, were standing on it, talking among themselves. It was the first time I'd seen the group of two women and four men. They were ordinary-looking people, mostly middle-aged, the women with shawls and the men in kerchiefs. I had probably passed most of them in one place or another.

A dais stood at the front of the stage, and a few steps behind it stood Rosamunde, in her long skirt and rust-colored shawl, looking over the throng, nodding to people occasionally, when she caught their eye. Next to her was Baptiste, in the bright blue jacket he'd worn at the Falls, when he'd helped extract Clive's body from the pond. His deep red kerchief contrasted nicely with the blue. He was leaning down slightly to listen to Juliette, who was at his side.

A familiar girlish voice piped up beside me. "Maybe somebody famous is coming," Kessie said. "A movie star. Or Princess Diana."

"That would be nice," I said, wishing it were true. At least, if the teenagers hadn't learned of the crisis, the information must not have leaked out yet.

Baptiste raised his hand, and the assembled Guzos quieted. Rosamunde stepped up to the dais. I didn't see any kind of sound system, and I wondered if her voice would carry across the square, but I needn't have worried. For a small lady, she had a powerful voice. "Fellow Guzos," she called out, "this afternoon we learned some troubling news. And we want you to hear about it from us, firsthand. Our master cheesemaker, Fred Haroldson, discovered that a wheel of cheese in the cheesery has been adulterated. It can't be eaten."

A shocked hush was followed by a rumble of voices. Rosamunde held up her hand, waiting until the noise had subsided.

"We don't know yet how many wheels of cheese were affected. And we have not identified the source of the contamination. Fred is on his way to Lyon with several wheels. They will be thoroughly examined at a reputable laboratory. We trust that the chemists will give us definitive answers soon. Based on this information, my fellow councilors and I will decide on suitable action."

"Was it an accident?" came a woman's voice from the crowd.

Rosamunde paused. "No, Felicity, I regret to say, we think the contamination was intentional." Gasps from the audience. "I know, it's hard to imagine anyone doing such a thing. But if we all cooperate fully, sharing what we know, I am certain we will get to the bottom of this."

A murmur rose then fell before Rosamunde spoke again. "Fellow Guzos, we will continue to give you information as we learn it. And we will try to do so in a way that will keep everyone safe. Are there questions?"

A man in front spoke up, and Baptiste repeated the question, so that everyone could hear. "Carl wants to know: How did Fred figure out the cheese was ruined? Was he dipping into the duchy cheese?"

Laughter erupted, breaking the tense mood.

"No, indeed," Rosamunde replied. "He was giving a tour of the cheesery to visitors. And may I point out that he is certain that the damage was done weeks or possibly months ago. So our recent visitors, Holly and Sebastian, are not active suspects."

Thank you, Rosamunde, I thought. What a wise friend she was.

Rosamunde nodded to Juliette, who stepped forward. "And now, our Sheriff has a few words for you."

Juliette's voice carried well, just like her mother's. "We have begun an investigation into the contamination of the cheese. As part of the process, I am interviewing a number of people. Don't be surprised if I, or one of my deputies, approaches you with questions. And please, come to see me if you have any information. Even if you're not sure it's relevant. I will hold whatever you say in confidence. Questions?"

A husky voice sounded from the middle of the throng. "Is this investigation going to be like the one to find Clive's killer? Seems like you haven't made any progress on that."

Juliette paused. "I understand your frustration, Daniel. I too had hoped we would have solid answers by now. At this point, we are still not certain whether Clive's death was accidental or deliberate. As you can imagine, we want to be clear about the facts before we start arresting people. But I promise you, Clive's death is still under active investigation. We won't give up until we find out what happened."

A woman's voice shouted out. "And when will that be? A year from now? Or ten? Or never?"

Before Juliette could respond, a deep, raspy voice shouted, "Maybe what we need is a real police department. And new leadership."

"Well said," cried a high voice, followed by similar sentiments.

Juliette raised her hand for silence, which came more slowly this time. "You are welcome to nominate a new council member, Hector. And you too, Harriet. In fact, everyone here is encouraged to do so. That's your right as citizens of St. Uguzo. These are all decisions for the council, but you all can have a voice."

A fellow pushed his way to the front, stood on a stair leading up to the stage, and faced the mass of Guzos. It was Bernard, Baptiste's younger brother, wearing a fiery red kerchief, his black hair tousled. "Maybe what we need is a duke," he shouted. "Like the old days. We need someone who's in charge. Who can get things done."

Baptiste walked over to him from the center stage, and they exchanged words.

Peter whispered to me, "I'm not sure if Bernard wants a duke or a dictator."

"You're wrong," Bernard said to his brother, loud enough to be heard. "This is exactly the right time. The right time and the right place." He faced the crowd once again. "We're having a rally on Friday night, at seven o'clock. Right here in the plaza. If you want a real duke, come and join us." He stepped down and was surrounded by young men, slapping him on the back and voicing their support. Excited voices filled the darkening air.

"Do you think Bernard wants to be duke?" I asked Peter.

He shrugged. "Yesterday I would have said no. Today I'm not so sure."

Rosamunde stood at the edge of the stage and raised her hand. Slowly, the noise subsided. "These are difficult times," she said. "I ask you all to remain calm. You have my word that the members of the council will listen to your concerns. And we will search for the best path forward. I would remind you, we have known dangerous times before, and we have always endured. We will do so again. Our greatest strength will always come from our unity in the face of genuine threats. From within or without."

Many people nodded, but grumbling came from several places as well.

She raised a hand. "Dear friends, we will meet again soon. In the meantime, peace be to you. And to all your loved ones. And God give you good evening."

And God give you good evening. A shiver prickled me, as if I'd been touched by some ancient breeze. Anwen might have uttered those words, or the sisters in the convent. And eventually the Wiskara must have said them, losing their language but not their identity. Too bad Rosamunde didn't want to be duchess. But I respected her for feeling at one with her bygone Wiskara ancestors and not with the squatters sent by the French king.

I looked at Peter, a direct descendant of Philippe and Anwen, the so-called squatters, and a guy who could legitimately aspire to be duke. At that point, I was a little biased, but I think most people would agree that Peter was a good man and a good Guzo. His devotion to the museum and duchy history demonstrated his loyalty, and he was the son of Duchess Anne-Marie's daughter. I thought back to the conversation I'd heard when I first arrived in the duchy. It seemed that several people had encouraged Peter to become duke, but to no avail. He didn't want the job or even a seat on the council. Why didn't he join the council or even become the new duke? And now it sounded like he was preparing to throw in the towel and leave the duchy. In some ways he was still a mystery to me.

The council members left the stage, and I turned to Peter, who looked glum. "Do you still want to rehearse tonight?"

"What? Oh, right. I don't see that we have much choice. It's the technical rehearsal. The lighting guy said he would be there." He gazed across the square. "In fact, there he is. I'll go have a word with him." With that, he strode off, leaving me with Kessie.

She turned to me. "You were on that tour, weren't you?"

"Unfortunately, yes."

Kessie's eyes widened. "Did you taste the cheese?"

"I'm afraid so."

"How was it? Gross?"

"Yes."

"I wish I'd been there," she grumbled. Of course. Kessie always wanted to be in the middle of the action. A girl about her age with a long, blond braid stepped beside her. "Guess what?" Kessie said. "Holly tasted the poisoned cheese."

"Cool," the girl said, clearly impressed.

A middle-aged couple standing next to us turned, and the woman speared me with her gaze. "It was you who discovered the tainted cheese?" she demanded.

"Well, I tasted it anyway. I'm not sure I discovered it."

"You're the Yank," the husband said. "Wasn't it you who found Clive's body?"

"We both did," Kessie said.

"So," the man said, eyeing me closely, "you uncovered the body and the tainted cheese too." The woman pursed her lips, as if she'd like to say what she thought of that, but she was showing restraint. Other people around us turned to gaze in my direction. I wanted to shrink away, but keeping a low profile is difficult when you're a foreigner, especially a tall one with long auburn hair.

A man in a paisley kerchief spoke up. "Oy, I hear you're a spy. For the CIA."

"She is not!" Kessie blurted. "That's a big, fat lie."

Inwardly, I glowered. How things had changed from yesterday, I thought, when everyone was kind and friendly. "What about my grandfather?" I longed to shout. "You know, the guy who saved all those lives." But clearly, these Guzos were not in the mood to hear about an old-time Yank. Not when they could find fault with a living, breathing one right in their midst.

Kessie pulled on my arm. "Let's go." We turned and wended our way through the mass of people now clearing out of the plaza. We soon found ourselves at the low wall along one side of the square. There, I saw Tony standing alone, his brows knit, looking deep in thought. Even so, I was glad to see a familiar face.

"Hey," I said, walking up to him, Kessie following.

He started. "I didn't wreck the cheese, if that's what you're thinking."

Apparently, I wasn't the only one under suspicion. "Well, I didn't either."

"Me neither," Kessie said.

"You sure?" Tony said with a lop-sided grin.

"Now that we've all established our innocence," I said, "I was wondering if you'll be returning to the play. Tonight is the technical rehearsal. We could really use your help with props."

"Maybe. I'll have to check with Sebastian."

"What do you mean? Why would you need his permission?"

Tony shifted his weight. "I'm working for him now. I'm his man. That's what he says, anyway."

I frowned. "You never seemed like the kind of guy who could be ordered around."

He stiffened. "I'm not. It's just that, well, Sebastian is arranging for me to enter an apprentice program for mechanics who work on Ferraris. It's very competitive, and he's pulling strings to get me in. So I do what he says."

I remembered now that Tony was eager to get out of the duchy. "That's very generous of Sebastian." And pretty manipulative, I thought. Was there really an apprenticeship waiting for Tony? "But aren't you a little young to be an apprentice?"

"I turn seventeen in December. That's old enough."

So, I thought, Tony is under Sebastian's control. I remembered what Juliette had said about Tony's outburst at the mead hall, how he'd said that Wilheard's hands were dirty. "Do you see much of Wilheard?" I asked. "I didn't think the two of you were especially friendly."

Tony gazed down at the ground. "He's okay. We get along."

I glanced at Kessie, who managed to look both uneasy and lovelorn. "Well," I said to Tony, "I hope I'll see you at rehearsal."

"Yeah. I'll see what I can do."

Later, as Peter and I walked to rehearsal together, I asked him the question that had been nagging at me ever since I learned the councilors were assembling that afternoon. "Will the council still meet tomorrow? They haven't forgotten my project, I hope."

"No. They're scheduled to meet at ten, and I'll be there to present your request. But Holly, I should warn you, the members are nervous, now that the duchy economy is in peril. The council members may not want outsiders reporting our problems to the wider world. I'll do my best, but your project may be a hard sell now."

I groaned. "But I'm only here to document the celebration. You know that. Tell the council that I will not write about the current political situation. Nothing about the tainted cheese."

"I know that's your intention," Peter said. "But I think you'll agree that ignoring politics is easier said than done. And the atmosphere surrounding the celebration is sure to be affected by Clive's death and the contaminated cheese."

"What if I give them final approval on what I write? I can delete anything they don't like."

"That might work," he said, but he didn't sound enthusiastic. Already, doubts and fears were bubbling up in me. How strongly would Peter champion me? Would the council refuse my request? This was beginning to feel uncomfortably familiar. Like having my academic career suddenly quashed by unfeeling faculty members, with no help from my advisor. Was disappointment my fate, just as Mom had warned me? I plucked up my flagging courage. "But you'll still defend my proposal, right?"

"Of course. You know I will. I just want you to be prepared for the outcome, whatever it may be."

"Okay," I mumbled.

He brushed my cheek with his hand, sending a pleasant shiver down my spine. "I'll do my very best. I know how important the study is to your career."

CHAPTER TWENTY-TWO

Day 12, Wednesday

I was on my second cup of tea the next morning when Peter joined me at the kitchen table. I had been worrying about the ten-o'clock council meeting, in which the group would consider my proposed project. I knew that Peter would do a good job of presenting it, but given the current troubles in the duchy, the decision could go either way. In my mind, I dwelt on the worst-case scenario, rehearsing how I would maintain my composure while reacting to the news that my project had been rejected. Would they really do that to me? Part of me refused to believe it.

"I meant to tell you yesterday," Peter said, pouring himself a cup of tea. "Mum called. She'll be arriving this afternoon. She reserved a car at the airport in Bois, so nobody will need to pick her up."

"Why the change in plans? I thought she was coming tomorrow." I was still a little nervous that his mother Lillian would dislike me, the American girlfriend.

"Rosamund called and told her about the cheese. Mum would want to know. I guess Mum also got a heads-up about my black eye and broken wrist. Apparently, Rosamunde told her that I look pretty bad, but I'm basically okay. So, my appearance won't come as a complete shock."

"Very thoughtful of Rosamunde," I said. The bruise around Peter's eye was turning yellow, but it was still pretty ugly. I re-heated bacon and eggs in the skillet, then served them to Peter, all the while avoiding any talk of my project. Instead, we discussed the previous night's technical rehearsal, which had run late into the evening.

Tony hadn't made it to rehearsal, just as I'd feared. Sebastian must have him on a tight leash. However, Alice assured me that her son would arrive early on the night of the performance. As it turned out, the lighting was no big deal. It depended on one stage light, which fortunately, had a dimmer attached, so the lighting choices for every scene consisted of bright, off, and somewhere in between.

Peter was pleased that the crew had worked well together, efficiently hauling the backdrops, five large pieces of painted plywood, on and off the stage and positioning a few pieces of furniture. The five backdrops were all charming, in a rustic sort of way, but my favorite was the last one, with its scenic view, featuring the Guardian and her sister peaks. Anwen and Philippe, those high-minded, young land-grabbers, would stand in front of that backdrop when they addressed the people of their newly proclaimed duchy.

A little before nine, Peter kissed me on the cheek and headed off to the museum, where he planned to work until the council convened at ten. I wanted to wish him luck, but I was afraid of jinxing the whole thing.

I was far too nervous to sit around, so I decided to clean the chalet, making it ready for Peter's mother. It was her childhood home, and I wanted her to find it shiny clean. I wished I had music to clean by, but I made do by humming old tunes from Broadway and Motown, which I had learned from Mom's old LP records. I swept and scrubbed, starting with the bathrooms and progressing to the kitchen and the upstairs bedrooms. I swept Gwen's room, but otherwise left it alone, hoping she would be back soon. Then I swept the large bedroom, which Lillian and I would share.

I was making up Lillian's bed, across from my own, when I heard the door open downstairs. A minute later, Rosamunde appeared at the bedroom door. One look at her face told me the answer to my question. I sank onto the bed. "Don't tell me. The council said no."

Rosamunde sat down next to me. "Peter and I both did our very best, but three of the members were adamantly opposed to your project. They were afraid of what would happen when outsiders learned of what was going on here. They have nothing against you personally. They just felt that St. Uguzo is in a very vulnerable situation, and we have to be careful about what news gets out."

"But the celebration sounds wholesome and patriotic."

"Yes, and most years there would be no problem. But right now, people are afraid and feelings are running high. Plus, a large amount of liquor will be consumed. It wouldn't be too surprising if fights broke out. Juliette is planning to deputize several Guzos to help maintain the peace."

"I understand," I said, retaining a bit of dignity, although I wanted to shout and hurl the pillow against the wall.

"But all is not lost," Rosamunde said. "Peter managed to strike a compromise." She took a deep breath. "Here it is. You will be allowed to write about past duchy celebrations, just not this year's. You can collect information about festivities from earlier years and write about those. Peter will be happy to help you with historical documents."

I wasn't thrilled, but I perked up a little. If I stayed a week or two after the celebration, as I'd planned, I should be able to collect enough data for a reasonably good chapter in Dr. Ferris's book. What's more, I would have time with Peter, without all the stress and commotion that surrounded the celebration.

"There is one condition," Rosamunde said. "You will have to leave by Friday morning. You can't stay for the celebration."

I stared at her. "You're joking."

"I'm sorry, Holly. People thought it would be too great a temptation for you to write about this year's ceremonies, including any kind of conflict that might arise.

"No," I wailed. "Didn't you tell the council they could have final approval on what I wrote?"

"Yes, we told them that, but trust is not running high these days."

"Why should this year's celebration be any different from the others?" I asked.

"There are always a few fights, with all the liquor imbibed. But people are frightened about the future, and they have wildly different ideas about how to move forward. Things could get ugly. That's what the council is afraid of."

I leaned forward, elbows on my knees, and lowered my head into my hands. Friday was the day after tomorrow, and today was half gone. I would only have one full day to gather information. Hardly any time at all to collect data or to be with Peter. Just as the far-flung duchyites returned to their homeland, I would be on my way out. How sad was that. "Where is Peter?" I asked.

"At the museum, pulling materials together for you," Rosamunde said. "Why don't you go over and have a word with him?" She patted me on the shoulder. "All will be well," she said, and left.

I sat there on the bed, bemoaning my bad luck. Why did I have to arrive around the time a murder was committed and the cheese was ruined? Now that my plans were dashed, I realized that my heart had been set on participating in the celebration. I wanted to watch the races and archery contest, look over the prized baked goods, listen to the yodeling, and watch the folk dancing, all the while scribbling down notes.

And I had looked forward to helping Peter with his museum tours and watching the play, if not acting in it. Then there was the stirring Ceremony of Allegiance, with all the patriotic Guzos packed into the plaza, lifting their knives. And afterward, what fun it would be to play my penny whistle with the band and dance with the local guys, including Peter, if he was up to it, with one arm in a cast. I had looked forward to it all. And now, I wouldn't be able to do any of these things. All because of those three pig-headed council members. (No offense to pigs.) It was way beyond unfair.

My sister's voice sounded in my head. "Having a little pity party, Holls?" Valerie wasn't given to self-indulgence, for herself or her little sister.

"Oh, shut up," I mumbled to my absent sibling, as I hauled myself off Lillian's bed. I shuffled over to my own bed, where I picked up my shoulder bag, pulled out my work notebook, and started skimming through it. I had been taking notes since my first night in St. Uguzo. There were pages of notes on duchy history from my tour of the convent with Peter, and more stuff I'd gleaned later, including facts about earlier celebrations. Just like my grandfather's journal, the last pages in my book were blank. But after going through everything, I realized that I had a good deal of information. Now, if I could just gather enough material on past celebrations, I should have what I needed to write a chapter for Dr. Ferris's book. And in return, I would receive an assistantship in the department and have some credibility in the department. My academic career would be back on track.

"You can do this," Peter said when I showed up at the museum fifteen minutes later. I set down my shoulder bag and gazed at the table by the window where I normally worked. It was half covered with files, and a tape recorder and cassettes sat to one side.

It was clear that Peter was making an all-out effort to support me with my study, and his kindness threatened to unglue me. Plus, I could hardly bear the thought of flying off and leaving him behind. I raised a hand to my lips, holding back a sob. He stepped around the table and put his uninjured arm around me. I buried my head in his shoulder.

"This sucks," I mumbled.

"I know," he said. "It's not what we wanted. But this compromise is the next best thing. And I believe it will work for you."

Peter spent the next half hour going through all the material he'd lain out, including two of his own articles from the Journal of Alpine History, which would provide good, easily-cited background information. He had taken out the old newspapers with special sections on celebrations and explained that he would make copies and send them to me next week, when I was back in the States. He had also pulled out my questionnaire, and we sat side by side, eliminating questions and adding a few more, now that we knew I wouldn't collect any current data.

Together, we compiled a short list of people who would probably agree to be interviewed. They included Rosamunde, who was ethnically Wiskara with educated parents; Rob, also Wiskara, but from across the valley; Peter's mother, Lillian, daughter of the late duchess, so definitely a Royal; Roderick, a Wiskara/Royal mix; and Baptiste, another ethnic mix, but with strong ties to France. It would be hard talking to them all in such a short time, but if I did, they would give me a reasonable cross-section of people. And of course, I could e-mail questions to Peter later.

"So, what do you think?" Peter asked finally. His brows had been furrowed all through this task, but now his expression was hopeful.

"It looks do-able," I said, trying to muster a little enthusiasm. "I'll get started with the interviews today. Maybe I can catch Roderick at lunch."

"Good idea."

"Thanks for putting all this together," I said, my gaze sweeping over the files. He'd clearly worked hard on it.

"I only wish I could do more. I can't tell you how fine it has been to have a colleague here. Another lover of moldy, illegible documents." He gave a half-grin.

"I've loved it," I said. "Every minute." Our eyes met, and for a second, I thought I glimpsed a flash of longing in his. Not the familiar, playful lust. Something deeper. Then it was gone.

My throat tightened, and I pushed back a lock of hair that had escaped from my ponytail. "And thank you for dealing with the council. It can't have been easy."

"It wasn't, and you're welcome." He rearranged a paper in front of him. "Well, then," he said, standing. "I suppose I should make you a plane reservation. You have a return ticket, right?"

"Yes," I said. "Gwen left the date open." I rummaged in my shoulder bag and pulled out my ticket in its stuffed envelope as well as my passport, both of which I handed to him.

We went into Peter's office, and he called a travel agent in Bois, whom he addressed as Carla. They talked in French, and a minute later, Peter looked up to me. "Is Air France all right?"

"Sure." Why not? At this point, I hardly cared what airline I took. They would all take me far away.

Peter made a series of notes on a notepad, then hung up. "Here you go," he said, ripping out the page. It contained the name and phone number of the travel agent, her agency, and a flight itinerary. "You'll leave Friday morning for Bois and take an afternoon plane to Paris. You should get home on Saturday." He handed me the sheet.

I stared at it, faced with the stark reality of my situation. I would leave the day after tomorrow. No way around it. "It's too soon," I squeaked, tears forming in my eyes. "I thought we'd have more time together."

"As did I," Peter said. He started arranging papers on his desk. "But if we're honest, we were aware from the start that you were only here for a couple of weeks." He aligned the sheets, matching the edges carefully. "What we had was good, but we knew it would come to an end." He paused, his eyes still on the papers. "And now it has."

"Of course." I was crushed. But Peter was right. All along, I had known my stay was temporary. It was only through sheer denial that I had convinced myself that our relationship was more than a fling. My mood, which had been sad and a little rebellious, now sank into utter desolation. "Thanks for making the arrangements," I said, holding up the paper with my itinerary and giving it a little flutter. "I'm sure Air France will work out fine."

We went back to the table in the main room. Silently, Peter put a couple of batteries in the tape recorder, then managed to rip the shrink-wrapped plastic off a cassette and inserted it in the machine. He pushed "play" and "record" simultaneously and recited "testing 1 2 3." When he played it back, his voice sounded clear, if a little high. It occurred to me that this sound check might be what I would have to remember him by. Well, c'est la vie, I thought, bracing myself against tears. I'd get over him. Eventually.

Peter went into his office and returned with a cloth bag. "Here you go," he said, holding the bag open. I lowered the tape recorder into it, along with several cassettes still in their plastic wrapping.

"Looks like I'm set," I said, trying to sound upbeat, and not as if I'd just been punched in the gut. I left the museum, walking blindly through misty eyes. What a fool I had been, thinking Peter really cared for me. To him, I was a cheerful colleague and a convenient, if temporary, girlfriend. Nothing more. Kessie had said he had a lady friend in Bois. The travel agent, Carla? They had sounded friendly. I supposed he would go back to her now, once I was out of the picture.

Who did I think I was? I was nothing to these people, a foolish American student thinking I was somehow important. Gwen had left, and now Peter was sending me on my way—with a lot of kindness, but still. He was probably always generous with clueless strangers and stray puppies. Mom was right all along. You had to keep your guard up.

I ate lunch alone at the dining hall, spooning down stew without really tasting it. An argument at a nearby table turned heated, the two men shouting at each other. Violet, the chef, went over to calm them down, but the air in the room felt charged after that. The duchy was turning into a tinder box.

Giselle, the blonde girl with the pierced nose, stopped at my table on her way out. "Oh, Holly, I just heard. I can't believe you are leaving. Just when we need you most." It was an odd thing to say, but I appreciated her sympathy.

Her expression darkened. "There are a few council members who should be throttled. I regret that I am a pacifist and cannot do it myself."

I laughed. "I'm sorry to leave, but I've enjoyed my stay here. Very much. I'll never forget the duchy."

Roderick was sitting at the goat herders' table, finishing his bread pudding, when I approached him a couple of minutes later. I asked if I could interview him about his family's experiences with past celebrations, and he readily agreed.

We left together and walked over to the plaza, where we passed a few women waiting for the bus, deep in conversation. No carefree chatting today. We crossed to the far corner of the square and sat on the wall in front of the evergreen hedge. Roderick was short enough that he had to hoist himself up, which he did easily, a feat that seemed to please him.

I took my notebook and pen out of the cloth bag and pulled out the tape recorder, which I placed beside me. I held down the "play" and "record" levers, then watched as the tape began winding around. "Can you tell me about your first memory of the celebration?" I asked, as I poised my pen over my notebook.

"Let's see." Roderick screwed up his wrinkled face, then relaxed. "I was seven years old. No, eight. It was back in the thirties. I remember I had a small knife my grandpa had given me for my birthday. A right beauty it was, with its own leather scabbard. I kept it on my belt, handy like. Well, my pals and me, we all went down to the plaza for the ceremony. We stood behind the men, and when they raised their knives and cheered, us boys did too. Pleased as punch, I was, to declare my loyalty to the duke. Old Leopold, it must have been. He had a fine, thick beard and a round belly. Oh, and he wore the gold medallion on his chest, the one with the salamander. That medal was a sight to behold, shining in the sun. Too bad it disappeared later. It was them damn Germans took it, or so they say.

Roderick reported that one year he had won a prize for the 100-yard dash. "I was right quick in those days." And his older brother regularly won a foot race to the top of a steep hill nearby. One year, his sister surprised everyone by winning at archery.

"But mostly the girls got dressed up and looked over the boys," he said. "Those girls were shameless, laughing and teasing the lads who walked by. Course, the boys had their chance to look the girls over and make their own cheeky remarks. Some of the young people didn't get into town much, so it was their chance to get a look at the available talent, so to speak."

It occurred to me that since the celebration only came around every five years, anyone close to marriageable age would need to take full advantage of this narrow window of opportunity.

Roderick then told me about a young aunt of his who was courted by a boy apprenticed to a cobbler. His grandfather was not pleased with the match. "We was Royals, more or less, and he was Wiskara. Back in those days, such things mattered, to some folks anyway. Not so much anymore. We're a race of mongrels now, Royals and Wiskara, all higgledy-piggledy. It's better that way, in my opinion."

"What happened to your aunt and the shoemaker?"

"Ah, well, the two of them met up at the celebration, on the sly, you might say. They were married a month later. Had their first babe in June. There was a lot of June babies back in celebration years," he said, winking at me. "Boys getting up their courage to propose, and girls saying yes. Who knows? Maybe you'll have some luck. That historian fellow is a likely sort. And I've seen the way he looks at you."

"Peter and I are friends and colleagues, nothing more. Anyway, I have to leave on Friday." Just saying it made my chest ache.

His face fell. "I forgot. I can tell you, If I was on the council, things would have turned out different."

"Yes, I wish you had been. I could have used another supporter."

Then we talked about his parents and grandparents and their participation in celebrations over the years. Finally, I clicked off the tape recorder and thanked Roderick. He said he was happy to help, the least he could do for the Yank's granddaughter. He grinned mischievously. And when had he ever turned down a beautiful young lady? he said. Then he ambled away to meet his friends, and I gathered up my materials and strode across the square.

I wanted so much to see the celebration. Did the girls and boys still scope each other out and set up clandestine meetings? Were the races still a high point for the young men? Did little boys stand at the back of the plaza and raise their small knives? I would never know now.

I was nearing the kiosk at the corner of the plaza when I saw a man tacking up a sign at the kiosk. At first, I thought he was a traditional Guzo, with his collarless shirt, beige vest, and kerchief of a deep brown hue. Then he turned toward me, and I realized it was Sebastian. Except for his usual khakis, he had gone native. Stepping closer, I saw that the sign was an announcement for the rally on Friday. He favored me with a bright smile. "Take a look," he said.

In large block print, the sheet read:

RALLY

GUZOS!

ARE YOU READY FOR NEW LEADERSHIP?

FOR A NEW AND PROSPEROUS DUCHY?

COME TO THE PLAZA ON FRIDAY, AT 19:00 HRS.

I did a swift calculation. That was seven p.m., the hour Bernard had announced earlier.

"Are you planning to come?" Sebastian asked. "It should be exciting."

"Probably not," I said. I didn't feel like admitting to Sebastian that I had to leave St. Uguzo on Friday morning.

Sebastian started tacking up another sheet, this one covering up the notice about chickens for sale. The sheet was typed, with "International Strategic Solutions, Inc." at the top in bold letters. The name of Sebastian's company. As I recalled, Juliette had found no record of it anywhere. And not a trace of Sebastian either. Or Wilheard. It was as if they had all appeared out of nowhere. But here they were, ready to wreak havoc, as far as I could see.

Farther down was a list of the services the company would offer to the lucky community that it chose for their new site. The list mostly included the kinds of infrastructure that Sebastian had told me about on our car trip to Bois several days earlier.

Investment opportunities for local businesses

Secure, high-paying jobs

Well-maintained, paved roads

Dependable utilities

High-speed computer access

A helicopter and helipad for emergency medical care

"Sounds promising," I said. "Remind me. What does the community have to do in return?"

He flashed his charming grin. "Just sign a contract allowing several wealthy, peace-abiding families to build homes here. By filling the newcomers' needs, we also fill the community's needs. It's a win for both parties."

"I thought you told me that the duchy wasn't in the running to be one of your sites. That it didn't meet your criteria."

"How things have changed, eh? Just in the short time we've been here. There's a groundswell of support for new leadership. Strong leadership." As I recalled, one of his criteria for a community was that it have a single leader who called the shots. Someone like Wilheard, if he were duke.

"You know," I said, "it might be easier to sell the duchy on your company if you gave us the name of another community where you have this contractual agreement. Where wealthy clients have moved in successfully."

"If only I could, "Sebastian said, shaking his head ruefully. "That would make this process a hundred times easier. But my clients insist on total anonymity. I know. It sounds crazy. But the uber-rich have a mania about privacy. I simply have to accept it."

Sebastian stroked his kerchief. "And I have to admit, I've fallen for this place. Haven't you?"

While I was coming up with a response, Sebastian said, "Oh, I forgot. You're leaving soon, aren't you? That's a shame."

"Not until Friday," I said hotly. I had suddenly realized that I was getting the boot while Sebastian—the other foreigner—got to stay. "How about you?" I said, just to be sure. "When do you plan to leave?"

"Right after the celebration. And if the Guzos are smart, I'll take a signed contract with me."

In three days? I didn't see how. But really, why should I even care? I'd be on a plane to Paris.

My conversation with Sebastian had put me on edge, but I didn't have time to brood over it. I had to think of my project. So, I headed for Juliette's office. Since she and Baptiste seemed to be an item, she would probably know how I could approach him about doing an interview.

I walked through the convent gates, and by luck, the door to the sheriff's office was open. Stepping inside, I found Juliette on the phone. She motioned me to a chair on the other side of her desk, and a moment later, after saying good-bye to the person on the phone, she wrote a check mark beside one item on what looked like a to-do list."

"What can I do for you?" she asked.

"This will just take a minute," I said and explained that I needed to set up an interview with Baptiste. "Any idea where I can find him?"

"Right here," came a deep, resonant voice from the doorway. Baptiste stepped into the office. I usually saw him from a distance, often on a stage. Up close, his dark good looks were even more impressive. I explained again about interviewing a variety of Guzos for my newly-altered project and asked if I might talk with him.

"I guess so. You want to do it now?" He looked at Juliette, who gave a "why not" shrug.

We sat in the convent courtyard on adjoining benches beside the small herb garden, the tape recorder between us. This late in the season, the parsley was leggy but still green and healthy, and the bluish rosemary needles emitted a delicious scent when I brushed against them.

My conversation with Baptiste flowed easily. It turned out that his family had been brewing mead and cider for generations, so the celebration was an especially busy time for them, as they kept the drinks flowing. "I only wish we could have a celebration every year," he said. "You know, keep the Ceremony of Allegiance for Guzos only. But we could invite people from the surrounding towns for the other festivities. Then we wouldn't be such a mystery to them, and we could drum up some interest in our economy. Maybe get more trade going."

"That sounds very reasonable," I said. "You're on the council, aren't you? Are the other members amenable?" It occurred to me that I was venturing into political terrain, but this information wouldn't go into my study.

"Some are. Some aren't. The old people are afraid our traditions will fade away if we open our doors to outsiders, that we'll stop speaking English and switch to French. But I say, if the young people all leave to find jobs, the duchy will die out, and the traditions will be lost anyway."

"Too true," I said. I'd seen enough moribund American towns to know that such a thing could happen. And there were far worse things than speaking French, especially given that a lot of people seemed to know it already.

"You want to run for the council?" he teased. I laughed and his face opened into a warm grin. It occurred to me what a fine couple he and Juliette made. Two mature, energetic, caring people. I wondered if Baptiste was one of Wilheard's supporters, but I stepped back from that political question. If he was, I wasn't sure I wanted to know.

I plodded up the road to the house, pleased with my two interviews. I'd taken plenty of notes, so even if the recordings didn't catch everything, I should be okay.

Entering the house, I heard voices in the back, Peter's and a woman's, in conversation. I made my way to the kitchen, where it only took one glance at the slim, middle-aged woman with the permed blond hair and upturned brows to know that she was Lillian, Peter's mother.

When she saw me at the door, she set down a teacup which she'd been sipping from, and Peter introduced us. "This is Holly," he said. "You'll be sharing the upstairs bedroom."

"I hope you don't mind," Lillian said in a soft British accent. "I don't snore. Or at least, I don't think so." Her eyes crinkled in a friendly smile.

"I'm glad to meet you," I said. "I understand you grew up in this house. I appreciate your letting me stay here."

"I am delighted to share the house with you. And that upstairs bedroom has seen many a gathering of girls. When I was a teenager and my cousins came to visit, we all spent lots of nights up there, talking about boys and laughing and getting very little sleep."

Why had I been afraid of this lady? Peter's mother was friendly and charming. Of course, I was no threat to her son, since I would soon be leaving the duchy.

Peter zeroed in on his mother. "Now," he said, "back to the play. I need you to play Anwen, Mum."

Lillian lifted an eyebrow. "Really, Peter, I know I've played the part before, but that was decades ago." She shook her head. "Besides, aren't you playing the young duke? You would have to woo me." She shook her head. "The gods don't like it when sons marry their mothers. You might remember Oedipus. Sophocles knew what he was talking about." I sympathized with Lillian. It would be weird for her to be courted by her own son. Even in a theatre production.

"Mum, I have no choice. Either you play Anwen, or I have to cancel the play."

"You're exaggerating. I can't be the only woman in the duchy who is able to play Anwen. Who has had the part up to now?"

"Gwen was the first. Then she left in a rush, and Eglentyne stepped in. I told you how that ended. Holly has been playing Anwen since then, but she leaves on Friday."

Lillian turned to me. "Oh dear. Couldn't you stay just two more days? Leave on Sunday?"

Peter explained about the council's decision, and Lillian shook her head. "What a pickle we're in," she said. "Rosamunde was holding back when she advised me to come early. I should have arrived a week ago. Or better yet, I should have stayed home entirely."

"You've heard about Wilheard Fosse?" Peter asked.

"Oh, yes, in some detail. I've visited my friends around town and picked up all the gossip. We can talk about it later. I don't suppose anything that I've learned will come as news to you. By the way, Rosamunde has invited us all for an early dinner next door. I brought wine, so we'll be well provisioned."

I went up to the room and collected my play book, then left it on the table by the front door, where Lillian could pick it up on her way out. The book had been passed around among Gwen, Eglentyne, and me. Now it was finally with its rightful reader. I felt a tinge of regret, which surprised me, since this was the result I'd wanted, a respected Guzo taking the part of Anwen.

Rosamunde's kitchen was cozy, with all of us sitting around the table—Rosamunde, Rob, Juliette, Peter, Lillian and me—eating our thick potato soup and drinking red Bordeaux. An unusual taste combination, but it worked for me. Kessie and Ozzie had been given permission to eat with friends, so we didn't have to watch what we said.

Juliette reported that Fred had returned from Lyon. The good news was that the chemical injected into the cheese was unpleasant in taste but not toxic. "So, you're in no danger," she told me. I was relieved. I'd had a lingering fear that the cheese I'd tasted had some kind of slow-acting poison. Or (and I know this was a stretch), it harbored a monster like the one in Alien. My sister Valerie and I had gone to see the first movie when it came out, and I'd hardly slept for a week afterward.

"Only two of the wheels of cheese had been injected," Juliette said. "And they were both from the front of the cheesery. Of course, we can't be sure yet, but it looks like the wheels stored in back are alright."

"That's good," Peter said. "But I suppose we'll still have to test them all, just in case." And after that, would anybody want to pay a high price for a wheel of cheese with a hole? One that had been suspected of adulteration? I was pretty sure I wasn't the only one wondering about that.

"And Fred was right," Juliette continued. "The cheese was injected at least two months ago."

"When did Wilheard arrive?" Lillian asked. She was catching on quickly.

"Right after the fire at Miller's barn," Juliette said. "A little over two months ago." Although I hated to think that Wilheard would intentionally harm the duchy, he was starting to look like the most likely candidate.

We finished the soup, and Lillian topped off our wine glasses. Then she proceeded to give us a summary of what she'd learned by chatting with her old friends. It was pretty much what we already knew or had guessed. The Guzos were all nervous, if not downright panicky. Clive's death had worried everyone. and some people started to have doubts about law enforcement in the duchy. But it was the "poisoning" of the cheese and the dire threat to the economy that really had people scared. Those folks who had been grumbling about the need for change, and that included a bunch of the young men, were now demanding it. Immediately.

"Then there's the rally on Friday night," Lillian said. "Everybody that I talked to expects Wilheard Fosse to be nominated as duke. And not just as a council member with ceremonial duties. No, they want him to be an old-fashioned duke with the power to sign contracts with no oversight from the council." She took a sip of her wine. "This is all so strange. Surreal even. What in the world is going on?"

Peter sighed. "Sorry, Mum, you're not alone in feeling lost. We still don't know how Clive died or who injected the cheese. But it looks like our present problems are connected, in one way or another, to Wilheard's boss, Sebastian. As we understand it, he is poised to have his company take over the duchy."

"You're joking," Lillian said.

Peter shook his head. "I wish I were. It's a company we know next to nothing about, but Sebastian assures us it will bring us prosperity and security. In short, it will solve all of the duchy's current problems. And to bring about this small miracle, all he'll need is the new duke's signature on a contract."

"Have you seen the contract?" Lillian asked.

"No one has," Peter said, "although Sebastian keeps promising to show it to us. I'd like to have a good attorney look it over."

"Sebastian wants the contract signed by Saturday night," I said. "Otherwise, another town will be chosen, and the deal is off. At least that's what he told me several days ago. He expects to leave with the contract after the celebration." I looked around, expecting everyone to agree that it wasn't possible to get it signed that fast, but no one was making eye contact with me. "It's crazy, right? Even if the council agreed to make Wilheard duke, why would they vote him special powers? That couldn't possibly be in their best interest. Not to mention going against duchy tradition."

"It's like this," said Peter. "Ordinarily, governmental decisions are made through the council. But there's one enormous exception. The duchy has a law, a three-part law, that allows the council to be bypassed. The rule has been around since long before we got a constitution. So, many people see it as a time-honored tradition."

"It should have been eliminated years ago," Juliette mumbled.

"And would have been," Rob said, "if certain council members had shown some balls."

"What's the law?" I asked, my patience fraying.

Peter cleared this throat. "Every five years, at the Ceremony of Allegiance, the assembled Guzos are allowed to approve a new council member. By a show of general affirmation. You know, knives raised and a shout of approval. That occurred once, about fifty years ago."

"Oh, I get it," I said. "So, for example, Wilheard could be named to the council, if he has enough support on Saturday." I wasn't a big fan of the man, but that didn't seem earth-shattering.

"Exactly," Peter said. "What's more, the Guzos can elect a new duke or duchess, although that's never been done."

I pondered this. "So, Wilheard could, theoretically, be made not just a council member, but the duke." Now, that was an uglier thought.

Peter nodded. "There's one more provision. Any adult Guzo may propose a law at the Ceremony. And if there's affirmation from the people present, the law will go into immediate effect."

"Really?" The whole thing seemed like a black hole in their governmental process.

"I'm afraid so," Peter said. "Originally, the measure was designed to override a council or sovereign that was ignoring the will of the people. But you can see its potential for abuse."

Rosamunde took a sip of wine. "The provision allowing a law to be passed hasn't been invoked for over a century. Well, it's been tried a couple of times, but it was never successful."

The implications gradually dawned on me. "You mean, if Wilheard gets the support of enough Guzos at the Ceremony, not only can he be proclaimed duke, but a special law can be passed. One that grants him the power to sign Sebastian's contract."

"That's right," Juliette said. "Without further deliberation. And that might be only the beginning."

Lillian shuddered. "The whole idea scares me silly."

"But surely most Guzos won't support such a plan," I said. The duchy was giving me the boot, but even so, I didn't want it to turn into Sebastian's private fiefdom, with Wilheard as titular head.

"Wilheard and Sebastian seem to be gaining a lot of support," Juliette said. "They tell people exactly what they want to hear. Folks think that if they accept the company's support, they'll have secure jobs and new business opportunities and computers in their homes. Who wouldn't want that? We just don't know what the price tag will be. I suspect some of us don't want to know."

Peter ran his fingers through his hair, a sign of his agitation. "We'll have a better idea of how successful Sebastian has been after the rally on Friday. But I don't suppose we'll really know until Saturday at the ceremony."

"I've always looked forward to the Ceremony of Allegiance," said Lillian. "But not this year." Judging from the dour looks around the table, I could see she wasn't the only one.

After dinner, Juliette and I offered to do the dishes, freeing Rosamunde, Lillian, and Peter to hurry off to play rehearsal. I had already decided to skip it. It would be too sad to watch the show that would go on without me. On her way out the door, Rosamunde promised to let me interview her the next day, sometime after breakfast.

As Juliette and I washed and dried the dishes, she taught me the three stirring verses of the duchy national anthem. Wherever I was on Saturday, she said, I could think of Gwen singing the anthem in the plaza and sing along. Or just play the tune in my mind. Juliette seemed confident that Gwen would show up in time. I hoped she was right.

It was after seven-thirty when we finished putting away the dishes. We shared a hug and wished each other good night before I hurried next door through the nippy evening air. Since no one was around to use the kitchen, I set up shop at the table, with my notebook in front of me and my tape recorder at my right hand, where I could easily press "play," "pause," and "rewind."

My interview with Roderick had gone well. But background noises that I was barely aware of—shouts, children's laughter, even the bleating of a goat—blared on the recording, often masking Roderick's voice. Even so, I was able to fill in my notes, completing words and phrases I'd missed. Baptiste's recording was even clearer, and I finished off my notes without difficulty. I only hoped that the other participants would be as cooperative.

By the time Lillian returned and climbed the steps to our shared room, I was reading in bed, under the covers with my pillow propped against the headboard. I would have to return *A Tour of the World's Thin Places* to the museum tomorrow, and I was re-reading the last chapter, where Framton discussed his fear that *Thin Places* around the world might be disappearing.

"How was the rehearsal?" I asked Lillian, as she unpacked her night-gown and toiletries.

"It would have been better if the leading lady had known her lines and blocking."

"I'm sure they were grateful to have you there," I said. She looked tired, and I admired her for participating in the run-through with almost no preparation.

"Also," she said, "two heated arguments broke out. They were about trifles, really, one actor standing in a place where he was blocking another, and somebody misplacing a prop. For a moment, I thought things were going to turn violent. But fortunately, Peter was able to defuse the situations."

"People must be getting edgy. The only problem we had before was when Wilheard demanded that we rewrite Philippe's lines."

Lillian hooted. "I can imagine how well that went over."

"Peter managed that altercation too." In fact, I thought, Peter was pretty good at dealing with conflict. Except when it came to Sebastian's mistreat-ing Kessie.

I went back to my book, and when I looked up, Lillian was in a calf-length white nightgown with embroidery at the neckline and wrists. She dug a paperback out of her bag and settled into the bed across from me, but she soon laid the book on her lap.

"I'm sorry you'll miss the celebration," she said. "Peter says you've worked hard on the play."

"It was a shock when I found out, but I'm getting used to the idea." Which I was, sort of. "I'll miss the duchy. I've enjoyed getting to know the people and learning about the history. This is a fascinating place."

Lillian drew up her knees under the covers and folded her arms around them. "I think Peter has found it so. I'm sure it wasn't easy for him, giving up his life in England, and coming here. And heaven knows, his job is far from perfect. I can't say that Guzos are always easy to get along with. But they have welcomed him, I think, and most folks value his work. That's important too, to have supportive people around you."

I considered my own situation. "My department isn't very supportive," I confessed. A few professors had been encouraging, but Dr. Ferris had dumped me with no remorse. In the end, I was on my own.

"Oh, I'm so sorry," Lillian said. "I do hope that will improve. From what Peter has told me, the academic world can be rather cut-throat." She threw me a commiserative look, then returned to her paperback.

I stuck a bookmark in *Thin Places* and leaned back into the pillow. My thoughts turned to my study of past celebrations. I was finding it rewarding, even more than I'd expected. The interviews were providing me with an intriguing glimpse into duchy history and culture. However, I reminded myself, even if the study was successful, and I managed to get a chapter in Dr. Ferris's book, I would be going back to an unwelcoming place.

The study, which I'd begun in a last-ditch effort to save my academic life, was turning out to be deeply satisfying. My nosy questions and observations were giving me a unique window into duchy culture, one I could never have gained as a casual tourist, assuming I could even have gained entrance to the duchy that way.

With those thoughts tumbling through my mind, I said good night to Lillian, turned out my bedside lamp, and scooched under the covers. It wasn't until I was dropping off to sleep that I remembered Giselle's odd statement. "I can't believe you are leaving," she had said. "Just when we need you most."

CHAPTER TWENTY-THREE

Day 13, Thursday

I awoke at dawn with the dismal realization that this would be my last full day in the duchy. On the other hand, I reminded myself, I would spend a good part of the day conducting interviews that should provide me with interesting and important information, a thought that cheered me.

But first things first. I stood up and stretched. Before I got down to work, I would visit the glade one last time. The prospect filled me with both excitement and trepidation. Who knew what the thin place might hold in store for me today?

Quietly, so as not to awaken Lillian, I pulled on jeans, a long sleeve shirt, and my coat. Downstairs, Peter's door was open. Apparently, he and Bonnie were already out on their run. At least he was loyal to his dog, although I have to say, the idea wasn't all that comforting. Ten minutes later, warmed and stimulated by a strong cup of tea, I hurried up the road. At the stream crossing, I leaped from stone to stone. The sun had risen over the mountain peaks, and the sky was clear, the kind of deep alpine blue that I never saw in the Midwest, where there always seemed to be a layer of haze.

Striding up the path, I kept looking for my marmot pal, Monty, among the trees and on the rocks and boulders. But he must have been occupied elsewhere. I slowed down as I got close to the turnoff to the glade. Spotting it, I stepped onto the narrow path. From there, I gazed above me and to the right, where the Guardian's sharply faceted flanks caught the morning light. Over the last two weeks, I had come to depend on that mountain as a point of orientation. Even in the forest, if I could see the Guardian, I knew where I was.

A few minutes later, I stepped into the glade and took a deep breath to prepare for whatever was to come. Moving to the center of the clearing, I planted my sneakered feet firmly on the packed earth, alert to my surroundings. The feeling that I'd had last time of being observed was gone. I was alone. I closed my eyes and waited. The forest noises filled my senses—birds singing their morning songs, insects buzzing. A light wind fluttered the leaves and chilled my face, and the dusty smell of autumn mulch filled my nostrils.

But that was all. I felt a little unsteady, so I opened my eyes to the same scene as before. No heightened awareness, nothing out of the ordinary. I closed my eyes again and waited. And waited. After what seemed like a very long time, a soft, almost imperceptible vibration stirred inside me. But it was only a weak echo of the hum that had filled me last time. I raised my arms in a welcoming stance that I hoped would draw in the energy of the thin place. But the ecstatic thrum that had filled me last time didn't come. After a moment, the vibration dwindled until it was no longer there.

I opened my eyes, hoping for that glorious sense of well-being I'd experienced last time. Nada. I was the same old Holly. Nothing more, nothing less. Disappointed, I started back down the path. Well, I consoled myself, after such a lackluster experience, I was unlikely to be visited by a scary dream that night. When I crossed the creek and regained the road, I turned to look back at the forest. There was Monty, sitting on a large rock. But as I raised a hand in greeting, he jumped down and vanished behind some rocks. "Bye, Monty," I said, knowing there would be no chirpy reply.

As I walked down the road to Gwen's chalet, I saw Kessie and Ozzie emerge from their house next door and hustle toward town, knapsacks on their backs, no doubt on their way to school. I went to Rosamunde's kitchen door, knocked, and walked in.

"Good morrow," she said, looking up from an apple she was coring. Beside her, a pan was partially filled with apple slices in neat rows. "Have you broken fast?" she asked. It took me a moment to recognize that she was asking me if I'd had breakfast. When I said I hadn't, she motioned with her paring knife to a pot on the stove. "There's still a bit of oatmeal left," she said. "I'd be obliged if you'd finish it. There's milk in the fridge."

Smelling the oatmeal, I realized I was hungry. So I helped myself, and as I ate my warm, cinnamony meal, I told Rosamunde about my disappointing trip to the glade.

"It's a pity," Rosamunde said as she deftly sliced an apple and lay the chunks in the pan. "The hum has been weak lately. The other dreamers have remarked on it. When you had such a strong response last time, I hoped the energy was returning to us."

"Maybe the first time was beginner's luck," I said.

"Yes, perhaps. Or maybe this time the spirit knows you're leaving us."

That I'm abandoning the duchy. The thought came like a blow. Don't be silly, I told myself. It was the duchy abandoning me, sending me on my way. I was the powerless victim, as usual. Anyway, it wasn't a thought I wanted to pursue.

Rosamunde picked up another apple, which she began paring, the skin curling around in a graceful twirl. I washed off my bowl and spoon in the sink, then joined her at the counter.

"Can I help?" I asked. My experience at the glade had left me unsettled, and I welcomed Rosamunde's comforting presence as well as the calming effect of a manual chore.

"There's a knife in the drawer," she said. I found the other paring knife, picked up an apple, and set to work beside her, the apple's skin falling away in a ribbon.

"Does the hum fluctuate a lot?" I asked. "Get stronger and weaker?"

"Not usually. The last time it was this weak was a long time ago. In fact, it was during the war." She paused in her work. "During those long, terrible months. That was when the dreamers noticed that the hum in the glade was becoming fainter. I remember my mother commenting on it." She returned to coring and slicing the apple. "We thought it was because of the war, all the turmoil in the world. And the conflict right here in St. Uguzo."

"You had conflict here?" I shouldn't be surprised. I knew that hardship could bring people together, but it could also make rifts deeper.

"You see, when the Yank—your grandfather—arrived, we Guzos were divided. Everyone was hungry and scared. Some people said we should help the airmen and the refugees, and others said we shouldn't become involved, that it was too risky. Families turned against each other, and people grew hateful and sometimes violent. There was even a rumor that a Guzo was tipping off the Germans about the rescue missions."

I cringed, appalled at the idea. "Yes, we were terrified," she said. "Then, after your grandfather died, something changed in the duchy. People came together. It was Gwen's grandmother, Anne-Marie, who took the lead. She reminded us of the Yank's sacrifice, of his willingness to lay down his life for his friends and even for people he hardly knew; people who trusted him. Anne-Marie was just a young woman, but she had a kind of moral authority, even more than her father, the duke. She urged us to continue coming to the aid of those who needed our help." She paused. "I still recall her words. 'When this horrible war is over,' she said, 'Guzos will look back and remember that we stood tall, as one people. And we did what was right.'" Rosamunde set down her knife and turned to me. "And so it was."

"Wow." What an impressive person Anne-Marie was. My grandfather was fortunate to have counted her as a friend. "I see why people remember the duchess so fondly."

"Oh, there were many reasons to love Anne-Marie." She smiled wryly. "And a few reasons to find her rather irritating." She picked up another apple. "After your grandfather's death and the unity that followed, the hum grew stronger once again. Even though the war continued for another year."

"How awesome."

"Yes. We dreamers decided that the strength of the thin place came from a joint effort between people and spirit. Of course, the primary force rested with the spirit. But it also depended on the harmony of the people nearby. You can see why we are concerned that the hum has been grow-ing dimmer. It bodes ill for the duchy. And maybe for the world. I can't help thinking that the *Thin Places* around the world are necessary for our continued well-being."

I thought back to my experience in the glade the first time. Of Monty, the marmot, drawing me there. Of the powerful stirring that the place had elicited in me. And that night, of my dream of Gwen's murder. All signs that the thin place was strong and viable.

"Your initial response to the thin place was unexpected," Rosamunde said, as if she were reading my thoughts. "It made me hopeful that the spirit wasn't giving up on us. Not yet, anyway. But now, well, it's clear that the duchy is in for a difficult time."

I'd forgotten about my apple. I noticed a cutting board lying next to me on the counter. I pulled it over and cut up the apple, then laid the slices in overlapping rows in Rosamunde's pan.

But as I washed my hands at the sink, a feeling of failure came over me. For some reason, when I came to the duchy, the thin place in the glade had favored me with its energy. It was like grace, I mused, a gift that was undeserved, but given freely. I couldn't shake the feeling that I had somehow squandered that gift. And not only that, I had let down Rosamunde and maybe the other dreamers as well.

I thanked Rosamunde for telling me more about the thin place, then started for the kitchen door. I turned, a thought popping into my mind. "Rosamunde, when I ran into Sebastian yesterday, he said he was staying until after the celebration. Did the council discuss whether he should leave or remain?"

"No. I wish we could have sent him packing, but his name never came up in our deliberations. Besides, by that point, it wasn't really possible to get rid of him. While I was waiting for the council meeting to begin, I overheard one of the members say that he was impressed by Sebastian. In fact, he thought that Wilheard and Sebastian were the answer to all the duchy's problems. After that, I couldn't very well suggest that we oust Sebastian, not without a very strong reason."

"He's plotting to overthrow the duchy," I said. "Isn't that a strong enough reason?"

"Sebastian's activities are certainly suspicious. But we lack hard proof of his intentions. Without it, the council can do very little. Nor can Juliette or anyone else."

"By the time we learn Sebastian's intentions, it may be too late," I said. "At the speed things are moving, Wilheard will be duke, and Sebastian's company will control the duchy."

"It's all very troubling," Rosamunde said. "And the injustice isn't lost on me. You will leave and Sebastian will stay. But this is not your fight. You must let it go."

She was right and I knew it. When I got on the plane, would this all melt away? Would the duchy just be a memory? It was hard to imagine.

Rosamunde brightened. "Oh, by the way, Lillian dropped by earlier and said she would be happy to let you interview her. If you can catch her between her various tasks."

As if magically summoned, Lillian appeared at the kitchen door, looking cheerful in matching tan slacks and jacket with a colorful scarf. "I have the car outside," she announced. "Is the produce ready?"

It was then that I noticed two baskets and four crates lined up by the kitchen door. They were full of potatoes, cabbages, carrots, and apples.

"They're destined for the convent cellar," Lillian explained. "Peter is decorating the place for tomorrow's tours."

Lillian, Rosamunde and I hauled the produce from Rosamunde's house out to Lillian's rental car. Fortunately, the sedan had a decent-sized trunk, or boot, as Lillian called it.

"Come back for lunch," Rosamunde said. "We'll have apple crumble for dessert. And you and I can talk about the celebrations afterward." I thanked her, and Lillian drove us to the convent, a basket of carrots in my lap.

Peter met us at the gate, and we hauled everything to the convent kitchen. In the corner of the room, he pulled open the trapdoor with his one good hand.

"The staircase is rather narrow, isn't it?" Lilian said in a strained voice.

"A little," Peter said. "Look, Mum, why don't you stay here? Holly and I can handle this." He turned to me. "Mum is a tiny bit claustrophobic."

"I am not," Lillian said. "I just feel a little uneasy in confined spaces."

"Mum, I've seen you break into a sweat in a lift."

It took me a second to realize he was talking about an elevator.

Lillian cast him a withering look. "Lots of people get nervous in lifts. You never know when they might break down. And there you'd be, stuck in the middle of a dark shaft, for God only knows how long."

"I'll go first," I said. "I've been in the cellar before." I picked up one of the smaller baskets, this one containing bright red apples. Standing at the top of the stairs, I allowed my eyes to adjust to the murky light from below. Then, hanging onto the heavy basket with one hand and the railing with the other, I descended to the lower level. Lilian followed me, stepping slowly, a penlight in hand. Peter came last.

At the bottom, we reconnoitered, and Peter suggested that we form a chain. He would be at the top, where he would move the crates and baskets into position, using his one arm and both feet. I would then move the produce down to Lillian, who was at the bottom of the stairs. I did a lot of climbing back and forth, but finally we'd passed everything down. Peter and I joined Lillian, and he proceeded to give his mother a quick tour of the cellar while I arranged the containers on shelves and the floor. Even that little bit of colorful food made the place feel more like a storage area and less like a dungeon.

We climbed back up the stairs, and as Peter closed the trapdoor, Lillian's face relaxed. "Well, I expect that's the last time I'll see the cellar," she said. "I'll be busy traipsing around, taking care of people's aches and pains."

"A fine idea," Peter said. "You can chat them up while they're waiting, remind them of how grateful we are for any contributions they make to the museum." He thanked me for my help, although he barely made eye contact with me.

We left the convent kitchen and strolled back to the museum. "If you'll excuse me," Peter said, "I need to put up posters advertising the tours." He had left a small stack on the table near the door, and he held one up for us to see. It read: "Guided Tours of the Museum and Convent, including the Cellar. All are welcome. 10:00 Friday and Saturday."

"Excellent," Lillian said. "Simple and to the point."

"I thought I'd put up the signs at the convent gate, the kiosk on the plaza, the dining hall and mead hall, and the school."

We agreed that should work, especially with the help of the gossip network. "I'm off then," Peter said and gave his mother a peck on the cheek. I might have rated a kiss two days earlier, I thought with a twinge of regret. But the fling was now well and truly over. I couldn't help feeling used, but at this point, I needed to maintain my dignity and act as if I hadn't been dumped. At least until I got on the plane going home.

Lillian turned to me. "Is this a good time for that interview?"

I collected my tape recorder and notebook, and we stepped into the convent courtyard, which was filled with light and warmth, a welcome contrast to the cold, dark cellar. We settled down in the same spot by the herb garden where I'd interviewed Baptiste the day before.

Lillian started with a description of her grandparents, Duke Leonard and Duchess Renate. "They were very old fashioned, very Royal. But they enjoyed the celebrations. It was an excuse to dress up and chat with Guzos they didn't see on a regular basis. And they liked to watch the races and sample the baked goods. By the end of the day, Grandmum would be complaining about being seriously over-stuffed. Of course, they didn't think it was their place to compete in contests with the ordinary Guzos. But, they awarded lots of prizes, and their congratulations always seemed heart-felt. I give them credit for that, because they must have said the same words a hundred times."

In the evenings, Lillian said, her grandfather played his French horn with the band, and her grandmother sometimes sang. "She had a beautiful voice, like Gwen's, although she lacked any formal training."

"And your parents?" I asked.

"My mother was Duchess Anne-Marie. I imagine you've heard about her." I nodded. "She followed my grandparents' example and didn't compete in any of the contests. My dad was older than she, and I think he'd taken a number of athletic prizes when he was younger. Once he married Mum, he handed out all the sports awards." Her face relaxed into a gentle smile. "He liked to joke around with the competitors and they liked that."

A breeze came up, moving through the rosemary and basil and scenting the air around us. Lillian pulled her tan jacket closer over her white blouse.

It blew a strand of blond hair onto Lillian's face, and she brushed it back with her fingers.

"Where was I?" she said. "Oh yes. Well, this part is sad. I had an older brother, Andrew. He planned to take the title of duke eventually, when my parents were ready to step down. But then he and his wife died in a car crash while they were on holiday. It was dreadful. Well, you can imagine. Fortunately, their daughter, Gwen, had stayed behind. She was only six at the time. You know her, don't you?"

"She invited me here." But I would be gone by the time Gwen returned. I wondered if I would ever see her again. Would she be disappointed in me, leaving the duchy before the celebration? Abandoning the play? Well, it hardly mattered. Our paths were unlikely to cross again.

"Ah yes, of course. Well, Mum and Dad brought up Gwen, and everyone expected her to become duchess when she grew up. But as you know, fate had other plans. Oh, Gwen returns for celebrations. She played Anwen three times, and she always leads us in our national anthem. But she doesn't want to settle in St. Uguzo and be duchess."

"How about you?" I asked. "Were you active in the celebrations when you were growing up?"

"Oh, I loved them. I only wished they came more often. The celebrations were a chance to hang around with friends and cousins and have a good time." I pictured young Lillian in a gaggle of girls, mercilessly teasing boys, as Roderick had described.

"I'm afraid I wasn't much of an athlete," Lillian said, "at least not a competitive one. And my baking and needlework were nothing to boast of. So I didn't enter the contests. But the year that I turned sixteen, I was given the role of Anwen in the play. I was terribly excited." She laughed. "For some reason, it didn't occur to me until too late that I would have to memorize dozens of lines. Mostly, I wanted to wear a long, romantic gown and have my hair styled and wear lipstick. Plus, I had a huge crush on the boy playing the duke. Teddy. He's in London now, working for an import/export firm."

We heard a loud chirping and paused to watch a brownish bird sitting atop the stone wall that surrounded the convent. Whatever it was saying, the message would be recorded on my cassette for all time.

"That was the last time I acted in the play," Lillian said. "By the time five years had passed, I had finished my nurse's training, and I was a newly-wed, living in England. I've always come back for the celebrations, but I've never been asked to play Anwen again." She smiled ruefully. "Until this year, that is. I suppose we must be careful what we wish for."

Lillian explained that her nursing training always came in handy at the celebrations, where she dealt with the minor injuries that inevitably occurred when kids were running around and people were putting away prodigious amounts of alcohol. "It's a way I can be useful," she said. "Plus, I always raise a dagger during the Ceremony of Allegiance."

"Does your husband ever come with you?"

"John? No. He's never had an interest in the duchy." She lowered her eyes to her clasped hands, a shadow crossing her face. "Nor did my younger son, Brendan, when he was alive." She paused, and when she looked up, the sadness had largely retreated. "It was always Peter who wanted to come with me. So I would take a couple of days off my job and pull Peter out of school, and we would come together. He has loved the duchy, you see, ever since he was a child."

Lillian paused, her fingers rubbing a spot on her slacks. "Dad died ten years ago. Then, after Mum died last year, I thought that Peter would become duke. You know, he would wait a few months, then let people know he was willing. But after his brother Bren died six months later, Peter never stepped forward to take the title."

"Do you think he will?" I asked. He had certainly seemed reluctant, and it was getting late, with Wilheard ready to grab the title.

"He should. He is Royal, after all. And in the direct line of succession, whether he cares or not. But then, we can't tell our children what to do, can we? Not in this modern world."

It occurred to me that Lillian must be next in the line of succession. "Have you ever thought of becoming duchess?"

"Oh, it's entered my mind. But my life is in England now, and John would never leave his job or his football league to come here and be husband to the duchess." She cocked her head. "If you don't mind my saying so, I sensed a little spark between you and Peter." She lifted an eyebrow quizzically.

A spark? More like a dying sputter. Even so, I felt my cheeks flush. "Your son has been very helpful to me, but really, we're just colleagues. And friends, I hope. I'm here for a very short time, as you know."

When we had finished, Lillian told me she had plans to meet an old friend for lunch in Bois, then run a few errands in the city. "Can I pick up anything for you?" she asked, but I could think of nothing I would need before my trip home the next day. I would be short on souvenirs, I realized, but maybe I could pick up some French chocolate at the airport for M.J. and my other housemates.

I walked back up the hill and had lunch with Rosamunde, the usual bread and goat cheese, with greens for salad and apple crumble for dessert. The crumble was still warm, and we poured goat's milk cream on top. While we washed and dried dishes, I plied Rosamunde with questions about the celebration.

"How many visitors are likely to come?" I asked.

"There were almost a hundred at the last celebration."

"Quite a few." I pictured the decidedly unwelcoming sign beside the road at the duchy entrance. Apparently it hadn't deterred visitors to the celebration. "What kind of people come?"

"Mostly expatriates, Guzos who left the duchy to get a higher education or find a job. Often, they married abroad and settled there. Like Lillian,

Peter's mother. Most of the expats will come from England or France, a few from Italy."

"It must be a nice holiday for them."

"Yes. Most Guzo families have sons and daughters who migrated. The celebration provides an opportunity for a family reunion. Every five years, the expats bring their kids, and sometimes their grandkids, to reconnect with their roots. This year will be the first time there will be a museum and guided tours of the convent, thanks to Peter. And, of course, the visitors all like to raise a knife at the ceremony. It's just a quaint custom for the children and grandchildren. They can hardly pledge their allegiance to the duchy, since they don't live here. But the ceremony is often meaningful for those who left, or so I'm told."

I thought of Gwen. She was an expat of sorts, I supposed, with her apartment in New York City and her global travels. On my first evening in the duchy, we had stood beside her rental car at the overlook above the valley. And she had spoken with passion about her love for the duchy. Maybe the more you saw of the world, the more precious this place became. I was beginning to feel that way, and I had only been here two weeks. St. Uguzo was a beautiful place with fine people, and it was now vulnerable from forces both inside and out. How could I not care about it? And yet, I was going to leave.

After we finished the dishes, I spread out my recording materials at Rosamunde's kitchen table. There, she told me about her family. They were a contrast to Lillian's, Wiskara instead of Royal. Rosamunde's father had been an educated man, and for years he had put out the local newspaper, including the special supplements that I had perused at the museum. He also judged the essays that the school children wrote for the celebration, the best of which ended up in the supplements. According to Rosamunde, he looked for originality and skill with words rather than craven patriotism. Her mother often entered her pies and tarts in baking contests. The competition was stiff, and her mother was a good sport in those years when one of the Fosse ladies won.

According to Rosamunde, her parents never joined the crowd in the plaza for the Ceremony of Allegiance. They were loyal to the duchy, of course, but they were staunch Wiskara, and the idea of pledging their support to a duke or duchess didn't sit well with them. But that didn't keep Rosamunde and her little brother from attending the Ceremony.

When we were finished, I turned off the tape recorder and thanked Rosamunde for her interview. "I'm grateful for your help with the study. And with everything else. I would never have known about my grandfather if it weren't for you."

"I'm glad I could be of help." She gave my hand a little squeeze. "Your grandfather would be so proud of you." Then she got up, put on her apron, and busied herself around the kitchen. It was my cue to gather up my equipment and leave, but I remained at her kitchen table, absently turning the pages of my notebook.

"Rosamunde," I said finally, "what if I gave up my study? Could I stay for the celebration?"

"Give up your study?" She gave me a long look, her dark eyes peering into mine. "Isn't that what you came here for? To gather information and re-launch your career?"

"That's what I thought I came for," I said. "Now I'm not so sure."

She lowered herself onto a chair facing me. "As I recall, the Council was only concerned with your plans to publish what you observed here. They didn't want our troubles broadcast to the world." She paused. "I suppose...I suppose if you agreed not to report any of your findings, the council would have no objection to your staying."

"That's what I was thinking."

"It's a big decision, is it not? If you decide to give up your study, do tell me, and I will inform the council members. I'm quite certain they will let you stay for the celebration. After all, you are Gwen's guest. And mine too. But Holly, you must be very sure about what you really want. Because there will be no turning back."

By supper time, I'd decided I really had to leave the duchy. It was my only hope for getting back into the department and resurrecting my moribund academic career. I was rummaging through the fridge, collecting the ingredients for a cheese omelet for dinner when I heard footsteps behind me.

I turned and faced Peter, who looked at me warily.

"What is it?" I asked.

"Mum is in Bois. The friend she's visiting has had an emergency. A daughter in the hospital. Anyway, Mum won't be back until later this evening."

"Oh, that's too bad," I said. And then I understood what this meant. Tonight was the dress rehearsal. "No. You can't ask me to play Anwen."

He pursed his lips. "Holly, there is nothing I want less than to ask this of you. But you see my position. Please. Be Anwen one last time."

"Merde," I said. At least I'd picked up a little French in the duchy.

Once inside the gym, I crossed to the stage, aware of a nervous buzz in the air. The cast and crew clearly shared dress rehearsal jitters, everyone aware that this was their last chance to pull their act together before the performance on Saturday.

Peter stood on the stage and announced in a calm voice that Lillian was unavoidably detained, and I would fill in as Anwen for this rehearsal. People glanced in my direction, and a wave of murmurs rose and ebbed.

Alice Cotton approached me, a rich green velvet gown draped over one arm, and I realized that Peter must have already notified the costume committee that I was substituting for Lillian.

"Since this is a dress rehearsal," Alice said, "we thought you should wear a costume. I believe this might serve." Alice held up the gown so that its shoulders touched mine. "It's a little short, but that shouldn't be a problem for tonight." She touched my hair, which I had pulled back in a low ponytail and secured with a polka dot scrunchy. "The emerald color is lovely with your auburn hair. And it brings out the green in your eyes."

I looked at the gown dubiously, reluctant to dress for a part that wasn't even mine. "I don't know," I said. "Is it really necessary? I'm just a stand-in."

Alice placed her free hand on my arm. "You've worked so hard on the play. You deserve this. Let's go backstage and try on the gown. This will be your performance."

The dress did indeed fit pretty well, with a neckline that was low but not too revealing. The waist was loose, but Alice was ready with needle and thread. She made a couple of small tucks, which took care of that problem. The worn velvet was soft against my skin, and the skirt draped gracefully. I'd worn my black ballet flats, and my ankles showed above them. Alice assured me they were hardly noticeable.

Obediently, I sat on a chair while Alice brushed out my hair, so that it hung just below my shoulders.

"Let's leave it long," she said. "We haven't time for anything fancy, and anyway, it's more romantic this way." She used a couple of combs to hold it back, then I sat still as she applied some rouge, lipstick, and a little mascara from the make-up trove that Tony and I had purchased in Bois. Finally, I stood and turned around in a slow circle as the two other ladies from the costume committee looked on. Alice smiled. "Very nice, my lady."

I thanked her for her kindness and strode onto the stage in preparation for Scene One, in which I, as Anwen, was summoned by the abbess.

Peter was standing on the gym floor, giving instructions to the crew. He glanced up and stopped mid-sentence, staring at me with what looked like admiration. I was pleased, but I reminded myself that I was nothing to him. Well, very little.

Until then, I hadn't seen Peter's costume. He took a step back, which allowed me to take it all in, and I had to admit that he was splendid as Philippe. He wore an embroidered black jacket over a white shirt, knee-length breeches, high socks, and modern dress shoes. A rich blue cape was draped over his left shoulder and arm, covering his cast. The costume was an odd mixture of fashion spanning the seventeenth to twentieth centuries, but who cared? He looked terrific. I was pretty sure that Ernest Merrywether, the nineteenth-century schoolteacher and author of the play, would have approved.

Fred was already on stage in costume, standing in front of a carved wooden desk. He was imposing in his flowing black habit, his bald head covered by a starched white bandeau and veil. At over six feet, the abbess was a figure to cause trembling in any young nun.

"Sorry," I said, feeling sheepish about playing Anwen again. "I guess I'm the understudy."

"You look lovely." He leaned over and whispered in my ear. "I always thought you were the best Anwen." His words melted me, and I beamed him my thanks.

I was carrying a copy of the play book, since I hadn't memorized all of Anwen's lines, and I glanced over my part, repeating the sentences in my mind as we waited for the scene to begin. I handed the book to a crew member offstage, trusting in my memory and my ability to ad lib a little if necessary.

Fred carried the scene with his usual finesse. When Peter entered as the dashing Philippe, he and I maintained a polite and guarded distance, which was appropriate for both our current relationship and the story.

It wasn't until we finished Act One that I began to get really nervous. In the next scene, Philippe proposed marriage to Anwen. How was I going to get through those emotional speeches with Peter? I always opened my heart when I was portraying a character, but under the circumstances, that could be hard. Just stay in character, I advised myself. You'll be fine.

While I gathered some fabric daisies from a prop box, the crew moved a woodland backdrop onto the stage, as well as a wooden prop painted to resemble a fallen tree trunk. I sat on the trunk, trying not to wobble it. Peter came onstage, looking as ill-at-ease as I felt. He stood next to me, and as the curtain opened, I began winding the daisies into a chain.

Following the script, Philippe and I made polite small talk about our long trip from Wales to France while I wove my flowers. He paced back and forth across the stage and finally stood facing me. "My dearest Lady Anwen," he said, "when I set out on this journey, I had only thoughts of devotion—to my beloved sister, who placed you in my care, and to those nuns in your order who await your arrival. My steadfastness has never waned. But I now find that my devotion has changed its object. I have examined my heart, and it is to you, my lady, that I now pledge my faithfulness. In truth, I am able to think of no one else." Peter paused, coloring under his makeup, and for a moment I wondered if he had forgotten his lines. But he continued.

"Sweet Anwen, if you are set on entering the convent, then I shall speak no more. But if you find in your heart a spark of affection for me, then I pray you, let not your maidenly reserve hold back your words."

I stood up from the tree trunk, my eyes cast down demurely, drawing together the words in my mind. "Kind sir, I too have examined my heart. As a child, I was convinced that I was destined for a life of saintly contemplation. But now I feel an even stronger calling. A call to a life of service and obedience to a man whom I esteem above all others. Who is second in my devotion only to my heavenly father."

Peter stepped closer. "I could hardly imagine…and yet, 'tis true. My affection is returned, and by the finest, most perfect lady ever to grace this world. My dearest Anwen, I have little to offer in riches or fame, but whatever I have, I pledge it to you. Freely and with all my heart."

"Dearest Philippe," I said, "I wish to share my life with you, in joy and in sorrow. And trusting always in the Lord to guide us in our rightful path."

Peter went down on one knee. "Lady Anwen, will you do me the honor of becoming my wife?"

"Yes, my lord," I said, allowing my emotions to flow. "I am, and will always be, yours."

Peter reached out to take my hand. Careful, I told myself. We are only friends. But his touch warmed me, sending a familiar glow through my body. Oh, treacherous heart, I thought, in a flash of Elizabethan passion. After a long moment, Peter released my hand and stood.

"Curtain," he called, his voice breaking. He cleared his throat. "Take your places for Act Three."

I was wrung out, physically and emotionally, by the time we got to the final scene of the play, where Peter and I stood in front of the mountainous backdrop, facing the Guzos, who were, in fact, the audience. We pledged our loyalty to our subjects, as the script required, and the assembled actors and crew cheered. Then we sang the Guzo anthem, took brief bows, and left the stage. We'd made it through to the end.

Rosamunde, Kessie, and I left the gym together when the rehearsal was at an end, and the props had been stored. Peter was having a quiet word with the actors in the battle scene, although it seemed to me they had performed quite well. We ladies had changed out of our costumes, but we were still wearing make-up. I could hardly wait to get home and wash it off.

It was a quiet walk up Dukesway to the plaza, apart from a rumble of voices coming from the mead hall. Kessie made occasional comments about her teacher and schoolmates, which Rosamunde responded to with a word or phrase. My thoughts turned to the rehearsal. Amazingly, I had made it through my lines with only a few small slip-ups, and it had been fun wearing the romantic, emerald-green gown. In the end, I was satisfied with the evening. Alice had been right. I had needed one performance of my own, even if it was only the dress rehearsal.

We arrived at the plaza and began the uphill trudge to our houses. On the way, I pictured Anwen, the young Welsh noblewoman who had trekked to St. Uguzo. Had she ever questioned her decision to go to the duchy? From everything Peter and Gwen had told me, I had learned a lot about the early days of the duchy.

Anwen and Philippe had arrived here to find the Wiskara, people with a well-established language and culture, who did not welcome a ruling family of outsiders. And not long afterward, the pair faced the task of building a monastery for a group of nuns and welcoming other Catholic refugees from England. Meanwhile, the duchy wasn't entirely secure; principalities around them laid claim to their land.

And then, in the greatest blow to Anwen, Philippe went back to his family in France, where he died, leaving Anwen in charge of three children and a duchy. It must have been a far greater challenge than she'd anticipated back in the days when she was a novice in Wales. Yet, somehow, she'd found the courage to survive and move forward.

I gazed at the houses alongside our path, first the tall, narrow ones crowded together in the town, then the chalets and cottages farther up the road. It was almost ten o'clock, but lights were still on in most of the homes, as Guzos made their final preparations for the big celebration.

I had come to love St. Uguzo, with its many charms and flaws. I hoped that I wasn't seeing the duchy in its final days. I hated to think what would be left if Sebastian and Wilheard had their way. Would Wilheard become a puppet dictator with Sebastian pulling his strings? I shuddered.

When I arrived at the house, I realized I hadn't even begun to pack for my trip home. Not that I had a whole lot to stuff into my bag. It could wait until tomorrow. There was plenty of time before the ten-o'clock bus whisked me away.

CHAPTER TWENTY-FOUR

Day 14, Friday

In the dream, I was above the glade, floating body-less at the level of the treetops. The Guardian rose high up to my right, and the circle of packed earth that comprised the glade lay below me. To one side of the clearing was a sign:

FUTURE SITE OF HELIPAD

PRIVATE PROPERTY

STAY OUT

Alarm shot through me. The glade was going to be used as a landing site for a helicopter? Surely, it couldn't be. The Thin Place was there. The Guzos would never allow it.

As I hovered, I became aware of a harsh mechanical noise moving toward the clearing. And then I saw it, a large machine with a big metal blade lifted above ground level and a cab above. A massive bulldozer. With a screech, the giant blade lowered, and I watched in horror as the monster moved slowly forward, heading straight for the clearing, scraping off soil, rocks, everything in its way.

"Stop!" I shouted repeatedly, but my voice was maddeningly soft. Inside the cab, the driver was a blurry shape, oblivious to my pleas. The noise grew louder, dust rising into the air, as the bulldozer reached the edge of the glade. "No!" I screamed in horror, as the monster ripped up the earth, destroying the circle. I wailed my helplessness and fury.

"Holly, Holly, wake up," came a woman's voice. I opened my eyes, my cries dissolving, leaving my breath ragged. Lillian stood over me, her face dimly lit by the grayish dawn light.

"Oh my gosh," I gasped.

Lillian sat down beside me on the bed. "It was just a dream."

I groaned, realizing the gravity of what I'd seen—the lethal assault on the Thin Place. "I'm afraid it was more than that."

Twenty minutes later, Lillian and I were gathered with Rosamunde around her kitchen table, each of us silently mulling over my vision and what it meant for the duchy, tea cooling in our cups and our bread lying uneaten.

As I sat there, mourning the imminent destruction of the glade, the strangest thing came over me.

An awakening.

I don't know what else to call it. The murkiness that had filled my mind — the doubts, the fears, the anxiety — were all gone. In their place was a riveting clarity. All my self-important goals had fallen away. I was no longer the ambitious young woman whose mission in life was to enter academia and climb through the ranks. The world did not need another Dr. Ferris.

Two things were certain. One, I was dumping my research project. And two, I was going to stay in the duchy through the celebration. I didn't know what I could do to help save St. Uguzo from a takeover by Sebastian's company. Maybe nothing at all. I was an outsider, after all. But the Thin Place had chosen me to receive its revelations, gut-wrenching though they were, and I would not abandon it. I would not give up on the duchy.

I thought of my notebook, full of pages of my happy jottings. My decision to dump the study was easy, but it certainly wasn't painless. I had loved immersing myself in the past duchy celebrations. I felt like a true explorer, uncovering information buried away in the archives and in people's memories, and piecing together the patterns that tied together duchy society. Of course, everything that I had learned would stay with me, and that was some consolation. But it would remain hidden away in my notes. Possibly forever.

I took a sip of my lukewarm tea, grimaced, and replaced it on the saucer. My thoughts turned to my grandfather, that homesick young man who had left behind not only the Air Corps and his buddies, but also any future life back home that he might have imagined. He had known something about letting go.

"What do we do now?" Lillian asked.

Without even thinking, I said, "we gather the Dreamers."

Rosamunde looked pensive, and I remembered her saying earlier that it wasn't the Guzo way for Dreamers to meet. I waited anxiously, knowing in my gut that we needed to share what we knew. Finally, Rosamund nodded. "Yes, quite right." She glanced at the clock on the wall and eyed me. "Are you packed for your trip?"

"I'm staying," I announced.

Lillian grinned and patted my hand. "Well done, my dear."

"I'll tell the council," Rosamunde said.

Lillian sat back. "We'd best get busy and let the Dreamers know that we're gathering. What do you say? Shall we meet this afternoon at the glade?"

"Two o'clock," Rosamunde said. She cocked her head, a tiny smile appearing as she gazed at us both. "It will be our first circle of Dreamers. At least the first one in a very, very long time."

I started down the road, heading for the museum. I hadn't seen Peter that morning, and I needed to let him know my change of plans. I wasn't looking forward to it. After all, Peter had worked hard gathering materials on former celebrations so that I would be able to leave. He might have let me down emotionally, but he'd supported me as a scholar from the start.

For the first time since I'd arrived, I had to walk close to the side of the road, in order to avoid occasional cars driving down to the center of town. The far-flung Guzos were arriving for their celebration.

As I approached the plaza, I was struck by a cacophony of sound. A dozen or so people sat on folding chairs, tuning up instruments of various kinds. It was the band, I realized, getting ready for Saturday night's big dance. And I'll be here, I thought. Maybe I could sit among the musicians and play my penny whistle. The idea cheered me. If we were very lucky, we might even have something to celebrate.

I crossed the bridge and saw several cars parked alongside the road across from the convent. Fred's cheesery van and the sheriff's van now had company, four cars with license plates with an "F" for France and one with an "I" for what I thought was Italy on the strips to the left of the tags.

I walked through the convent gate and was half way across the court-yard when I stopped in my tracks. On the museum door, Peter had put up a sheet announcing his tours of the convent. But above it was a flyer for the rally at seven o'clock that evening in the plaza. Did Peter know the sign was there? I stormed into the museum, where Peter was staring out one of the mullioned windows. He turned when he heard me. "I thought you'd be packing," he said.

"Did you know there's a sign for the rally on your door?" I asked, fully expecting him to be horrified.

"I told Sebastian he could put it up."

I stared at Peter. "You must be joking."

"I'm not supporting the rally," he said, "just letting people know it will take place."

"Just helping out Sebastian, you mean." I crossed my arms. "If I'm not mistaken, this is the guy who attacked Kessie and gave you a black eye, the one who told everybody I'm working for the CIA, the guy who is doing everything he can to make Wilheard, that wannabe Guzo, the next duke."

"I know. I know." Peter sank into a chair by my former work table, his gaze toward the window. "I'm not fond of him either. But you know, his company might not be all bad." He glanced at me and swiftly looked away. Not surprising given that my eyes were beaming death rays. I sat next to him, breathless to hear what kind of crap he would come up with next.

"Sebastian was telling me about the wealthy residents who will settle here. One is a fellow who is very keen on history. He has funded historical projects in the U.K. and the States. And he was a major donor to a museum in Los Angeles. It seems he is interested in the duchy. As a center of alpine historical study."

I could practically feel the excitement pulsing from Peter. It was exactly what he wanted for the museum, to make it a center for serious research. I wanted to join him in his enthusiasm, but I couldn't. "And what's the price for gaining a world-class museum? What if the price is watching the duchy become a dictatorship, with Wilheard Fosse at the helm?"

I watched with alarm as Peter's face reddened. He crashed his fist onto the table. "Have you any idea, any idea at all, how hard it is to keep this place funded? Not to mention bringing it up to international standards. And bringing our artwork home from the University of Leicester." He thrust his fingers through his hair, raising spiky tufts. "And now that Gran is gone, it's only Rosamunde who supports me on the council. No one else gives a rat's ass what happens to the museum or the work I do here."

I gulped, well aware that I had touched a raw nerve.

"So, yes, Holly, perhaps the idea of a wealthy donor doesn't sound all that bad. And if attracting him means letting Wilheard be duke, maybe I'm just willing to consider it."

I could hardly believe my ears. I gazed at him warily, as he slumped back on his chair.

"The duchy is going down the tubes," he said, "right before our eyes. People are practically up in arms, and without the cheese, our resources are very few." He raised an eyebrow to me. "Anyway, what do you care? By tomorrow, you'll be on a plane, flying back to the U.S."

"Actually, I'll be right here. That's what I came to tell you. I've decided to stay for the ceremony."

His face brightened for a second, then his brows knit. "What? What about your study? The council will never give their approval."

"I'm giving up my study," I said. "I'm sorry. I know you worked hard to help me with it. But I can't leave now." I told him about my dream of the bulldozer tearing up the glade. I didn't mention the gathering of dreamers that afternoon, since I wasn't sure how he'd react.

Peter had sat silently through my narrative, and now he lowered his head into his hands. I waited, and a moment later, he straightened and rose. "Well, then," he said in a stiff-upper-lip way, and he strode across the room to the entrance. Jerking the door open, he ripped the rally sheet off and tore it into strips, dumping them into a trash basket near the door. Good, I thought, but at the same time I worried about Peter, who was acting a little unhinged.

"If you'll excuse me," he mumbled and strode back to his office, closing the door. Several minutes went by as I wandered around the museum. I was reluctant to leave right away, since my relationship with Peter was on such shaky grounds. Doubts assailed me. Had I pressed Peter too hard? Was I too belligerent? But what choice did I have? I halted at the scribe's wooden lectern, where I slowly paged through the photocopy of the illuminated manuscript. Its beauty calmed me.

When Peter emerged from his office, I was relieved to see that his complexion had returned to its usual color and his hair no longer stood up in tufts.

"I'm sorry," I said. "I didn't mean to dismiss your concerns. I know the museum really needs money."

"No need to apologize. That big donor was probably all a lie. I mean, since when have we been able to trust Sebastian and Wilheard?"

"True."

"Let's forget about the evil duo," Peter said. "At least for now. I have something for you." He passed me a manila envelope. "It was to be a farewell gift. In fact, I was getting ready to take it to the bus stop. But you may as well have it now."

I opened the envelope and drew out a ringed binder with a plastic cover. The title page read:

A Journal of World War II

by Albert Becker Fleming.

Introduction and transcription by Holly Hewitt.

"We can add your middle name later," Peter said.

"No, it's perfect the way it is," I said. "Thank you." I sat and began turning the pages, one by one, starting with my introduction, and continuing through the transcriptions of my grandfather's diary.

Peter sat across the table from me. "Mum had the pages photocopied and bound when she went into Bois yesterday."

I turned to the final page, a finely rendered pencil drawing of my grandfather's tombstone. "Oh," I murmured. Peter's signature was at the bottom. "It's beautiful."

"I'm no artist," he said. "I also took some photos, both of the tombstone and a few of the original journal entries. The film should be developed by Monday, if you're still around then."

"You thought of everything," I said. "You and Lillian. I'm grateful to you both."

"I'm keeping the originals here," he said. "They aren't mine to give away. But your family deserves a copy. I read it through, and you did an excellent job with both the transcription and the introduction."

"Thanks," I said, pleased that he had found my work worthy of praise.

He cleared his throat. "I'm sure you know by now that your grandfather was a very fine man. Your mother and sister deserve to know that too."

"They do," I said, blinking back tears. "This means a great deal to me." And even more because Peter had assembled the book for me. Maybe I had been a little more than a fling to him. I slid the binder back into the envelope.

"I'm glad you're staying," Peter said.

I quirked a half-smile. "So am I."

He ran his fingers through his hair again, more gently this time. "Holly, I know I said some things about us, about our relationship. But I want you to know — "

"No," I said, "there's no need to explain." The last thing I wanted was to hash over our brief affair. "Let's just leave things as they are. You and I are colleagues and friends, and that's more than enough. And as you said, I will be on a plane soon." I picked up the envelope. "That reminds me. Could I ask you a favor? Would you call up the travel agent and change my return ticket from tomorrow to Sunday?"

He looked like he was going to say something, but he stopped and nodded. "I'll do that now."

I left the museum and exited the convent gates, only to see a dozen people heading down the road toward me. A glance at my watch revealed it was almost ten o'clock, time for Peter's first tour of the convent.

Kessie was in the first group, along with three other girls, all laughing and talking in high, girlish voices. She greeted me excitedly, saying they had heard that the cellar was haunted, and they wanted to check it out. Man, I thought, between vivid dreams and visions, the duchy was full of spirits. Why the excitement over a haunted cellar? But I just smiled and wished them luck with the ghosts.

I nodded to the people who followed, including Wilheard and Eglentyne, whom I hadn't expected to see at Peter's convent tour. He had been right. The rarely-seen cellar seemed to be a big draw.

Shortly before two o'clock, Lillian and I set out for the gathering of Dreamers, hiking up the road to the rocky crossing in the stream.

I wondered who would show up for the meeting. Rosamunde had said there would probably be a half dozen or so Dreamers, but she hadn't named anyone. "Is Peter a Dreamer?" I asked Lillian. He had been dismissive of vivid dreams earlier, saying they were useless, but he hadn't actually denied their existence.

"He had a couple of vivid dreams when he was a boy, although we never called them that. He found them a bit scary. Besides, his father only believes in the material world. If something can be measured, it's real. Naturally, the boys picked up on his skepticism. I told Peter about our gathering today, but I would be surprised if he showed up."

A few minutes later, we turned onto the narrow path to the glade, Lillian in the lead. The forest was quiet, aside from leaves whooshing softly in the wind and occasional bird calls. I caught a flash of movement to my right. A bushy-tailed, caramel-colored marmot sat on a boulder. Monty. He met my gaze, hopped down, and disappeared behind a stand of pines. Maybe it was the marmots who were the real guardians of the duchy.

It wasn't long before we'd made our way out of the cool, shady forest and stepped into the warm sunshine of the glade. Having adjusted my eyes to the gloom of the forest, the brilliance of the sunny glade made me squint.

When I looked at the trio of Dreamers assembled, I broke into a grin. We were preceded by Roderick and Oswin, my favorite goat herders. And next to them was Giselle, with her spiky blond hair and her silver nose piercings. Not only did I like her, but I was relieved that I wasn't the only young person in the group. The Dreamers might be small in number, but we weren't a dying breed. Not yet anyway.

Lillian and I had just stepped into the circle when I heard footsteps behind us. I turned to see Rosamunde with Violet, our dining hall chef. In the dappled forest light, Violet's eyes, always stunning, were a deep shade of blue, almost cobalt.

After we had greeted one another, Rosamunde said, "I believe this is everyone."

I counted. Seven in all. I hoped it was a lucky number. I remembered that Rosamunde had said earlier that there might be Guzos who were reluctant to admit being Dreamers or had not yet recognized their ability.

"Shall we form a circle?" Lillian suggested.

When we had arranged ourselves in a cozy ring, Rosamunde invited us to share any dreams or visions we wished to recount.

"I'll begin," Violet said. "I have a confession. I saw the cheese injected."

I gasped.

"Well, I'll be jiggered," Roderick mumbled. "Who did it? I don't suppose he showed his face."

"Afraid not. It was a few months ago. I couldn't see much in the dream. The scene was dark, with just a beam of light, from a torch maybe.

A flashlight.

"I saw a big needle, like a hypodermic needle," Violet said. "In the dream, a hand stuck the needle into a round of cheese. I can't even describe the hand because it was gloved."

"And you told no one?" Roderick asked.

"I should have. I can see that now. But it seemed so inconsequential. Like I'd watched some kind of ordinary lab test. Who would have guessed that someone would sabotage the cheese? Besides, I had received a tetanus shot a few days earlier. I decided it was my subconscious mind processing that. Eventually, I forgot about it. Until, that is, Rosamunde announced that the cheese had been tampered with. Then I knew what I'd seen. But it was too late to warn people."

In a way, it was a comfort to learn that I wasn't the only one having vivid dreams. The Thin Place was working on other people too.

"It's my turn, I suppose," Rosamunde said. About a year ago, shortly after Duchess Anne-Marie died, I had a vivid dream. I told Gwen and Giselle about it, but no one else." In her dream, she had seen a tall young woman with auburn hair standing behind a counter, with funny-looking hawks perched above her on a shelf.

"Oh my gosh," I exclaimed. "That was me, at the Hungry Hawk Café. The hawks were toy mascots."

"That's what we figured out, finally," Rosamunde said. "You'll remember that Daniel McCleary had been keeping an eye on you, so we knew where you were, more or less."

Daniel, I recalled, was the pilot whose life my grandfather had saved. He was also Grandma's friend, and I'd met him at her house a few times. "Wait," I said. "I thought that vivid dreams would only predict events here in the duchy."

"Usually they do," Rosamunde said, "but not always. They just need some connection to an individual here. I dreamt once of a flood in a town by the sea. I discovered soon after that my niece's house in Cornwall had been carried away in a storm. She and her family survived unharmed, praise God.

"Anyway, Holly, I took the dream as a sign that it was time to bring you to the duchy. So Gwen and I concocted a plan to lure you here. As you may recall, it involved a concert at your university. And even after all that finagling, the plot nearly didn't work."

"I declined Gwen's invitation at first," I told the group. "But I had eaten a slice of the duchy cheese. That must have been working on me, because at the last minute, I agreed."

"Yes!" Giselle said, pumping her fist. "I told Gwen to be sure to take cheese." Everyone nodded their understanding. Who could resist duchy cheese?

"Of course," Rosamunde said, "my dream occurred months before our present problems began. I thought we were bringing Holly here to learn about her grandfather. And she did." She turned to Giselle. "I think you had an early premonition that something larger was going on."

"I couldn't be sure," Giselle said, "but I'd been having dark dreams. Not vivid dreams exactly, but dreams with shady, cloaked figures and desolate landscapes. Nothing like the duchy, certainly. But every morning I'd wake up with a sense of impending doom, and it hung over me all day. I wasn't my usual self at all. Grandpère can testify to it."

"True enough," Roderick said, and with that, I realized that Giselle was his granddaughter. A family of Dreamers.

Giselle continued. "I was excited to think that Holly was coming. I hoped she would bring some new energy." She turned to me. "I wondered if you might be a Dreamer. I'd heard that your grandfather was."

"Good grief," I said. "Did everyone know I was Albert's granddaughter?"

Giselle grinned. "Everyone in this circle did. Or we suspected, anyway. I was dying to tell you, but I was ordered to hold my tongue." She glanced at Rosamunde, and I could guess who had given the command.

Rosamunde coughed lightly. "Holly, perhaps you could tell us about your recent dreams." I described my first visit to the glade and the dream of Gwen's murder that followed.

Violet clicked her tongue. "So that's why Gwen left so quickly, and without a word. It was so unlike her."

"I wanted to tell you all," Rosamunde said, "but I was trying very hard to keep it under wraps. Gwen told no one where she was going. That way, we couldn't let the location slip out. And we wouldn't have to lie about where she was."

I then told about that morning's dream, the horrible scene with the bulldozer ripping up the glade. A hush fell over the group.

"It's that Sebastian fellow behind it," Roderick said. "He's a sly one, all right. And us Guzos—we're too trusting by half."

I stood there, musing over Guzo gullibility until Rosamunde spoke up. "Well then, does anyone else have a report?"

Our gazes soon converged on Oswin, Roderick's buddy. "An-to-ni-ti, an-to-ni-ti, an-to-ni-ti," he chanted.

"What is it, mate?" Roderick asked.

"An-to-ni-ti, an-to-ni-ti," Oswin repeated, his voice more agitated this time.

We looked at Roderick, but he shrugged helplessly. "Can you tell us more?" he asked his friend. But Oswin only halted and shook his head. He was silent for a moment, then he mumbled, "Loo-kout, loo-kout," worry etched into his wrinkled face.

"You're right there, mate," Roderick said. "We'd best look out if we want to keep our glade safe."

Lillian was standing beside me. She had been silent during the reports, but of course she had lost her younger son several months earlier. That could have eclipsed any warnings about the duchy. The fact that she had returned for the celebration and was here with us now spoke tons about her resilience and her loyalty.

She addressed the group. "It seems we have our work cut out for us, if we want to save our duchy. Shall we join hands?" She clasped hands with me and with Oswin on her other side. One by one, we linked hands until we had closed the circle. Following Lillian's lead, we shut our eyes, and after a moment I felt a small but reassuring hum course through me and through my fellow Dreamers. Then it was gone. We opened our eyes, released hands, and met each other's hopeful gazes.

"Mo-row," Oswin said in a surprisingly clear voice.

"Just so," Rosamunde said. "We'll meet here tomorrow. Say eight-thirty?" The Dreamers all assented.

"Right," Violet said. "We'll see what more the Thin Place cares to reveal."

"No more heavy machinery, I hope," I said.

"If I may," Giselle said, "I am going to tell my friends and kinfolk about Holly's bulldozer dream. Anyone who is open to such things. We must get out the word." Roderick gazed at his granddaughter approvingly, and I had the feeling that authority was being passed to the next, spiky-haired, metal-pierced generation.

"You're welcome to tell anyone about my dream," I said. "I expect the news will travel quickly. Whether it's believed or not." If there were more Dreamers tucked away in the duchy, they at least should give credence to my vision. And perhaps support us at the Ceremony of Allegiance.

"But let us keep our circle of Dreamers a secret for now," Lillian said. "We don't want any thrill-seekers or curious tourists to descend on us."

Rosamunde nodded. "Good point." She turned a kind gaze on each of us in turn. "May the Spirit be with us all," she said. And with that, we turned to go, leaving the glade in single file. I took one last look at the clearing before I stepped onto the path. The Thin Place didn't always reveal its secrets in the most helpful ways. I'd seen that already. In fact, its revelations seemed to be kind of hit or miss. I suspected our small band would have to search out our own path forward. The celebration was tomorrow. Whatever we were led to do, I hoped we wouldn't be too late.

I spent the rest of the afternoon at the museum. Peter was looking for some way to entertain the children who visited, and it occurred to me that they could do a small art project using the letters used in the illuminated manuscripts. I found a bunch of plain note cards and a few boxes of crayons. Carefully, I wrote out given names on three of the cards, experimenting with "Holly," "Peter," and "Lillian." But for the first letter of each name, H, P, and L, I drew a simplified form of the elaborate capital letters that began paragraphs in the manuscripts. Then I drew flowers and vines around the border of the cards. Finally, I colored the letters and border illustrations with crayons. The name cards were actually quite pretty, and I thought at least some of the kids might enjoy making their own.

Peter, Lillian, and I arrived at the plaza a little before seven o'clock for the rally. The square was already buzzing with excitement. Not only had Guzos turned out in force, but it looked like some of the visitors were there too, most more fashionably dressed than their Guzo kin. Juliette and Baptiste stood off to the side, silver badges on their jackets. It was the first time I'd seen this emblem of the sheriff's authority. Behind the plaza, several children, including Ozzie, Juliette's son, ran back and forth. I looked for the other Dreamers and caught sight of Giselle standing nearer the front, next to an older couple.

At one end of the plaza stood the long wooden stage that had been set up for the next day's festivities, including the Ceremony of Allegiance. Near the center was a dais with a covered microphone on a stand next to it. The structure lent an air of decorum to the rally.

Several people stood at the back of the stage, including Baptiste's two younger brothers, Bernard and Bruno, in their bright red kerchiefs. They were in conversation with Sebastian and Wilheard, who were dressed much like traditional Guzos, with loose vests and matching deep blue kerchiefs, although their clothing was clearly new. They didn't look like they had ever herded goats.

A young woman with rosy cheeks and a deep pink shawl appeared at my shoulder. "Hello. You're the American, aren't you? I'm Sophie, a friend of Giselle's. She told me about your dream. I just want you to know that we will not let anyone destroy the glade." I thanked her from the heart for letting me know, and she moved away to join a good-looking young man with a goatee and a brown kerchief. I was encouraged to know that Giselle was getting the word out.

A few minutes after seven, Bernard stepped up to the dais and uncovered the microphone. He looked nervous, and Sebastian quickly appeared beside him, testing the mike, and handed it back.

"Welcome, fellow Guzos," Bernard said, his voice booming across the plaza and probably the whole town. He seriously didn't need the sound system. He started talking about the grievances that had brought him to the rally, including how slowly the council moved and the lack of modern conveniences. Once he'd hit his stride, he spoke passionately about the failures of law enforcement in the duchy, pointing out that Clive's death had yet to be explained, and that they had no idea who had tainted the duchy cheese.

I glanced over at Juliette, who had affected a poker face, revealing no emotion. But beside her, Baptiste looked seriously irritated at his younger brother.

Most importantly, Bernard continued, the economy of the duchy was in peril, and no one was taking charge. The council members were sitting on their hands, he said, with no clear leadership of any kind.

A number of young people in the front clapped and shouted their agreement with each of Bernard's points. The people farther back, in my area, were quieter, but many nodded and occasionally called out their support. It was hard not to agree. Everything that Bernard said was true to a point, although he could have been more understanding of the difficult position the council was in, especially since these revelations had come so close to the time of the celebration. And Juliette was working hard with very limited resources. He didn't mention that.

"I'd say we're ready for change," Bernard called out. "Am I right?"

"Yes!" shouted Guzos around the plaza, although a few stood silent, arms crossed.

"We've called you here today because we have a solution," Bernard said. "A way to get out of this rut. To move forward with prosperity and security. And I want to introduce a man who has the right plan to bring this about." He motioned Sebastian forward. "And here he is, Sebastian Elliott, a friend of our own Wilheard Fosse, and a man who I've come to know and trust."

Sebastian walked up to the mike and raised his hand in a modest wave.

"Go, Sebastian!" shouted someone from the front.

"Greetings, Folks," Sebastian said. "As many of you know, the last place I expected to be tonight was here on this stage. In fact, I came to St. Uguzo for a quiet, peaceful holiday. Can you believe it?"

"No, I can't," I mumbled.

Sebastian's expression turned earnest. "Little did I know that I would soon be involved in the most important work of my career. But let me begin by telling you about the company I work for, International Strategic Solutions. It's a mouthful, isn't it? But don't be put off by the name. It's an organization that helps fine communities just like yours."

He proceeded to explain how his company settled law-abiding, financially comfortable people in communities that could benefit from state-of-the-art infrastructure, good jobs, and a revitalized economy. I'd heard it all before, the day Sebastian drove me to Bois and dangled a glitzy job before my trusting eyes. It was almost two weeks ago, but it felt like a year.

Peter and I exchanged a look. "Snake oil salesman," I whispered.

His hazel eyes crinkled in mirth. "Indeed."

I looked around me. Most of the other Guzos were watching Sebastian with rapt attention and hopeful expressions, although here and there, small clusters of people looked skeptical. They may be our only hope, I thought, only too aware that the doubters appeared to be a small minority.

Sebastian went on to explain the two reasons that he had originally rejected the duchy as one of their chosen communities.

"Problem number one," Sebastian said. "Leadership was too diffuse, with no one person in charge. If we needed a fast decision, who would we go to? Know what I mean? And second, the duchy is a delightful place. I love it here. But it is also very traditional. Maybe a little too traditional for those folks who'd like to catch up with the times and move forward." A rumble of agreement rose from the crowd.

"Friends, I have to confess that two weeks ago, I didn't think there was a chance in hell that things here would ever change." He shook his head. "Man. Was I wrong. I see now that St. Uguzo is standing on the verge of a transformation. One that will ensure the vitality of the duchy for generations to come. And let me tell you who can bring this about, who can shepherd you to this new level of prosperity. My good friend and colleague, Wilheard Fosse."

Wilheard stepped forward to an avalanche of applause. He looked genuinely pleased at the adulation of his fellow Guzos, and he waved and thanked everyone for coming. His speech was short, but he carried it off well. He talked about how he had always dreamed of coming to the duchy and becoming a real Guzo. Then, through great good fortune, he had found a job with Sebastian's employer, Strategic Solutions. And he had seen first-hand what a difference the company could make to a struggling community. A place like St. Uguzo. He now saw it as his life's mission to make the duchy the best place it could be. And that meant joining forces with Strategic Solutions. "Fellow Guzos," he said, "have no doubt, the future is in our hands." Applause followed, and Wilheard thanked everyone again. He stepped to the side, allowing Bernard to replace him at the podium.

"What do you think?" Bernard asked the crowd. "I'd say we have just heard from our next duke." Gasps were followed by hearty applause and hoots of approval. In front, several young people jumped up and down. Bernard quieted the crowd with a raised hand. "Tomorrow, at the Ceremony of Allegiance, we will nominate and elect Wilheard as our next duke. And we will make sure he has the authority to get done what needs to be done."

A woman in the middle piped up. "And just what kind of authority is that?"

Sebastian stepped forward and took the mike. "I'm glad you asked that. Our success will depend on having a strong and confident leader, a duke with the support of his people. And the duke must be enabled to sign a contract. A contract that allows the duchy to form a partnership with Strategic Solutions. That's your first step to prosperity."

Beside me, Peter called out. "Nobody has seen this contract. When will we see it?"

"It's on its way from headquarters," Sebastian said. "Coming by special courier. I'll let you all know as soon as it arrives. Then you can take a good, long look."

"It's already too late for that," Peter grumbled quietly to me.

Bernard and Wilheard joined Sebastian at the center of the stage, where Bernard led the crowd in several rounds of "Wilheard for Duke!" while

Wilheard waved like a champ. Peter, Lillian, and I were silent, which caused us to get a few critical looks from the revved-up people around us.

The rally ended, and people began leaving the square, talking animatedly. "I've certainly heard more than enough," Peter said. Both he and Lillian spotted some old friends among the visitors.

"Come join us," Lillian said, but I declined. I would be uncomfortable as an outsider at her happy reunion. I looked around for Giselle, but she must have already left the plaza. That left me standing alone, the shouts of "Wilheard for Duke" still echoing in my head.

I supposed I should head over to the dining hall for a bite to eat, but a lot of people were streaming in that direction, and I didn't want to be in the middle of another crowd. On the other hand, I wasn't ready to walk home, so I headed for the wall at the far corner of the plaza, where I could sit and reflect on the horrible rally and what it portended for the future of the duchy.

The day was waning, but the sky still glowed a rich gold over the darkening mountains. The outdoor lights hadn't yet come on in the plaza, and the section of the perimeter wall under the evergreens was in shadow. As I neared the wall, I saw the glow of a cigarette and the outline of a man sitting on the wall. I was about to switch directions when I realized that I knew the smoker. It was Tony, Clive and Alice's son and my fellow Jedi knight from our excursion to the toy store. I walked over.

"May I join you?" I asked. Tony gestured to the space beside him, and I boosted myself onto the wall. Having stored up the sun's heat, the stone was pleasantly warm against my jeans. We both watched as the plaza continued to empty. Considering Tony was Sebastian's "man," I didn't detect much enthusiasm in him. In fact, he looked about as despondent as I felt.

"I'm not sure the Force is with us tonight," I said.

"Doesn't look that way."

"You think Wilheard will become duke?" I asked.

"Could be." He took a long drag on his cigarette and exhaled slowly. "I heard you're staying for the celebration."

"Yeah," I said. "I couldn't leave now. Not before the yodeling contest."

He flashed me a wry smile.

"No, I mean it," I said. "I've always wanted to hear alpine yodelers."

"Don't sit too close. They can get pretty loud."

"Right." I scooted myself back on the wall and let my legs swing. "So, it looks like we'll be working props together for the play after all."

"Sweet."

My thoughts turned to Juliette's comments a few days earlier. She had been at the mead hall when Tony became furious with Wilheard. According to her, Tony had claimed that Wilheard was in no position to criticize Clive, since his own hands were dirty. But she had never found out what Tony meant. Nor had anyone else, as far as I knew.

"You know," I said, "I suspect you don't want Wilheard to become duke any more than I do."

Tony snorted. I took that as a yes.

"Look, Tony. I think you know something about Wilheard. Something that could cause him problems, maybe even keep him from becoming duke."

"Could be." He took another drag on his cigarette.

This was frustrating. For the life of me, I didn't know how to get past Tony's barriers. "Does it have something to do with the duchy cheese?"

"That's part of it."

I made a wild guess. "Did Wilheard inject the cheese?"

"Yeah. I think so. But there's no solid proof, if that's what you're looking for."

Wow. I hadn't seriously expected Tony to say yes. But he had, sort of. I couldn't say it was a huge surprise. Wilheard had been pretty high on my list of suspects. He was an outsider, who had arrived in the duchy about four months earlier, not too long before the cheese was contaminated. Still, I didn't like to think that Wilheard would stoop that low. I had thought that somewhere in his grinchy little heart he truly cared about the duchy.

"Proof of guilt would be excellent," I said, "but at this point I'd settle for just knowing what's going on. What makes you think Wilheard injected the cheese?" I was frankly astonished that he had the skill to pull it off.

"Because of something I saw."

"Which was?"

"I can't talk about it. Sebastian would find out, and I'd be in trouble."

That lousy Sebastian. Always in the middle of things. When he wasn't lurking in the background. "Okay," I said. "So Wilheard sabotaged the cheese, but you can't talk about it. You said that the cheese was just one part of Wilheard's problem. What was the rest of it?" Whatever it was, I hoped Tony could talk about it more openly.

"It doesn't matter now. It's all in the past." A look of world-weariness had spread over Tony's face, making him appear older.

I took another stab. "Wilheard had dealings with your dad, didn't he?"

"Yeah."

I swallowed hard. "Did Wilheard have something to do with your father's death?"

Tony slowly exhaled a stream of smoke. I could feel the tension in his muscles. "It's nothing I can prove."

Yikes. I was getting closer to the truth. If only Juliette were here. Or anyone who was good at talking to teenage boys. But I couldn't wait around for somebody better to take over. This conversation might be our best chance to get to the source of the duchy's recent tragedies. Not to mention defeating

Wilheard. What's more, I sensed that Tony really wanted to get this information off his chest.

"That's okay. Just tell me about Wilheard and your dad."

"I can't. I told you."

I half expected Tony to hop off the wall and leave, but he didn't. I sat there, the heels of my sneakers thudding against the stone wall. How was I going to get the story out of this kid?

"Look, Tony, you and I both know that Wilheard shouldn't be duke. He shouldn't be a dogcatcher. And Sebastian is a scumbag. Am I right?"

Tony smirked. "You could say that."

"We can stop them. I'm sure of it. Tell me what you know."

"A lot of it is just guesses. You know, like educated guesses."

"Give me your guesses."

He took a last puff on his cigarette and dropped the butt to the ground. "If I tell you, you can't pass it on to anyone else."

I sighed. "You know I can't promise that. But if I give the information to Juliette, or anyone else, I'll ask that your name be kept out of it. Just like I did when you told me about your dad selling the cheese in Bois."

Tony gazed out over the square. "All right. But if anybody asks me, I'll deny everything I'm about to tell you."

"Understood." It wasn't a great agreement, but I was pretty desperate to get Tony to talk.

He reached into his jacket pocket and took out a pack of Gauloises, the cigarette brand I'd seen a few other Guzos smoke. He shook out a cigarette, then offered me one, his last. I shook my head. He lit up and inhaled, then breathed out the smoke slowly. "Here's what I know. My dad usually nicked cheese at work. He'd wait until Fred was gone from the cheesery, and he'd slice off a wedge. But one night he needed to lift some cheese right away, and he wanted a lookout. So he told me to go with him to the cheesery and stand guard. I didn't want to do it, and I told him so. But he was my dad, and I finally agreed." He took a long drag.

"Okay. So we walk over to the convent and stand against the wall, the one facing the cheesery. You know, to make sure we're alone before Dad goes in. There's an oak tree there, so we're hidden. Sure enough, a couple minutes later, we hear footsteps coming our way. It's that plonker Wilheard. But no problem. We figure he's out for a stroll, and he'll be gone soon. So we just wait there. But then he surprises us. He walks up to the cheesery door and fiddles with the lock. It opens and he walks in. He must have had a small torch, because we can see a beam of light moving around inside. A few minutes later, he slinks out of the cheesery, locks the door, and hurries off."

"When did this happen?"

"About three months ago. Yeah, I know. Around the time the cheese was injected. But we didn't know anything about it then."

"You didn't report Wilheard breaking in?"

"Nah. We figured it was no big deal if he was eating a little cheese on the side. He wasn't the first person to have a weakness for it. Of course, they didn't usually break into the cheesery to get it. Anyway, Dad said it was all a bit of luck for us. If anyone discovered that there was cheese missing, we could blame it on Wilheard. I mean, we already knew the guy was guilty."

The events surrounding the attack on the duchy cheese were getting clearer. Tony was an eyewitness to Wilheard's break-in, if he could just be convinced to talk. "What happened next?"

"Okay. So, Dad went in and grabbed some cheese. Then we went home. I told him I was finished. I wasn't going to act as lookout again. And I wasn't going to make any more deliveries. At first, he wasn't happy about it. But the next day, he said he wouldn't be needing me anymore. He was going to pay a visit to our light-fingered friend."

"Did he actually say it was Wilheard?"

"No, but who else could it be? The next day he gave Mum enough money to pay off our bills."

I pondered this. Clive sounded like the kind of guy who wouldn't be above a little blackmail. "You think your dad asked Wilheard for money? In exchange for his silence?"

Tony nodded. "I never asked him for details. In fact, I didn't want to know. But Wilheard had plenty of money. He was always sauntering around, acting like a big shot, buying rounds at the mead hall. He could have come up with the coin."

Tony shook the last cigarette out of his pack and lit up. "Everything was okay for a while. Then one day Dad went into Bois and came back very late, looking wasted. Mum and I figured he'd been gambling again. And losing.

"Not long after that, Mum needed some money for groceries. Dad said not to worry, he'd get some. Dad liked to confide in me, you know, brag a little. So that afternoon he took me aside and told me he was going to pay another visit to 'our light-fingered friend.' When he got back, he said, our money problems would be over." Tony took a drag. "That was the last time I saw Dad alive."

Oof. I hadn't seen that coming, at least, not so abruptly. I could see tears welling in Tony's eyes, but he brushed them away. "I'm so sorry," I said.

"It's okay," he said, his voice shaky. "I knew it was a bad idea, hitting up Wilheard for more money. But I never thought the guy would hurt Dad. I never thought he'd kill him."

So, Clive had tried to blackmail Wilheard again. But this time it didn't work. Poor Clive. He was no hero, but he could have had no idea what he was getting himself into.

Tony took a long drag. "Then, when Rosamunde made her big announcement about the cheese, I knew. Wilheard hadn't been stealing cheese. He was poisoning it."

"Did you tell anyone about your suspicions?" I asked.

"No. I wanted to. I meant to. But then Sebastian offered me the intern-ship in Italy if I kept my mouth shut. So I did. Dad was dead. I couldn't bring him back. And I just wanted to get out of the duchy. I still do."

"I understand." I stared, unseeing, across the plaza. I could imagine how Clive's murder could have taken place. It would have been easy enough for Clive and Wilheard to set up a meeting in an out-of-the-way place, like the Falls. Instead of paying off Clive, Wilheard could have pushed him over the cliff. I had no doubt that Sebastian was somehow involved in the whole thing. But if there was little proof against Wilheard, there was nothing against Sebastian. He had arrived a couple of days after I did.

"Look," I said. "I can see why you kept all this to yourself at first. But now we know that there's even more at stake. Wilheard is almost certainly a murderer. And that's terrible. But he isn't stopping there. Now he's trying to take over the duchy, hand it over to his pal, Sebastian. A guy that neither of us trusts."

Tony looked away. "I know."

The shadows were lengthening in the plaza and the street beyond. Soon the lights would go on, illuminating Tony and me. Our private talk would be over. "Listen to me," I said, "it's okay that you didn't say anything earlier. But now is the time to speak up. Tell Juliette or Rosamunde or anyone on the council."

He shook his head. "Don't you think I've considered it? But in the end, what I've told you is based on guesses. I can't prove it."

"Oh, Tony," I said, truly sorry he had to face such a painful decision. "Maybe you could just say you and your dad saw Wilheard break into the cheesery three months ago. People could come to their own conclusions. At the least, they would have to re-think making Wilheard the new duke. That might be enough to defeat him."

Tony shook his head. "No. You and I made a deal. I'd tell you what I knew, but if anyone asked me, I'd deny everything."

"I know, but—"

"Look, Holly. If I start making accusations against Wilheard, all I'll do is drag my dad's reputation through the mud. Besides, Sebastian says if I turn on him, he'll see that I never get a job outside the duchy."

"What! There's no way he can do that."

"No? What if he can? Anyway, Sebastian has promised me the internship with Ferrari, and he pays me good money for helping him out. So, everything is cool." He hopped down from the wall and crushed the remains of his cigarette under his sneakered foot. "I gotta go. And don't bother Mum and Jenny about this. They don't know anything." He strode away.

"Okay," I said. I had meant to thank him for telling me what he knew, but by the time I'd formed the words, he was half way across the plaza. I sat there as the lights came on around the square, casting a garish light around me.

I looked for Juliette in the area around the plaza, but she wasn't there, and no one that I asked had seen her since the rally. Desperate to pass on Tony's information, I raced over to the convent, but the doors to both Juliette's office and the museum were locked. Finally, I hurried up the road to Juliette's house, propelled more by adrenaline than energy. Unfortunately, Rob reported that Juliette and Rosamunde had both gone out, and he wasn't sure when they would be back.

My shins ached after my race up the hill, and I trudged next door, where I had better luck. Peter and his mother sat at the kitchen table, drinking tea. "Join us," Lillian said, gesturing to a can of cooked ham, a few slices of bread, butter, and half a bowl of cabbage slaw.

I pulled out a chair and sat. "I think I know who killed Clive Cotton," I said. "And who injected the cheese. It was Wilheard. Tony told me."

Lillian gasped, and Peter's eyes widened. "My God," he said. "Is there anything Wilheard isn't guilty of?"

I proceeded to tell them everything I'd learned from Tony—how Wilheard broke into the cheesery, how Clive blackmailed him, and how Wilheard presumably killed Clive.

"It's all beastly," Lillian said. "But you know what this means. We're saved! Once word of this gets out, Wilheard will never be made duke. In fact, he'll have to flee the duchy. He and his evil boss."

"Not exactly," I said. "Here's the bad part. Tony says he won't repeat this information to anyone else. And if we report it, he'll deny having said any of it."

Peter and Lillian stared at me. "Why?" Peter asked. "If Wilheard killed Tony's father, surely, Tony doesn't want to see the fellow become duke."

"No, but he has reason to remain silent. A few days ago Sebastian promised Tony an internship at Ferrari. Tony is dying to leave the duchy, so he grabbed it. But there's more. Now Sebastian is threatening Tony. Says if Tony reports what he knows, he will see to it that Tony never gets a job outside the duchy."

Lillian scowled. "What utter rubbish. But I'm sure the boy believes it."

Peter glowered. "The carrot and the stick. Sebastian is adept at using both. And the louse is only too happy to employ them to manipulate a vulnerable boy."

My stomach rumbled audibly, and I viewed the food spread out before me. Now that I had shared all my news, I realized I was hungry. Lillian set down a plate in front of me, and I made myself a ham sandwich while she poured me a cup of tea.

"I feel like we're in the midst of an appalling movie," Lillian said. "I only wish I could leave the theater."

"At least we're getting closer to the truth," Peter said.

Lillian clicked her tongue. "Such malice. It's almost beyond comprehension. But then the Fosses have never been trustworthy, at least not Wilheard's branch of the family. Your grandmother had some choice words for them. And Juliette told me about the photo of the medallion. The one in Eglentyne's album." She turned to me. "You saw it, didn't you?"

I swallowed a bite of my sandwich. "Briefly," I said. "It was gold and embossed with a salamander under a crown."

"Exactly. It was the French king's gift to Philippe. Wilheard's family must have stolen it at the end of the War. I see no other explanation for it showing up in the U.S. years later."

"I agree," Peter said. "But unfortunately, we have no proof that the medallion in the photo is the original. And Eglentyne isn't about to show the picture to anyone else. So we can't accuse Wilheard's family of stealing the medallion. Anyway, Wilheard has moved on to far worse crimes."

"I suppose you're right," Lillian said. "Although that was a very fine medallion."

Peter moved his chair back and crossed one leg over the other. "All right. Let's summarize what we know so far. And what we surmise based on Tony's confession." He paused. "First, Wilheard managed to open the lock on the cheesery door and snuck in, presumably to inject the cheese."

I nodded, laying down my sandwich.

Peter continued. "Clive and Tony saw Wilheard breaking in, but they assumed he just wanted to satisfy a craving for cheese. Clive didn't report the offense, thinking it was no great crime. But not long after, Clive found a way to take advantage of the situation. We all know he was short on money, due to his gambling debts. So he decided to blackmail Wilheard. I'm guessing that the first time, Wilheard handed over the money without too much difficulty."

"Yes, I can picture it," Lillian said. "Clive was a good-natured fellow. He probably teased Wilheard about his weakness for duchy cheese, and they both had a laugh about the local customs."

"Just so," agreed Peter. "But later, Wilheard, and probably Sebastian, began to worry. They figured out that once the news broke about the contaminated cheese, Clive would put two and two together, realize that Wilheard was the guilty party, and denounce him."

I helped myself to slaw, while my mind worked through Peter's scenario. "Wouldn't that be risky for Clive? I mean, he himself was a thief and a blackmailer."

"Possibly," Peter said. "But Sebastian couldn't risk having Clive turn Wilheard in. Clive would have to be eliminated before word got out that the cheese had been contaminated."

Lillian grimaced. "By eliminated, you mean killed."

"To put it bluntly, yes," Peter said. "When Clive demanded more money, Wilheard must have arranged to meet him in an out-of-the-way place. That's where Clive met his death."

I shivered, remembering the decomposing body under the Falls. Had Wilheard shoved Clive over the cliff? Wilheard was certainly unpleasant, but I had a hard time seeing him as a cold-blooded killer. On the other hand, Tony had made it clear that his father had disappeared after going to meet his "light-fingered friend" the second time. "Do you suppose Sebastian ordered Wilheard to kill Clive?" I asked.

"Very likely," Peter said. "Of the two, I would say that Sebastian is not only more cunning, but probably also more ruthless."

I thought back to my conversation with Wilheard a few days earlier at the soccer field. He had confessed that he was upset by the way Sebastian treated Eglentyne. When I asked why he didn't send his boss packing, he said, "It's too late for that." I had wondered what he meant at the time, but now the words had an ominous ring. By the time I met Wilheard, he was already a murderer. And if I wasn't mistaken, there was something more, some secret from his past perhaps. "I think Sebastian is holding something over Wilheard," I said. "I would sure like to know what it is."

"As would I," Peter said. "The rally made it perfectly clear that Sebastian is aiming to take over St. Uguzo. But to do that, he first had to destabilize the duchy. And for that, he needed help, someone who would relocate to the duchy."

"And inject the cheese," Lillian said.

"Just so. Sebastian must have been thrilled to find Wilheard—a Guzo he could use for his own purposes. Who would do whatever he asked. You're right, Holly. I believe Sebastian has some kind of hold on Wilheard. Of course, Wilheard's desire to be duke has made his manipulation all the easier."

We sat for a moment in gloomy silence, brooding over the whole sorry situation. Then Lillian poured the last of the tea in our cups, ran more water in the kettle, and lit the flame under it. She sat down again, then suddenly slammed her hand on the table. "This has all gone too far." She turned to her son. "St. Uguzo needs a duke, a real duke. Someone to get us out of this bloody mess. When are you going to step up and do your duty?"

Peter groaned. "Not you too, Mum."

"We simply can't let the Fosses take charge."

"I know. They're dreadful. But not only do we have no proof of Wilheard's misdeeds, he also happens to be the man of the hour. His followers are blinded by his promises, of money miraculously finding its way into their pockets. And by the prospect of security, now that the cheese is contaminated, and most of our foreign income is likely to dry up. But let's be realistic. What have I to offer in place of his promises? I have ideas, naturally. For an upscale inn and a traditional music festival and several other things. But where is the funding to come from? I have no wealthy corporation to back me."

Lillian clicked her tongue. "No wealthy corporation to control you, you mean. Wilheard will be a stooge. At the beck and call of foreigners. Even if he weren't a puppet of Sebastian's, he would still be a wildly unsuitable candidate for duke. His parents may have been born here, but there's nothing remotely Guzo about him. A kerchief doesn't make a man a Guzo."

Peter's lips curved up in a reluctant smile. "The same could be said of me. I was born in England, and I still have a British passport."

"That may be," Lillian said, "but you're a true Guzo and always have been." She turned to me. "Do you know that when Peter was a lad, he spent three summers with the goat herders up in the high pastures? He begged me to let him go."

Peter frowned. "You needn't make me sound like the village idiot. My friends were all going. And it was a good learning experience, as you know."

"Exactly. There's nothing like caring for goats to teach you the Guzo ways. Anyway, I'm not giving up. You should be the next duke, and you know it. If you sit back and let Wilheard take over, your grandmother will come back and haunt you." She caught my eye. "The duchess was strong-willed that way."

"I can imagine," I said. Lillian herself had a certain amount of grit. Now Peter had to access his.

We were clearing the dishes when Juliette appeared at the kitchen door. I recounted my conversation with Tony as Lillian poured Juliette a cup of tea.

"Well done, Holly," Juliette said when I'd finished.

"Thanks. If only I could have talked Tony into speaking up publicly."

"Well, you did better than the rest of us," Peter said. He was drying the dishes that Lillian had washed.

"Very true," agreed Juliette. "And I have to say, it's a relief to know who was responsible for Clive's death. Even if we can't bring the villain to justice. At least, not yet."

I was warmed by my friends' praise, although I was certain that my discoveries had little to do with any true skill on my part. "Who would have guessed that being on the props committee would end up being so helpful?" I said. I had met Tony at a play rehearsal, and it was our Jedi battle at the toy store that had bonded us.

Juliette leaned back in her chair. "I feel a proper fool. All this time, while we were preparing for the celebration, Sebastian and Wilheard were plotting to overthrow the duchy." She shook her head. "If only we could make Tony's information public. It would end Wilheard's campaign to become duke. But without the boy's testimony, our hands are tied."

Lillian brushed her fingers through the blond waves at the side of her face. "I suppose we could spread a little gossip, let people know what we've learned, without mentioning any sources. We wouldn't need real proof. I could mention to a couple of friends that I'd heard Wilheard was seen breaking into the cheesery. And right around the time the cheese was tainted."

We all gazed at each other. The idea was appealing. The information was true, so we wouldn't be spreading lies. And news of all kinds traveled fast in the duchy.

"Sorry," Juliette said. "As sheriff, I can't be party to such a thing."

I looked at Peter, wondering if he would second his mother's proposal, maybe offer to send out some gossip of his own. Sometimes the ends really did justify the means, didn't they?

"I don't know, Mum. Sooner or later, people would start to seriously wonder who had seen Wilheard at the cheesery. They might well bring up the rumor at the Ceremony of Allegiance. When no one admitted they'd seen Wilheard break in, the rumor would be quashed. And as members of the opposition, we might well lose our own credibility."

"Very well," Lillian said, "but we had better come up with a better idea soon. The Ceremony is tomorrow. Our time is drawing short."

I went to bed, grateful that I was still in St. Uguzo, under my warm quilt, with Lillian tucked away in her bed across from me and Peter downstairs. The conversation with Tony had been tough, but at least we now had a better idea of what was going on. Our challenge was clear. Somehow, we had to bring down Wilheard and Sebastian.

"Lillian," I whispered, not sure if she was still awake.

"Mm?"

"Do you think the Dreamers will come up with something useful tomorrow?" At that point, I was hoping for some kind of miracle, a revelation that would rescue the duchy from Sebastian and Wilheard.

"I don't know. The thin place has never solved our problems for us. At most, it's given us a heads-up about what could take place. Even so, I'm glad we're all going to meet again. We will surely need each other's support."

She was right about that. Maybe it wasn't the thin place, with its mysterious visions, that I should be counting on. Our strength might come from the Dreamers themselves. I smiled at the unlikely thought of Dreamers saving the day.

Lillian and I said good night and wished each other pleasant dreams, knowing that the reality could be quite different, if the thin place had anything to do with it.

CHAPTER TWENTY-FIVE

Day 15, Saturday

When I woke up the next morning, the sun was already shining through the patio door. I wasn't surprised that I'd slept in late, since worry over the duchy and the prospect of another vivid dream had kept my mind racing into the early morning hours. But I had been spared another horrifying dream. Two nights in a row might have been more than I could handle, although I had been willing to suffer through another dream if its revelations would help to save the duchy.

The Dreamers had agreed to meet at eight-thirty, and by a quarter to eight, I had showered and drawn my hair back with a scrunchy. Determined to look my best for the celebration, I pulled my only skirt and petal pink blouse out of my armoire. But to my horror, I discovered a large greasy spot on the back of my skirt, one that must have been there for a few days. How it had gotten there, I had no idea, but I would have to wear my navy slacks instead. Together with my blouse and cream-colored cardigan, I should be presentable.

I found Lillian in the kitchen, making a big bowl of yogurt with granola and berries. No vivid dreams had come to her in the night either. Like me, she was both relieved and sorry.

"I picked up a flyer yesterday with today's schedule of events," she said, pointing to a sheet of paper on the table.

I skimmed the list. Sporting events, including races, archery, rock throwing, and children's games, would be held on the field outside the high school from mid-morning into the afternoon. Competitions for baked goods, embroidery, wood-carving, and the like would be held inside the school. Peter had scheduled a tour of the convent at eleven, and the museum would be open from ten to two. The folk dancers were performing on the plaza at various times, and the yodeling contest was scheduled for one o'clock.

I hadn't been kidding when I told Tony that I was looking forward to the yodeling competition. I had wanted to learn to yodel ever since I was a little girl, when I used to listen to a country-western music show on Grandma's radio whenever I visited. There was one cowboy in particular whose yodeling skill was awesome.

Near the bottom of the flyer were the featured events: the Ceremony of Allegiance in the plaza at five o'clock, followed by the play, Our Noble Beginnings, at seven, and ending with a dance in the plaza with local musicians, at eight. "All are welcome!" the sheet announced. What the flyer didn't mention was that Wilheard would be nominated and possibly named the new duke of St Uguzo, and he might be given the power to sign a contract with Sebastian's company.

"The times are all approximate," Lillian assured me.

We were sitting down to breakfast when Peter appeared in the kitchen with Bonnie, his border collie. She gave a friendly sniff to Lillian and me before racing over to gobble up the kibble that Peter was pouring for her.

"What time is the gathering of Dreamers?" Peter asked. "Eight-thirty, did you say?"

"You're coming with us?" I asked, surprised.

"All hands on deck, Mum says. In her maritime way."

"Too right," Lillian agreed. "We leave in ten minutes."

Three cars passed us, heading down the road into town, as Peter, Lillian, and I hurried up the road to the stream crossing. There was still a definite chill to the air, and I buttoned up my cardigan. Like me, Lillian was wearing slacks, but she had a warm shawl crossing her blouse, in the Guzo way. Peter had changed into slacks and a sweater that was loose enough to pull on over his cast. He must have taken a quick shower because his hair was still wet, although neatly combed.

The sky was blue, with only a few wispy clouds, an auspicious sign for the celebration. We leaped across the rocks over the stream, and jumped onto the opposite bank, then strode up the path into the woods.

As we neared the turn-off to the glade, I slowed. "Should we tell the Dreamers about Wilheard injecting the cheese and killing Clive?"

"I wish we could," Peter said. "But we can't make serious allegations like that without providing some kind of proof to back them up. And we can't betray Tony's trust."

"It's a pity," Lillian said. We exchanged a regretful look. I was dying to tell Giselle.

I had thought we might meet Rosamunde on our way to the glade, but she was already at the clearing when we got there, as were the others. It was the same group as yesterday, with the addition of Peter, who was greeted warmly. Above us, in the distance, the Guardian's flanks were catching the morning sun. I became aware of an expectant energy emanating from our little group, and perhaps from the thin place itself, although I felt no hum.

"It is good to see you all again," Rosamunde said. "Anything to report since we last met?" I shook my head as I looked around at the others.

"Go ahead, Grandpère," Giselle said.

"It was razor wire that I dreamt of," Rodcrick said, "coils and coils of it on top of a wall. Ugly stuff, like you might see on a prison. Gave me the willies."

God help us, I thought. Was there razor wire in the duchy's future? Was that the company's idea of security?

"This probably isn't much help," Giselle said, "but I had a vision of a sporty car dashing up the road. It was dark out, but I'm pretty sure it was red."

"Sebastian's Ferrari," Peter muttered.

"I don't suppose you saw a contract on the seat beside him," I said.

"Sorry. All I know is, the driver was in a hurry."

"At least we know Sebastian won't be sticking around," Peter said.

We stood for a moment, waiting for more revelations. Finally, Rosamunde spoke up. "Any other visions or dreams?"

We turned to Oswin. I had noticed earlier that he was trembling slightly, but now his hands began to shake like leaves in a brisk wind. "An-to-ni-ti, an-to-ni-ti, an-to-ni-ti," he chanted, just as he had the day before.

Roderick looked as frustrated and confused as I felt. "Antonito. Is that a man? Or a boy?" Oswin shook his head vehemently but continued with the same chant, his voice rising in volume and speed, until he finally halted, his shoulders slumped in defeat.

We stood silently for a few moments. I could hardly believe it. Was that all the guidance the thin place had to offer? Dreams of razor wire and Sebastian's Ferrari, followed by Oswin's nonsense syllables? How would any of that help us? I was the one who had suggested that the Dreamers gather together. But for what? We were no closer to defeating Wilheard and Sebastian than we had been before we gathered. I looked around me, but no one appeared as distraught as I felt. Maybe their expectations had been more realistic than mine.

Once again, Lillian invited us to hold hands, closing our circle. Gradually, a small hum arose and vibrated inside me. But there was something more, I realized, a warmth that passed among us. The warmth of friendship, a steady glow, that told us that no matter what happened, none of us would be alone.

As we filed out of the glade, I consoled myself with the knowledge that no one had seen a murder. That reminded me, Gwen should be returning today. I fervently hoped she was safe.

A few minutes later, Giselle and I were walking side by side down the road. She was heading for the dining hall, where she had promised Violet to make sandwiches for hungry visitors, while I was on my way to the museum, to help out Peter.

"I was hoping the thin place would reveal more," I said.

She shrugged. "Me too, but it was not to be. You know, sometimes I wonder, does the thin place have a kind of intelligence? If so, it is very different from ours. Perhaps the Spirit is thinking, Ah! These humans are incorrigible. They have everything they need to live a good life, but somehow they always screw up."

"Yes," I said glumly. "Maybe we're as inscrutable to the Spirit as it is to us."

I dashed into my house to pick up my shoulder bag, then rejoined Giselle on the road. She gave me an appraising look. "Holly, you must cheer up. It is our big celebration day. And who knows what may occur?"

I tried to look cheerful, but Giselle only laughed. "That is a truly pitiful smile."

"Sorry. But I'm worried. What do you think will happen? Do we have enough support to stop Wilheard?" Giselle should have some idea of what her family and neighbors were saying.

She sighed. "Perhaps. There are others like us, who do not trust Wilheard and his evil boss. When the time comes, we will see how loudly they speak up." She sighed. "I fear it will not be easy. Wilheard's followers are forceful."

We strode down to the plaza, where our paths diverged. Giselle and I exchanged a quick hug. "Courage," she said, before heading down the Dukesway.

Peter had left the glade ahead of me, and I now found him inside the museum, preparing to open the place to visitors. I stepped into our small restroom, which I had cleaned the day before, and I put a couple of extra rolls of toilet paper on a small table beside the loo (as Peter referred to it). It wasn't the soft American toilet paper that I was used to, but it was what people were accustomed to here. Looking into the mirror over the sink, I applied lipstick and put in the small hoop earrings that I'd tucked into my shoulder bag.

Back in the main room, I set to work on my children's project, hoping it wouldn't prove to be a total failure. I set a pile of books in the middle of one of the round tables, and against them, I propped the three name cards I'd made the day before. Then I laid out copies of four pages from the illuminated manuscripts, so that the young artists could refer to them. Finally, I arranged note cards, pencils, and a few boxes of crayons around the table, which seated six. I hoped that at least a few children would find my little project appealing.

A few minutes later, Peter opened the door, and the museum gradually filled with visitors. While Peter took visitors on tours of the convent, I told guests about the scriptorium, showing them copies of the illustrated manuscripts the nuns had lovingly produced back in the seventeenth century.

A few people regarded me warily, and I had the sense that they were suspicious of an outsider spouting duchy history. How was it that I knew more than they did? But most seemed happy that a foreigner was taking such an interest in their homeland. An American, even. In chatting with the adults, I learned that many expat parents were excited that their children had a chance to learn about Guzo history for the first time.

With a little encouragement from me, several children (mostly girls) made name cards. They drew elaborate capital letters for the first letter of their names and filled the cards' borders with flowers, trees, bunnies, and even swords and a fiery dragon.

At one point, I overheard two of the children's mothers conversing about the ceremony to be held that afternoon. "I had no idea that the poisoned cheese had put the whole duchy in such an uproar," said one. "Thank goodness that international company has come to the rescue." I flinched. Naturally, I wanted to jump in and explain what a really bad idea it was for the duchy to invite Sebastian's company in, but I didn't feel like it was my place, as an outsider, to intrude.

By noon, the museum had mostly emptied of visitors. After the last of the kids finished their name cards, I tidied up the materials and sat down at one of the tables. My legs were tired from standing, but I felt satisfied with my small contribution.

I turned to the front door in time to see Lillian walking in, her first aid kit hanging on a strap over her shoulder.

"Any injuries?" I asked.

"Just a twisted ankle. An onlooker in the rock-throwing contest was jumping around and took a tumble."

Peter arrived a minute later, fresh from his eleven o'clock tour. There had been lots of good questions, he reported. "Before this week, I had no idea the cellar was haunted," he said, laughing. "Not that anyone has actually seen a ghost, but no matter. A duchy myth is born."

Rosamunde was the next to appear, carrying a bag of goat cheese sandwiches, apples, and ginger cookies, the simple lunch fare being offered at the dining hall.

"You're a godsend," Peter said. "I'll make us a pot of tea," and he headed for the kitchen. A few minutes later, Peter, Lillian, Rosamunde and I were sitting elbow-to-elbow around the desk in Peter's office, the food set out before us.

Peter suggested that we compare notes on the morning's activities, and I agreed to go first. Around thirty people had come through the scriptorium, including several children, I reported. Seven kids had made name cards, a few of them quite artistic. Also, several visitors were pleased to discover tools and other artifacts on the shelves, usually items donated by a grandparent or great-grandparent.

"Glad to hear it," Peter said. "We were hoping the exhibits would help the expats to feel more of a stake in the duchy." Twenty people had toured the convent, he said, and more were expected for the one o'clock tour. What's more, several visitors hoped to read up on duchy history and return when they had more time to look around.

"And I'm happy to say there were no major injuries among the athletes," Lillian said. "Although I should tell you that Sebastian and Wilheard hung around the playing fields, chatting up the onlookers. From what I heard, they were laying it on thick, drumming up support for Wilheard as duke. And they weren't the only ones. When Bernard and Bruno Bonnet weren't racing, they were talking up Sebastian's company and how it was going to bring the duchy into the twentieth century. I asked them if they had seen the famous contract that's supposed to link the duchy to Sebastian's company, but they admitted that they still had not."

"Now that you bring it up," Peter said, "several people asked me what I knew about Sebastian's company. They were excited about the idea of the duchy opening up to outside investment. A couple said they might move their families back here if opportunities arose. I told them that we knew next to nothing about the company, and it would be a huge risk to sign a contract with them. But it wasn't what people wanted to hear. Apparently, they had been warned about dinosaurs like me, Royals who didn't realize the world had moved on and who would try to talk them out of supporting Wilheard."

"Jerks," I muttered. As far as I was concerned, people skeptical of Wilheard's plan included anyone with an ounce of sense. "Can the expatriates vote?"

"Indeed," Rosamunde said. "If someone is born in the duchy, we have always considered them a citizen, even if they have relocated elsewhere. But voting has never really been an issue. It has been decades since an important proposition has been approved or rejected at the celebration."

"Until now," Peter said darkly.

"Can you vote?" I asked him.

"Certainly. I am a Guzo by descent, and I've lived here for the past four years. Besides, I applied for Guzo citizenship and got it. So did our friend, Giselle, by the way. She was born in France, as were her parents, but she has lived with her grandfather here for several years. Everyone regards her as Guzo."

"If the expats vote, do you think they'll be with us or against us?" I asked.

"Hard to know," Peter said. "But they tend to be young and progressive. They're fond of the traditions, but they would like to see the duchy increase its contact with the outside world. Unfortunately, from what I saw this morning, that means they are eager to believe Sebastian's promises."

A heavy silence fell over us as we turned to our lunch. The courtyard outside was quiet, but a hum of voices wafted on a breeze from the plaza and beyond. A car drove by, churning gravel, and a minute later, we heard happy voices, both mature and childish, all speaking French—a family hurrying by the convent walls.

Peter set down his mug. "If we can just get past this...this political aberration, if we can get rid of Wilheard and Sebastian, we can bring the council around. Open up the duchy enough that families can return and prosper. But we'll do it the duchy way. With the voices of local people and through the council's direction."

"Hear, hear!" Lillian exclaimed. "I, for one, have mentioned to everyone I know that I have very serious doubts about Wilheard as duke. I didn't mention that he is a thief and a murderer, of course. Although it took every fiber of my being to resist the temptation. But I pointed out that he is practically a stranger to the duchy." She lowered her voice. "And he is from the dodgy branch of the Fosses."

Peter laughed, Rosamunde smiled, and the tension among us eased.

"Just what we don't need, Mum. Discord among the families. But I have to admit, in this case, the Fosses have brought it upon themselves."

"Too right," Lillian said.

I reached for a ginger cookie. "I was hoping to go to the yodeling contest this afternoon at one o'clock, that is, if you can spare me."

"An excellent idea," Rosamunde said. "I can stay and help out. You must not miss out on the opportunity." Peter agreed that the museum would be in good hands. And I should get at least a taste of the celebration. It was high time I acted like a proper tourist.

We were finishing lunch when a couple of people entered the museum, and Rosamunde went out to greet them.

I glanced at my watch. One o'clock. "I should probably be off," I said.

"Yes, go along," Lillian said. "I can tidy up here."

But before I had even picked up my shoulder bag, Peter launched into a small lecture on yodeling in St. Uguzo. The best yodelers, he explained, were men from across the valley who lived in the more remote hamlets. They yodeled to convey messages from one hilltop to another. "They've been doing it from time immemorial," Peter said. "I used to yodel a little. It came in handy when I was herding goats in the upper pastures. But I was never in the same league as the fellows who compete here."

"I would love to hear you," I said.

"I assure you, it would be embarrassing to us both."

"Actually, I'd like to learn to yodel." I wouldn't have admitted it back in the States, at least not outside my friends in The New World Rovers. But I felt comfortable saying it here. "If women yodel, that is."

"Of course," he said. "Actually, Gwen is quite good at it. Or at least she used to be. She won a prize when she was a girl, if I'm not mistaken."

"Maybe I can get her to yodel for me," I said. Assuming, that is, that Gwen made it back to St. Uguzo. And the duchy didn't fall into the hands of Wilheard and Sebastian in a few hours. Peter must have guessed what I was thinking.

"Some things won't change," he said, "no matter what happens at the ceremony. Guzos will still sing and dance. And yodel."

"Yes, I'm sure you're right," I said, conjuring up a smile.

"You'll have to come back, and we'll set you up with a teacher. In fact, Rob, Rosamunde's husband, grew up in a yodeling family. He might give you some instruction."

"I'd like that." It hadn't occurred to me that I might return one day. I guess I had assumed that I'd received a one-time-only invitation. And if I did return, would Peter be here to welcome me back?

As I hurried to the plaza, it was clear that the yodeling contest had already begun. In fact, I could hear "odle-odle-odle-oo" sounds as soon as I left the museum. The undulating melody grew as I exited the convent gate and walked along the road—now lined with cars—to the bridge. When I got to the plaza, one contestant had just stepped back from the front of the stage (no microphone needed here), and another was preparing to come forward. Three rows of metal folding chairs were arranged half way back from the stage, probably to protect listeners' ear drums. Most of the seats were full, but there was an empty chair on the aisle in the third row.

"May I?" I asked, pointing to the seat.

"Of course," the woman in the next chair said. I slipped in beside her, noting that she was fortyish, with stylish blond hair, a satiny blouse, matching wool skirt and jacket, and no shawl. Clearly a visitor.

She turned to me. "Ah. You must be the American my aunt was telling me about. The Yank's granddaughter."

"Yes, I'm Holly Hewitt. Albert was my grandfather," I said, pleased that she knew of him.

"And I am Clara Fanucci." We shook hands lightly.

"Fanucci," I said. "I don't think I've heard that surname. Of course, hardly anyone uses their last name here."

"Yes. That's a very Guzo custom, using only the first name. It's very democratic, don't you think? No last names or titles. Except for the Duchess Anne-Marie, when she was alive."

The next yodeler began, and I settled in to listen to a weathered-looking fellow as he worked his way through three yodels, followed by applause from the audience around me. Finally, he gave a little bow and waved, before leaving the stage.

I turned to Clara. "Are you a native Guzo, if you don't mind my asking?" I couldn't help wondering if she was an expatriate with a vote.

"Oh yes. I grew up here. But I married an Italian and moved to Sant'Antonio. It's a town a few hours from here, across the Italian border. I always try to come back for the celebration. I still have family here, my great-aunt and uncle, and a few cousins."

"Are they competing?"

"Not in the yodeling. But my grandfather loved to yodel when he was alive. I suppose that's why I keep coming to the competitions. And my great-uncle Oswin was a champion in his day. Small but mighty."

"Oswin? I think I know him. A goatherder and good friend of Roderick's?"

She broke into a smile. "That's him. Oh, he's such a sweet fellow. He had a stroke a few years ago. I'm afraid it affected his speech. But he's still sharp as a tack."

I wished I'd known Oswin in his prime, yodeling his heart out. And Roderick too. They were both cute now. They must have been quite the heartthrobs when they were young.

Another contestant began, an older fellow with a strong voice and amazing control, judging from the way his voice leaped across octaves and trilled melodiously. He finished to enthusiastic applause. Clara and I agreed that he deserved a prize. He was followed by three more yodelers, who varied in age and skill.

"Is your husband here?" I asked Clara, when there was a break in the proceedings.

"He and the kids are watching the track and field events. I have a cousin in the archery contest. They will be cheering her on."

I noticed a slight upturn at the outer corner of Clara's eyebrows, so that they resembled Peter's, Gwen's, and Lillian's. "You must be a Royal," I said.

"Heavens. Is it that obvious? Oh, not that it means much these days." But I could tell she was pleased.

I touched the outer edge of my eyebrow, and she laughed. "That's the giveaway, isn't it? The eyebrows. Yes, I am a great-niece of Duchess Anne-Marie."

"You'll be staying for the ceremony later, won't you? I expect you've heard, it's very important."

"I wish I could, but we have to get back for a christening. I'm leaving as soon as my husband comes to fetch me."

"Oh no," I moaned. I was hoping to recruit Clara to oppose Sebastian. As a Royal, I thought she might support Peter and Lillian. "There's a fellow, Wilheard Fosse, who wants to be the new duke. His plan is to bring an outside company into the duchy. It will all be decided at the Ceremony of Allegiance."

Carla frowned. "What kind of company is it?"

"An international outfit, Strategic Solutions, Inc. They want to settle a bunch of wealthy new residents here. They're promising to provide infrastructure and jobs that the duchy could use. But I don't trust them."

Carla's face darkened. "You must be very careful. Such a company came to our town. The name was a little different, Residential Solutions, they called themselves. They came with lots of promises. New roads. Computers. Jobs to keep our children in the town. How could we say no? So we signed a contract, and the company took over our town."

"And then?" I could barely breathe for my sense of foreboding.

"The company brought many of the innovations they had promised. But they also turned the town into a police state. We have a wall surrounding the town. It dates back hundreds of years. They ran coils of razor wire on top of it."

I thought back to Roderick's dream of razor wire, and a chill ran down my spine.

There was a delay in locating the next contestant, and Clara continued talking, more quickly now. "The company erected a big gate at the town entrance. Uniformed guards manned it at all hours. We couldn't imagine what was going on.

"Then gradually we found out. Our new neighbors were indeed wealthy, but they were also the scum of the earth. One was a deposed tyrant who had skimmed millions from his national treasury. Others were criminals from different parts of the world, villains who had managed to buy their escape from prosecution. And they were all obsessed with security."

Clara clenched her hands on her lap, her expression grim. "They stripped us of our rights. We Antoniti had to carry an I.D. at all times and obtain permission to come and go."

Antoniti. An-to-ni-ti. That's what Oswin had been trying to tell us. Look at the people of Sant'Antonio, he was saying. The Antoniti. "But you got rid of the company?"

"Yes, but we were in the courts for three years before anything was done. Finally, the State stepped in. The Carabinieri arrived and forced the company to leave. The rich residents went too. We pulled down the razor wire ourselves. By that time, many of our neighbors and dear friends had left. Some came back. Others didn't. I tell you, we still bear the scars of such tyranny in our town."

"Clara," I said, "the same thing is happening here. I'm sure of it. Look. You have to stay for the ceremony and tell the Guzos what happened to your town. They need to hear it from a first-hand witness, someone who lived through the ordeal." I stood up and looked around to see if anyone from the council was in the audience, but there was no one. I sank back onto my seat.

Clara sighed. "I'm sorry. I really am, but I can't stay. My husband and I are standing as godparents at the christening, so we can't be late."

"But this is so important," I said. "Maybe you could talk to your husband. Explain that you must remain to save the duchy."

"It will be no use. People in Sant'Antonio want nothing more than to forget the whole ordeal. My husband included." She paused. "To be honest, there were threats made against anyone who spoke out publicly against the company. I wasn't too concerned at the time. After what we'd been through, I couldn't imagine any town in Italy welcoming them. It didn't occur to me that they might target the duchy."

Just then, a man in a gray bush hat and two lively, dark-haired boys appeared beside me.

"Ready?" the man said to Clara.

Reluctantly, I stepped into the aisle so that Clara could get out, and she followed. "Won't you reconsider?" I pleaded.

"I'm sorry. Truly I am. But I am a wife and mother. The well-being of my family must come first. You know how it is." She kissed me on the cheek. "The story is in your hands now. Tell people what I told you. And be careful."

Her husband took her arm, and they strode across the plaza, their two sons chatting excitedly about the races.

As the next yodeler stepped forward to sing, I grabbed my bag and ran. At the intersection with the Dukesway, I looked in both directions for Juliette. No sign of her. For the second time in two days, I raced around, stopping passersby to ask if they'd seen the sheriff. No one had. I checked my watch. A little after two. Time enough to alert the council members and put a halt to Wilheard's power grab before the five o'clock ceremony. I decided to go back to the convent. Juliette might be in her office, and if not, Peter should still be at the museum. He would know what to do.

I was crossing the bridge when I spotted Sebastian standing at the other end, arms crossed, staring at me. I considered turning around and going back into town, but he began walking toward me, and I knew there was no avoiding him.

"Holly. Just who I wanted to see," he said when we were face-to-face. "I hear you're spreading tales about some bulldozer tearing up the duchy. Total nonsense."

"It was a dream. You're welcome to think of it as nonsense, if you like." I stepped to the side, intending to pass him, but he blocked my path.

"You would have been smart to leave," he said. "But now that you're here, I have some advice for you. Enjoy the celebration. Watch the contests and the play. But when it comes to politics, butt out."

I started to ask him just who he thought he was, ordering me around, but he cut me off. "You're going back to the States soon. You'll be competing for jobs and funding. Right?"

I stared at him mutely, a bad taste in my mouth.

"The company could help with that. Or it could put up obstacles, invisible ones that you'd never see. Money can do that. Make things a lot smoother or a great deal harder."

I swallowed hard. "Are you threatening to sabotage my career?"

"Let's be realistic. Right now you have no career, am I right?"

I said nothing, bracing myself for whatever nastiness was coming.

"Just as I thought," he said with a smirk. "And it will stay that way for a long, long time. Unless, of course, you stop interfering in duchy affairs. Which are none of your business, anyway." He started to brush past me.

"Is that what you told the people of Sant'Antonio? That you would destroy their livelihoods if they spoke up?" The words had blurted out, seemingly of their own volition.

He stepped close to me, so that I could feel his stale, warm breath on my face. His eyes were flat, like a snake's, and I shifted my gaze down to his mouth with the bisecting scar. I was already regretting my words.

"Watch yourself," he said. "One person has already died." He turned and strode across the bridge, toward the plaza.

I stepped backward on the bridge, my heart pounding in my ears. Out of the corner of my eye, I watched as Sebastian strode past the plaza and crossed the street to the Dukesway, greeting people along the way. If only they knew what kind of man he really was.

I waited until my heartbeat had returned to normal, then I hurried toward the convent. Had Sebastian really threatened me with murder? And with the end of my fledgling career? Part of me wanted to pack up my things and take the next flight home, put thousands of miles between me and Sebastian. But that was how Sebastian worked, wasn't it? Make enticing promises, then move on to intimidation. I was now at Step Two, intimidation. It was clear to me that once Sebastian made threats, no one would stand up to him—not Tony or Clara or Wilheard. Would anyone have the courage?

I passed several people leaving through the convent gate and remembered that Peter's last tour must be ending about now. Inside the museum, half a dozen people milled around, looking over the manuscripts and other artifacts. I even saw a woman who looked, from the back, like Eglentyne. I remembered that she had gone on the convent tour the day before. Maybe it had piqued her interest in duchy history.

I didn't see Rosamunde, but Lillian was in an animated discussion with two older women. She took one look at me and excused herself from them. "Is something wrong?" she asked.

"I have news. It's important."

Lillian looked at her watch. "Peter should be finishing his convent tour." We turned to the door just as he entered the museum, engaged in conversation with a middle-aged couple. Lillian waved to him urgently, and he joined us a moment later.

"What's up?" he asked.

"I've learned something you both need to hear," I said. We headed for his office, where I sat on one of the straight-backed, cushioned chairs. I realized my hands were shaking, and I clasped them tight on my lap. Peter took the chair next to mine.

"I'll keep an eye on the visitors," Lillian said, and stationed herself at the door to the office, a spot from where she could converse with us while keeping an eye on the scriptorium.

I decided my death threat could wait for now. I had to tell them first about Sant'Antonio. "Do you know a Guzo named Clara Fanucci?" I asked.

"I know her," Lillian said. "She's a cousin, once or twice removed." She scrunched her forehead. "Or maybe a niece. Sometimes it's hard to know. I believe she married an Italian and moved to a town in Italy several years ago."

"That's right," I said. "She moved to Sant'Antonio. It's a few hours from here. The people call themselves Antoniti." I said the name slowly, and Peter straightened.

"Antoniti?" he said. "Like Oswin's Antoniti?"

"Exactly." I told them about meeting Clara and what she'd told me about her town, how it had endured a horrendous experience with a company that sounded a lot like Sebastian's. "Unfortunately," I said, "Clara and her husband are now on their way back home."

"What?" Peter exploded. "You didn't stop them?"

"I tried," I said. "Believe me, I tried. But they had to attend a christening. Besides, the townspeople were warned against talking about the company. Threatened. They're still scared."

"My God," Peter said. "This is exactly the kind of evidence we've been hoping for. But we need someone to confirm it. Someone with authority."

Lillian turned to face me. "Not that we don't believe you, Holly."

"It's okay," I said. I certainly didn't want to stand up in front of all the Guzos and pass on a story I'd heard from a stranger at the yodeling competition.

Besides, it hadn't escaped my attention that I always seemed to be the bearer of bad news. Clive's dead body. The tainted cheese. Wilheard's likely involvement in Clive's death. And now this. I was already well on my way to getting an unfortunate reputation.

Peter covered his face with his hands. Then he lowered them, an "aha" look on his face. "Wait a second. I know the priest in Sant'Antonio. We spent a summer together in Florence, studying art restoration. If anyone can tell us about what went on in the town, it's Father Anselmo."

Peter sat down behind his desk, where he had an old-fashioned Rolodex, and he quickly found the card for Father Anselmo. "Whew. I have his phone number. But this could take a little while."

After conversations with two telephone operators and a housekeeper, Peter finally connected with Father Anselmo. Lillian sat down beside me, and we both leaned forward, straining to gather what we could from the conversation, a tricky task, given that Peter was speaking in fluent Italian. He looked up from the phone from time to time, passing on tidbits of information to Lillian and me. Apparently, the information that Clara had passed on to me was true. But it was hard to make sure the company was the same, given that the name was different. And its agent was a tall, slender man named Gerald, with a beard and dark hair. That seemed to rule out Sebastian.

"Wait a second," I said, remembering the narrow scar that ran downward from the base of Sebastian's nose and bisected his upper lip. "Ask about any scars on his face."

Peter nodded to me and turned back to the phone, where he asked a question that contained the word cicatrice. Scar. Lillian and I both watched raptly as the priest responded. Peter's eyes flashed, and he nodded to us. "Gerald has the same scar as Sebastian."

Lillian and I both whooped. "They're the same man," Lillian whispered to me, her blue eyes sparkling. We raised our hands in a high five. So, I thought, Sebastian went in for disguises, not surprising in his line of work.

Peter thanked Father Anselmo profusely, then hung up. Quickly, he summarized what he'd learned, the information matching what Clara had told me, with some additional details. "Father Anselmo was apparently instrumental in getting the company kicked out. In the process, he received a couple of death threats."

Lillian clicked her tongue. "Well, we know that Sebastian isn't above murder. But he clearly hasn't carried out his threats against the Father."

I felt a smidgen of relief. If the priest had survived the company's pursuit of vengeance, maybe I didn't need to worry. Much. "Sebastian threatened me too," I said. "First he said he'd destroy my career. Then he reminded me that one person had already died. I guess I'm supposed to be the next victim." I shuddered at the memory.

Peter moaned. "I'm sorry he's gotten you in his clutches. But you'll have to queue up for your chance to be assassinated. He's already threatened me." Lillian gasped.

"Really?" I said. "When?"

"Last night, after the rally. He didn't appreciate my asking about the contract. Look, Holly, I suggest you stand back from this. It isn't your fight. Sebastian's threats may be hot air, but in any case, your life certainly shouldn't be at risk."

"Peter is right," Lillian said. "You came to see the celebration, not to sink into the political mire. Anyway," she said brightly, "it's all over now, isn't it? We can easily take Sebastian down with this information."

Peter nodded. "Father Anselmo has offered to come to St. Uguzo tomorrow, if we need him. In the meantime, we are welcome to convey this information to everyone. And that is exactly what we will do." He stood. "And now, it's time to close up the museum and find the council members."

Only a few people still lingered over the exhibits, and they were good natured about leaving when Peter announced that the museum was closing. Lillian had just ushered the last visitor out when she was nearly knocked over by a figure rushing in. It was Eglentyne, breathing heavily and looking distraught.

"It's Kessie," she said. "She's had an accident. In the cellar. I think she's broken a leg."

CHAPTER TWENTY-SIX

Day 15, Saturday

"Oh no," I exclaimed. What was Kessie doing in the cellar, of all places?

Lillian picked up her first-aid kit. "Peter, go and find the council members. Tell them about the Antoniti. Holly and Eglentyne and I will see to Kessie."

Eglentyne looked panicky. "No, no, we'll need everyone. She's stuck, you see. A wall fell down, and she's buried."

"Come on," Peter said, and we all hurried out, following the stone pathway along the convent corridor until we came to the kitchen. "My God, I just had a tour group down there," Peter said. "I had no idea the walls were unstable."

From the doorway, we could see that the rug that normally covered the trapdoor was piled up to the side. And the trapdoor leading to the cellar stood open.

"I closed that after the last tour," Peter said, as we rushed to the corner of the room. He faced Eglentyne. "What the hell was Kessie doing down there?"

"I don't know," she squeaked. "I just heard her calling for help. And I ran to get you."

Lillian stood at the top of the staircase and bent over. "Don't worry, Kessie," she called. "We're coming." There was no response.

"She's at the back," Eglentyne said. "In the last room. I'll follow you."

A box of mini flashlights, no doubt left from the tours, stood on a window ledge, and we all grabbed one. Peter led the way down the stairs, followed by Lillian and me. I expected to hear Eglentyne behind me, but when I got to the bottom step, I realized there was no one at my back.

"Eglentyne?" I called. "Are you coming?" But instead of a voice, I heard a creaking sound and a resounding crash as the trapdoor shut above me. I gasped and looked around for Peter and Lillian, but they had already disappeared farther into the cellar.

I raced up the stairs. "Eglentyne!" I shouted. "Open the door!" But I heard something heavy scraping across the floor above me. It stopped over the trapdoor. My heart skipped a beat. I tried to push on the door, but it wouldn't budge. Above me, I heard two pairs of footsteps retreating across the room.

"Oh no," I moaned. We were trapped. As I headed down the stairs, I realized that the Ceremony of Allegiance was less than two hours away, and the only people who could definitely stop Sebastian and Wilheard from taking over the duchy (us!) were now stuck in the cellar of the convent.

Peter and Lillian appeared in the entrance to the room. "There's no sign of Kessie," Lillian said, looking confused.

"Or damage to the walls or ceiling," Peter added. He looked around. "What was that loud noise? And all the yelling?"

"We're trapped," I said, "duped by Eglentyne." I pointed to the top of the stairs, where the trapdoor was closed.

"Bloody hell!" Peter cried, and rushed up the steps. He tried to push open the trapdoor, his shoulder to the wooden doorway, grunting with exertion. I joined him, pushing with all my might on the count of three. Several times we shoved, but the door didn't budge.

"I think Eglentyne pushed something on top of the trapdoor," I said.

"Like a grand piano," Peter muttered.

We plodded back down the stairs. "Let's look for a way out of here." But he didn't sound optimistic.

I peered up at the two small, dusty windows at ground level. They must have been ten feet up. Even if we figured out how to get up there, none of us was small enough to squeeze through one.

"If we can climb up there, we can bang on the windows," I said. "We might get lucky. Somebody could enter the courtyard and hear us."

"Good idea," Peter said. "Except the windows down here don't look onto the courtyard. They face the hill that leads down to the stream. Nobody is going to be walking by there, or even looking in our direction."

"I'm going to climb up and take a look," Lillian said, and headed for the shelving unit below the nearest window.

"Wait," Peter said. "Let's try one of the windows in the third room, nearest the end. That will put us closest to the bridge and the plaza."

We hurried to the last room, and I saw that Peter had arranged a couple of straw pallets and a low stool in front of the shelving in one corner of the room, re-creating the appearance of the cellar when refugees and airmen— including my grandfather—stayed there during the Second World War.

Lillian strode over to the shelves under the farthest window. "Brace the ends, will you?" she said. Peter and I raced over to lend our weight to the structure while Lillian began climbing up the shelves. Even as trim and petite as she was, the structure creaked and shifted. Fortunately, her sturdy cotton slacks had enough give for climbing.

"Is she safe?" I whispered to Peter, as I leaned against an upright post.

"I expect so. Mum's a mountain goat. She's been climbing since she was a tot."

Lillian halted on the next to the top shelf, where her eyes were at window level. She leaned forward and wiped off the window with her hand. "Oh dear," she said.

"What is it?" Peter asked.

"I can't see much of anything. There are weeds and bushes outside this window, and it looks like they extend down the building."

Rats. I knew what that meant. If we couldn't see out, no one looking in our direction would be able to see us.

Peter cursed under his breath. Lillian leaned closer to the window, stretching, so that her nose was inches from the glass. The shelving unit creaked, and I pushed harder to keep it upright.

"I can see the near end of the plaza," Lillian said. "It looks full of people. And the band is playing."

I could picture the scene. Everyone would be in the town square, listening to the music and watching the dancers, or at one of the venues with food or contests. Having a great time. All were waiting for the Ceremony of Allegiance. I looked at my watch. Three-twenty. An hour and forty minutes until the ceremony began at five. Wilheard was probably practicing the acceptance speech he would make when he became duke. The thought was too depressing to contemplate. "I wonder if Gwen has arrived," I said. She had to sing the duchy anthem in order to open the ceremony.

The shelves groaned as Lillian leaned to one side, peering out.

"Careful, Mum," Peter said.

"I can't make out the stage from here. Too far away and too much shrubbery." Slowly, she climbed down and brushed off her hands, which had picked up a layer of dust.

"What if we break the window and shout for help?" I asked.

"We could try," Lillian said, "but I doubt that anyone would hear us over the band. Then there's the stream below us. The rushing water would muffle any noise we make." She sighed. "Gwen is probably here already. Looking for us, wondering where in the world we've gone." She gazed around her. "And here we are. In this god-forsaken dungeon. Where no one in his right mind would ever think to look." Her expression darkened further.

She raised her arms, her fists clenched, and made a high, strangled noise of sheer frustration. I recoiled, as the sound reverberated off the stone walls.

Lillian turned a fierce eye on Peter. "You know, don't you, that this was all entirely avoidable. Entirely. All you had to do was to declare your intention to be duke. But you just wouldn't do it."

A heavy silence fell over us.

"Let's all sit down," Peter said. He slowly lowered himself onto one end of a pallet, moving awkwardly due to the cast on his arm. I sat down at the other end, and Lillian took the stool.

"Very well, Mother," Peter said. "You want to know why I didn't agree to be duke? I'll tell you. It's because I'm responsible for my brother's death."

I barely stifled a gasp.

"What rubbish," Lillian said. "Bren died in an avalanche in Switzerland. You were here in the duchy, nowhere near him. How could you possibly be responsible?"

This felt like a private family conversation to me, and I started to get up, although I was more than a little curious.

"Stay if you like," Peter said glumly. "You've heard this much. You may as well hear the rest. And in a way, it concerns you too." Even in the pale light, I could see that his face was scoured with grief, making him look ten years older. I settled back onto the pallet.

"I had a dream several days before Bren's accident," he said. "A vivid dream, as you call them. In it, I saw the figure of a man buried under what looked like a blanket of snow. I couldn't make out his features, but I knew it was Bren." He shook his head. "I could have called him that morning, warned him. But I didn't. I convinced myself that the dream was meaningless, a trick of my subconscious. Maybe the vestige of some old resentment. And I put the image out of my mind." He closed his eyes for a moment. "Then, several days later, I got the call from Dad. He said...he said Bren had been skiing with friends. And died in an avalanche."

"Oh, Peter," Lilian whispered.

"What's done is done," he said. "You can see why I can no longer trust my judgment. Or let anyone depend on me. Not for anything important. I certainly can't be duke."

Peter looked utterly forlorn, and I ached for him. It was clear why he had been dismissive of the thin place when I'd first brought it up. It wasn't that dreams had failed him. He had failed his own dream—possibly the most important one of his life. And now he was living with the awful consequences.

We all sat silently, staring into space, Peter and I on the straw pallet, and Lillian on the low stool. The cellar's damp chill was invading my bones, and I pulled my cardigan closer around me.

Lillian straightened and turned to Peter. "Since it's confession time, I have one for you. There's something I've never told you, or anyone else, except for Rosamunde, long ago." She looked down, as if collecting her thoughts. "About a week before Bren was born, I had a vision of a candle with a beautiful flame, burning pure and bright. In my dream, I watched the flame, mesmerized. Then suddenly it went out. Not gradually, as the wax melted down. It simply extinguished, while the candle was still tall. I tried to convince myself that the flame had nothing to do with the baby I was carrying, but I knew it did. I knew in my heart that the flame was the spirit of my child.

"Well, you can imagine how I reacted. I absolutely panicked. I knew I would do whatever I had to in order to keep my child alive. I determined to protect him from anything that might threaten him—stray animals, germs, motor vehicles." She sighed. "But then Bren was born, and I knew from the first day that he was a force of nature. You remember what he was like. He climbed high up in trees, jumped into streams, fought with children twice his size. For Bren, the more danger, the better."

"I know," Peter said. "You were always whisking him off to the hospital, to get stitches or have a bone set."

"Yes, and I'm afraid you were rather left to your own devices. Oh, Peter, I was so grateful that you were a quiet, sensible child. Another son like Bren, and I would have ended up in the loony bin."

Peter was certainly logical and disciplined, as befitted a historian, but I thought of him launching himself at Sebastian in Eglentyne's parlor and wondered how different he really was from his brother. He too had his wild moments. And he could be genuinely passionate.

Lillian sighed. "Then the worst happened. Remember? Bren was ten, and he went off on that ski trip with his best mate."

"I do remember," Peter said. "When he came back, he sold his football gear and who knows what else. Bought himself a pair of skis. After that, he lived for the slopes."

Lillian smiled ruefully. "I'll never forget that family ski trip we took, after endless whinging from Bren. That's when I understood how utterly hopeless my situation was. That infuriating child chose the most challenging slopes, tried out the riskiest moves. Truly, I couldn't watch."

"In the meantime," Peter said, "I was my usual stodgy self, sticking to the intermediate runs."

Poor Peter, I thought. It had to be tough, having such a dynamic younger brother.

"As you may recall," Lillian said, "I never got past the bunny slopes. And your father watched football games on the big screen at the lodge."

She stood up and walked nearly to the wall, where she gazed up at the windows, then came back. "Bren and I talked about death one day. Did he tell you?"

Peter shook his head.

She pulled the stool over close to Peter's end of the pallet. "It was before that underwater cave excursion he went on. You were away at the university.

When he told me about this trip he was planning, I was terrified. I was utterly convinced he was going to get himself killed. Well, Bren got fed up with my dire warnings. He sat me down and told me he didn't fear death. He knew that one day it would come. But in the meantime, he intended to live life to the fullest. He told me I needed to relax. Then he offered to share his marijuana with me."

Peter covered his face, his shoulders convulsing. At first, I thought he was sobbing. Then I realized he was laughing. "And did you?" he asked through teary eyes. "Smoke weed with Bren?"

"I'm not saying," she replied smugly, causing me to picture her puffing away alongside her youngest son. "Anyway," she continued, "that's how he lived, like a bright flame. He lived his best possible life, and he wanted the same for us."

Lillian's last words echoed off the walls. She had lost her beautiful youngest son, and now she was trying to save Peter from a life stunted by regret.

"I understand what you're saying, Mum," Peter said. "Still, I should have warned Bren."

"Probably, for your own sake. But what if you had? You know your brother. What would he have said?"

Peter's lips quirked up in a crooked smile. "Bren would have said...he would have said, 'Stop being such an old woman.'"

"Precisely. And he would have hit the slopes without a second thought. You know, there were unstable conditions in the mountains that day. I heard about it later. The authorities had posted warnings about the threat of avalanche. But that didn't stop Bren and his foolhardy friends. I couldn't protect him, and neither could you. It's a miracle no one else in the group was killed or injured."

Lillian leaned over and squeezed Peter's hand. "Bren loved you. It would have broken his heart to see you blame yourself for his death."

Peter nodded, as if he was slowly coming to terms with her words. "I hear you, Mum. And thank you for telling me about your dream." He scooched forward and kissed her cheek. "Bren was lucky to have you as a mother. And so am I."

"You're very sweet. Now then, will you agree to be duke?"

Peter threw back his head and laughed. "I'd forgotten that's what this was all about." But he was already sitting straighter, as if the burden he'd been carrying was now lighter. "Yes. I suppose I will. Of course, it will do us no good now. We'll never get out of here in time for the ceremony."

A thought occurred to me. "Isn't there a tunnel?"

CHAPTER TWENTY-SEVEN

Day 15, Saturday

Igazed expectantly at Peter. It was he who had told me about the tunnel. He shook his head. "Supposedly there was one, but I've never been able to locate it. In fact, I'm not even sure the tunnel starts in the cellar. In any case, it hasn't been used for half a century. It could easily cave in, if it hasn't already. I didn't even mention it to the tour groups."

I turned on my flashlight and focused the beam on a section of stone wall in the corner, one of the few places not covered by tall shelving. Could stone blocks have been removed to build a tunnel there? "How hard did you search for the opening?" I asked.

He shrugged. "Well, I could have been more thorough, I suppose. I did examine the accessible stone blocks. To see if there were signs that any had been moved and put back in the last fifty years. But I couldn't see any indication of recent masonry. And of course, I looked between the shelves wherever I could. But as you'll notice, most of the units are boarded up in back. To keep objects from falling off, I suppose."

I beamed my flashlight at the farthest wall, the one closest to the road. Three racks for wine barrels, all with wooden backing, were interspersed with three shallower racks for cheese or bottled rosehip wine. The shallow racks were widely spaced, one at each end of the room and one in the middle, between two racks for wine barrels. Peering between the shelves, I had a glimpse of the stone wall behind them.

"There's a long, narrow aisle between the shelving and the wall," Lillian said. "I saw it when I was looking out the window."

"The space was likely left there for ventilation," Peter said. "Is there enough room for a person to stand in?"

"I should think so," Lillian said, "although it would be tight."

"Can't we just walk back there?" I asked. "Look around for a tunnel opening?"

"We could," Peter said, "if there weren't tall planks acting as bookends at the end of each row.

I walked over to take a look. "Oh, I see. That's not very helpful." The planking made the shelving more stable, but it prevented us from entering the passageway from either end. And there were only a few inches between the racks. Not enough space for a person to squeeze through."

"I'd say that leaves us with one alternative if we want to check out the wall," Lillian said. "We'll have to crawl under the racks, the ones that aren't backed."

I crouched beside one of the backless cheese racks. "It looks like the lowest shelves stand about two and a half feet off the ground. I think I can crawl under on my hands and knees."

"So can I," Lillian said.

Peter rubbed his cheek as he gazed at the nearest cheese rack.

"You'd best sit this one out," Lillian said. "That cast is a definite impediment."

"I suppose you're right," he said.

After a brief conversation, we decided to begin our search in the present room, since it lay at the end of the convent. A tunnel from there would require the shortest route from the cellar to the cave in the hills. Besides, this room was farthest from the stairs, where German soldiers might have entered the cellar looking for hidden visitors.

Peter's brow furrowed. "Unfortunately, we don't know exactly where the grotto lies. But there are some caves above the cemetery. Since they would be closest to the convent, I wouldn't be surprised if the tunnel goes under the graveyard."

I shuddered.

"It sounds ghoulish, I know," Peter said, "but digging under there should have been feasible."

We all stared at the wall I'd been examining, the one parallel to the road and the graveyard. "We may as well start here," I said.

Lillian nodded. "What do you say we crawl under the racks at either end and take a look at the wall from there?"

I walked to the farthest rack and stuck my mini flashlight into my waistband, freeing both my hands. Then I got down on all fours and started crawling underneath.

"How is it?" Peter asked.

"Not bad, aside from a lot of dust and some mouse turds." I sneezed, proving my point. In fact, the fit was overly cozy. After hitting my head on the shelf above me a couple of times, I remembered to keep it low. From the other end, I heard Lillian humming the martial theme from The Bridge on the River Kwai, and I remembered that she was probably battling feelings of claustrophobia.

As my head emerged from under the rack, I faced the narrow passageway that Lillian had told us about. Clearly, standing up would be possible, but not easy, and I stayed where I was, on all fours. Looking both left and right, I saw no evidence of the opening to a tunnel. No hole and no material to cover one up. Just stone blocks, expertly fitted together to form the cellar walls. Lillian's head popped out from under the other backless rack.

"Whew," she breathed. "See anything?"

"No tunnels, I'm afraid."

Lillian looked up and down the stone wall, with the same result. "Pity," she said. "Now I suppose we'll have to crawl backwards out of here."

After shouting our disappointing findings to Peter, we crawled back and were soon standing up, brushing dust off our hands and the knees of our slacks.

"I don't know why I bother tidying up," Lillian said. "We're going to have to go through this all over again."

I was grateful that my skirt had not been fit to wear that morning, and I'd been forced to wear long pants. Peter hung back, looking ill at ease. I was sure he would prefer to be crawling around with us, in the thick of things.

I looked at my watch: five minutes to four. A little over an hour until five o'clock and the beginning of the Celebration.

Quickly, we identified two unbacked racks on each wall in all three rooms. Lillian and I crawled under the units that were farthest apart, and we made a visual sweep from underneath the shelves. It was always the same. On the other side of the aisle, the stone wall extended with no sign of a tunnel.

"Maybe it was all just a story, like an urban myth," I said, as the three of us stood in the center of the third room, the one farthest from the stairs. "You know, the phantom tunnel."

"I'm pretty sure it was real," Peter said. "Although I'm less sure where it started." He shook his head. "Where could the bloody entrance be?"

"Maybe we should break open a window and scream for help," Lillian said. "It seems like our last resort." We all knew how ineffective that would be. The suggestion was a sign of our desperation.

My gaze gravitated to the cheese rack standing next to me, an unbacked one. We hadn't bothered to crawl under it, since we'd already looked up and down the stone wall behind it from either end. On a whim, I got down and started crawling under the lowest shelf. My jacket and slacks were already filthy, and my hair, drawn back in a ponytail, was undoubtedly matted with grime. What harm would a few more dusty mouse turds and desiccated insects do? And we were out of good ideas.

As I emerged at the back of the shelf, I looked up to face more smooth stone blocks. Well, what had I expected? As I was preparing to back out, I looked to the right, toward the dark space behind the backed shelving next to me. I paused. Now, that was odd. The stonework protruded a little, maybe an inch or two from the rest of the wall. The other masonry was so level, it seemed strange the craftsmen had permitted this imperfection.

I crawled forward, out from under the shelving, and managed to stand up in the narrow aisle, then took a couple of steps to the right. And gasped.

There it was. A large, dark hole, starting just above floor level, extending up about four feet, and wide enough to let one person squeeze through. I could see why the tunnel had been invisible to us. It was in a shadowy spot, and the opening was obscured on all sides by the slightly projecting stone slabs that surrounded it. Stepping closer, I slipped my flashlight out from my waistband and pointed the beam into the hole. Sure enough, the opening extended back, beyond the wall.

This was the tunnel.

"You guys!" I called.

"What is it?" came voices behind me.

"You were right, Peter," I shouted. "The tunnel is real."

"I'm coming," Lillian called, and a minute later, she was standing next to me, scrutinizing the hole. It took a few more minutes for Peter to reach us. He'd scrunched through, commando style, his forearms and legs flat on the ground, his cast thunking on the dirt floor. As I helped him stand, I couldn't help noticing a wince of pain. He never talked about his broken wrist or any other injuries from his fight with Sebastian, but I had observed the occasional grimace when he thought nobody was watching. Lillian must have noticed his discomfort as well because she asked Peter how he was feeling.

"I'm perfectly fine," he replied brusquely, before shining his flashlight into the tunnel. A minute later, all three of us stood, crammed together around the opening, sharing our observations. It appeared that six or seven large stones had been removed from the wall to create the opening. Behind it, soil had been cleared out, forming a tunnel with walls shored up by thick planks of wood. The space was large enough to allow a person to step in, then walk hunched over.

"Why couldn't we see the entrance before?" Lillian asked. "I could have sworn we'd taken a good look."

"Because we were observing from the far ends of the aisle," I said. "Look. The stonework around the tunnel projects outward, just enough to hide the opening from view. I saw it this time because I was looking from a much closer angle, right next to the entrance. People who knew where the tunnel was would be able to find it without much difficulty. Otherwise, it would have required extraordinary tenacity or as in my case, dumb luck, to find it."

Peter scratched his head. "The tunnel looks pretty solid, but we can't know if it's truly safe."

"Okay," I said. "Why don't I climb in and go back a little ways? See how it looks?"

"I was just about to do that myself," Peter said.

Lillian coughed politely. "Be a gentleman, dear. You can go after Holly." I appreciated her support, although I wasn't sure the ordinary rules of etiquette applied here.

"Yes, all right," Peter said, sounding a little miffed. He eyed me. "Don't go far. Take a look around and come right back. Then we'll talk it over."

I stepped through the opening, ducking to avoid clunking my head against the low ceiling. Although I'd tried to act confident in front of Peter and Lillian, it took only two steps for the tunnel walls to seemingly close in around me, and the cold, earthen damp to seep into my nose and skin. I aimed my flashlight down, where the beam revealed a dirt and gravel floor. At least it wasn't slippery. Shifting the light upwards, I made out hard-packed walls, supported at intervals by wooden planks, both vertical and horizontal.

Suddenly, my mind flashed to the cemetery the tunnel would almost certainly pass under. All those corpses of the long dead and possibly more recently deceased. A shiver wracked me. Get a grip! My grandfather had once traveled through this tunnel. If he was frightened, he must have overcome it. So could I. Ahead of me, the path was straight for a few yards, then became a blank wall. I walked forward, my flashlight beam playing off the surfaces around me. Where the tunnel seemed to end, I saw that it had simply veered to the right, around a large boulder.

"Holly," came Peter's voice from the entry. "Come back."

With some relief, I headed to the opening, where I climbed out.

"How does it look?" Peter asked.

Part of me wanted to say that we should stay in the cellar, which now seemed quite pleasant in contrast to the narrow, dark tunnel. But I explained instead that the structure appeared sturdy enough.

"Even so," Peter said, "it was excavated half a century ago. We have no way of knowing how it has stood up all this time. For all we know, it could be ready to collapse at any moment, especially if we go barreling through it."

"Peter is right," Lillian said. "It seems too risky, much as I hate to admit it."

They were correct, of course. The sensible choice was to give up on the tunnel. And yet, something in me refused to admit defeat. I have to admit, I surprised myself. When did I become so brave? Or so foolhardy? I thought of my grandfather, who had guided refugees through the mountains, past armed soldiers. Maybe some of his courage had filtered down to me. Besides, the stakes were high, the very existence of the duchy as we knew it.

"The tunnel scares me too," I said. "But you know what really scares me? The idea of handing over the duchy to Sebastian and Wilheard. I heard what Clara said. They'll turn it into a police state." Peter and Lillian said nothing, but I could see from their anguished expressions that I'd hit a nerve. "I don't want to live with the knowledge that I could have stopped those two scumbags, but I backed down."

Peter straightened. "Right you are. That's why I'm going through the tunnel." Lillian took a sharp inhale, then covered her mouth with her hands.

"What?" I squeaked. "No. I was only speaking for myself. Not for you. I'm the one to go." What had I done? I hadn't meant to shame Peter into taking on the tunnel, but what if I had?

"No, Holly," he said. "You're only a visitor here. You have no business putting your life in danger. But I'm Guzo. And someday I may even be a duke, if Sebastian doesn't destroy the duchy first. If anyone should go through the tunnel, it's me." He turned to Lillian. "But I will be very, very careful, I promise. At the first sign of danger, I'll turn back."

Lillian looked stricken. She was in a tough spot, to be sure. She had talked her son into being duke, a position of leadership. And now he intended to act like one, possibly at great cost. I wondered if the same stark thought was going through her mind that was going through mine. If anything happened in the tunnel, we had no way of summoning help. After a moment, she nodded her assent. "I'll hold you to your promise."

"Well, I'm going too," I said. "I'm an experienced spelunker. I've crawled through caves, so I should be able to handle a tunnel." To say I was experienced was pushing it. Three caves made me no expert. Still, I wasn't especially claustrophobic, and I didn't have an arm in a cast.

Peter gave me a long, hard look. "You're sure?"

I hesitated. Did I have the guts to go through with this?

Lillian stepped close to me. "This is a big decision, not one to be taken lightly. You need to think for a minute, really consider what you're taking on." Peter nodded his agreement. "And Holly," Lillian said, "there's no shame in changing your mind. If you decide to stay here with me, I will applaud you for your good sense." She placed her hands on my shoulders and turned me around. "Take a moment. Have a good think about it."

I wanted to cry out, "No, no, we have to get started," but I could see the wisdom of Lillian's advice. There are decisions that you don't want to make in a moment of passion. I took a few steps away and stopped at an unbacked shelf.

What was going on? Why was I so determined to take on a challenge that I never could have imagined in my former, pre-duchy life? And why was I willing to accompany Peter, a man who had made clear his lack of feelings for me, into a possibly unsafe tunnel? I ought to prefer the easy and undoubtedly wise choice—to stay in the cellar until someone came to get us out.

But I didn't. And then, in a flash of insight, I understood why—why I was willing to take such a huge risk, even put my life on the line. For the first time in my life, I was surrounded by people who supported me. Since coming to the duchy, I had found a circle of people who truly believed in me. Rosamund and Juliette and Giselle and Roderick, they had all supported me from the start. They understood my soulful connection to the glade, and they recognized my grandfather as a brave young man, not the coward I'd been told he was. The Guzos—well, most of them—had welcomed me with open arms and warm hearts, gladly sharing their family stories with me.

And maybe because they believed in me, I had begun to believe in myself. Somehow, over the last two weeks, I had stopped seeing myself as a failure, a person deserving of abandonment. After all, I was the person that Tony confided in about his father's transgressions and his own failings. I helped to hold the play together, working props and standing in for the duchess as leading ladies fell away. I drove Peter to the hospital. And meanwhile, I had interviewed Guzos about their families' past celebrations, eliciting information that would be useful to the museum in the future. Not to mention transcribing my grandfather's journal.

Through it all, I had begun to see myself as a competent woman, a person who could live up to high expectations, my own and those of the Guzos around me. In my heart, I knew that I hadn't come all the way to St. Uguzo to sit in the convent cellar and count down the minutes until the duchy fell to Sebastian's evil company. I was going to traverse the tunnel, at least as far as it took me. If fate existed, this fate was mine.

I turned and strode back to Peter and Lillian, whose expressions were a mix of hopefulness and anxiety. "I'm ready to go through the tunnel," I said.

Peter must have been holding his breath, because he exhaled deeply. A wobbly smile turned into a grin, and he nodded his assent. "Very well. Let's get moving. Holly, you can bring up the rear."

"Yes, sir," I said and gave him a small salute. He raised an amused eyebrow in return.

"I'll get my medical bag," Lillian said. "Then we can get you kitted up." She crawled under the shelving once more and returned with her bag. A minute later, Peter and I were as well outfitted as we were going to get. We had ace bandages, gauze, band-aids, and antiseptic wipes. I wasn't sure what good they would do, but you never knew.

I thought back to my spelunking gear. "I don't suppose you have matches. If we aren't sure we're on the right track, we can light a match. The smoke will be drawn forward if there is an opening to the outside world ahead."

"Oh, clever," Lillian said as she rummaged through her bag. She pulled out an old matchbook, which she handed me. "I knew these would come in handy sometime." She also had a small flask of water, which she gave to Peter. "Make sure you share it," she said, ever the mom. He rolled his eyes.

My gaze darted to my wristwatch. Four-fifteen. Surely that would give us enough time to make it through. Wouldn't it? I wished we hadn't taken so long to find the entrance. Even if the tunnel was sound, and we made it out the other end, we'd have to find our way out of the grotto and down to the convent to free Lillian, before dashing across to the plaza to tell our tale.

Peter laid his hand on his mother's shoulder. "Would you mind if I had a moment alone with Holly?"

A tingling sensation coursed through me. It was part hope, part fear, and part annoyance that Peter would slow us down now, when we needed every moment. What could he possibly have to say that was so important?

"Of course." Lillian sent me a quick glance, then hurried off to the end of the aisle, where she began humming the tune from "My Favorite Things." Apparently, she was a Sound of Music fan too.

Peter raked his fingers through his hair before finally looking me in the eye. "Listen, Holly, there's something I need to explain. Back on Wednesday, when I told you that our relationship was just a temporary fling, well, I wasn't being entirely honest. My feelings for you were rather deeper than that. Quite a lot deeper, in fact."

I gazed at him, hardly daring to breathe. Had he cared for me all along?

"Please believe me, my intentions were good. I knew you had to leave and return to the States in order to complete your project. And I knew how important that was to you. Under the circumstances, I didn't want our relationship to stand in your way. So I suggested that we were just colleagues who had had a little fun."

"Oh," I said, conjuring up that horrible conversation in the museum. He had flung out the seemingly offhand announcement as he gathered historical materials for me to take to the States.

"I could see you were hurt," he said, "and I was sorry. But I thought I was looking out for you, acting in your best interest." He cleared his throat. "I suppose I was also a little frightened at the strength of my feelings for you. The fact is, I could hardly bear to see you go."

Something eased in me, a tightness in my chest that I didn't even realize was there. I hadn't been deluding myself. Peter had been truly fond of me, after all. "I wish you'd told me this sooner."

"I tried to tell you yesterday, when you told me you were staying. But you wouldn't listen."

"Oh." Was that only yesterday? It felt like a week ago. But he was right. He had started to tell me something, and I had cut him off mid-sentence. "I guess I was still feeling a little tender."

"Anyway, I wanted you to know how I feel before we set out on this trek. I didn't want a well-intentioned but foolish lie to stand between us."

My carefully constructed defenses against Peter started to crumble as I looked into the clear hazel eyes below his royal winged brows. There was more to say, more to delve into between us, but it would have to wait for a better time. "Thanks for telling me," I said and kissed him on the cheek. He tilted my chin upwards and returned the kiss with one on my lips. Even in my anxious state, his warmth melted me.

A moment later, at Peter's summons, Lillian strode back to us, teary-eyed, but looking upbeat. "Ready then?" she said. She pulled Peter into a big hug. "You will be careful, won't you?" she said.

"Of course. You know me. Cautious to a fault."

She gave him another hug, then turned to embrace me. "Look after each other." Her voice lowered. "Don't let him do anything foolish. I'm counting on you."

"We'll come back at the first sign of trouble."

She smiled, but I saw the fear in her blue eyes. She had lost one son. Now her other son was putting himself in harm's way. I had to admire her for not throwing herself across the tunnel entrance and forbidding him to go.

Peter climbed into the tunnel, and I followed, feeling a little more sure-footed since I'd walked here before, at least for a few steps. We could do this.

CHAPTER TWENTY-EIGHT

Day 15, Saturday

Peter led the way through the tunnel, bent over at the waist, like me. He directed his flashlight to the floor in front of him, while I kept mine tucked in my jacket pocket to conserve batteries. We soon took the first curve, bypassing a boulder embedded in the ground. Then the tunnel returned to its original course. We headed forward, keeping as brisk a pace as possible in the cramped space. At times, dustings of dirt filtered down, causing Peter to halt and beam his light over the walls up ahead, checking to see if they looked safe.

I soon realized that the shoring materials varied. In some places the vertical supports were a single plank of wood. In others, reinforcement was provided by several smaller planks. The ceiling was braced by heavy sawn timbers. All looked stable, as far as my untrained eyes could see. Our path veered to both the right and left, as we encountered more underground boulders in our way. The miners must have wished they had dynamite, as they would have had in their mining operations. At one point, Peter picked up an empty cigarette pack. Lucky Strikes. An airman must have dropped it. Peter stuck it in his pocket, and I imagined it appearing in a future museum exhibit.

After fifteen minutes or so, the tunnel began to slope upwards, a sign that we were past the cemetery and climbing into the foothills, presumably heading for one of the grottos. In spite of the damp cold around me, I began to sweat from exertion, and my back ached. Peter raised a hand. "Let's take a break," he said. We both sank to our knees and stretched our spines. He handed me the small water bottle. My mouth and throat felt clogged with dirt, so I took a sip, swished it around in my mouth and spat it out, before taking a real swallow.

I pressed the tiny knob on my wristwatch to light up the dial. Almost four-thirty. Half an hour until the celebration began. My gut twisted. "How much farther do you think it is?"

"Hard to say. We must be more than half way, but the gradient will probably get steeper."

Peter was right about the elevation. When we resumed our trek, my leg muscles started to ache, and I huffed, breathing in the stale, dank air. Many of the vertical supports now consisted of undressed tree trunks, no doubt cut from the nearby forest.

Peter came to a halt as a massive rock rose before us, blocking the tunnel from left to right. It was as high as my shoulders, but there was a gap between its surface and the ceiling. The builders had managed to continue their forward progress over the top of the rock, making use of a crude ladder still in place.

"Let me take a look," I said and started climbing the shaky ladder. From the highest rung, I crawled onto the top of the rock, pulled my flashlight out of my jacket pocket, and looked down. "Oh no," I murmured. On the other side, there had clearly been a cave-in. The tunnel was still open and supported by wooden planks, but the floor was much higher, leaving enough space for a person to crawl but not walk.

"What is it?" Peter asked from below.

"Bad news." I climbed down the ladder. "See for yourself."

Peter climbed up one-handed. "Merde," he mumbled when he got to the top. A moment later he was beside me, shaking his head. "Sorry, Holly. We have to go back."

I bristled. "What? But we're so close. I know you can't crawl through there with a broken wrist, but I think I can. The beams are still intact."

"It isn't safe. And let's face it, we don't even know if the opening to the grotto is still open."

I considered that. "I'm going to climb over and light a match. If the smoke is drawn to the back of the tunnel, then there has to be an opening up ahead." I went up the ladder again, crossed the rock and dropped down to the tunnel. Pulling Lillian's matchbook out of my pocket, I lit a match, blew it out, and watched. The smoke rose but showed no clear direction. Darn. Maybe if I just went a little farther.

I crawled forward, aware of gravel biting into my hands and knees. I had turned on my mini flashlight, shoving it into the waistband of my slacks. The tunnel walls seemed to press in on me, and I wondered if Peter was right. Perhaps we should just go back. But then what? Sebastian and Willard would get what they wanted. We couldn't let that happen. More determined than ever, I scrambled through a curve in the path and stopped, dragging out the matchbook once again.

This time was different. When I blew out the match, the rivulet of smoke rose and was drawn forward. There had to be an opening up ahead. Excited, I directed the flashlight beam over the walls and ceiling. The wooden supports looked intact. I crawled backward to the rock and made my way over it.

"Ready to go back to the convent?" Peter asked.

I explained about the smoke. "I want to go forward." Peter frowned. "No, really," I said. "It looks like the tunnel is still sound. Anyway, if the path is blocked up ahead, I'll come back."

"I don't like you going by yourself. If anything happens..."

I could guess what he was thinking. If anything happened, there was no way to get help. But we had been aware of that from the start. I laid my hand on his good arm. "I know. This is scary. But we could be close to the end. There's too much at stake to give up now."

"Holly…"

"I'll be careful." I perched my flashlight behind my ear. "Help me secure this thing, will you?"

Peter scowled and mumbled something under his breath that may have contained the word "headstrong." But he took out an ace bandage and rolled it over the top of my head and under my chin to fix the flashlight in place. It wasn't as good as a miner's lamp, but it would have to do. We both took a long swallow of water, then Peter dropped the bottle in my pocket. "You can use it to wash up when you get out."

"I'll do that." Assuming I made it.

He managed a lopsided smile. "I'll be waiting for you here."

I liked the idea of having Peter within earshot, but it wasn't very practical. If I managed to get out, going back to tell Peter would just slow us down. If he followed me through the tunnel, the crawl would be very slow, not to mention painful. "Maybe you should go back to the cellar and wait for me there."

Peter shook his head. "I'm not leaving you, Holly."

"Look. As soon as I get through, I'll run down to the convent and get you and Lillian out. If you're already there, it will save us some time. And we don't have much of that."

Neither of us pointed out what an enormous understatement that was. It was four-forty by my watch. Twenty minutes to crawl to the end of the tunnel, enter the cave, unblock the entrance to the outside—assuming it had been blocked—run down the hillside and over to the convent. From there, Peter, Lillian, and I would have to sprint to the plaza and plow our way through the crowd to the stage. All the while praying that we weren't too late to stop the duchy's takeover by Sebastian and Wilheard.

Peter raked a grimy hand through his hair. "I suppose that's our best bet," he said finally. "I'll head back to the cellar. Wait for you there with Mum."

We kissed. A promise of things to come. Then one more kiss. "Three for luck," Peter said, and we kissed again, then hugged.

I clambered up the ladder. When I looked back from the top, Peter was already hurrying back toward the convent.

It hadn't been that hard to keep my fear at bay when I was following Peter through the tunnel, but now I was completely on my own, and a creeping terror was my steady companion as I crawled along the cramped space, the musty smell of tree roots and burrowing animals filling my senses. I tamped down my brewing panic by keeping my focus on the task before me. Hand, foot, hand, foot, one step after another. Steadily, I crawled up the tunnel. To my dismay, the angle became even steeper, so that my pace slowed. I had to resist the urge to look at my watch. I was moving as fast as I could, faster than my burning muscles and lungs would have liked. It wouldn't help to watch the minutes tick by.

At long last, the light from my flashlight disappeared into an open space. A shock went through me. The tunnel was at its end. Ahead of me lay the grotto!

I crawled to the edge and looked down. In the dim light, I made out an irregular space about six feet across and bordered by craggy stone blocks that must have tumbled down the hillside in one of the landslides Peter had told me about. The rocks had piled up against each other and formed this underground cave, this grotto. I maneuvered into a sitting position and stepped down the foot or so from the tunnel to the floor of the grotto. To my relief, there was room to stand.

But the light was still faint, and my doubts assailed me. If there was an exit to the outer world here, shouldn't it offer more light? But then, maybe it was partially hidden. I unwound the ace bandage from around my head and removed the flashlight from behind my ear, turning it off, so that I could locate where the small amount of light was coming from. It seemed to be a little brighter at the far left side.

As I walked across the stone floor, I finally spotted the opening to the outside, and my heart sank. It was a hole at ground level where a small animal had burrowed in. That's where the light and air were entering. No wonder the smoke from the match had drifted so feebly. This was not a real exit, certainly not one for humans.

Now that my eyes were adjusting to the pale light, I realized there was another source of light, pale needle-like shafts that squeezed through a barricade of wooden planks at the front of the grotto. The boards filled a three-foot wide space that must have once offered a natural exit. Now it was a seemingly impenetrable barrier. I swept the flashlight across the stone walls that rose up around me, although there was little point. The Guzos had made sure that no unwanted visitors would enter the tunnel here. Or exit from it. Once again, I was a prisoner. Only, this time I was alone.

I peered at my watch. Five minutes after five. Down in the plaza, the Ceremony of Allegiance would be underway, Gwen singing the duchy anthem to the throng of Guzos. Meanwhile, Peter should be back in the convent cellar by now, anxiously awaiting my arrival, along with Lillian. But I wasn't coming. The horrible reality came crashing down on me. I had failed. I'd tried and I'd failed. The duchy would fall to Sebastian, and there was nothing I could do about it.

A wave of exhaustion and despair overcame me, and I sank to the stone floor, pulling up my knees before me. I ached all over—my arms and legs and shoulders. My hands stung from crawling on gravel.

I lowered my head, too emotionally gutted even to cry. What a fool I'd been, what a delusional fool, to think that I, Holly Hewitt, could save the duchy. Why had I ever thought I could follow in my grandfather's footsteps?

I'd known from the start that all our best efforts might end in failure, but this, I realized, was more than one isolated piece of bad luck. I had failed in this task, just as I'd failed at everything in my life. Never once winning a school prize. Spending prom night watching movies with two girlfriends, graduating from college with a degree in history preparing me for exactly nothing. My tedious jobs paid little more than minimum wage. And I'd been dumped from my graduate program. In fact, I'd only come to the duchy in a sad, last-ditch attempt to revive my academic career. Then, for a brief, heady moment, I had imagined I was the kind of woman capable of achieving fine and noble things. Now I recognized what a pathetic illusion that had been.

The sweat that I'd generated in the last uphill slog had now turned to a bone-chilling damp, and I began to shiver. Wrapping my arms tightly around my body was little help. I pulled out my nearly empty water bottle. A small gulp helped wash through the sludge that had lodged in my throat. I'd better be careful with what little water remained. I could be here for hours, days. I shuddered, sinking back into despair.

Several minutes must have passed when a high-pitched whistle sounded from outside the blockaded entrance. A marmot whistle. Montie? My spirits lifted fractionally as I pictured my furry friend. Could his territory possibly extend this far?

I dragged myself up and approached the wall of thick planks. "Hey, Montie," I called. Another small whistle came from the other side of the boards. Absently, I ran my hand across the unfinished planks, and I gradually realized that not all the boards were equally sturdy. At the left edge was a relatively thin one, and after fifty years, the wood was starting to warp. Was it possible? Could I find a way to pry it loose?

With sore hands, I started to pull at the deteriorated wood. After several yanks, it began to give—just a little, and then a little more. I gave the board a vicious kick, nearly falling backward in the process. Grunting with exertion,

I pulled on the wood until finally a splintery piece cracked and broke off. Behind it, there was light and fresh air. I still couldn't get through to the outside, but at least I could see it. Smell it. I was too late to save the duchy, but at least, someone would have to come by sooner or later. I wouldn't be trapped here forever.

As I worked at enlarging the opening, I pictured Peter and Lillian in the cellar. Was it possible that somehow, against all the odds, they had been rescued? And what was going on in the plaza? Were any of the Guzos resisting Sebastian's plan? Rosamunde would oppose it for sure, but she was on the council, and I didn't know how much she could involve herself in the vote. The other members of the dreamers' circle were well aware of the danger. But would their voices be enough to overcome Sebastian's relentless drive? Not to mention the Guzos' pent-up desire for change. If only Peter and I could be in the plaza! For all I knew, the vote could have taken place already.

Then, I heard the faint sound of people talking in the distance. Two or three folks, speaking a mix of English and French.

CHAPTER TWENTY-NINE

Day 15, Saturday

At the sound of the voices, I pushed my face to the narrow opening. "Help!" I shouted. "Help! I'm trapped in a cave!"

"Did you hear that?" came a faint woman's voice. "Someone's in trouble." The voice was familiar, with a French lilt.

"Giselle? It's me—Holly," I shouted. "I'm stuck in a grotto."

"Mon Dieu. Holly? Keep talking," Giselle called. "We'll find you."

Leaves rustled to the rhythm of footsteps. "Can you still hear me?" I shouted.

"Yes. Keep talking."

I stood there, my forehead against the wooden plank, my mind drawing an absolute blank.

"Sing something," called Giselle.

"Are you going to Scarborough Fair?" I sang at the top of my lungs.

"We're getting closer," Giselle said. "Don't stop singing." The steps hastened as I sang "parsley, sage, rosemary, and thyme."

A moment later, Giselle's face appeared in the small opening. "Holly, what are you doing here?"

"Giselle! I am so, so glad to see you!"

Roderick's face replaced Giselle's. "Well, I'll be jiggered. Our little Yank. We'll have you out of there in a jiffy." He looked around him. "We just have to move a few rocks and some old boards." He grunted and I glimpsed him rolling a large rock away from the entrance. He was assisted by a good-looking young man, whom Giselle introduced as her friend Jacques.

"Bonjour," Jacques said, waving.

"What are you all doing here?" I asked. "Is the ceremony over?"

"It hasn't begun," Giselle said, stomping at some weeds.

"But it's after five."

"Yes, but Gwen refuses to sing the anthem until Peter arrives, and no one can find him. I'm not sure how much longer she can delay the opening of the ceremony. Sebastian is furious. As you can imagine."

Good old Gwen! She must have realized there was something fishy going on. "I know where Peter is," I said. "He's trapped in the convent cellar, he and Lillian both. I was stuck there too, but I managed to crawl through the tunnel."

"Well, I'll be danged," Roderick said. "The tunnel they dug in the War? I went through there when I was a lad. You're lucky it didn't crash down on your head."

"I know," I said. It was a risk that I maybe shouldn't have taken, but now I was glad that I had. "We have to get Peter out of the cellar right away. He has news that will stop Sebastian and Wilheard from taking over the duchy. That's why we were imprisoned in the cellar. To keep us from talking." I quickly explained about Clara and Father Anselmo and how their town had been turned into a police state, complete with razor wire.

"Just like Grandpère's dream," Giselle said.

"Exactly."

Jacques took a mighty yank at one of the smaller boards and it came off in his hands.

"Go ahead," Giselle said to the men. "I'll finish freeing Holly while you liberate Peter."

"Right you are," Roderick said. He peered at me through the opening. "We'll meet you at the plaza." After a quick conversation among them, he and Jacques were off at a run.

A couple of minutes later, Giselle and I had managed to open up a space that was large enough for me to squeeze through. "Thank you!" I cried as I emerged into the world. Then my knees buckled, nearly toppling me to the ground.

Giselle grabbed my arm for support. I straightened and looked out at the valley below me, finally able to get my bearings. It was a major mental adjustment, going from a constricted, subterranean world to the vista before me, mountains and valley illuminated by the slanted rays of the early evening sun. Five-thirty according to my watch.

I could see why the tunnel had been so difficult to ascend at the end. I was standing on a ledge above a steep, rocky incline. Some twenty yards below lay the cemetery, spreading downward to the convent and cheeserie. And to my right stretched the forested area, running from the rocky incline down to the plaza. From where we stood, the square was mostly obscured by trees, their autumnal colors muted by shadow. A narrow road snaked down the hillside, between the cemetery and the forest.

"Look!" I cried. "It's the guys." Roderick and Jacques were jogging along, off to the right and about a third of the way down the steep road.

"They are the best," Giselle said fondly. "Oh, but they'll be at the convent soon. We'd best hurry if we are to reach the plaza in time for the ceremony." My legs were still a little wobbly, and she took my hand as we made our way across the rocky hillside.

By the time we reached the dirt road, my energy was flagging, and Giselle stopped. "We need to clean you up a little," she said.

"I have water," I said, pulling out the nearly-empty bottle. Instead of a shawl, Giselle had donned a turquoise kerchief, knotted at a jaunty angle, similar to the men's. She pulled it off, then poured water on it.

"Hold still," she said as she scrubbed at my face. The scarf was dark brown when she finished.

"Oh, your poor scarf," I moaned.

"Mais non," she said. "This is its finest hour. It has come to the service of a true heroine of the duchy."

I cringed. What a sorry hero I was. Ten minutes ago I was sunk in an abyss of misery, certain that my life was a complete failure. It was amazing what fresh air, friends, and good news could achieve. "You are the heroes," I said, "you and Roderick and Jacques, for getting me out of the cave and liberating Peter and Lillian."

"Ah. Just wait. There will be plenty of credit to go around, I think. Deserved or not."

We started down the pathway bordering the cemetery, sliding occasionally on loose gravel. Giselle confided that Jacques was more than just a friend, and she was really hoping that he would like St. Uguzo. Soon, we spotted Roderick and Jacques at the bottom of the road, where they jogged left onto the intersecting road that ran in front of the convent.

The back end of the plaza came into view below, and we could see that Guzos had spread out from the square into the road next to it and down to the bridge. Guzos everywhere.

A blast of sound filled the air. "The alphorn," Giselle said. "The ceremony is about to begin."

CHAPTER THIRTY

Day 15, Saturday

I had seen the six-foot-long alphorn in a collection of musical instruments in the museum and could see how the sound would carry for a long distance. "But how can the ceremony begin?" I asked. "Peter isn't there yet. Roderick and Jacques haven't had time to spring him."

"Maybe the council couldn't wait any longer," Giselle said.

We stepped up our pace, even as we kept our eyes on the road in front of the convent, expecting to see Roderick and Jacques entering the place soon. From our position over half-way down the road, we could still only see the rear of the plaza, but it was clear that Guzos had spread out beyond there to the road and across to the cemetery. Already, they were close to the bridge below. If we joined them, would we be able to see and hear the action in the square? good

"Look," Giselle said, pointing to a small grassy area to our right. It was below the trees and far enough above the plaza to afford a full view, including the stage at the far end. And with the sound system, we would be able to hear everything. A number of families were already spread out on the grass, and we found a spot mostly clear of rocks next to a young couple with a boy of about three.

We sat after clearing away a few rocks. I looked down at the stage. Gwen wasn't there, but the six council members were seated along the back of the stage, looking official in their bright red sashes. To their right sat Wilheard and Sebastian. As usual, Sebastian looked composed, but

Wilheard's legs were jiggling at a frantic pace. I examined the crowd from one end to the other, but I didn't see anyone resembling Peter, Lillian, Roderick, or Jacques.

Rosamunde stepped forward to the podium and picked up the mic. "Thank you all for your patience," she said, as the assembled Guzos quieted. "The order of our ceremony will be different tonight. We have decided to postpone the anthem until later. Instead, our fellow Guzo, Wilheard Fosse, has asked to address you all on a topic of interest."

Wilheard walked up to the podium. "Greetings, Guzos," he shouted, raising his hand in a stiff wave. Many in the audience returned it. He then immediately introduced Sebastian, who came forward, beaming.

Sebastian picked up the mic, holding it like a pro. "A lot of you know me already," he said, followed by a few cheers from the audience. "But for those of you who don't, I am here to make you a once-in-a-lifetime offer that will bring prosperity and security to your beloved duchy."

An excited stir rose from the crowd. Beside us, the young husband turned to his wife. "This is the guy I was telling you about. Just the leader we've been waiting for."

"I'm not so sure," the wife replied. "I heard he wants to bulldoze the forest."

Sebastian launched into his now-familiar spiel about his company and the miracles it would bring to St. Uguzo. The crowd buzzed with excitement.

Just then, a deep voice rose from the back of the plaza. "Make way. Make way," it boomed. Giselle and I leaped to our feet.

"Grandpère!" Giselle cried. Sure enough, a small figure was clearing a path through the crowd, his floppy gray hat visible from above. He was followed in a line by Peter, Lillian, Jacques, and finally Juliette, her gaze sweeping the scene. My heartbeat quickened as Giselle and I clasped hands, grinning. The Guzos in the plaza, who were already pressed together snugly, parted to make room for the procession.

At the stage, Peter, Lillian and Juliette climbed up and were met by Rosamunde and Baptiste. The other council members joined them as Peter held forth, his hands gesturing boldly. Beside him, Juliette added comments while Lillian nodded with feeling.

I peeled my eyes away from Peter for a moment to see Sebastian standing behind the podium, silent and red-faced with fury. I wondered if he was carrying a dagger, like many of the assembled Guzos, who were waiting to lift their weapons in the Ceremony of Allegiance. I certainly hoped Sebastian was unarmed because he appeared disposed to stab Peter.

Wilheard cowered at the back of the stage, looking like his greatest wish was to disappear. He flinched and stepped backward when Sebastian snarled something at him. Then Sebastian strode over to the council members and began haranguing them, his face in Baptiste's, then Rosamunde's. She stepped back and must have said something appeasing to Sebastian, because he puffed himself up and followed her back to the podium.

Giselle and I sat down, along with the people around us. "I'm surprised that Sebastian and Wilheard don't high-tail it out of here," I said. "They must know their time is running out."

Giselle nodded. "Don't underestimate Sebastian. He is wily."

The audience had become noisy as they speculated on what was unfolding before their eyes, and Rosamunde had to insist that they direct their attention back to Sebastian. He then replaced her at the podium, a confident expression plastered on his face. His voice oozing with conviction, he explained that Guzos were only a few minutes away from a new and glorious future. All they had to do was raise their knives to signify their election of Wilheard as duke and then give him the authority to sign a contract with Sebastian's company. He waited expectantly, but there was only a smattering of applause, as most people's focus had returned to Peter and the council members at the other side of the stage.

Baptiste stepped beside Sebastian. "I do not believe we are ready for a vote," he said. He thanked Sebastian, who retreated to the back of the stage with ill grace.

"Some new developments have arisen," Baptiste said. "Here to explain them is our duchy historian, Peter Bowman, and his mother, Lillian, the daughter of our late Duchess Anne Marie."

"Here we go," I whispered, my heart racing. Was Peter up to this? It had been an exhausting day. Giselle put her arm around my shoulder, and we leaned into each other. I was glad for the warmth and support.

Peter stepped forward and picked up the mic, while his mother positioned herself behind him and to the left. "Fellow Guzos," he said, "just a few hours ago I spoke to a friend of mine, a priest in Sant'Antonio, a town in Italy, not far from here. He had a shocking story to tell."

As Peter related his conversation with Father Anselmo, I began to relax. He explained clearly and concisely everything that he had learned from the priest—how a company had taken over their town and stripped its citizens of all their rights. If Peter was nervous, he hardly showed it; his historian's natural authority lent his speech gravitas. He had to pause now and then as gasps and cries of outrage erupted from the assembled Guzos. The parallels between the company that took over Sant'Antonio and Sebastian's company must have been clear to everyone.

I supposed Peter would say something about our being imprisoned in the convent cellar and tunneling out, but he didn't. It was probably just as well. People were already riled up enough. When he described the razor wire, a rumble of discontent traveled through the crowd. I glanced at Sebastian, whose expression had turned smoldering.

"Father Anselmo is prepared to come here tomorrow to tell you all this in person, but I hope you will accept my word that it is all true," Peter said. "Are there any questions? I'll do my best to answer them."

Sebastian strode forward and shoved Peter out of the way, grabbing the mic. "I have a question," he said. "I am appalled by how the company you describe treated the people of that Italian village. Why in the world would you think that company is mine?" He stared at Peter. "Does it have the same name?"

"Not exactly."

"Not at all, I'd wager. And did the good Father mention by name?"

"Well, no."

Sebastian smirked, addressing Peter. "Just as I thought. Some unscrupulous company shows up in an Italian town and manages to take it over from the gullible locals. I am frankly insulted that you would think that my company would stoop to such a thing. This talk of yours is nothing short of libelous." He faced the crowd. "We all know why the historian is telling you these lies. He doesn't want to see change come to the duchy. He is one of those dinosaurs who fears progress for St. Uguzo."

"Hear, hear," cried someone in the audience, and others chimed in their agreement. Public opinion, which had favored Peter a moment earlier, was fast leaning toward Sebastian.

But Peter was not finished. Facing the audience, Peter said, "Some of you were probably wondering why I was so late arriving. Well, I'll tell you. Shortly after I got off the phone with Father Anselmo, my mother and I were accosted by a lady from one of our most respected families, Eglentyne Fosse."

A strangled cry came from Wilheard, whose hand now covered his mouth.

Peter explained how Eglentyne had lured us to the cellar, under the pretext of helping an injured child. She and another individual had then pushed a heavy table over the trapdoor, blocking our exit. Guzos shook their heads and mumbled their outrage.

"Someone put her up to it. You can count on that," snarled a man behind us.

"I am only here now, "Peter said, "because our friend Holly crawled through the tunnel leading from the cellar to a grotto above the cemetery. I hardly need mention that she did this at great personal risk. She then sent Roderick and a young friend to free my mother and myself."

I scrunched down on the bench, mortified. Did Peter have to mention me by name? Giselle gave my arm a small squeeze.

Wilheard had shuffled forward, and I could see from the shock on his face that Eglentyne's trap was news to him.

Sebastian shook his head emphatically. "I am shocked," he said. "Shocked that Miss Fosse would do such a thing. But I have to take some of the blame. I was aware of how passionately the lady felt about our cause, how devoutly she wished for her brother to take his rightful place as duke. But I never dreamed she would take measures into her own hands." He shook his head, as if pondering in confusion what had happened. "Let us be honest with one another. Eglentyne Fosse is a fine woman, but she is, how shall I say it? A little off balance mentally. A trifle 'bats in the belfry.' I'm sure her cousin will concur." He turned to Wilheard. "Isn't that right? Here. Step up." He jerked Wilheard forward and thrust the mic into his hand.

For a long moment, Wilheard stared down at the floor. Then he looked up and mumbled something. We all strained forward to hear. He glanced at Sebastian, then said slowly and clearly, "Everything that Sebastian has told you is a lie." He pursed his lips, as murmurs sounded throughout the audience. "At least, he never told the whole truth. My boss lures people in with big promises. But he doesn't tell them the cost. He told me I'd be duke of St. Uguzo. But he didn't tell me that he would take over the duchy. Turn it into a dictatorship. Destroy everything good in it."

A rumble rose from the crowd. "Oh my gosh," I murmured. "Did he really say that?"

Giselle whispered in my ear. "Sebastian went too far. He never should have insulted Eglentyne."

Wilheard's voice rose, as if he were drawing on some inner strength. "I'm not proud of what I did here, misleading you all. I only wish I could take it all back." He straightened. "And for your information, my cousin may be overly trusting. But she is as sane as anyone here."

Beside him, Sebastian's face was livid with fury. "That's it," he spat. "I'm out of here." He cast a withering look at Wilheard. "You'll be sorry," he said in a way that made my blood run cold. Wilheard flinched, but he stood his ground as his boss strode off the stage and vanished behind it.

"Good riddance," I said as the crowd erupted, some in shouts of anger and others in applause at seeing the end of Sebastian.

Giselle put her hand through the crook of my arm. "Now I suppose Sebastian will take off in his little red Ferrari."

"Just like your dream," I said, and we exchanged a smile.

CHAPTER THIRTY-ONE

Day 15, Saturday

When Sebastian had left the stage, Rosamunde and Juliette approached Wilheard and had a quiet conversation, during which Wilheard's gaze remained lowered. I was happy to see him squirm, although I realized now that he was as much a hapless victim as well as a perpetrator of crimes. More than anything, I wanted to know what part he had played in Clive's death. I would never forget the sickening sight of the body smashed against the rocks at the bottom of the Falls. Alice, Tony, and Jenny Cotton deserved some answers, and I was pretty sure that Wilheard had at least some of them. Juliette had the authority to hold him, so I hoped he would realize his best way forward was to volunteer to stay and come clean.

A chilly breeze washed over me, and I shivered, remembering that I badly needed a shower and clean clothes. I looked across the valley, to where the mountain ridges rose in the distance. The sun was dipping below tree level, a pink and orange afterglow illuminating the sky.

A moment later, the electric lights came on in the plaza below. Clothing that had been muted now brightened. Kerchiefs and shawls splashed red, gold, blue, and green. Several knife blades, apparently unsheathed, shone under the lights.

Baptiste took the podium. "This has been a day for surprises. Both good and bad. And for heroism of various kinds. And now, I want to pass on another piece of news." He glanced over at Peter, who nodded. "Peter

Bowman, grandson of our late Duchess Anne-Marie, has agreed to accept the nomination for duke."

Gasps rose, then "hear, hear" from several people, and applause from others.

"Thank goodness," said the young woman next to me. She planted a kiss on her little boy's head.

"Just as well," her husband said in reply. "I always knew there was something dodgy about that Sebastian."

"Call for a vote," shouted a man in the back of the crowd, and voices both high and low burst forth in a chorus of "Vote! Vote! Vote!"

They quieted as a man climbed onto the stage. It was Bernard Bonnet, with his startling red hair and in his bright blue Alpine Rescue jacket. "Hang on a minute," he said. "You all know me. I have great respect for Peter and his family. But there's something I want to know. That is, will our next duke be a force for change, or will he hold us back? We have more than enough stodgy traditionalists on the council."

He stepped down from the stage, accompanied by a rumble of "aye" and "well said."

Oh dear. Peter had only just been nominated, and now he was going to have to present his economic and social platform before a whole crowd of Guzos. Did he even have one? I searched his face as he stepped forward, and was glad to see mostly confidence there.

He hesitated only a second before picking up the mic. "A fair question," he said. "And one that's been on my mind for some time. But please bear with me. I didn't realize I would be here this afternoon, sharing my thoughts with the entire duchy."

A few chuckles from the audience. "Go ahead, Peter," called a woman. "We are behind you."

"Well, then," he said, "I think we all recognize that the duchy must move forward if we are to survive. Not just survive, but thrive. If we ever had any doubts, the last couple of weeks have made that clear. First of all, we must diversify our economy. We can no longer depend on duchy cheese as our sole source of outside income. Those days are over."

"Just so," a deep voice called from the audience.

"Thank you, Hal," Peter said, smiling. "You have children and grand-children, and I understand how important this is to you." His gaze swept the assembled Guzos. "As it is for many of our beloved older Guzos. I know we have the ability, and the desire, to create a stronger society for the next generation and the ones after that."

"Hear, hear," Bertrand shouted, lifting a fist.

"We must open up to outside investment, but do it transparently and responsibly. I myself would like to see good roads throughout the duchy and access to the internet. Plus a few inns and restaurants. Possibly festivals that bring in outsiders and support arts and music."

In the audience, people were nodding and speaking quietly among themselves.

"I warn you. Change always comes at a cost. And there may be times when we would like to turn back the clock. But it is not really an option, is it? Nor has it ever been. If I am on the council, I will try to see that we keep what is best about duchy life but welcome the kinds of change that will keep us strong." He turned to Bertrand. "I hope that is enough of a response for now."

Bertrand nodded. "For now. And we will hold you to it, Peter."

"Have no fear," Peter said. "If I falter, the spirit of my grandmother will be at my back, warning me to pull myself together. And as you all remem-ber, Duchess Anne Marie had no patience with fools, especially those in her own family."

I heard chuckles from a number of elderly people in the audience and even saw a few tears.

Peter stepped back while the council members conferred. Then, Rosamund stepped to the podium. When she spoke, her voice was strong and clear. "As acting chair of the duchy council, I hereby call for a vote of the people of St. Uguzo. All present, please stand." Most Guzos were already standing, but Giselle and I, and others sitting on the fringes, rose. Many people fingered their knives.

Rosamunde's gaze traveled over the gathering of Guzos. Apparently, she found everything in order, because she said, "All those in favor of making Peter Bowman the new duke of St. Uguzo and member of the duchy council, raise your knives."

A sea of weapons, daggers mostly, but table knives and butcher knives as well, were raised, their blades glinting under the lights. Beside me, Giselle's dagger was lifted high, as were all the other knives I could see.

"Thank you," Rosamunde said. "Please lower your weapons. And sheathe them, if you will. Now, all those opposed to making Peter Bowman the duke of St. Uguzo, please raise your knives." We all looked around us, but no knives were raised. None. Either everyone backed Peter, or nobody wanted to let their dissatisfaction be known to their neighbors. I hoped it was the first reason.

An expectant silence ensued, and Rosamunde raised her voice. "By the power vested in me as acting head of the duchy council, I hereby pronounce Peter Bowman the duke of St. Uguzo and a member of the duchy council." All this time, her expression had been stoic, but now she beamed broadly, as Peter came forward and shook her hand.

The crowd erupted into a riotous mix of cheers and stamping of feet. Everywhere, people embraced their neighbors. Along the edges of the crowd, babies cried and dogs barked. Giselle and I hugged and laughed for joy. The tears that had eluded me earlier now streamed down my face.

"We did it," Giselle cried out, laughing. "Sebastian is gone, and Peter is duke."

Slowly, I became aware of a hush falling over the assembled Guzos. I looked down at the stage and saw why. Gwen, beautiful in a long, golden gown, stood at the edge of the stage, next to an elderly Guzo man with a violin propped under his chin. Gwen nodded to the musician, then began singing the duchy anthem in a pure soprano stream. "Sweet duchy of our dreams, guardian of our souls..." And then hundreds of voices lifted the song into the air as hands covered hearts, and faces lifted upwards.

I knew the anthem because we had sung it at the end of the play rehearsals, so I sang along, swept up in the emotional swell. The anthem lasted only three verses, then Gwen and her accompanist brought it to a long, sweet end. They made a small bow, and everyone applauded, not raucously, but with depth of emotion that brought tears to my eyes. Standing next to me, Giselle looked rapturous. She wasn't even born in St. Uguzo, I mused, but the duchy was infinitely dear to her. As it clearly was to the other people there. What a gift it was, I thought, to love your home so deeply. And now we knew it was in good hands.

Turning to the people around us, we shook hands, one by one, congratulating each other with, "Well done, neighbor," and "Well done, indeed."

As the plaza started to empty, Giselle looked at me, apparently taking stock of my miserable condition. "Poor thing! You look wretched. How are you feeling?"

"I've been better. I really want to clean up."

My hair was stiff with dirt, my jacket filthy, and I'd torn holes in the knees of my slacks. I wasn't presentable enough to see or talk to anyone. We detoured to the house, where I told Giselle I'd meet her at the gym later to watch the play. Privately, I wasn't sure I'd make it. I was exhausted, and every joint hurt.

I felt much better once I'd stripped off my disgusting clothes and soaped myself from head to toe. After pulling on a pair of pajamas, I lay down on my bed, promising myself a ten-minute nap.

CHAPTER THIRTY-TWO

Day 15, Saturday

"Get up, dear," Rosamunde said. "The play starts in fifteen minutes." I pried open my eyes to see Rosamunde hovering over me. "I think I'll skip it," I said closing my eyes again. All I wanted to do was fall back into delicious sleep.

"I'm afraid you can't. You're playing Anwen."

"What?" The idea shook me out of my torpor. "Nooo. Get someone else. Lillian. Gwen. Anyone." Every muscle in my body ached, at least every muscle involved in crawling across a football field and crashing repeatedly against a solid wall. I wasn't going anywhere.

Rosamunde whipped back the quilt. I grabbed for the sheet and pulled it over myself.

"Come along," she said. "Everyone is expecting you. Alice is here with your dress."

I couldn't believe it, but it was true. Alice was standing in the corner. In her arms was the green gown I'd worn for the dress rehearsal.

"I've added a border to the lower hem," she said. "It's just basted on, but it should do for now." She held up the dress, and I saw a lighter green band at the bottom. My ankles would be covered. If I put on the gown. Which wasn't going to happen.

Rosamunde perched on the bed beside me. "I know you're tired and achy, and you deserve a good night's sleep. But right now, you have to get up and get dressed. Monique is waiting outside with her car, so you won't have to walk to the gym. But you must rise quickly. Your underthings are here," she said, gesturing to the bed side table.

I lay there, willing her to go away. For everyone to go away.

"I'm going to turn around and count to ten," Rosamunde said, her voice calm but steely. "By the time I get to ten, you will have put on your undergarments. And you'll be ready for Alice to help you with the gown." She turned around. "One."

I groaned and heaved my aching body to a sitting position. "What about Lillian? She knows the part."

Rosamunde shook her head. "No. She refuses. And before you ask, Gwen won't do it. She's a perfectionist, and there's no way she will walk onto the stage unrehearsed. I'd say that leaves us with one option."

"But I'm not even Guzo. People won't want to have a Yank playing their duchess. They would never accept me."

"They will. You might remember that Anwen was not a Guzo when she arrived here. She was a young woman from a far-off country, and she must have been feeling very insecure about the whole thing. Rather as you are now."

It was true. If anyone could empathize with Anwen, it was me.

"I don't know," I said, but my defenses were crumbling. I didn't stand a chance of convincing Rosamunde, and as if to reinforce that thought, Alice took a step forward, holding the gown out towards me. "Let's get started," she said. "We don't have much time."

I glanced at the clock and was shocked to discover that I had slept for almost an hour.

Before I knew it, I was at the gym, dressed in the green gown, which I had to admit felt rather lovely, at least compared to my earlier outfit. I was shivering with nerves, and not just because of the play. My chest fluttered when Peter came over to talk to me.

"Thank you for doing this," he said. He was adapting to dukedom rather well, I thought. His hazel eyes shone and he seemed to be a couple of inches taller, although that was only my imagination.

"I don't think this is right," I said, ready to roll out my previous objections. "I'm not even a Guzo."

"Holly, please. The Guzos won't care about that. What they want most is a duchess who is young and fresh and beautiful. Someone they can fall in love with."

I lowered my gaze to my feet, blown away that Peter would say such a thing about me, even obliquely.

"Well, that counts me out," I muttered.

"No, it counts you in." He took my hands in his and stared deep into my eyes. "I need someone who can make the speeches, not just by rote, but with conviction and heart. You're the only one who can do it. You're the only person in the whole bloody duchy who can pull this off." His eyes beseeched me, and my weariness evaporated in the promise they held.

And so I agreed. What else could I do?

The play was, by all accounts, a great success. The audience clapped and cheered for five minutes after the final curtain, and we all went back on stage to take more bows. I'd never experienced the thrill of tumultuous applause before. It was exhilarating. And even more exciting was the touch of Peter's hand, warm inside mine, filling my body with frissons of anticipation.

After the applause had finally died away, the actors dispersed to join their partners and families in readiness for the post-play party. Everyone was smiling, and the mood was joyous. Peter and I were the last to leave the stage, still holding hands. Peter led me to a secluded corner, out of sight of the stagehands, who were busy sorting props. There, he looked at me so intently my heart jumped, afraid of what he might say.

"Holly," he said tentatively. "I... oh, damn, I can't wait." He bent his head and kissed me, a deep, searching kiss that created a strange vibration in my body. It began at my toes and shimmered its way to the top of my head, washing away all the hurt and the doubts of the past few days. It wasn't exactly the same feeling I'd experienced in the thin place, but the effect was equally glorious, a sparkling, uplifting sensation of intense happiness.

He kissed me again, and I enjoyed every second until I had the feeling that we were not alone. I opened my eyes to see a figure moving towards us. Reluctantly, I pulled back. It was Gwen, stunning in her golden gown, her blonde hair flowing loosely down her back.

"Sorry to disturb," she said. "May we talk?" She gestured to an empty bench, where we all settled. I gathered my green gown around me as I sat down, and smoothed the skirt into neat folds. A long dress was an unfamiliar garment for me, a big change from my usual jeans or slacks, but I found I enjoyed the way it made me feel. More elegant and sophisticated. Not words I, or anyone I knew, would have applied to me before now.

"I owe you an explanation, Peter, about why I left," Gwen said.

I swallowed hard, dreading what was coming, not wanting to remember that horrible nightmare.

"Holly dreamed that I was murdered." Gwen shuddered. "Garroted."

"Good grief." Peter's eyes went wide.

"Just so." Gwen went on. "Rosamunde told me she believed Holly is a vivid dreamer, so she took the dream seriously enough to convince me to go somewhere safe."

My stomach cramped. Peter had told me he didn't believe in vivid dreams. Would he think less of me for having one? Was our beautiful new love affair about to be squashed? Strangled at birth? No, I told myself. He only felt that way about vivid dreams because he'd had one about his brother and ignored it.

Gwen peered at me. "Are you alright?"

Peter looked at me, then, a look of concern on his face.

"I'm fine," I said. "Just remembering that dream is upsetting, but I'm so happy you're here now and safe."

"You think Sebastian would have killed you, given the chance?" Peter asked Gwen.

"We all know his goal was to overturn the status quo in the duchy. The more upheaval and instability, the better. He would step into the breach and convince the Guzos that he could restore peace and order. Getting rid of me would be a major step in that direction."

"He threatened Peter, too," I said.

Gwen perfect eyebrows shot up. "He did?"

"And Holly, as well," Peter said.

Gwen's face paled. "But you both stayed. You didn't run away."

"There was no time," I said. "It was just before the ceremony. Besides, they were just threats. For you, it was different. That dream I had could have come true if you hadn't left. Rosamunde was right to persuade you to go."

"Holly saved your life." Peter appeared a little shell-shocked, but at least he wasn't mocking or discounting my dream.

"And, Holly, I want to apologize. I felt terrible, running out on you," Gwen continued. "Especially as I was the one responsible for bringing you here. I expect you've heard the whole story by now."

"I have, and I'm grateful that you came to the States to find me." Grateful was something of an understatement. Overjoyed was more like it. I stole a glance at Peter, feeling my cheeks grow hot.

Gwen clapped her hands together. "I knew you two were meant for each other."

My face flushed even warmer with embarrassment, but Peter laughed. After a moment, I began laughing, too, and Gwen joined in. We were laughing with relief, mostly, that the ordeal with Sebastian had passed, that Gwen was safe, that Peter and I had a future together. One still to be sorted out, but I knew it would work. After years of distrust and self-doubt, it was marvelous to feel such certainty. Such love.

"Is this a private party or can anyone join?" Juliette strode across the gym towards us.

"Please do join us," Peter said. "Is something amiss? You look very serious."

"No. I have good news, for a change. The Italian police arrested Sebastian after he crossed the border. They're holding him on charges related to his activities in Sant' Antonio. And they're working with me, with the duchy, I should say, on the investigation into Clive's murder. I expect them to press charges against him for that in the coming days."

"Excellent. Good work, Sheriff," Gwen said.

"Hardly. I couldn't have done anything without the help of Holly and Peter and Rosamunde. It was a group effort, believe me."

"And what of Wilheard?" I asked.

Juliette smiled. "I think his future here will depend on the good graces of the new duke."

Peter nodded thoughtfully, got to his feet, and held out his hand to help me to mine. "We'll worry about him later. For now, we have much to celebrate and should join everyone else."

Not long afterwards, still holding my hand tightly, he strode into the hall, every inch the confident leader. The Guzos inside rose to their feet and cheered us both, delighted that the duchy's future was finally secure.

EPILOGUE

The sun was setting over the mountain tops, painting the sky pink and gold. There was a faint chill in the air, and I pulled my shawl more closely around my shoulders. Beside me, my mother stood, gripping the hand of her new husband and still looking a little overwhelmed by the events that had brought her here. My sister, Valerie, on the other hand, was flushed with excitement. She'd never seen mountains like these before, and had fallen in love with the duchy the minute she arrived.

We were assembled in the courtyard outside the museum where I had first read my grandfather's journal. Most of the older St. Uguzo residents who still remembered the war had come to pay respects to the man whose bravery had saved so many lives, including that of Roderick, who stood behind me with a group of his friends. Peter's father and Lillian stood next to me with Gwen and her new fiancé, a dashing orchestra conductor. Kessie gave me a big wave when she saw me, while Ozzie stood quietly between Juliette and Baptiste.

Peter, handsome in his duke's robes, stood at a lectern set up for the event, with Rosamunde at his side. He gazed at the assembly gathered in front of him. "We are here today to honor the memory of Albert Becker Fleming, and his courage in the face of great danger. On his last mission, he saved six lives, including four American airmen."

He nodded towards Danny McCleary, one of those men. Danny's grandson, tall, straight-backed and in an Air Force uniform, smiled widely at

Peter who talked for a while longer, recounting the stories Roderick had told us about those terrible times.

As Peter talked, my mother's eyes filled with tears. She had grown up believing the worst of the father she'd never met, and now she was here to celebrate him as a hero.

After Peter finished, Rosamunde stepped forward and took the microphone from him. Her voice filled with emotion as she spoke. "It is thanks to Albert that my father survived the war. He was one of those six airmen Albert saved that day." Her voice broke, and she took a moment to recover. "It is with great happiness that, on behalf of the Duchy Council, I hereby declare Albert Becker Fleming a citizen of The Duchy of St. Uguzo." Gathering her shawl tightly around her shoulders, she invited my mother and me to approach and presented us with a hand-written copy of the proclamation.

"Albert isn't an honorary citizen," she continued. "He's a genuine citizen, and that means his grandchildren can be too, if they choose to live in the duchy. And as his granddaughter, you, Holly, are eligible for a wedge of cheese at Christmas." She smiled at me. "You could even be elected to the council, or become duchess. Of course, it would help if you married a duke."

Peter's eyes met mine, and he smiled. Valerie squeezed my arm. She'd already promised to visit me at least once a year.

We stood quietly while Peter turned to secure a copper plaque to the wall of the museum. Under the outline of a WW2 airplane, the plaque bore my grandfather's name and two single words, "With Gratitude."

Overwhelmed by emotion, I hugged my mother and, together, we stared at the plaque. Gradually, a smile came to her lips, her eyes brightened. "Dad," she whispered.

The commemoration was to be followed by a public ball in the plaza. "We have rightly honored the dead, and now we will celebrate the living," Rosamunde said, as she led the assembled crowd out of the courtyard.

I joined Peter, and we talked with some of the men as we walked. Danny McCleary and his grandson were planning to fund a new brewery, while one of Roderick's family members had made a donation to the museum. Peter was actively, but cautiously, reviewing various investment opportunities that would, we hoped, bring new life and financial stability to the duchy. I had been surprised to find myself both interested and adept in business affairs, a far cry from the academic world I had now happily left behind.

In the plaza, an accordionist and two fiddlers were already playing lively tunes that had people twirling and dancing. On tables set up outside the mead hall were pitchers of mead, cider, and spring water alongside platters of cake and, of course, cheese.

As the night sky rolled over us, and I spun around in Peter's arms, I could have sworn I heard my little friend, Monty the marmot, whistling in time to the music.

THE END

ACKNOWLEDGMENTS

I am grateful to readers who have expressed their enjoyment of *Reading the Knots*, and *Unraveling the Threads*. This is not a continuation of that story line, but I hope readers will enjoy visiting the Duchy of St. Uguzo just as much. My deep thanks go to members of my on-line writing group: Carrie Bedford, Maryvonne Fent, Gillian Hobbs, and Diana Corbitt. They smoothed out numerous rough spots and encouraged me along the way. Many thanks to my ever-supportive husband, Jan Michael, who offered suggestions for what a medieval cellar, and a secretly dug tunnel might be like. And special thanks to Jan and Carrie for finalizing the book, proof-reading, and getting my last book into print the way I would have liked.